Cold Running Creek

ALSO BY ZELDA LOCKHART

Fifth Born

Cold Running Creek

A NOVEL BY

Zelda Lockhart

LaVenson Press

HILLSBOROUGH, NORTH CAROLINA

LAVENSON PRESS

This is a work of fiction.
Names, characters, places, and incidents either are the
product of the author's imagination or are used fictitiously,
and any resemblance to actual persons, living or dead,
events, or locales is entirely coincidental.

Library of Congress Control Number: 2006934001

HARDCOVER
ISBN 13: 978-0-9789102-0-4
ISBN 10:   0-9789102-0-6

SOFTCOVER
ISBN 13: 978-0-9789102-1-1
ISBN 10:   0-9789102-1-4

First LaVenson Press hardcover edition January 2007
First LaVenson Press trade paperback edition January 2007

10 9 8 7 6 5 4 3 2 1

Manufactured in the United States of America on recycled paper (50% pcw).
Book design by Dave Wofford of Horse & Buggy Press.

For information regarding special discounts for bulk purchases,
please contact LaVenson Press at 1-866-643-4002,
www.LaVensonPress.com, or LaVensonPress@aol.com

To my children, Travis and Alex,

two powerful souls

who have helped me re-member myself to my freedom

Author's Note

I'd like to thank the two women who over the years, I have forgotten to thank, the ishkis, mothers in my life who have nurtured me, and offered their own special variety of guidance: Elnora Lockhart and Minnie Yancey. I'm grateful to my Great Aunt "Suddie" Martha Jane Taylor for being generous with her shoe boxes of photos, and for telling me the secret: that the free boy did not marry, but stole the girl. Thank you to the women whose desire for freedom runs though my veins, my Grandmother Annie Laura Petty, and my Great Grandmother Lillie Kilburn.

Thanks to the women who helped me "to just keep writing," while the ill ecology of economics churned like a typhoon just outside my window: Alicia McGraw, Teri Hairston, Kia Carscallen, Joy Weber, Candace King, and Riggin Waugh.

Thank you Leslie Bode, Susan Kemp, Clare Brown, and Halle Meyer for tirelessly reading with such dedication and love.

Angela Walton-Raji, thank you for your expertise and contacts around the history of the time and people in Cold Running Creek.

Jerma Jackson, thank you for going to the library when necessary, and cheering me on at the end of the marathon.

Dafina Blacksher Diabate and Christopher DelCollo for whispering trade secrets in my ear, for your insight and generosity with information and connections.

I appreciate all of my students who inspired me and opened themselves up to giving and getting. And thank you to the members of my love circle, who provided everything from child care to reams of paper.

Thank you to Sally Wofford-Girand for standing ringside with a cool towel while I went in round after round in seeing the novel through to publication, and to Andrea Chapin, who came in and sprinkled her much needed editorial fairy dust on the manuscript.

The song on page 214 is originally titled *Raise a Ruckus Tonight*, and appears in Black Writers of America: A Comprehensive Anthology. Barksdale, Kinnamon. Macmillan Publishing Co., Inc. NY, NY. 1972. pg 235.

Part One

Fall 1834

ISHKI HAD FOUND THEIR HOMES with her bare feet, sensing the fertility of the earth where she walked. The other mothers said she was a seer, often looking into the distance, her eyes shiny on the surface like the water of a still pond, her black pupils not visible beneath the reflection of the sky. Her hair early in graying, like two streaks of clouds in a dark, starry sky.

"From so much worrying," the oldest aunt believed.

The two sisters often sat on the perch of the square fire pit. Ishki, dark and slender, her face fierce but gentle like the eagle's. Her sister, twenty years Ishki's senior, was quiet and squat, her head and body, even her feet were round like river rocks.

"Fear can unsteady the sight, make images cross each other like the dance of confused spirits. 'Who is it? Who is it?' she will start to say, and find herself blind. Yes, that is your Ishki's plight," she told the others of their clan.

One morning Ishki looked off into the coming day, then looked back at Raven coming out of the cabin. "Betrayal is on the wind," she said to her only daughter, and walked off toward the square pit where Raven's father had stood early that morning. Her vision was never clouded, until now.

Ishki's brow furrowed in the sun after that day. She looked off into the distance, or looked long and hard across the fire at her husband, his eyes quiet, staring into the square pit.

"Mind your step, child," she said to Raven one afternoon, stopping her in chasing the other children, their newly carved sticks held high and coming down to swing against the deer-hide ball in a game of ishtaboli.

"Yes, Ishki," Raven responded, respecting the base drum beneath her mother's voice, but spinning lighthearted in play, her long hair and spindly body free in the early fall breeze of new leaves, sweat, and sun.

Raven's father was the great hunter of the clan. They called him Inki, Father, for his commitment to protecting the clan and the grace with which he hunted their food—the same grace with which he commanded the circle of men in the drumming. His head was a solid square bone like his horse's. When he smiled it brought light to his wife who bore the heavy responsibility of staying sharp to any approaching danger.

Each morning he sought the two pointed fingers of each hoof, then the clustered dark droppings filled with seeds from the thorned blackberry twine that had just hung in the tough, tanned thick of his exposed shin. The arc of his cupped hand reached for the fallen hawk feather at the end of a smooth dogwood shoot and carefully chiseled flint arrow. In the gray light of dawn there was movement among the herd of deer before the arrow struck precisely in the tender part of the skull. They just stared in disbelief that this fate befell one of them again, then leapt toward the thick camouflage of woods.

One morning Inki sat at the fire pit and quarreled with his wife about heading back to Fort Adam's Port. "We are citizens of this state. White men can't just decide that we are a nuisance and remove us. I am not subject to the decisions of some mixed-blood traders of land and heritage. Within their negotiations was the promise of land for those who chose to stay. I intend to get it." He turned to his wife, who sat looking at the coming light in the east.

She spoke in a voice respectful of sleeping children. "You know as well as I that they didn't mean their words, or else they wouldn't have forced us to begin that journey. There's a big difference in choosing to stay and escaping." She pulled the thin shawl away from her shoulders; the cool air of dawn had already gone warm. She lit her pipe from a twig still smoldering in the night's fire.

Her husband stirred in the square pit with his best walking stick, the peppery cedar smell of morning blended with sweet smoked wood. "I intend to look them in the eyes like a man looks another man in the eyes and let them know we will no longer tolerate these shifting truths." His hands were red, the veins stressed. He turned to his wife and watched her calm herself with the smoke. And he went about shoving the dried deer meat, flat bread, and his buckskin vest into the satchel for the journey. "We need to either get what belongs to us or get back onto the journey of being with the others. Otherwise, Ishki…." He looked at his wife, and she looked back, each of them remembering the day they were wed, the warmth of skin, the smell of sun in the hair. He went back to his task of leaving. "I mean you no disrespect, but we can't just keep moving around and dying away. I have a responsibility to my people."

"And I don't?"

Inside the dark musty cabin, Raven did not move where she lay with the sleeping children. The short mumbling rhythm of the conversation kept the other children sleeping; their little bodies rested warm next to Raven's, her newly slender figure against their chubby hips; their bodies held in the bed like berries held together in a cluster; and she listened intently above the sound of her aunts and uncles stirring in the next room, and the sound of field mice scampering.

The pause that followed her mother's words meant conflict, and Raven sat up to hear in the space of their silence. She leaned to see beyond the frame of the door to where her father was walking away from Ishki's whispers. Raven sprung from the bed, all hair, nightshirt and bare feet, and chased after him calling, "Inki, Inki."

He didn't turn to look at his precious daughter, the child pitch of her voice invoking the feelings of defeat for not offering her something sound, a childhood of freedom or a childhood of fighting. She stood near the fire pit, her off-white nightshirt and her long black hair limp around her long figure. Raven hoped he'd motion for her to come.

"Stay, Raven, stay," he mumbled.

Raven turned to her mother hoping she'd stop him, but Ishki went to the porch, her body thick like one of the posts that supported the rotting roof. Cedar, smoldering wood, damp morning of early autumn. Raven saw her mother's body age as she ascended the stairs. Her father disappeared into the still vague light of morning. The birds called louder, a screech owl joined the chorus, and Ishki sang beneath Raven's earshot a song without drums. Raven ran to and forced her shoulders beneath her mother's heavy arm.

Inside the damp cabin they sat on the window bench. Raven rested on the pillow of her mother's warm breasts. They watched the light of day come. Not a word was spoken, but her mother's thoughts were loud like a chorus of wailing demons, so disturbing to the spirit that the children stirred in waking. The screech owl's call quieted, and Ishki lit and smoked her pipe to calm her racing heart as the sun rose in the east window.

Raven rested her head on her mother's lap and slept a gentle sleep. She dreamed high walls, men scurrying, her father approaching with his head down; no pounding of his drum in the back of his mind the way he went out hunting on mornings before the sun kissed the sky. No, in the dream he did not return thanking the ancestors. Raven could see him coming out of a wooden gate with a chicken bound at the feet, feathered, and the head was that of a child, peaceful, her arms folded against her body. She dreamed his powerful shoulders in silhouette to the dust raised by the white men riding on horses while the dark ones raised dead trees to erect the walls of protection.

Inki quieted his thoughts with the intention of his stride. He walked through tall grasses that stood erect in the already hardened earth. Seeds flew before his steps that would destroy their parent roots; tubers red beneath the caked earth; their tendrils hugged cool rocks and sent the message to distant grasses that a man's destructive footfall was above them. Inki pinched the sprig of disconnected grass between his teeth. His muscular jaw held the stress of indecision. The blood of green seeped into the open pores of his mouth.

As the reality of the morning sun went bitter on the grass stem, spit and sweat came forth to cool him. From the unprotected flesh of his temple, the first sweat rolled down. He remembered his own father's words. *Life, brother and sister of death.* His father, who would always be remembered smiling a sun-wrinkled smile the day he left to ride against the Okla Tannap Choctaw, who honored a contract of easier and better things offered by the Spanish, then the French. His father, of Okla Hannali, neutral; neutrality being unpredictable, a threat to warring nations. He remembered his father's parting words: "The Chahta people have become so divided that it is hard to trust your brother for fear he may bring your enemy to our feast."

The green grass blood on Inki's tongue went bitter.

Life and death, mother and father, child and child. Life and death, untamed, neutral, unpredictable, some mornings better left to choice than fate.

He remembered the smell of the blood that covered his newborn daughter, waterlogged from her dead life sack, like the smell of a deer gutted and left to dry in the sun; the deer that would give his wife the strength to nurse the new life. *For my daughter,* he thought. Inki picked up his pace. Reverent grasses bowed quiet in his wake, and he ran into the blinding glare of morning, the heel of his moccasin boots on the earth like the shudder of his mallet on the drum.

Late that afternoon he returned, slow in his stride, and when Raven went to collect the berries from the heavy thorned bushes, he came to her in the clearing of trees where the blackberry reached up and over to snag the ungraceful deer or small child.

"You are the oldest child." He held her face and looked deep into her eyes.

Raven saw a desperation and fear in his eyes that felt shameful to witness.

He whispered, "If we get separated in these days, know that I will wait for your spirit in the ancestral place."

Her mother's voice, "Mind your step," blending in harmony with his "I will wait for you." The sound of fear pounded in her chest.

"Be brave, child." He asked her to listen carefully and watch as he sketched in the dry earth. "Still water," he said," where many things lay unsettled, tall trees with their roots above ground for fear of digesting the sins that lie beneath. This is the swamp. This is a safe place. You have never been there, but if we are separated, look for the flat green nuts of the water hickory and follow them to the swamp. "Do you understand?"

Raven answered, "Yes," quickly, trying not to let her voice waver.

He went on, "In this place of exile, you will find safety. If there is trouble, you must take baby Dove and your brother, Golden, and run to this place. Are you listening?"

"Father, what about the other children?"

"They will be your uncles' charge. Listen to me, Raven," he scolded her, and the tears burned in her nose. She held her breath to keep the sorrow of her father's harsh tone from breaking her.

Change had been hard for her, never allowed to cry, the oldest child. "Be brave" he had said to her the day they escaped the relocation to the new Territory. Her clan eluded the army in a torrential rain that lowered like a veil. The army men called for a halt because the noon sky had turned evil, a rumble of thunder, an explosion like cannon fire, and the rain came down in gray sheets. It filled the dips and gullies with churned water that sunk the wagon wheels. Flashes of lightening spooked the horses.

Most of their clan was on foot behind the wagon. The army's men called for the assistance of every able-bodied man and woman to free the wagons from the deepening mud and to get the horses to safety. The rain hushed their commands and made the color of Choctaw skin and the color of white skin indistinguishable. Raven's inki knew that the confidence in the army men's voices was a mask over their anxiety, for they had not left territory familiar to Choctaw hunters. He did not need to say to Ishki what would come next. He and his wife unhitched two horses, one of them his own, and set them beneath the high pines near a deer path; the grandmother, two little cousins, Raven, with baby Dove on a crib board rode on one horse. The most recently walking child and Ishki on the other. "Be brave," he said before slapping the soaked hide; his wet hair and the horse's mane trailing in Raven's memory. The aunts and uncles ran with him, carrying the supplies they could gather quickly, and they were gone, shadows beneath the sheets of gray rain, between dark tree trunks, up a deer path, gone, to this place where Raven stood. Change threatened to stampede through the comforting rhythms of her new life again.

Raven's inki spoke solemnly now. "I am entrusting you with my plan for your survival. You must listen." But fear gripped in her chest, and her mind lingered on "survival," having seen that word wrapped like a blanket around death.

He stroked her hair, explaining to her horrified eyes, "There is nothing left for our people but to stand up to our enemy and fear not the truth. They will either come with what I have demanded or they will come to fight, and you will need to get away. You must take your sister and brother and run."

"Inki," Raven spoke, though the words were twisting inside her body. "Mother says always stay with the children. What about the others?"

He tossed his head to the sky and she could smell the sun and codfish oil in his hair. Raven could hear him speak, harsh and frustrated with her insistence, but his words did not resound above a hiss as she sunk away from the hurt. *Inki, hold me. I'm afraid,* she would have said, had her focus not turned to the sky. The evening sun told her *Hush,* as it stooped down to hide behind the thick and thin trees; a tribe of mixed pines and elders. *Hush,* they said as the sun brushed their top limbs with orange light.

Then her inki was quiet. He squinted though the sun was below the shadow of leaves, and touched her face; her jaw strong like his. Inki thought of what to tell Raven in the event that life and death collided, or in the favorable event that nature played her trick, danced her dance, and did not repeat her steps to the benefit of her neglected children; the takers giving back, the prayers answered.

No words came, and a tear swam out from the corner of his eye and laid itself wet and open to roll down the rugged side of his solid face, and he laughed and cried in one quake, then set himself right again at the sight of Raven's eyes cast down to the bed of needles and leaves, the juice of blackberries showing on the sides of her mouth where a shaft of sunset lit her face.

He laughed again, intentional, using the cloth that hung out of his boot to wipe her face. "Let's have a good meal. Smells so good, doesn't it?" He stood tall and opened his chest to the evening air.

Raven was relieved that the spell was undone, that Inki was Inki again. "Mmm." She raised up on her toes. "Smells so good, Father."

She could be his child again, comforted by his amusement with her, comforted by the sameness of things.

They walked carefully from the snarl of thorned vines, Inki smiling a forced smile. Raven walked next to him pretending to be hungry but fighting the queasiness from blackberry pits in her belly.

At the edge of the woods they both stopped and watched her mother, whose frown seemed to say, *The business of elders is not to be entrusted to children.*

Against the log cabin, their pots and pans were scattered in a relaxed pattern of belonging. The few chickens scratched around the stone fire pit of the square dwelling. The mothers moved in a dance around the children, trying to prepare for the meal in the absence of the oldest child.

"Raven!" her mother called out, her stout body agitated as she hauled and spilled water. She went to the fire and turned the rabbit meat from Inki's hunt without looking up. She wore a thin cotton dress that had been traded for hide tanned by her strong hands. She frowned with deep concern remembering the things she had foreseen; Inki's defiance of her advice to wait and negotiate for the promised provisions for Choctaw who stayed behind.

"Raven," she called out again. Raven and Inki watched without response. The smoke from the fire vanished Ishki for a moment.

"Enough has been said," her father whispered and squeezed the back of Raven's neck before taking a deep breathe and walking. He held her hand, his raised calloused cuts against her soft damp palm. Lifelines mirrored inside their grip. Raven felt blood and memory across those lines for an instant, and her father let go.

The two of them walked separate now along the edge of woods hoping to avoid her mother's sight. They were tall in who they were: long dark hair, thick boned.

"I am here, Ishki," Raven called out, and ran toward the last evening.

After the meal, the taste of lima bean and green corn stew lingered, like the taste of creek water on lips. Raven was quiet. *"Minti!"* Come here! Her mother called her to the wash water at the side of the cabin. In the peach light of evening their hands disappeared beneath the reflection of the water; the sky, the clay bowls, their skin all one shade of golden evening light.

"What are you thinking about, Raven?"

"Nothing, Ishki, nothing."

Raven hummed the evening lullaby for the children, to keep sound above the thoughts and images in her head. *Will I disrespect my inki and tell my ishki what he has said? Will I disrespect my ishki and hold secrets away from her?*

The sun set dramatic in a peach-and-purple sky. The men sat around the pit warming and bending their arrows, "For a big hunt," Inki said, arousing no suspicion with his overzealous explanation. The women collected the remains of the meal. A hint of summer drifted on the autumn breeze, crickets and cicadas hummed weak in the waning light, and the sound of children's laughter was sweet on the changing air.

When the children are sleeping; that's when I'll tell. When the men are out at the fire and the women are smoking, I will join the mothers and tell them what my father has said. Movement beyond the transparent tunnel of smoke that danced before her musing interrupted Raven's thoughts.

In the distance, a horse-drawn wagon appeared in the light sky. A man sat high on the buckboard. He towed another wagon, empty, pulled by two horses. He turned toward their camp slow.

Inki smiled halfheartedly and said gently to the uncles, "They've come with what I've demanded." He stood and gripped his daughter's shoulder in assurance. The uncles nodded, new pride in their bodies. Inki left his quiver of arrows and the bow made from an ash limb warming by the fire. He looked at Raven; his eyes round like the moon, and smiled, relieved that Raven wouldn't need the instructions he'd given. He repeated his words loudly for the mothers who stood on the porch. "They have come with our provisions to move on." Raven's ishki clasped her hands and squinted toward the horizon before turning with the other women to bring the supplies from the house.

Raven directed the children in collecting the items around the brick pit; pots and containers were stacked and placed gently on the bear hide. She was relieved that this moment was different. She had imagined that someday they would have to leave this place, that the babies would cry first at the sight of odd things stacked together; a quiver of arrows, moccasins, the wooden loom and the hatchets. Baby Dove would spot the odd pile baking in the sun, and her cry would shriek out past the uncles, and the mothers bending over in the task of packing, past the elder mother sitting with patient hands and bright, knowing eyes. Another cousin would pick up the cry, then another. The newly walking cousin would throw down her rattle in protest. Raven and her brother, Golden, would find something to be discontent with and start pouting and disobeying, and her father would go to Baby Dove, the first screamer, pick her up, and hang the straps of her crib board on a low limb, where movement could be amusing to her.

But it wasn't the way Raven had imagined. Everyone moved as if they understood the gift approaching but did not sense it.

Out beyond the man with two wagons the line of trees seemed to move, until it was clear: ten soldiers on horseback.

The wagon stopped in front of Raven's father, and the white man driving looked down from where he held the reins. "I hope you don't mind I brought some of my old friends. They claim we don't owe you, but that you owe the government a couple of horses. Say you stole; say you ran off, did ya; and took some things that didn't belong to ya?"

Inki's eyes darted to the hatchet standing ready in the chopping block, and then over to the men approaching in uniform, and then to the children lined up like birds in leafless trees.

The man's eyes were small blue shadows beneath his hat. Raven had never seen eyes like the sky. A lump hardened in her throat. Her father turned to her in the new glow of dusk, his eyes apologetic.

The ten horses galloped now. The uniformed men sat high and erect, pulling down on the bills of their caps to keep from the wind. They were like the men who Raven's clan had fled in the torrential rain. They stopped, raising dust in the place where the chicken scratched. They pulled on the reins to steady the horses, and didn't say anything at first. Then Raven looked up to see their bearded faces, which showed copper in the light of the setting sun. The one with no uniform hopped down from his wagon and walked around, looking the children over. His blue eyes stopped on Raven, just as the six mothers were exiting the cabin.

"Look at this one," he said, turning in the direction of his companions. And in the cold soft bones of her young body, Raven understood the word "evil."

The blue eyes, the dirty suit coat too high up his arm, the fermented smell of corn whisky in the oil of his skin and sweaty hair. He threw a few green logs in the fire pit for better light. The mothers stood alarmed to see not only the wagons hauled by the blue eyed man, but ten soldiers on horseback circling their children like wolves. The women were silent, their eyes a blank stare of fear and disbelief, their arms filled with bedrolls, pipes, pitchers, and bowls, their children far from reach.

The green logs popped violently in the high blaze, and the bowls that Ishki held crashed earth on earth. She ran for the hatchet from the chopping block.

With the hatchet prepared to swing from her midriff, Ishki ran past Raven. Her voice whispered like a storm wind through high pines. "Run to the swamp, children. Raven, take the children and run."

Raven saw her mother's hands, aged; the handle of the hatchet; her mother's lips, red with fear and aggression. Raven had not moved from the place where she had stood thinking of when she would tell her Inki's secrets.

Toward the reared hooves of horses Ishki flew. The sounds of the men, their voices like locusts, the sound of her mother's bare feet against the earth, the force of her body passing. Her ishki screeched like a hawk descending. Raven still did not move. She turned to see the uncles struggling to fetch the arrows warming luxuriously by the fire, their eyes behind them on the soldiers, on the women flying into the storm, dark hair, round warm arms; the uncles' eyes pleading as they moved fast, as they moved too slow to save their women.

Raven could not move. *This cannot happen again,* she thought from some place ancient in her soul, ancient in returning over and over to find her standing quiet among the herd of deer, not believing that this fate would befall them again.

The sounds of her mother's cry cut the air, the babies were still silent, and Raven cried out first, "Ishki." A soldier grabbed her arm. She struggled and her mother turned away from the horse's hooves and ran to her child, but the soldier pulled Raven into the chaos, and her body was lost in the panic of her mother's sight; sky, fire, and mud flying up from a horse's hoof. *Where is my child?*

Where is my mother? Raven tried to breathe and open her eyes wide to see her ishki. Then she saw her mother's hands raised above her head, above the screams, the hatchet held high to strike a blow to a head of corn silk hair, but another small hatchet, of metal, not stone, struck and caught in her mother's skull like a blade chucked into a block of wood, rusted blade past dark hair, red flesh, and white bone, a sound that dragged Raven quickly and safely to the memory of her father; with the rock, surprising the rattlesnake that focused on her bare ankles dripping with water from the creek on the day of sun and rain.

Ishki fell to the ground, and Raven fell with her. She felt her body give way from the hands that constrained her; ishki, mother, and alla, child, both falling as if the cord still connected them, their flesh gone numb.

Raven's limp body lay on the ground. Sharp rock cut her legs. She heard her brother, Golden, scream, "Ishki," heard her mother's voice again, "Run to the swamp, child, run," softer now, like cicadas going quiet in the autumn night. Raven joined the younger ones, scattered like the chickens in the coop when her mother went to take one for their dinner. They ran avoiding hands, hooves.

Raven could smell the deep earth, mint of water-hickory nuts crushed beneath horses' hooves, but she could not remember her father's words, could not decipher the code of flat green water-hickory nuts that floated before her vision just before her dinner erupted in her throat.

Her cousins broke from the chase and Raven scooped her sister and brother and ran inside the cabin. Her hands grabbed the bearskin that had been laid out to wrap her father's drum. She pushed the little ones beneath the bed, hid them beneath the dark brown fur. She did not know she was running around the cabin looking for her own place to hide, but heard her bare feet like field mice on the dry wood, heard her own breath inside her head like tornado wind.

The blue eyes arrested her. He grinned with yellow teeth. The bear-skin quivered with two small bodies.

Raven heard the eldest aunt grunt one time; holler for the sake of gathering energy to kill a white man. She jumped at the explosion of rifle fire, and then the sound of her aunt's last breath ascending. The man approached her frightful dance and backed her against the cabin wall. The room went black. Hot embers floated up to alert the Spirits, but it was too late. Raven's eyes darted past the images, weeding them out for some glimpse of her father, in hope of seeing his dark eyes standing in the cabin door, but there were the blue eyes, the yellow teeth, the smell of corn whisky and sweat, laughter, the smell of the rust on the tool that had sharpened the hatchet to kill her mother, the same tool for making a spark against flint for the first fire. The sharpening tool, splin-tered steel, hooked in the warm untouched flesh of her insides, as the man worked the tool and spit on her over and over. Raven screamed, but no sound came, just blood, and images; smoke, the babies' faces, burn-ing embers, the color red, new crops, shooting stars all melted together until things went black again.

The last sound was the wagon wheels leaving, roughly, over hard earth and clumps of dry grass patting against the wagon bed. Raven faded in and out as her bleeding womb swelled and throbbed so close to where her heart beat, so close that she was nothing but the rhythm that held her in the land of living. She saw herself running to the place of still waters and trees with roots above the earth, running into the dark-ness to join her father, but when she came conscious, she was still lying on dry boards that smelled like the sweet musk of the warm bodies that now lay dead beyond the open door.

It will be dark soon, and darkness will comfort you, she heard a spirit sing.

In the light of dawn she drifted on consciousness while she watched the image of her mother leap from the porch into the sky; her tears became stars as she flew over the fields, the fort, over the graves of the promisers and the promised, over a dark Mississippi path once blazed by the hunter people of her fractured ancestry.

Then the sun rose in the east window and Raven awakened to the eyes, living beneath the quivering bearskin.

Spring 1850

RAVEN SLEPT SNUG against her husband's body. Grey Fox held her, their figures contoured like two newly carved wooden spoons. Husband and wife, they resembled male and female of the same soul; long body, narrow face, angular jaw line beneath the toasted skin. Her breasts were the two moons that gave definition to man and woman, where they lay on a bed of sun-crisp linen, in a room decadent with rugs and drapery, held up by white pillars, windows of hand blown glass that revealed them, vulnerable in their prosperity in a white run Mississippi.

She woke from the dreams to find him gone each morning, to find that the faint light of dawn had absorbed the blanket of black, star-sprinkled sky. Out of the darkness the yard became visible; the stump hedges in the garden, the stable, the grassy hill that led down to the fields of LeFlore plantation. From her heavy-draperied window she watched Grey Fox begin his morning exit at the side door below her and go to the stable in the vague luminescence of dawn. His long legs made a shadow like the stick dolls her ishki once made. His hair fell neatly to the shoulders of the dark suit that he insisted on wearing to the fields. *It will be warm soon,* Raven thought, and smiled at the stubbornness of a Choctaw man.

Have a good day. I love you, she said inside her head every morning for sixteen years to wish away the awful fantasy of his cream-colored horse, Spirit, flipping him over the split-rail fence at the edge of the cow pasture, his body landing on a jagged rock, or a tornado wind coming across an open field and whipping his long body into a dark thunderous tunnel; she was plagued by the awful thoughts of losing him the way she lost the world one day.

Occasionally Raven snuck one of Grey Fox's cigars and pulled her knees in tight; a lace cotton nightgown blanketed her; and she took short puffs, then long rhythmic drags, to soothe her nerves the way the pipe once calmed her worried ishki.

Some nights Grey Fox brought a snifter of brandy to the imported mahogany bedside table and collapsed in exhaustion before taking a sip. Those mornings Raven would say the repeated prayer for her husband's safety and dismiss the thought of hatchets, hooves, and stray arrows by turning up the globe of amber whisky. She let herself cry to release the pain before donning herself in the dress of a Southern lady. But on the mornings of this chilly spring, the walls of her heart were disintegrating, the pain bleeding out into her days.

She had seen the prominent men of southern society prosper from the war against the Mexicans. They had their way and did not have to see their women and children affected by their conquests. But the new agitation in their voices, the way they were disgruntled with their Northern compatriots for prospering from their Southern brothers' battles for land, would turn to hatred, would build and manifest itself as justified killing. She knew that change was soon to come and disassemble the morning stars and place them in new arrangements.

Change did not come easy for Raven. She was eighteen years old before she could settle into Grey Fox's touch, his flesh inside her body. For years she disappeared after the gentle kisses, but he did not know. He did not know that inside the story of the horrible massacre of her clan was the memory of filth so deep that no amount of tallow soap, bean soap, lye soap could scrub it clean.

She loved him, loved the way they made sense to each other, comforting each other with belonging. Raven needed the pattern of things; at dusk he came home, dinner with Dove, Golden and herself, evenings in the sitting room, then to sleep, and in the morning he was off again to his work on the land just before dawn. But the political meetings took him away from the rhythm.

Change did not come easy for Raven, and this long season of change disrupted her body, her family; Dove and Golden no longer followed her lead, but looked away to pursue their own lives.

Raven questioned her family as if they could make sense of the shifting currents that carried them all along. She asked Grey Fox, "What's bothering you? I know something is wrong. Each morning you get up and run away from me; you don't even wake me to say good-bye. You run from me like the moon running from the sun."

When she became passionate and anxious, Grey Fox would dismiss her by going into a quiet place, tolerating her questions without ever answering them. "Please lower your voice."

"Answer me Tchula. Why are you leaving me?"

"Raven," He only shot her one look and was conservative with his words, before lowering the lantern wick for his short night's sleep. "It is a difficult job to keep up the land, the obligations, the stresses of being the man I am in a white man's society."

Raven listened for more, but his breaths came deep and rhythmic.

One morning Raven woke after the sun had risen and burned away the possibility for her ritual of prayers for her husband. The canopy of fabric over her bed dipped low to hide her from the transformations that permeated her body, her mind. Her nightdress was stuck to her body like a birth sack saturated with sweat, her long body waterlogged. Outside her chambers she heard the twin servant girls, Earleen and Emma, whisper, "Sleeping late, hot flashes, she's taking the change early." Grey Fox had long since gone to the duties of his day. Those days, even on Sunday, he was up and out before the break of morning.

Raven drank the liquor tincture at the bedside, which quieted her mind and the sound of heels outside her door. She dressed in a dry cotton blue that matched the spring sky and went downstairs to the veranda, where she could inhale the scent of spring; frogs new and wet, dragonflies swimming in the larvae of the creek, the earth sweating away its frost and relaxing for seeds to be sown. She inhaled deep and smelled the moist earth that took her back to the creek banks of her childhood where she scooped clay with her aunts. The smell of rich damp earth and the lingering taste of brandy comforted her.

She remembered the clay pots beneath the wash water; her and Ishki's hands, the dishes after the last meal, her ishki's question, "What's bothering you?"

Raven's mouth and eyes watered, and tears rolled down, cooling themselves in the journey over her angled jaw. She was crying there on the veranda when Nathan, the stable hand, saw her, his skin the color of his black work pants, his hair speckled with age. He dropped the wheelbarrow and ran to the place just below the porch. "Missus LeFlore, is you all right? Can I get you somthin? Can I call Sybil for ya?" Most of the time he pretended not to see her looking out on the property like Grey Fox's horse, Spirit, when the half door had been shut to keep her in the barn.

Raven giggled at her own whim and dabbed the tears gently with her soft hand. "Good morning, Nathan, the pollen is just awful today."

She felt embarrassed at the loss of control, and a lie rushed in to cover her secrets. She composed herself and bid Nathan on to his work. She peered down the hill of trees at the slaves, single file going to their Sunday meeting at the barn. Her brother, Golden, rode behind them the way he did every Sunday, "No Sunday meetings without overseeing," Grey Fox had instructed.

Golden was proud and eccentric in his ways, keeping his hair long. Dungarees accentuated the length of his legs, the finest leatherwork boots a man could wear, and always a white shirt with the bright ribbons sewn on by the slave women, who found him handsome; and he was, as handsome as his inki had been.

The slaves marched along in their Sunday best; pants on the little boys, who usually wore long shirts like the girls. The slave woman Josephine had tended to sewing for the children, half of whom were hers.

How can they be so happy? Raven thought. *On Monday they will be back in the fields and have to spay and hoe, pick the mysterious new stones from last year's soil.* And she remembered looking down at her own bare feet as a little girl, laboring in the cornfield beside her parents, her body small enough to duck under the leaves for shade. Her little legs ached as she held her aunt's hand in the long journey to the creek for bathing.

She remembered the cousins, the lingering smells of fresh air and sweat when she played ishtaboli with them, the bark smooth wood against her hands as she reached up to the sky to catch the stuffed deer-hide ball and collide with the other little bodies.

The flat blue sky sheltered them, the same color as her dress of fine remnants; her father's voice sweet like tobacco. "They are your uncles' charge."

She didn't know the tears had rolled down her cheeks until they made dark spots on the cornflower blue dress. She used the lace paper fan on the veranda table to conceal her face as she walked past Sybil, her cook and maid, who brought the marmalade and bread to the table where Raven would soon eat silently with her sister, Dove, who always slept late.

"You all right, ma'am?" the dark, tall Sybil asked with false concern.

"The pollen is dreadful. Wipe down that veranda again." Raven's voice was so much like her mother's, but with a sharp tone for her husband's maid, whose mother had cared for Grey Fox like he was her own; her husband's maid had grown up with Grey Fox and gave subtle looks and gestures of superiority to undermine Raven's place as the mistress of LeFlore plantation.

The next morning Raven lay in her bed drenched, her hair heavy with the weight of vinegary sweat that cooled her. She thought and rethought the *why* of the slaves' happiness. She could hear them singing on the way to the field, heard the young girl Lula's sharp laughter, and imagined the children running with the seed sacks on their shoulders while she chased them playfully. *They do not know,* she thought, remembering the innocence of her play on the day that her mother said, "Betrayal is on the wind." *They do not know,* to be nervous around the new words of young white men and their fathers. *Secession. Separate. Separate.*

"The only way white men know," Raven's father had once said. Raven went to the window and watched from her perch while the morning air chilled her wet gown and left her skin cold with goose bumps.

She saw Grey Fox descend the hill on horseback, another day leaving for his duties before she woke to question him. She turned her head away from the window and took a long, soothing drag on his cigar to burn away the thoughts. "Change," she heard her own voice whisper; and felt fear seize in her chest. "It is on the wind."

She dressed slowly, first in the corset that hugged her long frame and made her stand erect, then in the white dress with small red flowers, her breasts concealed beneath the high neck that hid the suntanned light brown skin. She twisted her dark hair into a bun and descended the staircase, which split their home; down one side, the dancing room, dining room, veranda; down the other, the sitting room, study, kitchen, and maid's quarters.

Raven went down to the veranda, her feet bound tightly by fine shoes. She looked out on the manicured lawn, the hedges about to explode with yellow and fuchsia. The trees that bordered the hill that led to the quarters were light green with new leaves, and she was grateful for the safety of her life, for her husband, Grey Fox, for the cupboards of china, the fine wooden chairs, the doilies sewn by her and her sister's idle hands.

The white pillars of the veranda hid her from the dark ones, their movement between the light green of new leaves like that of black bears through swamp brush. They moved from the quarters to the fields that Monday morning, the air sweet with dogwood blossoms.

Six, seven, eight, Raven counted and stopped. She tried to remember the names of her slaves, but only remembered Sybil; the twin girls who worked in the house with her, Earleen and Emma; Nathan, the stable hand; Josephine, the slave woman who could work the fields like a man yet breed the most profitable hands for Grey Fox to sell at a price higher than any cattle; Lula, the child born the day Raven, Golden, and Baby Dove arrived.

So much time has passed? Lula is a young woman now, Raven realized, trying to remember if she'd seen Lula close up in the past few years. There was Burtrome, Lula's brother, and their mother, Harriett, who died last year, Raven thought, biting her bottom lip, but she could not remember any of the other thirty slaves who lived at LeFlore. Her ability to remember her own husband's name often escaped her along with the name of the sweet substance she wanted on her hot bread, the name of the undergarment that required an extra set of hands to lace, while the memory of things forced into exile in her mind sprung to life with the slightest stimulus.

How can that be? she thought, not wanting to imagine herself as the woman she was; clay still fresh beneath her fingernails, the scars of ishtaboli still on her knees hidden beneath the long dresses, the songs of the harvest, of planting time, on the edge of her memory. *Planting time, it is planting time, and I can't remember the dance. Why can't I remember the dance, like I remember the sound of the frogs singing in the bayuk when I was only two years old?*

She closed her eyes and listened through the sound of wind in the trees on the hill, listened to hear the songs the slaves sang on their way to the planting, but couldn't make out a melody.

That night the wind was still, the air cool. Wolves howled nearby.

Nathan reported, "They done took to beddin themselves down at night under the floor of the feed barn. Sure wish you would give Massa the word to shootem." Raven was fearful of the wolves but knew they'd be gone as soon as the puppies were born.

After she gave Nathan his leave to go visit in the quarters, she sat alone on the veranda, the lanterns unlit, and from her teacup she sipped Grey Fox's finest brandy; fresh tapped from its cellar barrel. The taste of wood and boring insects sharpened the flavor on the back of her tongue. Soon the house was quiet, but the quarters were lit and lively. Raven crept to her room for the black cloak Grey Fox had brought back from New Orleans, the one he had decided she best not wear, for his neighbor John Bartlette's wife had said it looked like a witch's hood. The wolves howled into the darkness, and she carefully descended the hill to the quarters.

She walked among the freshly plowed fields in hopes of remembering the planting dance; memories cataloged by the granules of dirt between her toes. She wanted to feel with her feet as her mother had.

Hidden by the moonless darkness, the cloak would keep her safe as the mistress of LeFlore plantation. She stood in the newly furrowed fields and quietly clapped and shuffled her feet with the slaves who danced around their Saturday night fire, the familiar sounds of fellowship from the days of her childhood; laughter, music, talking. She tried to relax her tall body and not consider the consequence if her husband returned from the meeting early and found her there in the fields behaving like the Negroes. She tried to loosen her body to remember the shuffle and step from her past that this movement resembled, but the voices of her husband's comrades interrupted her concentration like the pervasive call of the whippoorwill. *Democrats have a responsibility to claim the way of life that our father's intended for this land.*

The pending birth of South-and-North conflict brewed in a distant parlor where men plotted a course of action to increase commerce and ward off threats to their prosperity. *Quiet, quiet,* Raven said to her mind, but conflict brought images of black hair matted in blood, hands gone gray and swollen in the morning heat. Her heart beat fast like the day of the deaths she witnessed, quick heart, base like the lead drum, off rhythm.

Raven danced in the darkness beyond the firelight's reach at first, not allowing her body to move freely, then she remembered the scent of blood from her mother's body and her own strange blood mingled with zinc red earth the day her first moon arrived; and her body remembered the dance.

Raven's black cloak moved around her body as she flung her arms with the pulse of the drum, to throw the seeds to the earth. Her hair flew free from the bun that constricted it, and life surged up from the dormant pain of her injured womb, up the nerve cords of her spine. The energy of the dance rained out through the ends of her long hair.

She heard the whippoorwill's call and the laughter of the slaves as they tossed dirt on the smoldering ashes. Her movements went awkward, her hands pulled in close; the dance was over. Tears flowed heavy under concealment of the night sky outside the quarters, and with her hot feet she felt the hum of life and death inside the earth, and saw flesh molded over flesh, healed inside of her body, filling up the space where the man with corn-silk hair and blue eyes had scraped away the future of her child, the future that would have made itself round like the smooth bottom of a wooden bowl, waiting for fresh wild blue berries; but that future would hold no hope once change had come and drained her last blood.

Hatta Tchula, his Choctaw mother had named him. He was now Grey Fox to everyone except his father, who called him Tchula, and Raven, who called him by that name only when she loved or hated him deeply.

He dressed always in a suit and hat, even when he was surveying his property on horseback. The painting of his younger self and his father hung over the sitting room mantel; a declaration of belonging. His father was Jacques LeFlore, the Frenchman whose family befriended the Spanish, befriended the English, and survived all conquests for American soil with a sizable holding and no allegiances. His Southern comrades called him Jack Flowers.

In the painting, Jack Flowers concealed his right hand in his suit breast, his left hand placed on the shoulder of his son, who stood next to the embroidered claw-foot chair where now Grey Fox took his seat at the political meetings.

Jack Flower's smile showed an amusement with life, but his Tchula, ten years old, held a stare of ambiguous belonging. Both had dark hair cut in the short-bang style of a Frenchman, and not many glanced and rested long enough to see their differences, but Grey Fox often stared at the painting, wondering if the painter took the liberty of creating such anguish on his face when he didn't remember being less happy than his father.

He was forty years old now with daily responsibility that often made him dizzy with lists of things that never seemed to get done. Certain forms of personal maintenance became unnecessary, and his hair, once trimmed neatly, hung weighted and made the conservatism of his suit look awkward. The bones of his face narrow like carefully chiseled flint arrows; his jawbone solid like pelvic bone. He was handsome but maintained a stare as joyless as his childhood portrait.

When he was only twenty years old he was, by his father's standards, a capable man of mixed blood, and was given charge of LeFlore plantation, the place where the wallpapered rooms still smelled like the dried roots his mother kept private from her husband; behind the cool metal plates of the fireplace in summer, and inside the cold dark cupboards of the kitchen in winter. Her Tchula li, Little Fox, knew her secrets and kept them well.

"Own as much of yourself as possible," Jack Flowers said to his son, and he went to the Territory without Grey Fox. He intended to reclaim great portions of the land his own father had sold, in defeat, to the English.

Jack Flowers had been councilman to the Choctaw people. He had interpreted the proposed Treaty of Dancing Rabbit to the tribesmen, had stood under the muddy tents, laughed, gotten drunk, and danced with their women, had taken one as beautiful as his deceased wife into a tent and pushed his white flesh into her warm red flesh and made himself at home.

He had been councilman to the new state of Mississippi and was now a councilman in the Indian Territory. "You have to know your environment if you are to flourish in it. That is a real man's war, son."

Grey Fox was considered to be the perfect caretaker for the four hundred acres of woods, pasture, and fields cultivated by his father. "You are a good liaison," his father once said, holding Grey Fox's little face so resembling his Choctaw mother. "A liaison between prosperity and uncertainty. Together we can shape the alliance of landowners and the Indian people. A white man, a Chahta, you can be a great leader of great prosperity. When you are with them call yourself Grey Fox. They will respect a man with a name they can pronounce."

His father laughed stiffly, looking down to where his hand cupped the flame for his cigar, never looking to see his son's expressions.

So Grey Fox went about the tending of the land and slave stock, as committed to his duty as his upbringing called for. His father had given him the finest things and kept him by his side, though the boy's mother had been murdered when he was five. "Mistaken for a runaway mulatto," his father explained with no trace of a Frenchman's accent. "She was shot when she took a tree limb to a patroller's skull in defense of her own honor. We'll always miss her," he groaned, without touching or comforting the cold child who stood listening.

Grey Fox was a loyal son, never defying his father, never exploring the possibility of self-directed fate, until recently.

Lately he had taken to venturing to the place where once great fields of cotton sprawled, tended by the slave people of his boyhood, many of whom went in the caravan with his father.

"Say yes, Tchula, to all of them and you will be the richer man for it." But his father had not told him how to hold on to this oath when the heat of dissension sharpened the sight and senses of his fellow Southerners, whose allegiance he eluded.

Now, tall grasses covered the cotton fields of his youth. A sea of sweet beige tassels hid the dark-haired master from his slaves in his quiet thinking place where the grasses met the line of woods.

Ten species of cicadas hummed above and below his thoughts. *Why do I come here?* he asked himself where he sat vulnerable in the dry heat, resting his butt bones on the suit jacket turned blanket. He sat beneath the new leaves of poplar trees asking himself that question every day, watching the light of day come and burn away dew on the grasses until the sun threatened to set fire to his surroundings. He assumed some answer would come, but his thoughts tumbled numb without sucker feet to latch on to something solid.

His hair made movement and shadows in his corner vision, and he wondered if someone watched him there, but no one ever came, no humans, no spirits came to him there where the bugs sang in a painfully meditative pitch. The heat made parchment of his white shirt, and after several hours he threw his dusty suit jacket over Spirit's back and let his thoughts wander to the cool well water with lemon that Sybil's clean hands would place before him on the white linen as her mother had done when he was a boy.

Before mounting, he pulled his hair back to knot it beneath his hat. The twisting and twisting of his hair in his sweaty hand, the smell of his own body's oil; and he remembered it. He remembered running with her, his feet so sharp with pain that pain yielded to ice-cold ache. He remembered running and stumbling over roots entwined across the path she took in escape. He remembered the side of her face. "Bruises," he had said, crying and pointing at her when they stopped to drink from the hole revealed when she freed the roots of the sumac sapling from the orange earth. His mother knelt in the clothes that kept her warm; her husband's Frenchman trousers, his shirt loose around the shoulders. Her long hair was tucked beneath the squat hat.

"Bruises," he remembered when she used the shells of walnuts from earlier that day to bring the evasive water to his cracked five-year-old lips.

Spirit blew a warning from her snout, wondering why her master had paused so long before mounting her.

Tchula. He remembered the timbre of her voice on pitch with the hum of the cicadas. His hands shook hopelessly as he tried to grab the reins and steady his boot into the stirrup. He knew now why he had come to this place every day, and why he must not come again.

He tucked his hair beneath the hat not realizing he had repeated his mother's actions the morning she ran away from her husband in his clothes and tucked her hair under the hat.

Stop, stop, he heard his own boyish voice plead with his father.

He allowed Spirit to guide them home out of the overgrown fields. "Run, Spirit," he whispered to get distance from the place beneath the poplar trees, to get closer to his wife, and the sister and brother he'd adopted as his own. The certainty of their assuring faces across a solid oak table is what kept him forty years old in that moment.

Spring 1851

I N THE YEARS that seemed to promise division, there was quiet. Among the privileged there was unspoken concern for food, shelter, and belonging; things some had never been without, others had never taken for granted.

Before sleeping one night, Raven stood at her bedroom window, wondering at first where her husband was on a night when the crops had been planted and every head on the plantation rested in satisfaction of knowing that food would grow. She knew that the more her nerves were set on edge, the more he'd close himself away from her; never home while she was awake; and she wanted to be nonchalant like the mistresses of other plantations, keeping to their houses, their only concern the latest remnants from New York and London, the very cities their husbands despised for benefiting from Southern labor while abiding by Northern rules.

Why, she wondered, *aren't these women preparing for survival, while the men are preparing for war? Why aren't we coming together?*

That afternoon she had Nathan drive her to tea at the Bartlettes.' Missus Bartlette and Missus Campbell sat with their lips pinched and almost invisible as they sipped on their tea and gazed off into the distance, with little to say to the Indian woman except a terse dismissal.

"Dear, the tension will never come to that. Besides, Dear, war has brought us access to the finest things from other lands." The two of them laughed at Raven's concern for men's affairs, laughed, not threatening the integrity of the corsets that held the childbearing flab tight to their bodies. In the distance their children engaged in a proper game of croquet. The women continued to speak about things that did not matter, and Raven disappeared into a bell jar of estrangement as she watched the children play.

That night Raven sat up, again wondering about her husband. Noises from a distant bog floated in the humid air, grunts and screeches of mating alligators, and rarely seen birds. She imagined Grey Fox groaning in satisfaction somewhere in the darkness with some other woman, perhaps a slave woman, or the mistress of another plantation.

Raven closed her eyes and remembered the backs of the mothers; shoulders rounded with shawls pulled in tight where they sat at the fireplace, across the wide floor of the log cabin; whispers, and laughter from the pit of their bellies, soft hushing sounds when ideas were being contemplated. Her inki and the uncles out at the fire, their presence remembered only when they cleared their thoughts, acknowledgment that plans were being made.

Raven remembered the way her mother devoutly skinned the deer the day of a successful hunt; the bulk of her arms, muscle beneath the pillowy flesh. Her ishki pulled down hard on the vine to hoist the deer high enough to work on preparing it, the deer's gentle eyes round black domes of death, but her ishki tended this work as meticulously as she molded clay or bathed a child.

She remembered her father's eyes across the fire on the night she knew he would not trust the slow, negotiating ways of the women. She remembered her mother's look of knowing when she held the vine before tying it and was caught vulnerable by her daughter's stare; Ishki's eyes revealed denial over her husband's disrespect for the rhythm. The rhythm keeper, fallen prey to the awkward cadence of deceit.

Standing at the window, Raven shut her eyes tight against the memories and surrendered to the lesser pain; fantasies of Grey Fox gallivanting or dying a brutal death; the possibility of him leaving her someday without notice, for some fate he'd been secretly courting the way men do.

As her head became weighty with sleep, Raven drifted in illusion; the little girl she always wanted stirred on the sun bleached sheets in her imagination, like the memory of Dove playing all day near the stables with Nathan, then sleeping restlessly across the hall from her older sister's chambers. But Dove was a woman now, her brother, Golden, a man of his own thoughts, so different from her own. Raven, blew a sigh that released the tightly wound thoughts, and lay down on top of her own covers where she slipped quickly into a nightmare.

Fire burned so hot, so bright that her eyelids ached from where the lashes had singed away.

"Ishki," she was screaming but could see only glimpses of her mother's legs, down close to the ground beneath the flame. Raven crawled, coaxing her mind to withstand the heat, then the wall lowered, white hot, then cold pain in her bones, her teeth.

She startled awake to find herself on the floor, soaked in sweat again; the heavy drapery from the side of her canopy bed on top of her, her elbows and knees hot from the tight weave of the Oriental rug.

She lifted the drapery the same way little Golden had peered from under the bearskin. Raven listened for Sybil or someone to come and question the noise, but the house was quiet, the sky dark and humid with the sounds of frogs croaking deep. Staring up at the ceiling, she whispered, Ishki, Inki, and her heart seized in recognition of their pain; hatchet to the skull, chest blown open to rancid air and buzzards. Her body clinched remembering her own pain that day. *Run with the children,* she heard her mother say into the empty room where she lay in a fine white cotton gown soaked in sweat and urine, on a rug imported from a land she couldn't imagine.

Tears rolled into her ears. She cried for not running to the swamp, as her father had told her, for not birthing and raising a child and instilling in her the language and stories of her people as her mother had hoped when they bled together at the creek. She cried for the mended flesh in hard lumps inside her womb where the white man who smelled like corn whisky split her open and removed the seeds.

She curled into a ball and dreamed again. A slave woman stood on the other side of a creek, sun and shadow blending her dark features. She wore a white rag on her head, a black dress, and held a child in her arms, wrapped in a rag like the one on her head. The child squirmed and fell from the woman's arms. She was Choctaw, so tiny, her hair as long as her little body. In the dream Raven ran toward the rushing creek, and the three of them were one heartbeat beneath the water. There was darkness, and Raven could not see, could not breathe, until she felt herself rise up out of the water and fly away from where the child sat on a dry rock, watching.

Raven sat alone having her morning tea. A spell; the child. *I know I will meet her, that I have met her. I have seen her the way my mother saw. I must find her. How will I find her? Where will I go? How will I explain a journey, unaccompanied by my husband? Perhaps Golden will go with me. What will I tell him? What am I thinking?* she asked herself, and watched the perfect steel clouds for some shifting formations.

The sound of footsteps just beyond the French doors startled her. There stood a Choctaw man, his skin tight with fear and desperation. His eyes were hungry and tired. His ragged shirt was torn and hung long from his gaunt frame. The filthy gray trousers looked like they were held to his legs by the two sets of hands that clung there. A little girl and a little boy, twins; both of them in unwashed cotton shirts that were some shade of permanent dirt, no pants covering their knees, which protruded from the straight bone of their legs, no shoes on their perfect feet. The boy's head was rounder; the dominant twin with his straight dark hair lopped off above the ear in a jagged line. The girl's hair dangled limp around her shoulders and made her head look more narrow than it was. *Is this the child?*

Raven studied them, with her teacup still perched beneath her lips. But the girl's eyes were not familiar like the eyes of the baby in the dream.

"Ma'am?" The man spoke up above the rising wind that spewed milkweed into the air. "I heard about this place. We've been walking for a while, and are looking for work." Raven put the teacup down without taking her eyes off the man. He spoke up as if accused by her stare. "If you intend to send for the sheriff, let me know now, so I can keep on my way, ma'am." His words were lazy with weakness and he blinked, slow.

Raven imagined the bone on bone of the children's knees as they tried to escape men on horseback. "Sit," she said and led them into the dining room where he fumbled awkwardly, not sure if the fine fabric of the chairs would absorb the dirt from his clothes.

"It's okay, just sit down," Raven said, anxious to understand their plight.

The man rubbed his hands over the bumps and chafe spots of his face. "I ran off from some work 'cause the debt was getting higher every day, and we couldn't work any harder than we were working. The landlord came around looking over my daughter one day like he had plans to make good on what I owed by selling her off or something. I knew I'd try to kill him if he did, and if I succeeded I'd be killed; if I didn't succeed I'd be beat within an inch of death." Raven saw the raised welts on his lean arms. "That night I took my kids and ran off."

Raven held her hand up to arrest the man's desperate monologue. She was still standing on her side of the table in a delicate white-and-blue plaid dress. "Sybil!" she yelled in the direction of the kitchen. "Sybil, bring three more settings for tea." She looked back at the emaciated faces that now sat with eyes less dim. "And some biscuits, Sybil."

With more vigor, the man spoke up. "Ma'am, I can work for my keep. I just need a workplace for me and my girl and boy so we can earn enough to get on to the Territory." The smell of the biscuits quickened the man's words. "When I was ten, I was sold into servitude for a white family. I did what I had to do to get along there."

Raven focused on his strong forehead, how much it resembled her father's. She entertained the thought, *Perhaps he is the one who will help me find the child. Perhaps the child is in the Territory, and I will go there with him and find her. I can't leave Golden and Dove.*

"Ma'am?" The man stopped her thoughts. Raven sat down at the table and asked the question that had kept her from being able to listen. "Why did you come here?"

"Grey Fox is respected among the Chahta people who are still in Mississippi. I didn't know how true the conversations were, because I had been hearing about him since I was just a young man; a half-blood, no older than me, but master of his own plantation, the best trading corn in the state of Mississippi. I had heard about the place being five miles northwest of the gray swamp."

He listed the facts of his sudden appearance.

"So, ma'am, I didn't come to take advantage of your prosperity." The man sat up, dignified in his frail body. "I just need to know if there is work of any kind here for me, and a small corner of the barn or an empty slave cabin."

Raven chuckled and closed her eyes at his subordination. *Slave quarters?*

"What's your name?" she asked, somehow endeared to him; something about his lean face, his clothes the color of earth, and his constant rambling reminded her of an uncle who talked to the other uncles around the fire about his opinion on the state of the hunt, his opinion about the configuration of the stars as a sign of the time to plant, his opinion about the way to deal with white men. He talked even if none of the men were listening.

"Henry Trench." Henry sat up full in his chair now. "My mother and her mother were of the Okla Falaya, northeast Chahta." A chill went up Raven's spine and tightened the hair at the roots of her bun; she didn't remember the origin of her tense response. Again Raven held up her hand. To hear the language so fresh on his tongue made her hands and face go hot with fear of returning without warning to the day of her internal death.

"What are your children's names?" she asked.

"Samuel and Rebecca." The two looked up, brown eyes round in recognition of their names, and Raven smiled outside her own stiff austerity.

"Tea and biscuits," Sybil announced, opening the kitchen door with her backside. She swung the two plates of steaming biscuits in front of her, and placed them in the center of the table. She remained expressionless as she went to the china cabinet. She placed the saucers harshly in front of the frail, quiet children, startling them. She frowned, as if unimpressed by their performance, and placed the hot teapot directly in front of Henry Trench.

"Tea and biscuits, Mr. Trench," she said loudly, but barely parting her lips. "Good eating, Mr. Trench." She stressed his name again, asserting that she had heard enough of the conversation to know his name.

"That'll be all Sybil," Raven said. "Tell me Mr. Trench, what is your understanding of the current political situation?" Raven knew that any newcomer to Grey Fox's home would need to be a believer in Grey Fox's and Golden's politics, or there was no pleading his keep.

"The Southern rebels are making their own army, you know?"
he said, attempting to chew before swallowing, unlike the twins, who
were already eating the crumbs from their second biscuit. "It's secret.
The government just thinks they're still rebuilding after the Mexican
War. We got to keep the Yankees from knowing. It's coming along real
slow, but I give them five or six years and they'll have something. The
word is they're clearing out any Indians who don't mean to ally; keep
any of them from spying for the North. It's a blessing that your husband
is such a strong supporter of Southern culture, and a blessing that his
birthright is land that can't be taken away, because of his mixed blood."

Raven questioned his odd commitment. "As a man, once a sharecropper for Southern prosperity, what do you really think about it all,
Mr. Trench?"

"It's about business, ma'am. If I get myself to the Territory, I aim
to grow what I can grow. Cotton is king here, and, well, something's
gotta yield there. I'll own what I can own, and those too weak to be the
leaders can be slaves to my earnings."

Raven cocked her head slightly to one side, shocked by the conceit
that his returning strength revealed, conceit that didn't seem likely for
a man of his recent defeat. Raven thought for a while of how to ask
him to be more specific about his assertions, but Dove appeared from
the dancing room, and Raven's questions would go unanswered, until
Henry Trench's actions revealed him.

Dove had never experienced a swoon; a word she became so familiar with in her recent reading of Thackeray's "Lovel the Widower." So
intense was the feeling that all the blood in her body went rushing to
her core like a gush of water into a hungry mouth. Small stars appeared,
particles of the universe drew themselves into the vortex of her heart.
She felt her lips go numb, anticipating that they would soon touch his,
gently.

Life is what Dove felt, like a dead thing rising up from the rank-
est inhabited grave. Her heart sang like the first frogs in February, so
intense that the call was deafening. She looked into Henry Trench's
soft doe eyes and felt all the pain that he had ever known; from the

blinding and nerve-bending experience of air on his newborn body, to the thrashing he'd endured when captured by patrollers, his two small children turning away as the rags that held him were severed by the whip.

The fullness of love opened like a bud, deep and painful from its confines, and the current of emotion shifted from pleasure to agony; the memory of her mother's body colliding with the earth, blood from her mother's skull and milk from her breasts expelled with the impact. Above the sound of birds cooing on the veranda, she remembered Raven's cries, the smell of the bear hide; the warmth of Golden's breath, tears without sound.

As she stood in the doorway to the dancing room, Dove's skin melted away from her flesh as her whole body gave in to the swoon. The blood traveled quickly away from her head to deprive the surge of images. Her face was wet with tears and sweat, and the round, beautiful Dove felt the tilt of the doorframe that supported her. Henry stopped his ramble, and reached; one swift move from his chair to where Dove leaned. His dirty, musty arms caught her; the tightly knotted bun of her heavy Choctaw hair came undone, and her round face was peaceful, unconscious now.

The next week they were married; with dogwood pink and white in bloom. Petals rained from the twisted branches. A mix of Southern white and Choctaw tradition made the feelings of loneliness more profound for Raven, who watched in chiffon, standing next to her sister. Raven's face was in shadow and sun beneath the trees. A hot flash took her breath. *How, in just one week, does my sister have new family?*

Ribbons, red, yellow, flew on the spring breeze above the arch in the garden. Grey Fox sported a proud smile, as if some crop had born ripe fruit. The other man of his house, Golden, stood with his hands behind his back as if he wasn't sure how to look, what to feel. The white shirtsleeves were adorned with ribbons sewn by the slave girl Lula, who always halted in her chores to watch him pass; the shirt moved gracefully in the breeze, disguising his stiff body. He cast his eyes on the lovely couple because he didn't know where else to look.

Samuel and Rebecca clung to their new mother's legs, where the deer-hide tassels of her dress hung close to Henry Trench's new black trousers, and the couple engaged in a passionate, unchristian kiss.

The four of them were married like the wind and assorted petals are married in an unexpected dance before an unexpected storm.

Henry did not experience the same swoon when he looked at Dove, but saw only resurrection, saw the end of his suffering, saw home, safety for the children, whose arms were still much too spindly and much too pale for Choctaw children. He saw the opportunity to own what he could own, to be a strong victor over his old circumstances, saw himself forever on the proper side of the furrowed fields.

Henry's tattered clothes were to be burned beneath the laundering fire, where Sybil and the twin slave girls toiled on a cloudy Saturday morning, but they were stirred in with the lye soap and carted away on tops of heads, strong necks, one hand supporting the basket, one the skirt; they descended the hill to the quarters for the older boy to have some pants that Josephine didn't have to mend from feed sacks.

In his new clothes, Henry satisfied his hungering pride. The wind now blew freely through the places in his soul that sharecropping had clogged with dead weevils. His arteries opened on a diet of lean meat, fresh vegetables, pure sharp whisky that stripped away the pork fat of those years. He was free now, free to return his spirit to the virile life he had once known; the peaceful stillness of a quiet morning before sunrise, dampness, faint light, deer grazing on wet clover. On mornings of hunting, blood swelled in his veins resurrecting the ancient instincts.

When he returned from the hunt he thrust himself into Dove's virgin warmth where he exploded and felt in harmony with all the world's destructive forces and singular with all deities.

Dove shed the decadence of overwhelming fabric and became soft, a woman in easy-to-caress cotton dresses. Her hair draped like heavy seaweed. She gave up the hard-soled shoes and wore moccasins fashioned by the hands of a Creek woman indentured to a white man at the county trading post. She looked like the spirit of Henry's freedom.

Both of them clung to a lost or forsaken heritage; Dove through her new dresses, Henry through his new warrior pride. But they each enjoyed the comforts sustained by dark personas who passed cautiously like broken-spirited wolves, claws never drawn, teeth never baring, eyes cast down in submission, but feral someplace far back in their eyes.

"Feral," Henry often said, shaking his fork and looking up across the table at his new wife whenever Sybil left the dining room. He asked Dove about her complacency with such a crafty being in her presence every day. "Don't you wonder what docile creatures plan in their dens at night?" He recalled his own weary hands shaking in the dark barn where he tied the bundle of supplies before running in broken soiled shoes, away from the debt that grew and festered like an infected wound, threatening to turn his whole body and his children's bodies and souls into the sharecropper's debt.

His wounds were mended by the promise of General Thorpe, who sheltered him and his children when they were brought to him by the patrollers. The general agreed to settle the debt if Henry Trench agreed to follow his thirst for freedom to the land of the half-breed Grey Fox.

General Thorpe's voice was clear, his eyes intent on the desperate eyes of Henry Trench. "I have known his father for many years; we cannot trust him. He has never shown an allegiance to the South, nor has his father. His crops have set out for sixteen years without cotton. That is highly profitable soil. He has grown too quiet in the meetings, listening, listening with never a word of allegiance." General Thorpe paced the hot room, where a breeze refused to enter but lingered just outside the open window, tempting Henry to leave. But Henry looked at his hungry children and the coins stacked on the desk. The general paced before them in his gray uniform and hypnotized Henry into submission.

"I can do this. Yes sir. I will gain his trust and bring you any information that may lead to his legal removal."

"Good, then." The general placed the coins into a sack. The twins' sweaty black hair seemed to dry, and their mouths watered at the sound of the precious coins like pebbles tumbling over pebbles in the creek. "Good." The general held the sack out before Henry, "If you help me,

I will see to it that you are well cared for, and your children will be well cared for. If you cross me, I will have you killed."

"Feral," Henry said to his new wife, his voice slightly nasal in its new aristocratic tone, which he had affected after listening to Grey Fox on nights of monologue about Yankees, after the brandy took hold of Grey Fox's deep, dignified voice and left the lazy nasal sound. Henry secretly adored Grey Fox's loose submission of the deep tone and subconsciously adopted this sound for his own, to suit the new mended man. As much as a person could desire to be another, Henry coveted his new master, who accepted Henry Trench into his home without question, without question.

The next night, after the soothing brandy, Raven walked the corn-field and counted the raindrops, contemplating her life. The rain came at first in sprinkles, then a sobering cold shower fell down on her black cloak. She was drenched where she stood, and did not mind, for the sudden fevers had brought a flash that also drenched her dress beneath the cloak. Her feet rested there in the cold mud, memory of clay between her toes. She was ashamed of what she must have looked like there; Dove's words, "Sister, you better not let Gray Fox know you trudge down the hill to the fields like a woman of the night. He will swear you are mad in your changes."

From one of the shack windows came shifting lantern light, then a cry; like a goat kid longing for its mother. Raven moved closer, among the thin pines that made the wall between the fields and the shacks. Pine branches dripped heavy with rain like the pines that sheltered her family departing from the caravan of the relocated. She heard a banjo play in another cabin; metal strings, dry fingers, joyful. The rain hushed the turmoil of questions in her head and she stood still and quiet. Through the small window she saw Josephine; the breeding woman lay with covers twisted about her. The young tall field girl Lula dabbed Josephine's forehead with the cool rag. The lantern light shifted in the current of air caused by Sybil, who hustled about.

Raven inhaled deep, her chest taking in the wet air at the thought of Sybil coming down to the quarters and it not being a Saturday night.

Inside the warmly lit cabin, there was movement around the basin of water, and then the child, unswaddled, was handed down to where Josephine lay with her top around her shoulders.

The cold rain poured down on Raven's heavy cloak, a shivering breath escaped and fogged the glass where mother, *ishki* and *alla*, child, lay warm and exhausted. Raven was struck by the resemblance the child bore to her brother, Golden, when he was born. "Is this the child in my dreams?" she whispered to the glass that blurred her view.

In the morning Raven sat with Golden at breakfast. Henry Trench, Rebecca, and Samuel all took to Dove's lazy morning habits, and were still sleeping. Sybil poured their coffee and placed Golden's napkin on the lap of his faded work pants, as if he were still six years old. Golden sat up tall while he was waited on; thin stature, his tied-back hair, frumpled hat, shirt of multicolored ribbon, stiff, dirty pants, and high boots. Raven frowned, tilting her head in disapproval of her brother's spoiled behavior, which over the years was reinforced by his position as Grey Fox's second man at LeFlore, a position that he'd held since Raven was fifteen years old, when she was in love with her Grey Fox the way Dove was in love with Henry Trench. Golden had benefited from his sister's good fortune, and never showed gratitude. Their separate ironies of entitlement constantly pitted them against each other.

He was named Fallen Golden Feather by the aunts who were with his mother the day he came without enough warning. His ishki did not come in from the herb gathering before the pains came quick and sharp, and he fell from his mother's bleeding core into a patch of leaves, cold and wet; the cord of innards trailed down to where he lay.

Golden, was a shortening of his name that only Raven knew was more flattering than his given name.

"Brother?" Raven questioned. "The new slave child in the quarters, I have seen it through the windows." Raven did not hide the possible shamefulness of her voyeurism. "Is the baby yours?"

"Sister?" Golden laughed deep like a mellow drum. "You're a lady, and you have no business skulking about in the quarters. Besides, what difference does it make? All the slaves of LeFlore are your husband's property, to trade, sell, and treat as he pleases."

He went back to gulping his coffee and ripped the biscuits in a hurry to get to his monitoring of the work. He continued to chuckle, shaking his head, his voice deep and thick from where the laughter erupted in his chest and burst forth into the cool morning.

Raven loved him, but he was arrogant and disrespectful to her, to the elder woman in the house of his upbringing. Her tongue pressed against the cage of her clinched teeth.

"Don't worry, sister, these things happen. Children are born of simple desire and men's needs. Bloodline has nothing to do with it." Raven squinted one eye shut in a stressful pinch. "Besides," he went on the way he always did, testing the limit of his sister's emotions, "you have a spell on you from the voodoo woman. I don't think you're capable of yielding any additions to this bloodline."

Raven did not respond but continued to look in his direction, her mind dwelling in another time.

"Raven, what is wrong with you? You've been behaving so strangely fickle."

Raven spoke passionately now, the light powder on her face giving in to perspiration.

"Golden, the child does not look dark. The child looks like you when you were a baby in our mother's arms, clinging to her breasts with your pink lips. She is yours, isn't she, brother? Don't answer me, don't answer."

Golden watched Raven orchestrate a reality for herself, laying a foundation of questions and answers.

"Don't you see, brother, you've brought forth a child who is damned to be motherless? Grey Fox has told you not to mingle with slaves. You have stepped out of place, brother." Raven's voice was going hoarse with stress.

Golden tried to answer her without smirking or laughing at his sister's preposterous behavior; perspiring and fidgeting with her collar.

"Sister, this child..." He stopped and ran his fingers through his hair. "It does not matter, sister. They are slave women. The white men have the same slave codes about commingling blood, and they don't follow them. You know that landlords are truly the lords of their property. Grey Fox is no better than John Bartlette, and I'm not going to hide my face in shame for any occasional dealings I've had with the slave women." He tilted his head to one side.

"Things are no different than they've ever been, Raven. What's really bothering you?"

Raven shook her head and looked away from him.

"Raven, sister, if you think this way, then why do you mingle there at night, envying their nigger ways? Is it after a few goblets of brandy that you find such a journey befitting a lady?"

Raven wiped the morning lip color onto the freshly folded napkin and discarded it with disgust for her brother. She massaged the tension on the right side of her neck the way she did these days when she was having trouble explaining herself. She reached out for Golden's face, in the same manner that he had reached for hers, a gesture they both inherited from their mother, but he backed further away and nodded.

"This is not about me, is it? This is about Grey Fox, your constant obsession with him leaving you. Well, don't worry. As a man I can tell you, sometimes we just need warmth and comfort from an old mammy rather than always having a woman need us. Be glad he didn't seek that out away from LeFlore. There is some honor in that."

Golden chuckled again. "Your husband is a busy man sister, and has overlooked the corn basket hauled at the waist to conceal his own offspring." Raven broke the sound of laughter with the flat familiar openness of a mother's hand; she smacked the sun-tightened skin of his face, and sent his hat and hair ungraceful in their flight. He held his hand there to calm the sting.

"There is war in the air, brother. It might be far off, but it brings dreams, memory, fear of losing my husband, my kin." Raven reached for his hand. "And you are my brother. I still recognize you as the little boy who walked holding my hand for two days, running and walking. You were only four. Maybe you don't remember, but you were afraid, and I was injured, still bleeding. Do you remember the journey? I needed to rest, remember? The woman in the swamp, she was no voodoo woman. She harbored us for a cycle of the moon."

"Sister, I don't recognize you when you are like this. We were talking about the child in the quarters. What does memory have to do with this? The swamp woman did put a spell on you, sister. If not, then where are the children of your house? Where? Perhaps your husband has solved this riddle."

Something in the back of his mind told him to stop. At seeing the anguish in her face, he wanted to comfort her, but that would mean going with her on a journey that he denied remembering.

Raven dabbed the perspiration from the flash of fever, and pinched her eyes shut to focus her mind; her parents, and the child she wanted, danced in the dark lonely place inside her where all pain resided.

"I am the mother of this house. Any children who will come, will come through me." Raven looked away, and looked back at Golden with a new stern face. "The man that killed our parents took the children of my house; tore my insides apart, took the seeds of the children out, and left them to die in the sun." Raven unbuttoned the collar of her blouse and breathed in rapid pants. "The woman of the swamp harbored us, and when I was well she said she could no longer accommodate me; just like that, told us to leave." Raven put her hand to her forehead, where the sweat was threatening to drip into her eyes. She tried to focus her thoughts again.

Raven's voice fell into the isolated feelings. She heard the redheaded woman's words, *You got to leave here now.* She placed her brother's hand to her face and tried to steady her breathing as the images came fast, but Golden held his bottom lip in tight and looked slightly to the right of her face to show disinterest in Raven's trance, which he convinced himself was her ploy to win the argument.

Raven went on, lost in her pain, "I remember Mother's twisted mouth, the scent of wisteria blooming above the stench of death on the back of my tongue, when we ran, a day later. I was so weak. The woman of the swamp should not have turned me out. I was not well. I'm so sorry Golden I didn't know what I was doing, I didn't intend to leave the swamp and go back there. Dove was so heavy on my back, the crib board straps burned and cut my shoulders. I just wanted to go home. I'm sorry brother." Raven was lingering, somewhere on a ledge above a pit of torment. She stood above the flashes of memory with the crib board on her back, holding Golden's little hand, watching the shadows of vultures over her people's swollen bodies.

Raven's tears and sweat dampened Golden's stiff hand. "They are all gone, Golden, and I am the mother of this house, and you are a child in my house, your children are to be children of my house."

Golden gently raised her up from where she slumped limp. He held her soggy face in his rough hands. Raven looked into his eyes and remembered that her little brother was a man, and he did not need to say the words, but he did.

"I am not your child, sister, and I have no children."

The despair that welled up in Raven made the rest of her brother's words profound in their hurt.

"I respect Grey Fox like a father, but I am not his charge, nor the scapegoat for his errors. If war is in the air, then I will go away from both of you and fight, be my own man."

Raven gasped and moved his hands aside. They were the same height, same build, Ishki and Inki's children. Her voice took a high pitch, and she spoke in her mother's voice, "If you do, you will commit the same sins that have been committed against you, and you and I will be separate in the same house."

A cold chill ran up Golden's spine at hearing the first voice he'd ever known, come cold and dead across his sister's lips. He turned to leave their madness, to leave the overwhelming sweet, clean scent of wisteria memories that rolled in on a damp morning breeze. He fought back the helpless angry feelings of the boy who denied the memory of his parents' murder and his sister's rape. The sound of the soldier's boots echoed in his own steps as he walked quickly to leave the dining room. The damp floor where he and Dove lay shaking under the bear-skin; the sound of Raven screaming, her breath coming shorter until she was silent and the men talked among themselves as if they'd just finished a game of arrows. He had not slept that night, his eyes unable to close; his breath frozen, silent death, his baby sister's slumber, his older sister dying under the weight of the white-skinned monster. He remembered.

"Golden. Minti!" Raven called after him like his mother, but he stormed from the dining room of fine wood and china. He did not turn toward the calling of his name, but stopped at the mantel in the dancing room and yelled out, "Damned Northerners," and in one long sweeping of his arm knocked the vase of wisteria blossoms to the floor. Glass and tiny purple petals landed at Henry Trench's boots.

"Golden, are you well?"

"Yes, brother." And they took off to their day of managing the property.

Sybil stood on the other side of the kitchen door eating the last biscuit before the inevitable cleaning up behind the sorrows of Grey Fox's patchwork clan.

Raven went to the veranda, where already the morning was humid and her sister sat ridiculous in her task beneath the twin oaks. She had collected cane for a week, sheared it with one of Grey Fox's knives, her hand cut in the same place with every pass. Dove so looked like her ishki, a woman she did not remember, but in Dove's search for womanhood she faultily took up her mother's ways. She was now attempting to weave a basket. *She will always be a child,* Raven thought, *too young to remember that day.*

From the adjacent kitchen window Raven heard a quick giggle, and then, "Lord have mercy on my massas." Sybil watched Dove getting the cane strips stuck in her loose hair. Raven yelled out, offended at Sybil's judgment, "More tea, please!"

Dove looked up from where she sat in the yard, just above where the trees descended downhill to the quarters. Her round cherry face held the same look of her infant days. Simple red cotton dress with ribbon hastily sewn on the sleeves, and white apron like a servant in bright colors; she and Raven stared at each other in the distance, and looked away embarrassed at what they saw.

Raven plopped herself down in the big rocking chair. She rocked back and forth and imagined a child in her arms sleeping. She saw the child's sweet face against the backdrop of tulip tree blossoms pink and orange.

Disturbing her daydream, Grey Fox's horse leapt up onto the lawn from climbing the difficult hill. Raven assumed he was coming from his rounds in the quarters, but he had taken the field route back from his obsessive musing, from searching for answers he didn't really want, like picking at a scab knowing it would make the sore bleed again.

He had taken the difficult route home, because it was fast and he needed the familiar of home, of his wife, the smell of lemon verbena where it settled in the sweat between Raven's two breasts. He needed *home* after a morning of memory.

Raven stood up, waiting to hear his anger about the child born against his plan. He vigorously rode his horse past Dove and onto the tailored green lawn beneath where Raven stood. His face was handsome and stern. *Golden's words are true. Josephine, has somehow concealed the child,* Raven thought.

Their eyes were locked on each other in his approach, each looking deeper for understanding of the other's thoughts, then they recognized each other; some amalgam of fear and need melded in that moment. Grey Fox saw the Raven who had come to him broken, needing comfort and safety. He saw in her eyes a reflection of the boy who needed to save the one he loved from the plight she'd endured. They saw each other, and simultaneously conjured flesh against flesh, where just beneath their skin coursed different blood, like shifting currents of a river.

That's how they lay that afternoon, juxtaposed in separate needs for comfort; their lovemaking, dissatisfied fits of holding and thrusting in opposition. By late afternoon they lay side by side in the luxury of their bed, spent. He spoke first. "I hope Golden has made the rounds in the fields, checking the placement of seed. The kernels should be measured properly."

She said nothing.

"Raven," Grey Fox whispered into her ear. Raven feared he would speak some justification of the new child, but his mind had been hovering, tormented in the space of remembering his mother's words, *We have to get away from your father,* the words that came in memory after he'd refused the images of her sad face, like Raven's sadness, which consumed him. *I cannot make her happy,* he thought lying beside her, poised to speak to her about his torment. He could feel her anticipating his words, her grip sinking past his skin and moving through his blood, and he couldn't stand being near her for another second.

"See to it that Sybil and the other house girls prepare the parlor for tonight's meeting with General Thorpe and his gentlemen from the governor's office." He was standing with his pants already buttoned by the time he'd finished his sentence. His hair hung in his face so that their eyes did not meet.

Outside their chambers Raven heard a servant's fallen heels thud and echo in the lifeless halls of their home.

April 21, 1851

JOSEPHINE'S BABY was swaddled in light cotton, almost the weight of gauze. The days were cool in the morning, but stifling by noon. The baby girl's skin was honey colored just like her father's, her cheeks two semicircles that squeezed her tiny nose when she fixed her face to cry at night, but Josephine coaxed her purple nipple between the child's searching lips and kept her quiet. The next day the child slept, having been kept awake all night by Josephine's thump, pinch, tickle. In the day, the blankets were hung over the windows, the baby placed quietly in the little trough crib, and off Josephine went to the fields for early summer planting.

Josephine was so tired the next day. Every time she stood from breaking the clumps with the dirt rake, dizziness threatened to lift her up out of her body. She may as well have been a ghost. She did not remember dropping seeds into the last three holes she'd prepared, but she was sure she had as she drifted between dream and awake. She saw her new baby's face in each of the tiny rocks she flicked away from tilled soil with her cracking fingernails.

"Mama Josephine." Lula, the young girl who helped with the labor some nights before, spoke into the dream space. "Best wake up, Mama Josephine."

"Hush, child, I ain't sleepin." Josephine's voice was hoarse as if morning had not been driven away by noon.

The girl kept poking the smoothed poplar stick into the mounds, and dropping seed from the grain bag. She kept her pace slow and watched Josephine in her side vision. "The baby girl, she feed good last night, Mama Jo?"

"Yes, sure 'nuf." Josephine bent back to the sun and squeezed the tired muscles of her back. "Gonna keep her long as I can." Josephine's face was chestnut brown against the flawless blue sky.

"Sure 'nuf Mama Josephine," was all Lula said when she saw the way Josephine's tired face stretched out against the blue like a soul ready for rest.

Josephine took a deep breath and stepped with young Lula in the planting.

"Mama Jo, what make you think Massa gonna sell her? She ain't even been weaned."

"Child, I believe he was grievin about somethin awful that night. I believe he meant to lay with me too, but I don't believe a man of rules like him meant to bring forth no Massa slave baby. I love what God done let me have of my own want, but Sybil is right, once Massa know a baby came of it, he ain't gonna let that be."

"Maybe you can go live in the big house and be his special gal," Lula giggled.

"Hush gal. Shush." Josephine waved her arms in an attempt to keep the shame away from her; the shame that of all the unlikely women to ever lie with, Master Fox chose Mama Jo.

Josephine flailed at the air as if swatting annoying deerflies.

"I ain't studin him."

"What kinda spell he had on you Mama Josephine?"

Josephine mumbled, "The kind that say this ain't none of that breedin stuff; and I don't care what ya'll think. That night was mine; that baby mine. I ain't lying about you need to hush either Lula, so hush."

Little Man came down with the water. He was almost a teen boy, but he wasn't bigger than the little boys. Master Golden had set his tasks as running the water, running the cows back into the barn before a storm, running, because that's something he could put to use within the boundaries of those four hundred acres; a child bred to be a strong field hand, but he couldn't be sold. He had short legs, big feet, a stout body, could run over the furrowed fields like a bunny rabbit, and all the while keep the water bucket steady.

Josephine looked down on his nappy head, which glistened in her dizzy vision as he dipped the water. "You all right Mama Josephine?" They both looked up to see if Master Golden or Master Tchula was riding near.

Grey Fox did not know it, but many of the older slaves who went on with Jack Flowers to the new Territory had called him Tchula li, Little Fox, and although they called him Massa Fox in his presence, he was Tchula li in the fields, some compassion still left for the man who was once a sullen little boy, now just the steel-faced man with nothing on his mind but keeping the rhythm of crops and the rhythm of good commerce.

Josephine sipped a little from the clay cup, lips cracked, and she spilled the rest slowly down the front of her dress to blend the darkness of sweat around her collar with the leaking milk of her breasts.

"She wasn't crying, was she Little Man?"

"No ma'am, quiet as a little ole mouse."

She waved him on, retied her white head cloth, and went back to breaking the clumps, poking the holes and dropping the seeds that would soon burst through the finely worked soil.

October 1851

Fall weather came early.

The men's eyes danced slow, graceful around the room. From across the hall, lush piano chords resounded, played by the twin servant Emma, who had been told several times to dust the keys without making music.

The men were busy positioning themselves in the room and did not mind the music for their political dance. Only six years before, these same men discussed long into the night the conquests that led to the American-Mexican War.

A thin, sweet layer of cigar smoke just above their heads drifted from the window and out to where one slave carried the news of the evening to another. The information wafted down the hill to where the adult slaves were comforted by the damp smell of tightly wrapped tobacco, which meant news soon to come.

Grey Fox held to his father's tradition of hosting the meetings, a way to always take the pulse of pending conflict. The uniforms; gray against the pale skin of the bearded ones, the pale skin of the young blond ones and dark-haired ones. Most of them were Grey Fox's age when he was gifted with the burden of this property.

They laughed and lit the cigars as they settled into embroidered, upholstered chairs with cherry wood legs; their eyes danced, slowly assessing the camaraderie of the pack. Outside, an evening rain fell gentle at first, but heavy now that they were settled into the circle. The first ceremonial brandy burned in their guts, but Grey Fox's snifter of brandy was still half full, and that was the first sign of his neutrality.

General Thorpe spoke first and a leader was established.

"The vote. We must influence the vote. Every good Democrat will be necessary in securing our seats in the Congress." His uniform, tight across his chest, bound his shoulders and held him secure in the chair like a body after the passing, wrapped for anointing. He somehow managed to bend his arm and stroke the new beard; its first streaks of gray lay down straight like slumbering quills. He and Grey Fox were both forty, both approaching the conversation about slavery with territory to protect; General Thorpe's being the territory of Mississippi, of the South, of commerce, the ports to the east where trade of barrel upon barrel of brandy had been stopped, where the shipment of brown shiny-skinned Africans had been stopped, where one day killing would result over an attempt to arrest the shipment of the king's white crop. General Thorpe's territory was the territory of the South, where he had grown up hunting, skipping rocks in the creek, and staying within the parameter where white men guarded against the wild spaces that had not yet been tamed.

For Grey Fox, conversations about slavery were conversations concerning the territory he must guard, keep, watch, the land where his home had always been, where his demons and saints sat quiet inside the smoke-tinged walls of the sitting room where the men, including the esteemed newly appointed governor, John Isaac Guion, heralded by the *Mississippian and State Gazette* as a true Southern leader, smoked the finest cigar.

Each man was to speak his opinion, to vow his commitment with upstagings of outrage. The governor spoke up when all had been said. "Be damned the North, Yankee thieves benefiting from our struggles and our ingenuity. Their textile mills run on our cotton labored in our fields, by our slaves. They depend on it, the French depend on it. I say we threaten trade and force more slave states. They'll buckle. They wouldn't risk annihilating the source of their wealth." Then he proclaimed, after gulping his drink, "If war should come, I'll burn my cotton fields to save them."

He turned to Grey Fox. "What will you have us do, good man? What would a man of white blood and Indian blood have us do? Speak to us as a man who has held his own through storms of change."

The governor's theatrics threatened to rip the seams of his tight-breasted suit coat.

Grey Fox sat expressionless, not listening to the chatter until now. He had been contemplating the painting above the mantel again, imagining his form sinking into the same place his father once sat in this chair, in this room, wielding power and gaining allies with the lie of loyalty. How had his father known what to do at every turn of white politics, when it seemed that to merely keep one's affairs in order and survive was task enough?

Grey Fox replayed the question, his face sober, the other faces loose, leaning in. "Tell us, half-blood."

Outside the window, the moonlight reflected in the cold raindrops as they slid down the wavering panes of glass.

"Have your brandy, man; and speak," General Thorpe said with a spray of spit flying from his lips.

"I would say that we must fight for what is ours, for what we have worked hard to build."

The men lifted their snifters to the candelabra that looked over them; twenty tiny fires burning above their council, and they roared in drunken satisfaction. But General Thorpe and Henry Trench were already engaged in the drink. Their eyes over the dome of the glass conveyed the shift, brought on by Grey Fox's ambiguity.

Fall nights were cold and uncomfortable to the adjusting heart, but days were still hot, still thick, lush green, and unbearably humid. Corn continued to yield, and it was soon to be shucking time again. Josephine weeded with the spade under the heat of a cloudless sky. The bug noises down in the fields were so loud she couldn't hear a peep out of the baby if she wanted to. Her straw hat kept the shade and bobbed with the intention of her every stab. Keeping the child up at night and working all day had settled into a tolerable pattern. The little nameless baby remained free after six months of exile.

Josephine's strength full again, the earth shuddered while she worked the spade. And though she was happy with her new baby, she grieved at what would come soon; the field hand Burtrome was being sent that night to lie with her.

She would work the fields till the fall harvest was done, and as her womb and her agitation grew, she would be sent to sew and spin through the winter months. In early spring she would dye wool, and in summer her black body would yield a new brown crop to be kept healthy and clean for five years, then sold.

She stabbed at the roots of weeds. The little ones ran behind her but could scarcely keep up with the picking up of the discarded roots; chickweed, burdock, hemp weed, all to be secretly kept for medicine.

Little Man came running without the water bucket this time, his vest open. Sun baked the brown smoothness of his just-before-manhood chest, pants tied with hemp rope. He leapt barefoot like a scared deer over the harvested tobacco crop, to the cornstalks where Josephine worked among the leaves that rustled in her wake.

"Baby is cryin, Mama Josephine."

Josephine looked up and wiped her brow. She took a deep breath and held Little Man firmly by his bare hot shoulders. "You sho, boy?"

"Yes, ma'am. She sho' nuf cryin."

"Lord, it ain't but noon day."

Josephine looked up in the direction of Massa Tchula's house, but with the patchwork green of poplar and maple leaves going yellow, she could not see if there was dust raised by his or Massa Golden's horse.

From a few rows away, Lula hacked at the weeds but did not move along. "Mama Josephine, you done named her yet?" Lula's voice came from between the stalks of green; the sound of her spade came down, severing the root of red dandelion. "Best name her;" down with the spade again; "before he know, and sell her off to keep the Missus happy. Maybe she'll go with her name, and you'll find her when you get to heaben."

Josephine dug her hoe into the ground like she was taking the one good stab into Tchula li's septum, soft bone cracking under her pain, and she walked out of the cornfield, exposed to the house on the hill, sweat around her dirty collar, the two dark circles of milk like eyes on her broad chest.

Raven stood on the veranda where the heat could justify the saturating sweat that soaked through her undergarments and her dress. She peered down to where the baby's cry broke from the harmony of the bug hums. The cry echoed up the hill, reverberating on quartz, flint, the bed of the first fallen leaves. In the afternoon shadow of trees, moss made fuzzy covering for the rocks, but the baby's cry bounced over that cushion of quiet.

The cry reached the flat expanse of lawn below the veranda, rolled recklessly toward the white house, and shattered on the pillars that held Raven on her platform. The shudder tunneled up through the wood, through the hard soles of Raven's shoes, to the open palms of her Choctaw feet, straight up the bones of her long body to the plate of her skull, where dreams of the child had been reflected night after night.

Down in the quarters, Josephine ran across the yard. Sweat trailed down both sides of her head as she hurried to quiet the child, whom she would call Lilly, for the first and last flower of summer.

Raven took to her bed that afternoon, nauseous from the overwhelming yearning for a child. In the dusty heat of her bedroom she removed the dress, the corset, her aching breasts relieved to be free of the agitating material, and she fell into a deep sleep. She dreamed that afternoon of her body rapped in and around Grey Fox's, her body like a snake's threatening to constrict and devour him unless he released the seed that would bring her mother's wishes of a child to pass down the traditions. But when she awoke the light approached peach in the sky and peeked through the opening in the drapes to bring the reality of emptiness in her womb.

Her husband and General Thorpe were meeting again that evening, and Raven stayed in her chambers. She rang several times, pulling the corded rope that led to the kitchen, and Sybil brought eight snifters of brandy, one at a time on a silver tray, as if each time were the only time ma'am rang for a drink.

The whisky was not hot on the back of the tongue, but bitter like the deep root medicine of the redheaded woman in the swamp, whose solid touch Raven could still remember. The brandy was good medicine for washing away Raven's sorrow and calming the spasming walls of her womb. In the small porcelain basin, she soaked the menstrual rags in the brandy, making red clouds of where she bled her last true blood.

The next morning Raven woke to the sound of Grey Fox's horse, Spirit, snorting in the distance as galloping hooves took them both away from the house, the fields, the quarters. She pushed her head away from the pillow; the rancid liquor smell in her own sweat turned her stomach. She listened but could not hear above the hiss of late night bugs. *What, she wondered, did Grey Fox and the men discuss last night? Did he come in and tuck me beneath the covers, or was it Sybil? Did the men plan a battle the way my father did, leading our clan into death?*

Before she could tame her intoxicated thoughts she saw the eyes of her rapist, felt the rough hands on her pried-open thighs; the brandy from the night before rose up in her throat, and she swallowed back.

The redheaded woman of the swamp walked through the room with accusing eyes; the smell of mold from her cabin, the place where she, Dove, and Golden slept on a small round table away from the scurry of rats. Raven remembered the rancid fruit smell of the woman when she leaned over her each day to check the color of Raven's tongue, where the layer of leaves was placed daily.

She remembered the woman's words. *Each moon the blood will come heavy, but a child will never live in there, never.*

"Sybil," she yelled out, not bothering to pull the cord, and Sybil appeared. "Yes'm."

"Where has the Master Fox gone?" Raven steadied herself, her feet slung over the edge of the bed.

"To the fields this mornin ma'am. But it's noontime now," Sybil added in a condemning tone. "Would you like tea?"

Raven didn't answer.

"I'll bring tea." Sybil left the room with such force that the warm air outside the window rushed through the room and followed her sun-bleached apron out of the stale chambers of Raven's grief.

"Crazy," Raven whispered out loud questioning her sanity. She sat on the edge of the bed, and entertained obsessive thoughts about the slave woman Josephine, breeding with the seasons.

That night, after Grey Fox fell into a sleep of breaths so deep and quiet that death rested on his naked chest, Raven stole away to the quarters.

Josephine stood in the doorway to her cabin, her Bible black and sweaty in her hand. She had prepared her speech for Master Tchula, but was ready to give it to Raven or anyone who came for the child: "This Bible is mine. I cain't read it, but I know that the Lord's love is true. I know that love is freedom, and I love my baby and you cain't take that away."

Raven crossed the threshold into the darkness beyond the shaft of light cast by the lantern, still hooded in the black cloak. She had never been inside the cabins, and her mouth watered; a wolf smelling skin and hair and sweat different from her own, smelling new hair, skin, flesh of kin. Dampness and mold saturated the wood walls and floors of the tight space.

She hadn't planned her speech the way Josephine had, and was having difficulty standing in the sweet fog of her drunkenness. "Josephine" was all she said before sitting down at the only table, where the lantern lit a small space of the cabin. She allowed the hood to make a shadow over her face, as she listened to the sound of the baby girl sucking her mother's milk. A Bible in one hand, the child wrapped in a small white sheet in the other, Josephine loomed over Raven in the darkness of the cabin.

"Josephine, I won't let them sell her. I will keep her at the house. I will keep Golden's child in the house of his sister, and she will be safe."

Raven's concocted reality about the child's origins made its way into her negotiation. Nothing was said. Regretting, forgetting, foreseeing, whole lifetimes occurred in the silence. The same round eyes of her childhood shifted, brown pupils traveling across the whites of her eyes like moons swiftly over the years of her life. Raven's sweat dripped onto the table in the darkness.

"Ma'am, I know she don't look Negro, but she mine." The words were not the ones Josephine had rehearsed. The desperation in Josephine's voice snapped like the whip severing flesh. "I'll do anything for you and Massa, but don't let him sell her, she mine." Her voice cracked as she beseeched, as if saying a prayer, knowing she could not control the fate of her baby girl. Whenever she carried a child for Grey Fox's brown crop, he came to check on her with Sybil in tow. He came into the shack without knocking the same way Raven had, as if they were entering the horse stable. Master Fox would hold Josephine's head back, look at the whites of her eyes, and instruct his cook, "Make sure Josephine has the good cuts of pork leftover from the supper, and give her some fruit from Bartlette's trade, and remind Little Man to keep that calf from the cows so there's plenty of milk for her." Sybil would nod, hands behind her back, eyes cast down away from her friend. On the way out she'd turn and smile, she and Josephine both knowing she'd pinch an extra inch, and good rations for Josephine meant a little something for everybody in the quarters. They'd make the best of that special treatment that had nothing to do with Josephine but with the quality of the slave she would harbor for nine months.

She knew Raven's intentions, her gentle voice, was a trick to take the baby without struggle.

"I know that you will take her, and Massa will sell her. I know it, and she pretty, she'll be used as some man's bed pillow." Josephine's voice was raised to an almost hysterical pitch now.

Raven fidgeted in the darkness, swallowing the painful lump that formed in her throat. She wished she had stolen the child away in the heat of the day, in the obvious unsuspecting sunlight when they were all in the fields; come like a hungry wildcat and taken her. She startled at the sound of a small critter scampering in the darkness of the shack, and realized her head was pounding. She spoke. "Josephine, she's going to get sold as soon as my husband gets a good look at her, but I can save her." Raven focused her eyes, hoping to get a better look at Josephine in the darkness. She worked to convince herself that her need to fulfill the visions of her and this child together was not an evil thing, and in that moment the door to the cabin squeaked open.

"Ma'am," Sybil said quietly into the dark cabin. "Missus LeFlore, is there something you need me for here."

"What are you doing here?" Raven did not mean to yell, and tried to hold her peace in the moment as things became too confusing for her mind to grasp. "You are not to leave your quarters without my permission."

"Yes'm."

Sweat dripped into Raven's shadowed eyes and burned, and she fought back the tears that came and reminded her, like a guilty child remembering her purpose, that all she wanted was to be inside her house with the baby.

"Sybil," she whispered, blinking hard to compose herself. "Grey Fox will sell this baby, and I have come to save her."

"Why, ma'am?" Sybil questioned politely, but with resentment for Raven's privilege. "Aren't the babies always sold? Let it get on up in age then. Let Massa sell it. What you savin it for?"

"Sybil, please," Josephine pleaded to spare Sybil punishment.

"Ma'am, please let Sybil carry the baby up to the house." Her pear-shaped body on long stilt like legs, Josephine walked quickly to the small trough crib, leaving Raven's vision. Josephine's backside was the only thing visible, where the skirt bunched around her waist, as she bent over to wrap the child in more blankets. The muffled sound of Josephine's tears, like the sound of dark laughter, came from the corner. In the darkness she spoke to Raven, who still sat at the table, her face lit from beneath, "Please let me come and nurse her, ma'am, please." Lanterns glowed in the other cabin windows.

A breeze blew up from the darkness that hid the green stalks, their limp leaves rustling, heavy with mature corn. Josephine's face came out of the darkness like an injured animal coaxed toward healing hands, and Raven leaned in.

"I'll keep her and raise her, and she will be near. She will have a good life. You will be able to see her. I will not let her be sold." Raven's heart was racing now.

"Yes," Josephine agreed in the manner that she must, though she did not believe. She caught Sybil's eye in the darkness and whispered, "A fool." She outstretched her arms to Sybil, with the squirming life crying loud now, air passing through her body with the sound they all would have made had they not been women of Southern circumstances.

Raven stood and moved Sybil aside, and received the child.

"I called her Lilly," Josephine confessed, with her throat constricted and her mouth turned down; sun set in her heart at the sight of her baby in the candlelight. Raven's bitter mouth straightened. Both women with arms extended; tears dripped from their chins. "She ain't free no more." Josephine cried, defeated.

Raven pulled the child from her mother's grip and wrapped her in her cloak. She leaned out of the lantern light, and Josephine and Sybil became invisible again.

Raven fled like the bird of her name, across the dividing crops to the large house, up the crumbling slope, and the swamp woman's spell was broken by the sudden sound of the cabin door squeaking on its hinges in Raven's escape. It resounded in the quarters, where the sin was new and still unknown by the other members of the child's community, the slaves, who would soon become the strangers across the fields.

October 27, 1851

H ER HAIR WAS BLACK. That was all Golden allowed himself to see over Raven's shoulder, where she huddled over the child. He heard Grey Fox's proud report that Raven saved a child left on the porch, perhaps by Choctaw travelers poor and desperate. Golden knew not to speak of it, and the sight of the child sobered his fever for brown-skinned women.

Lilly was a child of Raven's house by blood, by secrets. Grey Fox was drunk with the idea of keeping the girl baby, an heir, keeper of his father's wishes. He knelt gently at Raven's side and kissed her face. He touched the baby's tiny hand with a gentleness he had never shown.

The lie of the found child was never spoken, and it became easy for Raven's mind to embrace the myth that she and Lilly were united by their ancestors; Raven's mother folding her back into the clan to uphold the old ways, to see and tell the stories of love and war.

Warm washcloths heated by Raven's hands, not the servants', cleaned the smell of Josephine's flesh from the little flower. Raven feared any slave holding her baby.

Her promise to Josephine was quickly forgotten. Josephine peered into the kitchen window, her breasts hard and painful. Each day she failed in all attempts to express milk for Sybil to take to the crying child. Josephine hid behind the house, or in the stable, Nathan and Sybil repositioning her to avoid their masters. Then Lula would whistle the warning that Massa Golden was coming to do the rounds, and Josephine would scurry down the hill over moss-covered rocks, over fallen leaves, over leaves covered with rain.

Long after the milk was dry, Sybil comforted. "We'll try again tomorrow." She held the back door open a crack to keep the cold draft from racing down the hall, where it would alert Raven. Then one day she looked down the back steps at Josephine and told her the truth, "Yo wool shawl and long skirt are for keeping the new baby warm, Josephine.

Your next milk is for the next child in yo womb. Go on down to the quarters and get outta the cold."

Lilly rejuvenated Grey Fox, let light into the place where the memory of his mother's trauma had set him into days and nights of questioning his father, his own understanding of what he remembered. The baby's new life; sweet cooing, little cries; made worries of political conflict seem foolish, but conflict mounted all around him.

As she sat on his lap, Lilly's new dark hair rubbed the chafed, skin on his face, and she opened the heart of a motherless boy.

He marveled over how much she looked like the mother who he had lost. Grey Fox whispered, "Found child," and vowed to teach her his father's and grandfather's ways. Lilly blew spit bubbles and affirmed her commitment to him. One day, when only Grey Fox was listening, Lilly spoke her first word, "Dada," and took two steps into Grey Fox's arms.

The next summer Josephine gave birth to the newest slave. She named her Tessa, just in case they would meet in heaven.

Summer 1853

GOLDEN SAT AT BREAKFAST with his sister, Henry Trench, and their twins, who approached puberty with gentle steps inside the house of their good fortune. Samuel was curious about everything said by the men, and Rebecca kept quiet and invisible.

Golden shook his fork. "It's Sunday, and I have to escort the Negroes to their worship, but I want to leave you with something to think about, Brother Henry. You too, young Samuel. Pierce may be a lame leader, but that is the very symptom that will lead to the Southern Democrats taking over the party, ruling congress, and putting an end to this nonsense of a free West."

Henry leaned in, placing his black suit sleeve in the marmalade bowl. Rebecca giggled. "Never you mind, little lady. Sybil!" he yelled out, and she came slowly and wiped the elbow without looking at any of them.

"I say this to you men, and you as well, Grey Fox." Grey Fox did not look up from his play in the next room with his daughter, but Raven sat in the rocking chair, knitting and listening for signs of war.

Henry deepened his voice, "The battle to keep this country running smooth on Negro labor is one that will have to be fought. Winning the Congress, the House, even the presidency won't change the fact that there is no labor to send west. The South is losing its labor force by sending too many Negroes to the new states, and the zealots that will die to see those states free, are undermining the labor force with their abolitionist missions. There is really only one answer. Open up the import of African labor again, and indenture any free mulattoes, half-bloods, any Negro who has managed to slide out of the system of labor."

Golden laughed. "You have the clearest ideas, brother. If only we could make you president."

Raven chimed in from the next room, "Can't you find anything else to talk about in the presence of the children?" For almost two years everything had felt perfect for Raven. There was the sound of children in the house, and her body had relaxed into its new era, found balance after the cessation of blood. Talk of war could only ruin her peace.

"Excuse me, ma'am." Nathan stood in the hallway in his driver's uniform, which he wore to Sunday meeting. His arms were full of a wooden toy for the child. Nathan used all the time he wasn't tending the horses to carve a rocking horse for Lilly out of scraps of lumber. In making it, he thought about the freedom she had, the life she would have endured as a slave, and gave it a great mane made of scrap leather.

Raven gawked at the thriftiness of the thing, but the child had already pulled herself up from the floor and was wobbling to steady herself and get one leg over for a ride. "No more nigger baby toys," Raven shouted, quickly, embarrassed by her outburst. She waved Nathan on with her jaws still tight and her back turned to the child's new toy.

"It's okay, Raven," Grey Fox mumbled.

"Yes'm." Nathan turned and left the scene.

Golden and Henry stood to depart for the day's work, and Henry offered his opinion again. "Looks like some of the Negros need more duties if there's time to carve toys."

Raven watched Lilly rock furiously on the shabby thing. "Careful. Don't get a splinter." But Raven was ignored. The toddler girl saw in her mind her father riding over the fields, the cream-colored Spirit carrying him wherever he wanted to go, her straight hair, still thin, wild like her father's.

And she rode and rode the toy, as the politics shifted and changed over who would dominate slave states, slave minds. And the little wooden horse shrunk beneath the long legs and tall body of the little girl, who one day discarded the old thing, and it became a relic down in the quarter barn, where it was repaired and came to life each Christmas for the children who lived in the place where she was not allowed to go.

April 1861

W HEN LILLY WAS NINE YEARS OLD, Grey Fox took her to the stable and showed her the gift, Little Spirit, named after his own horse, who'd finally been mercifully put down by his own revolver. His new horse, Chestnut, was a gentle mare who was patient with the young, sand-colored Little Spirit and her spirited girl rider. When Grey Fox watched Lilly ride, he remembered the joys of his own childhood, how he would hold the reins and coax his pony into a wild gallop.

When he walked hand in hand with Lilly, he remembered the comfort of holding his mother's hand, of hugging, crying, laughing without regard for who might judge. He had taught Lilly to read on their long excursions, had let her read small portions of the letters from his father; the greetings, the questions about her; but never the full content, which he kept for himself, tucked and folded dusty in the inside pocket of his short riding jacket. And when the child was off with her mother, he read the letters standing quiet at the line of trees that led to the cold end of the great creek; quiet there, he read among the birch and oak trees. His father's words added to the mound of worries he had packed away and ignored, not wanting anything to spoil the happiness he'd found.

Over the years he had continued to sit quietly in the meetings of the men who boasted and argued passionately; he had wanted his father's guidance so desperately, but could not ask him one question without asking the questions about his memories.

March 12, 1861

Dear Tchula,

I have read the reports of the presidential mess. How can we stand by and be governed by a nation who would be led by Lincoln, a man so fainthearted that he would sneak into the city of his thrown by way of a night train, and have the nerve to give an inaugural speech the next day which speaks of freedom for all men when he himself acts like the niggers who steal away in the night rather than stand and face the fate before them?

The Confederate's new president is just as useless. He has done nothing in response to the telegraph sent by myself and other land-owners about the renegade niggers who threaten to raid our homes and set our slave property free to roam senseless and unchecked. I am appalled by my own citizenship in this land and hold out voicing any allegiance to either side of this nonsense. I am embarrassed of the Southern politicians who I have supported with service on councils and delegations, and appalled at the cowardice of the Union. Five other slaves, including Grandpa Buck, oldest nigger I've owned, he was treated well here. He had such nostalgia for the plantation back home. Well, he disappeared with a bunch of marauders who stole him to make a mockery and insult of me; no regard for Buck, just to make a mockery of me.

If things get worse, son, I'm ready to ride the fields myself at night, relieve the patrollers of their job, so I can kill a few. I have sent my rider to the wagon depot with this letter, hoping he too does not flee post. I hope this letter finds you in good health.

Yours truly,
Father

Grey Fox refolded the yellowing paper and blocked the old man's agitated tone out of his thoughts. Old age did not hide the truth that Jacques LeFlore would have turned his own kin out to patrollers if they crossed him. Grey Fox blocked the rising feelings and memory, the feelings that made him heavy, and unable to get about his duties. He took a deep breath of cool spring air, looked out on the trees naked with tight buds that would soon open under the pressure of warming air, and sun that would push these clouds away. *Yes.* Grey Fox assured himself of good feelings and went to his days calm again until the morning of April tenth, when he retrieved the next letter from the county station.

March 30, 1861

Dear Tchula,

I see very difficult times ahead. Prosperity in this Territory may not last for your old French father. With the Choctaw agent Mr. Douglas Cooper's decision to give Choctaw support to the Confederacy, there has been an uprising of horse thieving. The people have less than they had in the days of the relocation. There will be no more allotments for the Choctaw from the government because of the choice that they have made to support the Southern cause. Though it is politically sound for them to do so, I fear that by siding with the South, they have shot themselves in the foot.

Trading in town has turned to robbery. Whisky has replaced any sense of God the Indians have. My men are spent, patrolling for insurrection and escape among the slaves, and now watching the steer pin, the horse barn. Last week fire was set to our stored grasses. I received a message, delivered by two agents from General Thorpe. He has urged that I declare my alliance with the Choctaw people or leave these parts, but I fear that it is a trap to integrate my belongings into a falling nation.

You must pledge your allegiance to the Confederacy in Mississippi and hold fast to our land, as it may prove to be your only inheritance. You must teach our Lilly to carry on your lot in life if things fail in this time. I have been advised not to send a rider to the wagon depot, for the possibility of him being murdered on the trails that are being fought over;

piracy, arson, this pending war will not be a gentleman's war. I will
continue to send a rider to deliver and retrieve letters. Notify me soon
of the state of our LeFlore. I hope soon to lay eyes on my only grandchild.

Yours truly,
Father

One letter had made him want to run from the very idea of his father, of his own likeness to him, but this letter had made him miss his father, to be near the man he hadn't seen since he was thirty years old. Jacques LeFlore had made his first return in the harsh travels of winter; an ominous stagecoach, out of place, out of character, the driver a bearded old black man who looked vaguely familiar but held no true resemblance to anyone Grey Fox had known. He stood at the bottom of the stairs with Nathan, awaiting the man who would step out, and it was his father. The goose bumps rose on the taut muscular arms beneath his shirt vest and coat. His father; relief, comfort, a letting go of some breath that had been trapped in the deepest pit of his belly for twelve years of uncertainty and loneliness; his father was there.

The words of his father's letters, *I hope soon to lay eyes on my only grandchild,* made Grey Fox feel out of control with grief, and longing to be with his papa, to dispense with any doubt of him, to be with someone who, when Grey Fox looked in a mirror, he recognized.

Grey Fox folded the letter and tucked it away in his breast pocket.

Three days later, Union forces in South Carolina fell to Confederate troops that took Fort Sumter. A civil war was officially waged in the nation that prided itself in freedom, in expansion, prided itself in forward movement that had encountered a dead end.

April 14, 1861

I N THE MEETING THAT NIGHT General Thorpe declared, "Our fathers, the English settlers, overcame their oppressor. This is no different. We may be few in numbers, less in land holdings, but one thing Southerners are is passionate about our convictions. That will take us up to the giant, and smite him with his own lies. They stand tall now, but oh they shudder when they fall."

Upstairs, above the fervor that stirred in the sitting room, Raven told Lilly often, "You are beautiful," and she braided her hair, refusing to let the fears of war rise up again and trample over what had seemed so good for the past nine years. Downstairs the men argued a case for riding into battle today. "To hell with strategy; strategy be damned." Raven heard their voices muffled by the walls and floors, and she spoke up louder to her Lilly.

"You have the same weight of hair as your grandmother." She wrapped the braids that hung long and free at night into a beautiful bun, like fresh-baked bread, and adorned the girl with taffeta and lace. That night she sat by Lilly's bed and told her stories about the first people, guarding against apocalyptic thoughts, but acting on the possibility; stories told with variation of memory. "Nanih Waiya, the sacred mound birthed us like a pregnant woman's body births her firstborn."

Lilly fingered the pages of *Oliver Twist* while she waited for her mother to finish pulling and twisting her hair. She waited for the stories of Nanih Waiya to end so she could resume the story of the orphaned boy from London.

In the kitchen, Sybil prepared the shortbread and molasses cookies, which never settled well with whisky, but each time the men had filled their lungs with the smoke and their bellies with the drink, she was instructed by Grey Fox in the same way that he as a boy had instructed her mother, "Make the shortbread and molasses cookies." She included extra molasses, and watched from the kitchen door when the men left the meeting one by one and ran with their lanterns to the outhouse.

Sybil had once been loyal only to her Tchula, playmate in her childhood. She had been hateful to the woman who came and disrupted that illusion, but Grey Fox's betrayal to her dearest friend had added to Sybil's resentment, and held strong long after Josephine's grief over "the stolen child" had subsided; long after she had urged Josephine not to live her life worrying after the child she was never allowed to be near.

Josephine saw Lilly only from far off, in the distance a flash of red in her riding coat, pink in her fine dresses through the trees at the top of the hill, having tea on the veranda with the missus, never within arm's length of her true mother, never in full sight of her true mother's stare.

"You have other babies, Jo. You best enjoy what you got. You never know, maybe Massa Tchula will sell you on down to the Bartlette place. Lately been smokin up the sitting room with talk of what they can trade in hard times. 'cause Bartlette and Massa Tchula as close as hog slop and hog shit in a hog pen." The two of them laughed in the way that they felt comfortable laughing only on Saturday nights, and Josephine set her thoughts on loving the girl she did have, her girl Tessa.

April 15, 1861

THAT NIGHT DOVE and husband Henry hosted a celebration of Southern heritage. Raven agreed to be present but had warned her sister against the ridiculous idea of a Choctaw-themed dinner party. It would insult the gentry and be a disgrace of a flop in hostessing. Dove had sewn with her own hands a dress with spring flowers for Rebecca, who was now a beautiful young woman, and moccasin boots for Samuel, who hoped to leave the next week to train at the fort. "What a ridiculous theme for a party, sister. Whites are not interested in your heritage."

"Sister, they will love the joy and celebration of the planting dance. I will teach it to them."

"How will you teach something you were never part of?"

"Henry has taught me many things. It's all in fun. And all in step with what is new. This is a new South, and the women love new things."

All of Dove's guests arrived in hoop dresses, Dove the only one among them in traditional dress, red dyed in berry juice that still stained Dove's feet, buckskin leggings and moccasins beaded, wrapped tight. The dances were a wrecked version of what had been. The white people stomped barefoot in a square dance, making a whooping noise to imitate Indians. *The stress of war,* Raven thought. *They have all gone mad.*

Raven stood against the wall fanning herself, refusing to correct them, because respect was of no importance when the dance was merely trendy amusement for the white aristocrats who mingled in the house of Choctaws.

Alone on the veranda, Raven watched the glow of lantern light on the trees. Lilly had been told to stay in her room and write with quill and ink the story of Nanih Waiya. Instead, she read from *Oliver Twist,* straining her eyes in order to live vicariously by his defiance. Raven closed her eyes and imagined Lilly all grown, a woman who spoke the old language, who brewed tinctures in a new clay pot molded by her own hands.

She tried to imagine Lilly pouring medicine into the mouths of children, their heads held back, from a scooped-out gourd grown in her own garden; poured to protect them from the white diseases of malaria, the diseases of the mind and spirit, and the diseases that sneaked in under the covers promising a life far from dirt huts, diseases that curled around the heart like honeysuckle, decorated with beauty and perfume while extracting life.

Raven closed her eyes in exhaustion and had not noticed the gentle wind and the spray of rain on her face and hair. She opened her eyes and turned to the French doors, where the guests laughed heartily as Dove, Rebecca, Samuel, and their papa danced clumsily, shuffling their feet now free of the moccasins. Mr. Bartlette's young daughters beat on the cast iron pots supplied by Sybil, who stood between the dancing room and the dining room pretending not to show judgment while she waited for her next duty.

Raven marveled at the spectacle. *We have all lost our minds, the well bred and ill bred alike.*

Grey Fox shut the doors to the sitting room, blocking out the noise of the guests.

"Good evening Grey, Fox." General Thorpe stood politely in the sitting room and handed Grey Fox the bottle of brandy he'd brought to intoxicate him for the gravity of the moment to come. His free hand was tight in a fist behind his uniformed back, hiding the nervousness of his duty.

"Sit, General Thorpe," Grey Fox instructed, pouring a snifter of brandy for both of them. Grey Fox joined General Thorpe in a drink. "So, to what do I owe the honor of this moment away from the festivities?"

"Is your father well? The insurrection has not affected his plantation?"

"No," Grey Fox lied, prideful.

"Well, Jack Flowers has always been a man to hold his own. It's good to know his claim on Oklahoma has held up well and he, unlike many others, has prospered."

Grey Fox tilted his head curiously. "Do you bring some news or concern of the Territory?" Grey Fox coaxed gently, not raising suspicion of his concern for his father.

"News? No," answered General Thorpe, smoothing his mustache before taking several indignant gulps of the brandy. He left the glass dry and placed it on the end table. He leaned forward and blew into his hands nervously as if it were cold in the humid room. "The army is preparing for battle."

"Yes, of course. It is what must be done," Grey Fox answered, staying calm. He sipped gently from his brandy snifter, wanting to be alert for the words that would follow General Thorpe's raccoon stare.

"Your father has always been a supporter of the Southern cause, and, well." General Thorpe stood and tugged on his uniform jacket. "We are asking that you donate the plantation for a training camp and a military post. It is the highest point in the county."

Settling into this unexpected request, Grey Fox stood and drank the remaining brandy. "Surely I will honor your need. How many acres from me and how many from my neighbors?"

"We need four hundred acres and we are asking that you offer your land to the cause. You will be given two wagons and supplies to take your wife, child, your niggers on to Oklahoma to join your father, where the landholding is plenty."

A roar came up in an impulsive fit of laughter. Shamelessly Grey Fox threw his body forward, holding on to his gut. His mind said, *No, be still*, but his nerves, reacting on their own, sent his body into ridiculous involuntary giggles.

General Thorpe was unmoved, and reacted sharply to the assumed ridicule.

"Get ahold of yourself. Do you take me to be your fool? This is a serious matter."

The general's tone was sobering. Grey Fox straightened his clothes. He saw in General Thorpe's eyes the same urgency with which his father entrusted four hundred acres to him.

"I can do no such thing, General Thorpe. I believe the evening of fine whisky has gone to your head. Good evening, sir." Grey Fox reached for the brandy snifter on the end table beside General Thorpe, who then rested his hand on Grey Fox's shoulder.

"I assure you I am not drunk, and I would not of my own volition have you removed in this manner. I personally believe you are not a threat, but I have my orders, and I am asking as opposed to ordering, out of respect for your father, Grey Fox."

A lump formed in Grey Fox's throat, and he spoke his mind without long contemplation. "I honor my father in saying I will offer my support, but the magnitude of the sacrifice you require is simply ridiculous, sir. Good evening."

The general squeezed the muscle and bone of Grey Fox's shoulder. "I strongly recommend that you do not question, but that you go on to the Territory, to where at least you have your father's holdings, and an allotment of your own as a half-blood."

The Territory. General Thorpe had never referred to the place where Jacques LeFlore staked his claim as the Territory; that was a designation for the five tribes, banished because their relationship with Southern land made them a threat to Southern progress.

Grey Fox let out another involuntary chuckle. It all made him slightly dizzy to think just moments ago he was clapping and watching the Bartlette girls turn a reel into a primitive dance.

"I believe you have forgotten yourself, General Thorpe. Forgotten to whom you speak. My father needs to hear from you. My father, who has taken part in the writing of this state's constitution, who took part in the writing of the codes by which the civilized Choctaw of this land and the land where he now holds great stewardship govern their slave property. My father, a great proponent of Southern economy . . ."

"Your father, a neutral man, a man of no allegiance, and a son who sits in the heart of conflict and remains silent in his own meetings. No sir, you and your father of different blood, but of similar tactics.

"You are a man who for years has stowed away three Choctaw who are rumored to have run away from obligations. I have been a friend, a knowing but silent friend, Grey Fox. Do not pit me against my duties to the Confederacy. You will lose."

Who, Grey Fox wondered, *has told this man that Henry Trench and his children are of no relation?*

"General Thorpe, this has gone too far. You are in my home and accusing me of nonpatriotic behavior. It's time that you left, and know that as I have said, you can count on my support, but not my surrender of my birthright." The very sound of the word "birthright" incensed General Thorpe, as he stared at Grey Fox, remembering that Indians were all heathens.

April 16, 1861

IN RAVEN'S DREAMS, her mother floated above a field of dead bodies. "Run, run, run." The chapped lips parted and struggled to speak the words. Raven sat up in bed. She refused to open her eyes. Was it morning? Night? Was she a child lying still on the floor afraid to awaken to find her mother and father slaughtered, herself bleeding slow like a hunted animal refusing death? She opened her eyes.

Grey Fox's place on the covers next to her had gone cold. He was away from the plantation before dawn, while the other men in the house grew restless.

At breakfast Golden and Henry discarded all possibility of politeness and dipped their biscuits into their tea. Golden spoke out to Dove, Samuel, Rebecca, Raven, and young Lilly who sang quietly to the porcelain doll while her uncle talked. "They are armoring their navy to use their industry against us; iron plated ships to block the ports so our cotton does not go to Europe. What shall we do? Take this lying down?"

"Brother, please." The tone in his voice made Raven's breath come short. She looked over to her daughter. Golden responded, "Everyone should know the truth of what the North has planned for us. Niggers alike need to know that freedom is being used to gain their allegiance with no intentions for their well-being. Just yesterday I met a free man who mistook me for an ally and declared he was on the run from Union service because the treatment was worse than the life his parents lived."

"Brother, please," Raven pleaded again, shaking her head.

Dove and Rebecca sipped their tea, while Samuel leaned into his father, and to Golden. "What shall we do, brothers?" Samuel asked.

"What would any man do to protect his family and his land?" Golden spoke with confidence, but turned toward the men, to avoid his sister's condemning stare.

The men whispered and laughed away the morning, going on and on about the nature of war, bolstering their individual prowess long after the women had left the table.

General Thorpe had urged Grey Fox to surrender his home, had trespassed on his relationship with his father, assuming his white father would forfeit land to a righteous cause that might fail. Grey Fox spent that morning riding to other plantations; John Bartlette's place, Bartlette's cousin Abram Campbell's, the Pickets', all white men's land, and all had been asked by General Thorpe for support if the time came; to give a portion of their crops to feed troops, to agree to house troops, to proudly send their sons to fight, but not one had been asked to forfeit land for training grounds. *This is ridiculous*, Grey Fox thought.

He wrote to his father for advice, knowing weeks would pass before a reply was possible. He hoped that the roads and trails into the Territory had not been seized, that his father would find a way to send guidance, despite the mounting obstacles. Grey Fox carried his burden in his eyes and in the stiffness of his body, but sat high as he slowly rode Chestnut back to the house, to fetch Lilly for a morning trot across the pasture.

"What's the matter, Father?" Lilly questioned.

His face always brightened at the sound of her voice, whether when she was two or now at nine. "Lilly, Lilly," he sang, looking over at his precious daughter. "The men of our country are preparing for war against each other. Things only seem peaceful here, but it is just a matter of time before everything changes. I am trying to figure out what to do before time figures it out for me."

The red of her riding coat made her face glow like embers.

"What are you talking about Father?" Lilly answered. "This war is not going to ruin my birthday, will it?"

Grey Fox was lost in the rhythm of the horses' cantor and did not answer for a long while. "You are as sharp and knowing as your mother, but don't let your mind tangle itself up in worries like she does. Forget what I have said. You ride lightly daughter."

"Is it the damned Yankees, Father?" she asked, in a defiant tone, and Grey Fox laughed out loud at her precocious nature, and she blushed and giggled deep like her true mother.

"It's the damned Yankees honey, and the reaction they solicit from good people, but we'll whip them if they try to get what we've got." He looked at her and she looked back, both of them with a furtive glance, and they whipped the hind flanks of the horses and galloped as if riding into battle. Headlong, they road into the morning wind toward the county station for a birthday present and to send Grey Fox's letter; the decisions of his coming days hinged precariously on a reply, but they rode playfully and hard with the sound of hooves and wind.

Lilly often went to the veranda to enjoy the smell of damp earth while watching the black girls her age come up from the fields, where the sun had scorched them all day and the rainfall was welcomed at dusk. Watching the little black slave children was her favorite hobby of boredom, like when she watched the ants from the bottom white step where the earth was manicured without a bump or groove. Watching the slave children was like watching those ants whose mounds of broken earth were trampled each day when Nathan swept the uneven debris into the lawn, but slowly they emerged again, thin, ancient black bodies all uniform in shape and shade, carrying the earth to build for another day.

Lilly watched the slaves from between the sheets of rain and wondered for the first time about their eyes. She always looked into Sybil's eyes when she spoke to her, but Sybil never looked straight into hers; yellow eyes with soft brown eyeballs, eyes like hers and her mother's and father's, but not like General Thorpe's. She wondered about the slave children's eyes; would they stay locked on hers if she spoke to them? The rain fell hushing the thoughts.

Sybil and President Lincoln have sad eyes, she thought, "Buffoon!" she remembered Uncle Henry shouting. *Is Lincoln a nigger lover because he has sad eyes, sad like a nigger? Is nigger loving like how I love my father and mother?* Lilly wondered as the rain washed the faces of the young slaves from her sight.

"I don't think you should be riding so far with your father, Lilly." Raven came onto the veranda speaking above the static of the rain. Lilly turned and looked her mother straight in the eyes.

"Why does Sybil look down when she speaks to me?"

"She's..." Raven paused to consider her rote response, the consequence of separating Lilly from others born as slaves, and the consequence of revealing to her the true kinship she shared with them.

"They are slaves' children, Lilly, and you are Grey Fox's child."

"Mother, I was thinking about the children as well, but was asking about Sybil. I've known her my whole life, and don't remember a time without her. When I'm speaking to her she speaks back, sometimes cleaning the spot where I have just made a mess eating, and I will ask her if the riding weather looks good for me and Father. I will ask her if we can please have biscuits for breakfast. I'll ask her, and she will answer looking at the stains she's washing away. She will answer me without looking at me."

Raven smiled and shook her head to show Lilly that these things were not for her to worry about, but Lilly spoke on. "In the distance, Mother, I see the slave women Josephine and Sybil walking on Sunday to the old shed, where they sing. I see them with their arms around the little children. I see the children run up and squeeze Josephine or Sybil tight around the knees, but Sybil won't even look at me, and the slave children are just slaves. Why won't Sybil look at me?"

"Lilly." Raven grabbed her around her delicate shoulders. "Where do you ride with your father? What is bringing these questions about?"

"Through the woods and around the back land of the fields to the creek for the horses to drink, Mother?" Lilly was agitated with being held in question and not having her own question addressed, so she lied about her daily ride, then continued with her inquiry, "Mother, let go, and tell me about Sybil. Does she not like me the way she likes the slave children?"

Raven let the child go and wiped her own brow; the smell of lavender in the soap she'd used to wash her hands made her nauseous in the thick humidity. "Mother, are you well? Your lips look purple."

"Not enough sleep, Lilly. I'm sorry for talking to you that way."

"Is it the dreams, Mother? I hear you speaking all the time even after Father has left for the morning. Do you miss your mother?"

"Child, please. Listen to me, you are my mother's grandchild, you are, and you remember that."

Lilly spoke softly in defeat, knowing Raven would not feed her curiosity. "But there's so much, Mother, that I don't know or understand. You tell me stories of things that seem so strange, but you don't answer about things I want to know more about, and Father speaks in riddles about things changing."

"You are just a child, Lilly. You are not meant to understand everything. You have a long time of life for understanding, for now just play."

Lilly walked away from her mother, leaving her with the rain on the veranda. For the first time in years, Raven was thirsty for the soothing properties of dark amber whisky.

April 17, 1861

THE NEXT MORNING RAVEN PUSHED open the kitchen door to remind Sybil about General Thorpe's favorite dessert, for he had planned another visit that evening. She found Sybil laughing in a relaxed way with her head thrown back, that way the slaves laughed in the quarters on Saturday nights when Master Fox was out and Raven was invisible, watching from the fields.

"You ain't doin it right, child."

"I'll try again." Lilly was bent over, hair hanging in her face, her nightgown hanging to her knees, slippers like sandpaper on the floor, her sweet voice singing.

Baby call her Mama Josephine,

Josephine,

Josephine.

Sister call her Mama Josephine.

Hop, hop, slide to the middle.

Sybil heaved back and forward, holding her gut with flour and biscuit dough still on her fingers. The source of her amusement stood giggling softly, and satisfied that not only that had she made such a stern servant let go of herself in the master's house, but that Sybil looked at her the way she looked at the slave children.

"I ain't never know'd you was so funny, Li'l Bit."

"Lilly," Raven yelled, throwing the kitchen door open. "Go to your room!"

Lilly's giggles turned to silence. Past Raven, she ran, and her cotton nightgown created a breeze that carried with it the scent of sweat and cow's milk, hair and skin like the scent of Josephine's cabin in the dark that night. Raven couldn't remember what she'd said that day to wield the child from Josephine's arms, but at the sound of Josephine's name resounding in Lilly's voice, she remembered this same feeling of her body going cold, and the goose bumps rising at the thought of not having her baby.

Raven stared at Sybil, whose teeth ground against teeth.

"Go ahead and throw something if you need to, ma'am," Sybil said in the same passive coldness that she had used to deal with her white benefactors since she was ten years old. Her own mother was proud to see Sybil in a life that was surely better than being a field hand, but in her mother's old age, she did not remember the heat from a cast iron oven on a one-hundred-degree day, when baked bread was a ridiculous luxury for the people who ate it only when it cooled. Her mother did not know the insult of having to call a nine-year-old girl "miss"; the insult of baking for the little miss biscuits on demand and knowing the consequence of not complying was a night out of the house in the quarters, where the provisions were scarce. "Better than a field hand," her mother had said.

But her mother did not know the sin of keeping slave-owner secrets. "Chahta Judas," Sybil cursed Raven under her breath. Her mother did not know the sin of what came after speaking such words.

Raven slapped her once, twice, and a third time, until Sybil cast her vision back to the floor so the jealous ma'am of LeFlore plantation would not take aim and slap her already bloody lip again.

"Maybe you best sell me on off ma'am, 'cause I sho don't think I best stay here."

"I'm not worried about you, Sybil. I'm better off knowing where you are at all times."

Sybil went back to preparing the strawberries for General Thorpe's special shortcake dessert. From her bitten lip she tasted the salt of her own blood and let it drip red on red into the bowl of sugared strawberries.

April 18, 1861

THE NEXT MORNING, at his wife's insistence, Grey Fox sold Josephine and her strong, nine-year-old daughter Tessa, to John Bartlette, the only man in the county with enough holding to actually continue purchasing slave stock. He was the only plantation owner who had not turned a cold and strange shoulder to Grey Fox for not taking a solid stand against the North.

Bartlette's overseer came and looked Josephine and the girl over, made his own estimate of Josephine's age, which was fifteen years younger than the truth. Grey Fox claimed he had not kept a proper record, so she was sold as a weaver, a candle maker, and to the surprise of Josephine and her friend Sybil, both mother and daughter were sold as breeders.

"Passionate people. Passionate." Henry Trench was proud to be a supporter of the Confederate cause. He stood in the sitting room the day after Josephine and Tessa were sold and made his face look sad, his body slump in order to mock President Lincoln's words, "The rebels will remove the blockade of Fort Sumter and allow the Union troops to restock supplies. For they will certainly not risk striking the first blow."

"Brilliant performance." Golden, John Bartlette's twin nephews, and young Samuel roared with laughter. Their excitement echoed in the halls of LeFlore. "Brilliant, just brilliant," Golden said over and over again.

He skipped up the stairs two by two to tell his sister the news. She had retired to her bed, and was fighting a sharp headache.

"Sister, I will be leaving this house to join the Confederate troops. I am offering my service as a man committed to an independent Southern nation."

Raven whispered, "You would leave your sisters; the women of your house for some foolish war that is not yours?"

"How can you speak against me, Raven? How can you stand in this room, servant bell on the mantle, and not send me with Godspeed to protect your comfort?"

Golden turned to leave and Raven followed him down to the open hall and cursed him. "You damned fool!" The damning echoed on the hard floors and ornamented ceiling to where her daughter played with the beautiful ballerina clothes her mother had ordered from Paris.

Adorned like her innocence in the soft chiffon dress and dance slippers, a birthday present opened early, Lilly pranced into the empty dancing room to find her mother wilted in a heap of ballooned cotton. The draft from the gaping dry fireplace kept Raven from fainting at the thought of her brother leaving her.

"Mother, Mother?" Lilly hugged her mother around the shoulders. "We'll whip those Yankees, Mother," Lilly whispered, "We'll whip them."

"I was fifteen, Lilly, when my family was destroyed. White men mean you nothing but harm. Don't side with them."

Raven felt herself prideful and wise like her mother, a shift from the desperation that, just moments before, collapsed her spirit, and days ago had caused her to lie to Grey Fox, telling him the slave Josephine had come to the house and threatened her; had caused her to lie the way she lied when she wanted the child; to lie as she lied for the first time, and answered her mother, "Nothing," when everything was bothering her. She was a desperate child in one moment and her mother in the next, and Lilly noticed the subtle shifting in Raven's behavior, and it made her wary of the woman she called Mother.

Lilly wrenched loose from Raven's grip and scooted back on the floor. "My father is half white, Mother, I am part white. Who would you have me side with; the niggers?"

"You listen to me, Lilly. You are no better than the slaves."

Lilly reared back in her first preadolescent defiance. "Nor are you, Mother, but look at us. If we are no better, then why do we respect ourselves enough to stay clean and be civilized while they allow themselves to be damned?"

"Lilly. Those are not my teachings, but your father's. I have told you the stories of your ancestry."

"Those bedtime stories of people sprouting 'out of a mound of dirt like flowers.' Mommy, that's not Christian for me to believe in that kind of nonsense. Father says I am a child of God, not created from some ancient heap of orange dirt. He says that might be where my body ends up, but not where it came from."

The cry of a screech owl sounded in the afternoon sky, and Raven remembered the omen of owls before death, bats before birth. She reached for Lilly's hand. "You are so confused. You only know what you have been taught."

"I am not confused, Mother. Everyone says you are confused and not well."

"Lilly, there are things I must teach you, things only you can pass on, things I must teach you before it is too late." Raven's eyes were glossed over while she spoke.

"I am a daughter of the Okla Hannali Chahta. Thirty years ago my family lived in a small village to the southeast of here. We were a self-sustained band who had warred in the past, but only with the Chickasaw and the Spanish who wanted the fertile land where we fished, hunted, and honored the old ways of gathering and harvesting corn, melon, beans."

Lilly struggled to get loose, but Raven tightened her grip. "By the time I was eight we had lost several of the men to skirmishes to protect the ever-decreasing land and to protect us children from becoming Chickasaw slaves, prizes from the French who were their new allies after the Spanish had been forced out by the new, English settlers.

"The children were the thriving force of our band, and the herb tinctures our mothers prepared, along with strong play in the sun is what my mothers said kept us healthy."

"A child only has one mother," Lilly replied.

"Only one mother who brings her into this world, but many who help her grow into a woman.

"My father traveled many days to discuss with a delegation his opposition to relocating to an unknown territory, but men like himself were outnumbered, and many who were on his side fell prey to the carousing that took place in those delegations; drinking, gambling, and things honest men shouldn't do. He came home angry and changed. He didn't walk with his head up, but the worry pulled him down. When the time came to leave, he led us in escape, and our family moved from location to location, re-creating the village of his childhood. My mother was worried about his ways but loved him anyway. She used her vision to lead us to a safe place. But one evening the men came for what they thought was theirs... killed for revenge on my father, who had eluded like koi."

"Mother?" Lilly stopped struggling. "Mother, let go," she whispered.

Raven was hot with a burst of heat that broke into a mixture of tears and sweat. She released her daughter from the pressure of her grip, and Lilly rested her head gently on Raven's shoulder, and they leaned against the stone framing of the quiet fireplace.

"Mother, what is happening to everyone?"

Raven did not answer but allowed the child to melt into her chest.

Outside the window Lilly heard the two slave children who brought the food up from the garden. "Can I go out and play before tea?"

"Absolutely not. What's gotten into you these days? Your father and my brother will kill me with their bare hands if I let you go off and play with slave children."

Raven frowned, realizing she didn't care anymore what they thought; leaving her, each of them. *They do not think of me the way I think of them, always considering their politics not wanting to make decisions that might embarrass them before the Bartlettes or Campbells.* She stared at her child from the daze of her shifting mind. She heard her ishki's voice, *Betrayal is on the wind,* and she set back limp again.

"Mother?"

Raven suddenly could not bear the tone of Lilly's voice.

"Go just go, go."

And Lilly stumbled clumsily on the newly polished wood of the dance floor as she headed upstairs to prepare for play with the mysterious children from down the hill.

Grey Fox spotted them crouched down in the corn like little gophers. He turned Chestnut around to meet them, intending to startle them and keep them humble as children. But Lilly saw her father; like looking into reflective water, she saw his approach in her mind and ran to avoid him. Her two brown playmates ran through the corn chasing after her. "Lilly! Where are you going?"

Grey Fox's horse was galloping now just outside the rows of corn. The children ran faster; Lilly ran as fast as the horse's gallop.

She exited the cornfield on the east side, which faced the quarters, where she had never been allowed to play. She stood there for a moment, breathless, observing the dusty state of things; worn wood shacks, no grass; and her blood ran cold in her veins. She took a step forward and the horse's mane caught her eye. Grey Fox sat high above her, his face a shadow with the sun so strong behind his head. Her playmates rode holding tight to him.

"Get down, and get to work," Master Fox demanded. The two boys ran barefoot as fast as their feet could carry them to the barn to hide. His voice was as stern as Lilly had ever heard: "Don't you ever run from me, Lilly, ever. And never are you to be found in the slave quarters." His voice quivered and he recognized his father's voice, "Don't you ever run from me!"

He held out a shaking hand, but Lilly ran back through the corn, her calico play dress like milkweed on a breeze through the green rows. The pain of hearing her father scold her as if she were a stranger's child carried her home.

That evening, all of the adults sat quietly at dinner, each with their separate worries. Lilly stayed in her room, refusing to talk to her father. Knives clanked against china, napkins were raised occasionally to soft lips, throats were cleared.

Grey Fox put his napkin in his lap. "She's ten years old tomorrow and much too passionate. Lately she acts like a heathen."

Everyone continued to eat; the word "heathen" passed out of his lips and over them like an omen. Raven was the only one who contested his words.

"She is my child, Gray Fox, your own daughter. Do not speak about her like she is a stranger."

Golden looked up for a moment, chewing on his pork steak, and went back to the task of cutting the meat.

"Do not dress her like a slave girl and let her run wild with Negro boys. I have to maintain my place with the other landowners. We are at war, woman. Don't you think?" He was shaking still, working hard to contain himself, but frightened at the sound of his father's temper coming out of his mouth.

Deep sighs were heard from Dove, when Henry spoke up. "I agree, it isn't ladylike."

Golden changed the subject. "Tomorrow, I leave for Fort Adam's Port."

Grey Fox's manner stiffened. "Golden, perhaps we should talk first. There are things that need to be worked out for this family, discussed with the general."

Raven added with an accusing look, "Tomorrow is your niece's birthday. You would leave on her birthday?"

Henry Trench interrupted. "I have discussed it with the general and will be joining Golden. Samuel will come too. We understand that you must stay as guardian of this land, but we must go."

Golden spoke again. "I was sure you'd be pleased, Grey Fox. Don't worry about the lack of hands. I've told Burtrome and some of the other slaves of shifts in their duties."

"Now just wait a minute, brother. Things are moving very quickly here. We must talk." Grey Fox wanted time to think about the general's demands, time to send an urgent telegram for advice from Jacques LeFlore. He did not want to voice the general's request before having time to work out a compromise. "Some things have shifted. I'm awaiting a reply from Jacques about the state of things in Oklahoma, and his opinion about things here."

Henry wiped his mouth and sat up straight. "Some things like what? What is there to think about? There's fight the bastards, or lie down and roll over. Are you afraid that some of the niggers will sneak off with them outlaws sent by that Frederick Douglass?"

"No, my slaves never had reason to run off, and there are extra patrollers out with the war on."

"Not for long if they're called to fight."

"Golden," Grey Fox called out across the table, "What would you be willing to sacrifice for an independent South?"

"Everything."

"Everything?"

"Yes, brother, everything, and I should think you'd feel the same."

"A toast," young Samuel shouted, barely shaven, eyes wide open, light brown skin clear and new, his hand around the glass to toast war like a man, when he had never used a gun except to shoot rabbits, fox, and quail for sport. "To independence! To whipping them Yanks back to where it's too cold to grow anything but iron."

They all laughed heartily and drank, while Grey Fox, Dove, and Rebecca sipped gently of the cool water from the creek. Raven fidgeted nervously, longing for the taste of whisky in her dry mouth.

The ruckus was interrupted by a slight and sleepy voice. "We'll whip them all the way back to the fool Lincoln's front door."

Lilly stood in the doorway wiping her eyes. The whole family burst into laughter, except Raven, who had continued to hold her peace until now, but her agitation could not be contained. "It's the root of her passionate behavior. Her ignorance is so easily bred in this house of red-skinned puppets who'd just as soon advance the cause of Jefferson Davis as defend a white marauder in Indian Territory. What of our kin who were pushed west against their will?" Raven hadn't remembered her father's voice until now, but her mind spoke in his voice this time, in his tone.

"Raven!" Grey Fox cautioned, standing at his place, but Raven stood and continued more passionately. "What of the Chahta who were prisoners, slaves to the Chickasaw? What of the Chahta with Negro blood?"

"Mama," Lilly cried out, scolding her own mother for speaking such indignation in her father's house.

"That's enough," Grey Fox demanded. "This family has gone crazy, everyone in it."

"Crazy? Speak for your wife, man," Golden spoke under his breath, arousing a giggle from the other men.

Grey Fox's head pounded from the stress, and the last swallow of pork steak sat lodged in his constricting esophagus. "I will not delay General Thorpe's visit any longer. Tomorrow evening we will host him, and the men of this house who will be going off to join him. I will speak my peace at that time about what will be done here for everyone including my brothers." Grey Fox stood with his shoulders back with the sort of confidence he had seen in his father, and lifted his wineglass and drank without toasting Samuel's words. The men smiled.

Lilly's smile sagged, "But what about my birthday?"

"That celebration will be delayed, child. Don't be selfish."

Lilly ran out of the dining room through the kitchen door to make a fast escape from her father's new agitation.

"He will come around," Henry whispered to young Samuel.

The glow on their faces was reminiscent of Raven's inki, and the uncles after the last meal around the fire pit just before dusk.

"Raven," Grey Fox piped up with bolstered pride, "see to it that Sybil prepares the sitting room for tomorrow's meeting. In the morning, I will leave to settle some business at the county station. I'll be gone for the day and will not return until shortly before General Thorpe's arrival. Make sure there is bourbon, cigars, and his favorite dessert."

Raven's face was stiff, her eyes lost in another time.

The slight opening in the kitchen door squeaked closed where Sybil watched and listened with one arm emotionless patting the quietly sobbing child. The family departed to their evening of packing and silence. The men's voices echoed in the hallway.

"Where do you suppose we'll be sent?"

"I'd like to go right into the heart of things, Missouri. We've got to secure it, force them to swing south."

"Right you are. We can't let them take Missouri, have to keep the river transport for the Confederacy."

Young Samuel didn't speak in the trailing off of bravado.

Raven was left to sit alone on the veranda. From the adjacent kitchen door she heard Nathan's deep voice attempting a whisper, but his words were clear.

"Josephine done passed on this mornin while dipping extra candles for Massa Bartlette to give to his nephews' company." Then silence from Sybil before she scolded, "Why didn't you say somethin this afternoon when you brought candles here?"

And Nathan's voice, high-pitched: "I didn't know. Lord, it's a shame, the whole thing a shame."

Raven turned to see past the veranda doors to the mantle where a small cluster of beeswax candles had been placed in the carved, ornamental cherry wood box that morning. She turned back and stared out on the moonlit night as if looking away from the open eyes of the dead. Nathan's dark personage walked across the yard back to the stable house, past the trees that sat above the hill that descended to the quarters where Lula's voice sang out loud in words against her masters, who might discipline her, but were too busy with the affairs of their war.

Might have my body locked up in chains
But cain't hold my soul down no more,
No-o-o
Cain't hold my soul down no more.

The tone was sorrowful: long, wailing notes, but Raven did not feel sorrow. Beneath the itchy cotton layers of the high-necked dress she felt heat rise anxious to the surface, and she was overcome with a fear of being left alone: Grey Fox riding to the county station and not returning till meeting time the next night. *Why is he going? Golden, Henry, Samuel, all going off to die; why is that a better fate than staying, standing, here?*

There was talking at the front door, and she listened to a Confederate rider speak harshly to Golden. "Where is Grey Fox? It is urgent that I have a word with him. John Bartlette has a claim against him for the knowing sell of a sick slave."

Raven prayed to any God for the peace she once knew. "Please make this all go away." She stopped short in her prayer at the sound of Lula's singing in the background.

What will I tell Lilly about the slaves mourning and wailing? She knew she would need to think to know what she would tell her daughter, who had made a new practice of watching the slaves and comparing herself to them. Just then, Lilly ran from the kitchen, still in her play clothes, ran from the haunting sounds of Lula's cry, up the stairs to the safety of her room of lace curtains and porcelain dolls.

Raven placed her left hand over her rib-constricting corset. She concentrated on steady breath, and she remembered being caught in the flood current when she was a little girl, her mother yelling from the occasional crest of water that buoyed her body up for breath, "Breathe, Raven, breathe," and her mind quieted, her body relaxed, and she found air above water.

On the veranda, Raven closed her eyes to deprive her mind of the sights and sounds around her; more voices in the quarter joined in the song, and lantern light was cast on the lawn from Lilly's window. Raven repeated the list of those who would leave her, in the same manner as the Confederate officer who stood at the county station and repeated the names of the dead, called them off in the same tone, cawing like a crow so all who stood around could hear. "Golden, Samuel, Henry, my Tchula li." She fell short of breath again, and struggled to undo the strings of the corset through the tight cotton dress.

"My inki, my ishki, my Lilly."

The list trailed off quietly with her struggle for steady breathing. She used the porch rail to steady herself in the silver moonlight.

She turned to see her own reflection, her petticoat revealed beneath the dress hem, her hair fallen from the bun. She looked taller than she really was in the high neck, with her hair around her long face. She saw her father, worn and tired the way he looked the morning he stood at the fire arguing with her mother before dawn. When the lantern light from Lilly's window was extinguished, the reflections faded, revealing the quiet dining room, the candle box on the mantle, full.

"Josephine is gone. Lilly knows, she will leave me," Raven whispered, confessing to the box. She blinked wearily and tried to straighten herself. The decision came without hesitation. *I will go to the woman of the swamp. She can give me something to help Lilly stay.*

Green, gray, brown, and black were separate and distinct in the glow of Raven's lantern as she journeyed. Her cloak above the green pasture. The moon held her in its light, and once Raven entered the swamp, brown, gray, black and green became one. Movement in the camouflage, a black bear, a shadow, the open rotten insides of a fallen tree, a shadow, a snake hung low, tree moss, fog, dense, in the distance an egret, a clump of grasses, tall, still brown from winter's death, red in the core, red in the movement. *Breathe.* Skin, hair, gray shirt, a woman came toward Raven, eyes blinked. She was mulatto brown and stood short and stout on the solid ground where water moved quiet beneath the earth.

One eye gray, one hazel-brown, the woman looked steady into Raven's eyes, and the familiarity quieted Raven. The redheaded woman didn't speak. Raven could hear their hearts beat in rhythm there in the swamp. The woman blinked, and Raven knew she was not a spirit. She wanted the woman to open her arms. She had come looking for answers on how to hold on to her child, to hold on to her own sanity, but she needed the woman to hold her.

She remembered long, comforting caresses from arms so much larger than hers, but the woman was small like a child now. Her dingy work shirt and work pants were held up with frayed leather suspenders.

"You drunk?" the woman said, and Raven did not speak, but pulled the black cloak over her head to keep the woman from seeing her blood-shot eyes.

"Is your name Josephine?"

"No," Raven responded. "No." She shook her head like a child not recognized by her own clan. She fumbled beneath the hood of the cloak to wipe a stray tear. "I was here when I was a child, so long ago, and I never knew your name."

"Hee, hee. Lord, and your life is still a mess." It was quiet. The woman still stared at Raven. "A bit late in the even'n. Yo husband know you out here?"

The woman picked her teeth with bitten-off brown fingernails. A slight breeze blew and Raven swallowed away the woman's smell of musk and the old smoke gone sweet in the oil of the woman's dirty clothes.

"Well, it wasn't that long ago. You came by way of the swamp islands and dry land bridges, not the gator holes, sand pits, and snake water. I remema that." The woman reached in the bluish light of the moon. "What you got for me?" The freckles and scars on the woman's hands, dots and textured lines like the roughness of birch bark. "Come on. What you got?" The redheaded woman motioned for Raven to reveal the offering beneath her coat.

Raven reluctantly showed her several candles of beeswax; dipped carefully by Josephine's shaking brown hands that morning. The redheaded woman closed her eyes there beneath the swamp and its shadows. She closed her eyes and held the candles with Raven. Together they saw the moment as things happened in Josephine's cabin.

Josephine clung to the table's edge before giving over to the dizzy head that had plagued her those days of her last pregnancy.

Raven's hands gripped the candle to pull them away from the redheaded woman. "Stop," Raven demanded, realizing that she was witnessing Josephine's death, but the woman put her hands over Raven's, and together they saw Josephine fall from her chair to the worn boards of the slave cabin. A round, faced Negro girl made a shadow over Josephine's strained expression. The girl shed a tear and in it they saw the births of babies coming like seeds from Josephine's chest, bursting into the spring days without her permission, their faces blending into the work of the fields, into the eyes of the Negro women, eyes like the colors of the swamp. They saw Raven's eyes when she first came to the swamp so long ago. They saw Raven's hands touching Josephine's dry hands where they both cupped Lilly's bottom, and Raven pulling Lilly away to have what she must have.

The redheaded woman let go of the candles and set Raven free. First the sobs came with a gentle shaking of the chest, the head bowed in guilt, then long howls that came up from the water that rushed beneath the earth where she stood. Raven's guilt spewed into the open air and then another voice came from her mouth. "Stop it!" Raven demanded her own silence, and a shock like the fire of lightening struck, shot down her arm from the center of her chest, and she could not breathe. Hidden birds shook loose from the cypress trees and took flight above the falling lamplight. Raven's body hit the ground and she pleaded inside her mind, *Stop it! Stop it!*

The woman's hands slowly reached out to hold Raven still where she now lay on the gentle floor of the swamp. She cupped Raven's face in her rough hands, placed her dry lips over Raven's soft mouth, pinched Raven's nose closed with the calloused banjo fingers, and breathed.

Raven's eyes showed nothing but the whites. The other voice ceased, and the woman held Raven's sleeping body on an island in the swamp, Raven's long thin stature folded into the stump frame of the woman. "Hush now," she whispered into Raven's ear. "You got to live so you can send the child on to her right home. Hush."

Well into the night Raven woke on the bed of green moss, alone. The moon set yellow on the horizon.

April 20, 1861

AT DAWN, JUST AS RAVEN was crossing the pasture for home, the moon set in Sybil's window, tempting early bird songs. Sybil drifted back to sleep and dreamed about Lilly; the child who did not know the voice of the woman who first called her that name, the child who stood on the veranda elevated up above the ground watching the men who had danced outside the slave shack of her birth.

She dreamed of the night of Lilly's birth. The baby did not move at first. Sybil squeezed the plug from her little nose and rubbed her fishbone chest fast as if she were rubbing the last stub feathers from a chicken's belly. Lilly's wet body moved with Sybil's hand until her arms flailed against the jarring and the tiny desperate cry came.

Sybil sat down on the floor that night. "She was a fright quiet, but she fine now." Then the voice of Lula, sniffling with the rag for Josephine's brow. "Lord, she got herself a free baby, free 'cause Massa cain't make a slave outta what he don't know nothin about."

Sybil dreamed of the cotton, gone to seed and blowing from the fields and catching in Lilly's hair where she stood on the veranda staring; her eyes black, her hair like fine web in the wind of the coming storm. The cotton lodged in the strands, and Sybil was the cotton flying and struggling to escape the black silk. Then the hair turned to tar-covered ropes that burned and cut with every movement.

In the dream, Sybil and Lilly stood, Sybil in black, Lilly in white, looking into the perfect grave, snug and secure, the walls orange-and-brown earth like the chocolate carrot cake for Lilly's tenth birthday. In the grave was Josephine—pinched eyes, and fists clinched over her stomach. She opened her eyes and a swarm of blue-and-black butterflies floated out, then the sound of the wings soft as they surrounded Sybil. All she could see was blue and black, and the child's small yellow hand slipped away, and Lilly fell into her mother's grave.

Sybil woke with her eyes hot and swollen. The sound of her own voice, "Lord, have mercy." She cried aloud in the small room behind the kitchen, hoping that her noise had not been heard through the thickness of the walls. She held her hand to her forehead where sweat rolled cold from under her cotton gray hair. "Shame," she cried, combing her aging fingers through the gray. "Shame."

The pink light streaked pastel then like blood in the dawn sky, bringing the sound of the screech owl's cry once, twice, then faint in the distance, and her heart beat out of rhythm as she heard Raven's steps light, like a bird's talons on the back steps.

Raven had been walking all night to find her way out of the swamp. She contemplated the horror of her broken promise to Josephine, contemplated the redheaded woman's advice to live and send the child home. She thought about Josephine's heartache ground into every handful of corn she tossed into the mill, woven into every sweater, dipped into the candles made by her hands. How many times, Raven wondered, had she eaten Josephine's tears? *Which of the children of the quarters were bred from Josephine's womb? How many were Lilly's siblings? How many?* She stopped to count and remembered that there had been a nursing baby sold with Josephine. Raven stood inhaling the damp air, trying to clear her mind to remember the facts of it, but she could not get the sights and sounds in her memory to order themselves.

Raven ascended the steps above where Sybil lay listening, both women tense with the burdens of the coming day. Shortly after Raven settled herself beneath the covers and drifted away to bird songs, Grey Fox returned home. Her body relaxed next to his assuring warmth, and both of them slipped into fitful dreams before sunrise.

In the dream, Raven watched as Lilly skipped from rock to rock seeing the shiny fish just below the water's surface. *Minti!* Come here! Raven shouted like her mother, but Lilly skipped on unconcerned about the black and tan snakes that coiled together in and around one another like chain links. Her feet danced gracefully just above the sur-face, and then an alligator's stare. Raven's eyes busied with the task of seeing where the gator had gone, her voice was paralyzed. She strained to see Lilly's feet. Her feet were still on the rocks, and the black and tan snakes coiled, constricted tighter and tighter around her ankles. Lilly's feet turned brown, bruised skin like the clay on the banks of the pottery creek of Raven's childhood.

Raven woke to find Grey Fox's spot in the bed warm where he had come and slept without her knowing. She grabbed her robe and ran. Her hand smoothed the polished wood of the banister as she flew down the stairs, and she caught him crossing the yard to the stable for his horse.

Lilly watched them from her bedroom window. Her small face was mixed up in the lace and dawn light, camouflaged as the two of them argued, whispering and shouting sometimes. "Josephine has died, and John Bartlette is very angry with you for selling him a sick slave. Tell me why you are going to the county station at a time like this. Please, stay here today. I know that something awful will happen if you don't."

"Raven, you know you have always believed that. Every day of our marriage I have been hostage to your fears. I will return. I have talked with Lilly, and assured her to stay put, that I will return this evening. I am asking you to follow my words as well."

Raven held the saddle strap now, but Grey Fox just stared off into the distance, not answering her. From her bedroom window Lilly watched and listened, and then the sight of her parents turned inward to waking visions. She *saw* as her grandmother's eyes had seen; she saw not like a little girl wanting silence from her arguing parents, but saw her mother, counting raindrops as they fell into a strange puddle where Lilly's night dress was soaked with mud. A horse whip cut the air and startled Lilly, and she opened her eyes there behind the lace curtains.

Grey Fox rode away from Raven, whose figure looked more slender than ever. Raven wrapped the thin white robe around her shoulders to brace against the dampness of a Southern spring morning, and looked up to where her daughter's face disappeared from the window.

No one had ever died in Lilly's house, and she wondered about spells and curses. Was her father right, that the slave people were not true Christians and were damned? Why had death come only to slaves, and never taken anyone of Lilly's family? She was lucky, she thought as she blinked against the morning weariness. She heard her mother's bedroom door shut, then silence.

Lilly crept downstairs, where she found Sybil working in the hot kitchen to prepare the biscuits that she knew Lilly would soon request. Despite the heat of the iron stove, Sybil wore her long-sleeved linsey-wool dress, because it was the only nice black garment she owned.

Lilly sat on the counter swinging her slippered feet and complained. "It's too hot in here, Sybil, and what are you wearing that heavy dress for?"

Sybil didn't look in Lilly's direction.

"Look at me. Come on, Mother is asleep. You can look at me."

"Gotta get the breakfast finished so I can get out to send the soul of my friend on, then get back in here to serve the breakfast." Sybil frowned and hurried about.

"Uncle Henry says you niggers have a party for everything. Josephine didn't even belong to us anymore. Why does she need a funeral here? Why on my birthday? And, did you ask Mama? She's in charge of things around here if all the men go fight."

Sybil didn't answer but pulled on her hair bonnet and looked down so far at the biscuits that she almost touched her chin to her chest to keep the girl from seeing the tears that fell salty into the kneading. Sybil had always been able to hold her tears and her laughter unless she had a sip of the spirit water, and she had, just that morning, gone to the place under the draped table that held the wash pan where she kept an old brown turpentine bottle filled with the leftovers from brandy snifters. She had said a prayer for Lilly that morning while listening to Raven sneak up the stairs to her bed, then she listened to Grey Fox follow. She had watched the morning light come and turned up the bottle and drained it just before putting on the wool dress and striking fire in the stove for Lilly's biscuits.

The drunkenness was still in her, and her mixed feelings were difficult to hide.

She turned away from the child's questions and drank a bit of the tonic from a tin water cup on the windowsill. She remembered Josephine peering through that window to catch a glimpse of the baby girl who she had thrown to the light, the days when Josephine's face was smooth and her dark brown cottony hair still solid in color. Sybil remembered how she would leave the kitchen door open, claiming that she was helping to draw the heat from the kitchen into the morning chill of the house. "Got to keep that new baby warm."

One morning Raven passed the kitchen door hollering for Sybil to bring the warm cow's milk with water for the baby. When Sybil turned to fetch it from the stove, Josephine stood flat against the wall, having expressed half a bottle of milk from her bare left breast. Her tears flowed only from the left eye and she slipped gently out the squeaky back door while Sybil hollered back, "It's coming right away, ma'am."

"Sybil?" Lilly looked up from reading *Oliver Twist* and realized Sybil was still staring out the window. "Aren't you going to take the biscuits out of that hot oven so they can cool down? I'm hungry."

"Yes I will, and in the meantime I wanna tell you somethin to remember." Sybil took off the apron and let the bravery of the drink speak. "You ain't better than me. Yo Mistress Raven ain't better than me, and the black folks is gone have they say one day. Best decide if you side'n with the Indian folk or the black folk, and best decide right now."

Lilly bit her bottom lip, and blood filled her cheeks. Her emotions wavered between bursting into tears like a child, or standing up to Sybil like the young heir of LeFlore plantation. "Sybil, I'll have my Uncle Golden tear your hide off for talking to me that way."

Sybil got close to the girl's face, so close Lilly could smell the whisky in Sybil's sweat. "Trouble's comin, little miss, and God ain't gonna spare you no more than he spare them who ain't done nothin but serve you. You think you know who you is but you don't, and shame is cain't no body do nothin about it without risking freedom of the whole lot. Why don't you ask your uncle and your father if they got any niggers in they family? If I was you, I'd be running on away from here befo' them who mad about what they been sold come to settle a score on your head." Sybil breathed heavy, trying to hold her peace with the innocent child.

"My father came to me before leaving this morning. He said trouble's coming, I know that. He told me to stay put till he gets back tonight for the meeting. He's got some figuring he's gonna do. Maybe he's gonna sell off a sassy-mouth nigger like you."

A knot hardened in Sybil's throat and the heat of the kitchen overwhelmed her.

"Get outta my kitchen before I smack you back to where you belong, gal. Get!"

Lilly hopped down off the counter. Anger made the straight black roots of her hair stand on end. She had grown tall for her age, the promise of a strong body like her mother's was evident at ten. "Soon as my mother wakes I'm telling her everything you said to me."

"You gonna be waitin 'till judgment day. That lady laying up there in that bed cain't help herself, let alone help you. You know just like me that she crazy as a rabid coon."

An hour later, the biscuits had cooled. Sybil had returned from the quarters and she served the breakfast, anxious to be relieved of the

LeFlore family's presence. Henry and Golden and Samuel ate their last breakfast before departing.

Raven picked nervously at her eggs. "Aren't you going to wait for Grey Fox? He said he'd be meeting and making some decisions for you all with General Thorpe."

"Sister, Henry and I have decided. He and Samuel and I will go, there is nothing to wait for.

"Where's my niece this morning, Raven?" Golden asked.

"She's decided not to say good-bye."

"Is she in her room? Maybe I'll just go up and steal a kiss."

Henry sat back in his chair and kept his gaze to the side of the table where Dove and Rebecca sat, eating their meals. Over the years Rebecca had begun to look like Dove, and Dove had grown to look more pensive like her husband. The look of sadness that came over Henry seemed contrived to Raven. She could not uplift her own sincere sadness, and realized in that moment that she had never liked Henry Trench. She had never trusted him, had never liked the veneer over his elusive personality. "I think she should be left to her room and wishes. If you are departing after breakfast, do so without disturbing her."

"Really, sister." Golden spoke only a few words but did not dare rouse Raven's unpredictable temper.

Raven skirted the edge of the unspoken stresses between them. "Does it bother you, brother, that your niece has not come down to have breakfast with you before you go off to war? Does it bother you that your own sisters, perhaps your only kin, will be here while you fight on the side of the men who killed our parents?"

Henry joked, "Don't act so glum, ladies. We'll be back in a couple of months, with prosperity like dewdrops on our sleeves." The three men tugged on the sleeves of handed-down uniforms and laughed in an explosion of falsely boosted morale.

Sybil started to clear the table in an old winter work dress, one she rarely wore even in the dead of winter, and Raven couldn't calm her mind to question. All day, Raven watched from both porches for Grey Fox to return, but saw no sign of him. Strange thoughts that had never plagued her, ate at her mind. *What if the slaves are planning something, as Henry has always warned? Should I heed the chills that run up and down my spine, the feeling that tells me to run with Lilly?* Her skull ached from containing the storm of thoughts.

Lilly played in the sitting room, rolling glass marbles across the wooden floor. Raven did not answer Lilly's intermittent question. "Will we have my party tomorrow?"

Lilly occasionally apologized for bouncing the marbles off her mother's shoe, rousing her from her trance.

Sybil came in and lit the lamps and the chandelier. "Ma'am, I done prepared for General Thorpe and Master Fox, and turned back the beds. If you don't mind me sayin, it's getting on in the evening, and maybe they's decided to meet somewheres else. I'd like permission to go on down to spend my Saturday night in the quarters."

Raven remained with her head leaning on her fist. She did not turn around in Grey Fox's chair to question Sybil. "How do you suppose you'll hear me ring if they get here and you're in the quarters merrymaking?"

"I'll watch for General Thorpe's buggy Ma'am."

Lilly was watching Sybil. "I wouldn't let her go, Mother. She doesn't respect you like you're the master of this place."

"Be quiet, Lilly. Go to bed."

Raven rubbed her temples and still did not turn to see Sybil, wearing now, a different work dress from the morning; double-skirted bottom, an apron beneath the skirt that held things from the kitchen that were too heavy for decent travel: the iron hooks that had been carefully tempered, hammered, and stretched into vines, the rusted biscuit cutter, the tiny washboard for cleaning the kitchen towels and napkins.

"Good night, Sybil," Raven whispered, and fell asleep in her husband's chair.

She was awakened by the sound of a coach pulling up. Raven crept to the front door with a lantern. Her sister, Dove, and Rebecca stepped slowly into a coach. "Sister!" Raven called out in a whisper. "Where are you going?" Dove came to Raven on the stairs in a plain cotton plaid dress with apron. "Henry has sent for us. I didn't want to wake you, sister. I will return in a week. I won't stay away. I didn't want to wake you, sister."

She held Raven's hand to her cheek. "You have been so restless and worried. I didn't want to wake you." She looked at Raven's dead eyes and looked away. Rebecca sat up in the carriage, waving slowly, her dark hair limp, falling into her face.

"I'll return in a week, "Dove whispered, shutting the coach door.

There was no wind down in the quarters that night while the slaves sat ready. The plan was to wait for General Thorpe and Master Bartlette to come and carry out the law; take the child born a slave to replace the damaged, dead property sold by the master of LeFlore.

"Guilty" in the Confederacy's eyes; a new government that wanted the land that housed the highest point in the state of Mississippi, strategic land for spotting coming troops. Henry Trench had reported to his benefactor, "General Thorpe, with some clearing, there isn't an acre of that land that you can't see from the house."

So the Confederacy had found just cause in Grey Fox wrongfully representing property as "good" when Josephine was in fact almost finished. The dishonest sell of property, a claim set forth by his maid, Sybil, who reported this deed to the payment of new shoes, which she would soon use to run with her kin of LeFlore. Sybil planned then to betray the giver of shoes for trusting in her docility. Once Nathan escorted the general's horse and wagon to the stable, he'd unhitch and bring all the horses to the quarters, load them up, and depart.

Henry was right; they should not have been trusted. Even he forgot to pay attention to Sybil's long-sleeved funeral dress; beneath it, silverware tied to her body with burlap string, which did not hurt worse than a slap or the whip that her mother endured at Jacques LeFlore's hands.

Sybil sat in the dark silence with the others; the carefully bundled belongings rested at their feet. She took long puffs on one of Master Tchula's cigars and repeated to herself, *They are counting on me, they are looking to me to be brave in leaving;* thoughts that helped to keep Lilly's innocence at bay.

Grey Fox sat in General Thorpe's office; the compromise to keep his land played over in his mind. He waited in the hot office, where the lanterns that lit the room made his weary head heavier from the heat, weary from a long day of riding from mail post to mail post seeking his father's words, between rides, sitting quiet beneath poplar trees to contemplate his plan.

He thought about his father and wondered if he were dead. He imagined the letter carrier riding to the nearest Oklahoma post, violating the Union order of no travels in or out of Indian Territory via Union trails. He imagined the rider being fired upon by a group of bored Union soldiers who were left to camp out, hungry, no orders, afraid. They fired on him, and the letter carrier fell from his horse like a limb from a tree; the satchel hit the ground first and its contents were carried on the wind of the chaos; Grey Fox's urgent letters requesting his father's advice, but the envelopes were scribed with *DECEASED RETURN TO SENDER!*; the envelopes that float down over the dead man and his horse.

General Thorpe, John Bartlette, and two shabbily clad soldiers entered, interrupting Grey Fox's thoughts. Acknowledging their presence, Grey Fox stood, smoothing his weighted hair. "General Thorpe." And at the other men he looked on curious. "Good evening, Mr. Bartlette. I do have a private matter that I would like to discuss with you, but I have business, a private matter, to discuss with the general."

Grey Fox fumbled with the hat he held in both hands. General Thorpe stepped forward, his uniform frayed where his hand so often covered his heart. His beard had turned from gray to yellow on the stresses of war. His skin was lighter between the wrinkle creases. He was exhausted, knowing his duty to his superiors: "Secure the four hundred acres by what ever means necessary." A duty that had been a concern ten years ago was now fulfilled.

"Grey Fox, I'm afraid Mr. Bartlette is sound in being here, and so are my men. We have matters that must be addressed." General Thorpe combed his beard with his fingers and looked up at the taller, older Bartlette. "With the sheriff and his deputies deployed in battle, Mr. Bartlette has come to me about your lawlessness. As well, Henry Trench has informed me of lawless behavior on your part."

Both young soldiers came toward Grey Fox, their short black militia wear ill-fitting, moth-eaten, handed down from men of the American-Mexican war. They each grabbed one shoulder and one wrist.

The general spoke up. "You are being imprisoned for the wrongful sell of property. The reimbursement of that slave property will be satisfied;" General Thorpe paused and looked out the black window; "by the enslavement of her child Lilly, who you have taken into your home against the very Choctaw slavery codes your father helped mandate. We will retrieve her, and she will be handed over to Bartlette immediately."

Grey Fox did not speak. His gaze was caught steady by a moth that flew into the window and batted and dived at the lantern on the desk until finally heat singed the wings and it fell into the glass dome. General Thorpe looked down at the scribed statement and looked away from Grey Fox as the memory of Lilly's playful voice echoed above the shifting of the two young soldiers' feet over the dirty wooden floor.

"You will receive ten lashes for breaking the Choctaw slave codes, and for making a slave child heir to your property, as is set forth in the Choctaw slave codes drawn by your father."

"Henry Trench," Grey Fox whispered from his waking sleep.

The general continued, "Added to these charges is the charge of harboring Raven, Dove, and Golden, three fugitives of the relocation, children of the Okla Hannali band of Choctaw, their father a hunter and a horse thief. You will remain imprisoned until such a time that a sentence is set by a county court for the three charges against you. During this time, you are to forfeit all landholdings."

At the end of the list of charges, Grey Fox began to struggle, and stopped at his own reflection in the raised pane of glass in the open window. He saw through the curtain of his own dark hair his eyes, and stopped there, looking into the portal of his own story. His mother argued in a tone where her words came in short breathes, her throat closed with frustration. *I won't do it anymore. I am not simply another stolen article in your list of stolen artifacts. Don't ask me to be here while you go to work your magic with my people, convincing them with the poison drink that they should walk away from all they've ever fought to hold on to.*

Tchula li and the little Sybil stood unseen, both of them clean and obedient. Tchula li stood straight; the girl's glance was cast to her master's nervous feet; the two of them cultivated by the habits of their parents. They watched Jack Flowers and his wife in the sitting room.

His father stood, neck stiff, stance proud, calculating without moving his eyes, without the pulse of the veins in his neck quickening. He reached for the cigar case like reaching for a soothing smoke, but sped his moves and slung the wooden box and its contents toward Tchula li's mother, toward her unsuspecting stare. "Stay in our room when the men come.

"Myrtle!" He called for Sybil's mother, his trustworthy maid, to come and clean the mess of scattered cigars and the spatter of blood that stained the papered wall.

In the reflection of the window Grey Fox watched General Thorpe and the square-faced John Bartlette exit the room. General Thorpe turned to his defeated associate. "You should have gone to Oklahoma when the chance was offered."

Nathan sat quiet on the shoeing stool outside the stable, the sound of his breath the only indication that he sat in the moonless pitch-dark of that night. He heard the clock up in the hallway of Mistress LeFlore's chambers. Twelve chimes. Nathan knew that something had gone wrong, that Master Fox would not return, that John Bartlette and General Thorpe would not meet him there. He could feel the tension inside the house, the tension down in the quarters. He knew that he must take Miss Lilly's horse, and Master Golden's horse, ever so quietly down to the quarters and make the run. That there was no turning back on a plan where things had been stolen, bundled, children had been told, and would speak if they were asked. He knew that they must go before the spell of that night opened up with the dawn and brought change that could never be undone. He sat for another half hour, not able to imagine leaving the two women alone in the house, then said a prayer. "Heavenly Father, forgive me if what I'm 'bout to do is a sin befo' yo eyes."

He walked; his and the horses' knees clicked where the cartilage was crumbling with age; around the slow decent of the hill to let their hooves fall on lawn, to avoid the windows of his masters.

With four hours before dawn remaining, the black bodies led by Nathan and Sybil; Lula, Burtrome, Emma, Earleen, Little Man, and the brown crop of big and small children, descendants of Josephine; left the sweet-fruit-smell, damp-fertile-earth home of LeFlore plantation, silent, the mournfulness of leaving in the slump of their bodies, the jubilance of freedom dormant in the core of their souls, which led them away. Slowly at first, and then swiftly in flight at the sight of a thing, thin and white in the darkness like the ghost of a great snake. Closer, Sybil rode on Golden's horse. Then, more swiftly they fled, realizing a loosened rope, loosened noose where decayed flesh rotted the loop, hanging still in the darkness, where white men might be gawking from the woods, predators to their passing.

In the distance behind them, two generations of Okla Hannali women, not white, not black, sat in the stillness before dawn.

April 21, 1861

LONG BEFORE MORNING lit the sky, Raven looked upon the sleeping face of her precious daughter. The candle cast a light that made Lilly's soft face glow orange, her cheeks red with the heat of dreaming. At Raven's feet was the valise stuffed tight with the clothes and a few belongings that she would take for her and Lilly. She let herself cry gently to release the pain of uncertainty. She touched her own face and marveled at the softness of her skin, the new wrinkles gone with the swelling of a night of tears and worry over those she might lose.

The hungry feeling in her belly twisted, and she sighed and touched Lilly's quiet hand that was so limp in resting. *If only my parents had not clung to the land like stubborn leaves in winter.* She cried now before

Lilly awakened to see her mother weak and uncertain in what she would demand of her daughter. She imagined herself speaking with Lilly's face between her hands the way her inki had spoken to her beneath the safety of the pine and poplar trees. *Run, run, run with me, Lilly. Death is coming and your life is in danger.*

Raven dried her eyes and slipped loosely into dreams of objects swirling in a violent wind.

In the dream she saw Sybil riding high, looking into the distance at the house, standing, waiting hesitant in her approach. "Lilly, Lilly," Sybil whispered, and then turned the reins in the direction of the rising sun.

"Mother." Raven was startled awake by Lilly's bright voice, the candle sleeping and the first hint of morning silver on Lilly's cheek, her voice playful and innocent. "Good morning, Mother. Did Father return last night? He and I must ride this morning. The air is good for flying." She laughed deviously, waiting for her mother to scold her for wanting to ride fast like a boy, but there was nothing, just the balmy, hesitant breeze of morning coming down from the North.

"Lilly, they are coming for you. I can see them, hooves making sparks on jagged rock." Raven hadn't planned to speak such words, but words and images merged and she could not distinguish between asleep, awake, and the space in between.

Lilly frowned. "They who, Mother?"

"You must listen to your mother, Lilly. Just listen this once, and don't ask questions."

Lilly's playfulness turned to the defiance that was new and solid in her. "I am to listen to my father as well, and he has told me to always wait, to be still. He talked to me before he left, you know? He said if you want to go on a trip, to stay, to wait for him. Even if you want to go to town, to wait. I want to stay and wait for him. I know they will come. I have seen it in my dreams too, Mother, but I will stand here and fight the Yankees with my father."

"Listen to me, Lilly." Only now did Raven feel the certainty, only now had she crossed the line of doubt, of knowing, of insanity, of clarity, knowing where time did not need the boundaries of the mind.

Raven listened and heard General Thorpe, Henry Trench, John Bartlette's overseer, two young soldiers, exhausted, determined to finish what they had started.

"Lilly, the men who come for you are Confederate. I can smell the sweat in their hair." Raven closed her eyes. "I can feel the grip on the reins. They mean to take you." Raven's words slowed. "They mean to take you."

Raven was sweating, her eyes pinched closed. Sweat soaked the underarms of the light blue cotton dress. She released the imprisoned breath, grabbed the valise in one hand, Lilly by the arm in the other.

"Mother. Stop, please. Father said you are changing with age, Mother: the forgetfulness, the speaking when no one is in the room." Raven had not known her daughter's strength, ten years old now, growing strong in her bone and muscle.

Raven heard a flood of noise, voices grunting. She saw in a flash of sight; blood streaking down a saddle skirt.

"Stop it, Lilly. Come now, come." Raven hurried her grip, threatening to pull the child's arm free from her body.

They stumbled to the top of the stairs, struggling. Raven shook Lilly, holding her shoulders. "We must run. Can't you hear them?"

"I want to fight them, Mother. I know where Father keeps his guns."

Lilly broke free and ran to the end of the hall, where the grand clock stood, cherry wood and shiny golden hands. She opened the pendulum door and behind it found a small arsenal, two bayonets and two small handguns. Before she could reach for them Raven hugged her from behind, pinned her arms to her body. She dragged Lilly down the stairs. Raven screamed for Sybil, and so did Lilly. The sound echoed in the empty house.

Lilly ran to the kitchen to find Sybil, but she was not there, offering a place to hide. Her heart beat wild in her chest as she flung open doors of the cupboards, and under the table that held the washbowl she scurried and closed the drapery and her eyes tight against the sound of the hooves that were so loud inside her mind and Raven's mind, and they both saw into the past; the men dragging Raven over dry earth, smoke rising in great billows to a sunset sky, the hatchet, the blood.

Lilly tore through the curtains of the table that hid her and found her mother staring out the French doors of the veranda, lost in the seeing of things passed. She grabbed the soft fullness of her mother's hand and ran out the servant door with the sun at their backs.

The spring peepers sang in the distance as night evaporated into morning, their calls shrill in the distance as Lilly and Raven fled.

It wasn't the end; Raven sensed that. She stepped high over weeds and smelled the damp air just ahead. Dawn gave everything the same purplish gray tint, but the sun rose and revealed colors; their faces, tanned skin, dark hair, cornflower blue dresses, tall thin woman and her young kin, whose face was darker, strong, capable of enduring.

The land around them grew thicker with green as dawn lifted and they ran closer to safety.

Out of breath, Raven stumbled and stopped near a stone wall that led down a hill.

"Lilly," she gasped, "I want to show you something."

Raven unbuttoned the high collar and unlaced her shoes.

"Mother, your feet will be raw."

"I want to show you the planting dance. I remember it, you know?"

Raven smiled at her daughter, still out of breath. She smiled in the new light of morning; teeth bared, though the men were in pursuit.

"Mother, you are not well. We should keep running."

"Look, look." Raven held up the front of her dress to reveal her bare feet and sun deprived legs. She kept her feet flat on the earth and shuffled.

"See, I'm plowing the earth, caressing it, asking my Great Mother permission to enter her." Raven's face looked relieved by the movement.

"Mother stop!" Lilly looked away, then behind Raven to the coming light. She closed her eyes to block the sight of her mother, who was lost in the trance of her movements, and Lilly saw in her waking dreams the hooves again with morning light. She called out, "Mother!" and arrested Raven's dance. The two of them stared into each other's eyes as Raven slowly returned to the moment.

"Mother, there is a stone wall. This is someone's land we can run to. Mother, please, they are coming."

"Lilly." Raven was out of breath, grinning, intoxicated with the satisfaction of having remembered the planting dance.

"Lilly, this is John Bartlette's land."

"Then we must keep running, Mother. I heard the men. Bartlette is looking for father." Lilly looked helplessly into Raven's eyes.

Leaving Raven's shoes and stockings behind, Lilly grabbed her mother by the hand, Raven's other hand still in a tight fist of dress hem as they ran.

The sun came full on them, and stripped the air of its coolness. They arrived at a great boulder creek. The two of them stood, staring up and down stream for a shallow crossing.

Raven jerked her head in the direction of a humid breeze, like a wolf catching the scent of death. "Mother?" she could hear Lilly say from far away, the shush of rushing water between them. Pain gripped in her chest and shot down her arm to the hand where she held Lilly's. They stood on the small rocks just before the place where the large wet rocks descended to boulders and rapid water.

Raven's eyes saw the sky, the trees, and heard the sound of the earth losing breath as her head hit the banks of the creek.

"Mother?" She heard Lilly's voice again, and saw her father next to Lilly. She saw a shorn lamb next to him, saw Josephine kneeling at the basket of wool, a spinning wheel turning, dizzying. "Mother?" she heard Lilly cry, and Raven heard her own slow breath inside her head, blended with the breath of the creek.

"Lilly," she said in a sweet song, her own voice sounding far away. She saw on the other side of the creek Josephine's spirit, a white rag on her head, an arm full of empty white blankets.

"Lilly." Her voice was almost smiling as she freed the words from her lips, going purple, "Josephine is your ishki. Josephine is your ishki. Go home," she whispered. "Run, run, home."

Raven floated above her own face and followed the cold tear that let go like the first fallen leaf.

"Mother?" There was a hand; the smell of dirt, sweat, young hand. Lilly called, "Mother!" and Raven was gone.

The sun burned the skin on the back of Lilly's neck, reminding her that she was flesh and bone, and she ran; air and breath moving through her body, like wind through reeds, she ran to catch her mother's spirit. She ran until her heart swelled and constricted to tell the mind to stop the body, and it was finished.

John Bartlette's overseer tied the rope in knots like knots for the caught wild boar. Her gentle lavender-scented flesh ripped under the roughness of tar dipped ropes, and Lilly screamed, "Mama!" The sound rushed through the sunlit trees, bounced on the wet boulders of the creek, and reached the body that lay miles away in an unknown direction where the evening waters of the creek rushed to the bank and took Raven's body home.

Part Two

April 23, 1861

I N T H E D R E A M, pleated wings fanned over me, and I stared long
in my confusion at the curtain of feathered brown until I recognized my own hair lying over my eyes.

The cabin was dim in the light of the lantern that burned on a table.
Beyond the veil of hair an old Negro woman knitted a square of blanket,
off-white like her eyeballs, and my eyes filled with tears, my body mourned
my mother's death, though I could not remember. Somehow, my body
understood the reality, before my mind, that I had been assigned by law
as property. The woman looked up, stern in her glance, her mouth frowning to one side, and my thoughts moved quickly past images of Hansel
and Gretel inside the witch's cottage, to my mother standing at the water
just before the men descended on us. "Where are my mother and father?"
I demanded rubbing the tears and exhaustion from my eyes.

"Dead," the woman said without missing a stitch, her voice so flat
that I was convinced she had misunderstood. I rubbed my eyes again to
wake from the dream, but the woman knitted without blinking.

"Dead," she said again, with little regard for my feelings. I called out
for Sybil, then I remembered the running.

I sat up in the bed next to the lantern, the thin hair on my arms
almost singed from the heat of the globe. The woman continued to
knit, and watch me as I first turned around to feel for the source of the
roughness beneath her. Straw poked through the thin sheet to my soft
thigh. Then I saw my wrists, my breath came in pants, and my hands
shook remembering the burns of the ropes, the sensation of flight, my
body thrown onto the back of a wagon, the pain in my left buttock
where I landed. The sight of the soiled cornflower blue nightdress, and

I gasped for air. "Mama!" I remembered, my mother, "dead," the image of her body near the creek, like a creature folded limp after a tornado. I remembered Bartlette's overseer's hands on my body, and I screamed a scream that dredged up the full memory of my capture; I screamed until the old woman frowned harder, shook her head and returned to her knitting. The pitch of my cry elevated.

The cabin door was the only sound above my noise. It squeaked on its hinges as a Negro man entered; broad chest, yellowing hair; his face was soft, old, and assuring. He came toward me, opened his giant hand, which smelled like biscuits and coffee, and covered my mouth; uncovered and covered it again until my screaming was over. I fell back, limp onto the straw mattress, my mind turning off after my soul's failed attempt to flee.

"Come and see where you is," the man said, pulling me up to a sitting position. My bare feet caressed the dirt floor like the hands of the blind feeling their way, questioning the absence of hard wood and fine Oriental rugs. I walked out the cabin door and my feet met the cool earth, and sent the message to my mind to flee for home.

Lanterns crossed in the darkness like fireflies, and voices trailed behind them. Men and women with voices deep like hummingbirds' wings, like Sybil's voice, like Nathan's voice. I stood at the man's shoulder letting my eyes adjust in the darkness; I noticed a few other sheds visible in the half-moon light.

"Am I in the quarters? You are not one of our slaves. Take me up to the house," I demanded.

"Little miss, you been sleep for two days."

I turned back to the inside of the cabin. "Then I missed my birthday party. Where are my shoes?" I asked the old woman, who looked at me and rolled her eyes away to her knitting.

I scampered beneath the platform bed, and shrieked at the bareness of things. When I lowered the tattered sheet, I saw my wrists again, red, raw, salve caked there. My throat closed: the boulders in the creek, my mother's spirit rising up over the water and flying away faster than the breeze. I felt myself fall forward.

"Now don't do that again," the man said. "You's at Massa Bartlette's plantation now. I'm gonna help you get some food." His tone was harsh, as he limped to a place in the darkness of the yard, where he fanned embers beneath a stew kettle, and returned with a wooden bowl. I sat on the floor between the dirt outside and the dirt floor inside. The woman cawed a response. "Lettin the skeeters and flies and everything else in. Shet the doe. You ain't got no servants around here to swat pests for you."

"Hush, Anna," he said and handed me the hot bowl.

She shrugged her shoulders and knitted with fury now. "Don't treat her like that. Things ain't gonna be that way for her. So don't start her out thinkin somebody gotta take care of her."

He waved his hands at the woman's comments, and looked back at me with the compassion for a wounded animal before he said. "You ain't gonna be goin home. You is here to settle a debt between yo father and Massa. All that other life of yours done faded on away to the past. This is home now." He reached for my face, and tears of full understanding, full memory flowed like sap out of my eyes, over his thick-skinned hand, into my bowl, and they kept flowing, day and night, as memories of home distilled into raw longing.

Nights, I sat by the fire, away from the Negroes, because every time I heard one of the slave children say, "Mama," I ached deep inside from the place where my navel inverted and met with my intestines, where the undigested pig's parts churned before settling heavy on my stomach.

Overseer Yates rode out to where the slaves sat, a ring of light in the darkness. He clodded in slow and wobbly on his old horse, that walked with a canter much like his own drunken stride.

"Where is she?" He called out, looking around the circle. I sat outside of the glow of the firelight. When a flame rose from new pine thrown on the fire, he spotted the dingy white of my blouse and my light skin. I tried to curl over and disappear into the wooden bowl I cupped in my lap. I concentrated on the sound of the crickets, and stopped chewing on the gristle of the pig's feet.

He came over to where I sat. "You a nigger now Miss Lilly." He let the whip come down in the dirt next to me, and the sound released a screech despite my prayer, *Be still, be still.* The warmth of urine escaped, and forced me to hold my body tight. *Does he want me to answer him? Does he want me to be quiet and just listen to him speak?* I didn't yet understand the rules of where I lived, still understanding slavery from the other side of the white pillars. I looked up at him in question, and our eyes met. I saw the weakness that told me, he was a landless peon, that he was beneath me in society, that he was a coward, *hattak mat,* my mother would have called him in her language.

My stare was broken by a wise and weathered hand that came rushing through the air and collided with my face, temporarily displaced my jaw bone, gristle on gristle causing a ringing in my ears that made things go black until my own cool hand held the stinging, slapped cheek.

I opened my eyes to see Old Raymond standing there. At the sight of him I remembered the kindness he had shown on that first day, then seeing his dangling hand, lax from the slap, I closed my eyes to hold back the tears, and shut myself away from him. He stood in the darkness between me, and the Overseer, whose horse trotted away. He rocked, as if unsteadied by his actions. His frustration was bellowed in a barrage of reprimands.

"You gonna bring bad down on yoself and everybody else, actin like that. You ain't Lilly LeFlore no mo. You just Lilly, and Overseer mean to prove it."

The wooden bowl fell with it's contents, and I used both hands to cover my face. Something kin to humiliation, but steeped in isolation washed over me. Old Raymond, bent down to pull my hands away. "Stop all that. I yelled at you 'cause I want you to understand that you ain't just a single somebody, but you effect the whole lot."

I wept into my hands, until Old Raymond surrendered and limped to his cabin. The others turned back to their conversation around the fire. One slave woman mumbled, "Somebody best teach her that them Missy Lilly days is over." A few chuckles resounded in the night noises, and I ran through the darkness to the safety of me and Anna's cabin.

I tried to push the memory of Lilly LeFlore down beneath my dreams until I did not wake mornings expecting the sounds of LeFlore, but the memories leaked out of cracks in my psyche, and I began to walk inside my sleep. One morning before dawn, I walked slumbering in my bare feet over grass lawn like cool moss between my toes, to the smokehouse, where the meat sent out a savory signal of salt and sweet to the back of my tongue. I helped myself to the ham that hung there.

From the smokehouse, with my belly full, I walked across the yard, my head lilting forward and back as the length of my hair draped and then fell back to reveal my glazed eyes. Across the Bartlette yard I floated, following the smell of bread which wafted damp on the morning fog. Up the back steps I walked leaving wet footprints on the smooth wood.

Bread kneaded by brown hands was cooling for the start of a new day, chestnut colored and shiny, buttery sweetness like Sybil's. The familiarity of smells, raised me out of the dream a bit, left me with waking illusions. I thought I saw Sybil standing there, and heard her say, "Come on in here child and eat it while it's hot."

When my mouth watered, I found myself awake, in Bartlette's kitchen eating the bread, barely allowing myself to swallow the thick dough before tearing away another piece.

The Negro cook Janie stared me down with her hands on her hips, which were as narrow as the stove pipe.

"What's you some kinda fool, child? Ain't gonna have folks think I'm coaxin you to act like you got some kinda special privilege 'cause you used to be somebody's Massa." She walked past me in her hard-soled shoes and cried out, "Oversee-a! I done caught the fox in the henhouse."

I whimpered all the way to the hitching post, fearing what would happen to me. The old scabs from the ropes that brought me to Bartlette's were reopened by the pulling, and Overseer Yates paraded me from the house to the quarters as if he'd caught a prized hunt. His foot fall conveyed the confidence he would bestow on himself by whipping the likes of Lilly LeFlore.

He passed Old Raymond in the yard and told him to get everybody from the fields, and Old Raymond carried his tall, thick self slow, into the rising fog. His hair was dingy white like sheep's wool, but his skin was dark like dried tobacco, and made his eyes look ghostly on his return, with the whole population of the quarters behind him.

Tears and the piece of smoked ham were still salty on the back of my tongue when I felt Overseer's hands on the back of my neck before he ripped my night dress open, and pulled until it fell around my waist. I flailed and sent screeches into the air like the monkeys I'd once seen in a traveling side show. I gripped the post to bear the pain of the first lash. Splinters broke away from where the wood made thorns in my hands. Eyes of old and young dark faces watched the reverse of my birth: this time the women waited for the crying to stop, because when it did, Overseer was no longer interested, and would leave me alone.

My mind slipped into a dark place where color did not exist, a place where there were no smells, where a hand brushed over thorns did not feel pain.

After the tenth lash, the baskets and bags were picked up, and I saw from where I lay on the ground, the worn shoes and bare feet returning to the fields. "She too young and way too little for all that. Just wasn't necessary to teach her her place in that fashion." Anna rubbed the salve on my back, and gave me a new blouse, tailored from an old night shirt. She did not concern herself with looking at me, though I sat on the side of her bed, numb with a belladonna stare. "Quit lookin like you done had your heart took out. Got that bad mojo look in your glance. May as well clear that up right now. I cain't say I like your uppidy ways neither. But, you didn't deserved to be punished like that. It's done now, and least you know something that you didn't know before: Overseer Yates is one of them whites that hates massas and rich folk more that the Negroes do."

Anna left the cabin for her work in the house, returned three times for things she had forgotten, and then was gone past the tiny cabin window. On her way up the hill, she hummed a tune with no melody to push away any concern for me. She looked behind her with every step toward the house, as if haunted by the memory of some other Overseer, a walk I soon adopted.

That evening I stood next to Old Raymond at the stew pot, weak but comforted by his smell of lard and onions, a smell that reminded me of Sybil. The evening air was cool, but my body was hot with fever from the open welts. On and off the tears flowed, and Old Raymond wiped them away like sweat.

Around the fire the voices of the others rumbled and broke into laughter in an unpredictable rhythm that caused my body to throb with pain, *Are they laughing at me?*

I quietly asked Old Raymond the question that had been on my mind since the first day. "What is a breeder?" I asked knowing the word meant something about life and death, something of the woman's body and babies being born. Like Oliver Twist's mother, I knew that once I was bred, I would die. I pictured myself floating in the quiet end of the cold creek where my mother died, the end that bent around the back acres of LeFlore, where father and I let the horses bow and drink. One daisy over each eye, my long hair like dark weeds on the surface of the water.

As I watched Old Raymond stir the pot, my thoughts drifted from the fantasy of my own death, to the fantasy of running. *Dusk will be a good time to go, run away in search of the stone wall and follow it to the rise above the creek,* and then, *I will not hold my breath to prevent drowning. I will let the loose debris of cattail reeds be my raft, dusk's, subtle light making the water a black blanket beneath me.*

Old Raymond's rough tone interrupted my musing. "You ain't been here but a little while, and you done stole, got beaten, and thinkin on strange ways to set yo self into the next life. I reckon you still full of notions of being somethin yo ain't no more. But breedin? You got time to know what that's about. You ain't got the bleedin yet. Before that happen, the war or somethin might find you a way out'a this mess. I'm hopin on that for every one of us," and he stirred the steaming cauldron of hot chitlins.

I asked again, "What's a breeder?" He did not answer me, but changed the matter, "It ain't important what you eat, child. Getting yourself beat for hot bread and smoked meat be a foolish thing. And ham?" He laughed deep, "If you gonna do a thing like that, I guess

you best skip the salt pork and go for the good stuff. Um, um, um."
His chuckling rubbed against the open welts on my back like splintery
branches, and the tears came.

"I know what it means, I have to do like the cows when Overseer sets
the bull out in the field, just stand still. But what's going to happen to
me then? Will I die?"

Old Raymond, hummed and stirred, in the pot, waving the smoke
with the changing direction of the wind, behavior that served to delay
the images that my questions provoked.

At night, I sat awake listening to Anna snore, and worrying about
bleeding time, about breeding time. Who? How? I wondered if the
blood would come in my urine, or from the hole for my bowels. I bit
my nails down to a bloody nub, and imagined myself asking Old Anna
or Old Raymond these questions that would surely make them look
off and ignore me. I wore my mind and body tired thinking at night,
time away from picking up behind the weeding, time away from learning to use a hoe, to carry a seed sack so the weight did not rip my arm
away from my shoulder. As the darkness gave way to a hint of light,
the worrying questions came more intensely: *Will I die from the weight of
the man crushing my ribs, or will death come after I do like the cow, drag the
sack along the ground, until the slime and the baby detach and break free?*

Old Raymond watched me, sullen, and quiet, "Latch hold of something Lilly, and stay around here, stay, 'cause if it be yo time to go, you'd
be gone already. Tomorrow take the clothes Old Anna put by yo bed.
It's good stuff that belonged to the Bartlette girls; good clothes."

My stomach knotted at the thought of wearing the old clothes of the
girls who I once played dolls with.

He shuffled two steps away from the pot to where I stood and raised
his musty arm to rest his hand on my oily flat hair, and I was grateful
for the first touch since my mother. "Put yo hand atop yo head, gal, and
look down at yo feet. Long as you know yo self chile, you home." *Home.*
He walked away, leaving the short breath of that gentle word lingering
in the stench of chitlin steam. It hovered like a hummingbird pausing

in a tense stare, and then disappeared like my mother's spirit into the unshackled distance.

Every night, I was obsessed with a fear of being bred, of who would be my bull. I wore extra long blouses to hide any impression of my body, and I learned not to look at any of the slave men, not to even go near them for fear that they may notice me the way men notice women, and request to be the one. Except Old Raymond, I stayed close to him, consoled by a false sense of my protection.

July 1861

THE NEXT TIME OLD RAYMOND went to the kitchen door for the scraps and rations, he took me with him. He pointed his ashy finger between my eyes. "Now don't do nothin foolish, hear? Less I ain't gonna do this no more. You lives on this side of the big houses now, and sooner you know that, the sooner you gonna be alright." He winked to soften the sternness. "Maybe I can get some fresh bread for ya."

He left me to stand at the bottom of the steps, outside the door. The Bartlette girls peered down at me from the window over the kitchen roof, behind glass in their nightdresses. The porcelain dolls that we once played with were under their arms. I looked up, and looked back at the kitchen door, remembering what Old Raymond said. I listened to Old Raymond and Janie exchange the news, overheard from the parlor the night before.

"Lord help us all. They done took the Union at Bull Run, big victory for the devil. They done declared a leader of it all and callin him Stonewall." My heart lightened; *a victory.* I strained to hear.

Raymond said, "Don't make no difference. They still is gonna fall, and we all gonna be free. I done seen it," and Janie whispered, "I know the slave-ownin people is gonna see punishment from God." I tried to fix my mind to understand my own feelings; wanting the Yankees dead, and wanting Bartlette and Overseer punished by Old Raymond's God. I quieted my thoughts and stared at the screen for a better understanding of things.

The girls tapped on the glass above my head, and stuck their tongues out at me, and I remembered the light bug inside the jar from the days that our mothers shared awkward conversation over tea, and Bartlette girls and I hunted the bugs whose green light gave them away in the elusive dusk. I forced myself to stare at the kitchen door and swallow back the tears.

Old Raymond was proud to see me there when he walked out. "Got a bunch for makin the food this week, chile. Apple peels is as good as apple cider." He wiped my tears without asking me what was wrong. The girls were knocking on the window now.

"Come on, Lilly. Hoist that bag up on yo shoulder, and smile. I'm 'bout tired of seeing yo face frowned up. You cain't let misery take over yo good looks." I raised my cheeks in a pained smile and tried to pretend I was not a slave girl, my feet rough from wearing no shoes, or wearing shoes that didn't fit well, my hair never getting a proper washing or brushing. I imagined I was with Grey Fox, returning to the house after a long ride, the smell of wind in my hair, my body tired with happiness. I remembered one afternoon when we stopped to water the horses at the creek, and I asked Father if I could take off my riding clothes and go for a swim.

"No, your skin will burn," and when I explained that I had been in my room in the wash tub, with sun coming in the window without being burned, he shifted on the rock and pebble beach nervously, and said, "It isn't lady like Lilly," and he reached down to relace the one boot I had already undone. I rested my open hand on the hot black of his coat, where the heat had penetrated and left a slight dampness beneath the layers of fabric. I remembered how my insides shuddered at the possibility of his bare back beneath his clothes. In our house bare skin was never revealed to kin, but the slave girls Earleen and Emma had seen each of us completely naked, had sponged my mother, my father and me close to the heart, around the places were coarse hair was now beginning to sprout on my body, but clothes helped to hide the changes from everyone, including myself.

Old Raymond stopped for me to catch up. He touched my shoulder to bring me along, and I flinched away from his naked hand.

Overseer circled from the other side of the field, like a hawk zeroing in on the tiniest mouse in the field. By the time we reached the little root cellar, he was behind me, the horse's breath at my neck. "Don't even turn around," Old Raymond whispered as he put the food on shelves, in jars, inside the iron box away from the rodents.

"Raymond, now you know this gal is here for a higher calling than being a lackey like yourself. She has got to be gettin strong in the field so she can bare a baby well. Strong body, strong hair." Overseer Yates leaned forward on his horse and reached to touch my neck. Without turning around, Old Raymond grabbed my hand in a staged show of his sternness with me. "Now finish up the job, I started gal. Get everything put away, and get to the field like Overseer say."

He stepped out of the dugout cellar, and talked at the horse's hooves, "Yes sir Overseer, I'm teachin her about the food fixin, for when she is too far along with child for the fields, and makin sure she is workin the fields all the while. But, Sir." Raymond looked further down on the ground. "You sure Massa want to be bringin children into these hard times. It's a lot of feedin them before they fit for any work?"

Yates sat up on the horse, with a frown of disbelief. And yelled into the dugout, where I stood waiting for him to leave. "Be sendin somebody soon, 'cause I know you little Indian bitches get to your menses early."

When he rode away, Old Raymond went back into the cellar, where the smell of hanging herbs, earth, and my sweat filled the room. "Look at ya chile, just shakin. You cain't let that vulture see you that way. He gonna feel your fear, and come for you himself just to prove somethin."

He snatched the carrots from my shaking hand. All the while I looked at the floor, rather than look right at Old Raymond. "Well he the one you ain't supposed to look at. When I'm talkin to you, I sure would appreciate see'n yo face." I looked up, and we stared at each other for a moment before he said, "Well, go on. Lord, I cain't make no field hand out of a fragile little ole mouse."

I hoisted the sack back onto my shoulder, and walked quickly to the field, where I would be without Old Raymond, but I wouldn't have to endure the likes of any other slave trying to talk to me.

I worked side by side with the others for months, dropping seeds, pulling weeds, and standing quiet in hopes that the water cup would come around to me, but it rarely did, and I didn't call out like the others, "Bring that water over here!" I just hoed, and picked with the rag tied tight on my head hoping that Overseer would not come.

No matter how alert I stayed. I would never see him coming: suddenly blocking the blinding sun, or from between the corn stalks, sneaking in his bare feet. He walked by me without looking at me, while calling out some demand to another slave, "Get this bail up and fill it. This ain't no holiday," and his hand would know that my body was covered by several layers, but would find and squeeze my new breast. Or, if my hands were crossed over my chest, with precision he would grab between my legs where hair held the sweat of the day, and then he'd moan between his commands, a code, just for me, that said, *I am everywhere. When you are sleeping, fear me, when you are awake fear me.*

One afternoon Bartlette sent his girls and wife away to someplace safe from the anticipated Union backlash. He kissed them on the cheek, and they boarded their carriage in the long wide-bottom dresses. The heat kept a constant swarm of flies around the two shackled horses. The Negro man held the reins, all dressed in black with a top hat sweat trailing down his face. Bartlette's precious ones rode away with their bellies full, weighing down the back of the carriage.

The wheels, smooth, rode over the earth sprinkled with water to keep the dust down. When the carriage reached the place where the road trailed off behind the cotton fields, I ran down to where the road was visible behind the trees. Though I often fantasized sneaking into the house at night and cutting off their yellow hair, the occasional sight of them on the lawn playing croquet or in the window laughing at me, was all I had left of the little girl I once was. They were young women now in fine dresses and parasols to shield and protect them from the sun that had turned me almond brown, my black hair brown from the bleaching sun. "Rag picker!" The two refined voices shouted from the carriage in unison.

I stepped toward the edge of the cotton field, my breath tightened in my chest, my head felt disconnected from my body, but told me to run, away from Overseer, away to LeFlore. Old Anna often reminded me about patrollers, men who hunted children, tied them in ropes, and dragged them miles from their dying mother. I looked down at my own feet, stockingless in the shoes, and I whispered for them to move, but fear had nailed my feet to the ground. The sound of the carriage faded, and I held my aching breasts tight to apologize for the fondling they'd endure as soon as Overseer passed.

Old Raymond stepped slow around the cotton stalks, his limp favoring him to one side. "Come away from here, Lilly."

"I want to go home, Old Raymond," was all I could say through the hard knot in my throat that held back sobs.

"Ya know, some of the slaves here is related to the slaves there, and sometimes it don't make no difference whereabout you lived. If you could get to know some of the folks here, who is descended from there, that would kinda make you have kin."

"I don't have anybody, Old Raymond. I don't have anybody. I don't belong here. I don't talk like anybody, nobody talks to me. I don't look like anybody. Did you know I can read old man? My father bought me all the great children's tales. I can read anything. I can read better than the Bartlette girls."

"You angry chile. Just angry that's all. That ain't no good sign, 'cause it makes me suspect you'll have the bleedin soon, but maybe somethin'll come about."

He limped back through the cotton field. I followed, both of us getting seared by the early autumn sun "Hmm," Old Raymond said, "Be time to pick all this soon. Time to go way down to the smokehouse to smoke the meat soon too." He looked back at me. "If you get told to work the smokehouse, you get down that way without a worrying about Overseer and his old nasty ways."

For days I worked at the smokehouse with two slave women, Overseer, who watched perched in the saddle picking his teeth, and Tessa.

The girl Tessa understood survival in a way that took pain and suffering and made it into mischief and trickery. I wanted to hide in the shadow of her two puffy ropes of braids. Her face was round and soft with shyness until she opened her mouth to talk. Her voice was like the caw of a raven, and she spoke directly to the goodness or badness of a matter with a chuckle. Something about her way, made me believe that she could walk away from Bartlette's whenever she got a mind to, but I was bound there, a fool by comparison. She was a year younger than me, and I was glad that I had that over her, and I was glad, most of the time, to be near her.

The women were not allowed to carry the woodchips in buckets. Overseer told us we must carry them in the apron of our skirts. I wore one of Old Anna's skirts taken up in the waste, so there would be plenty of slack. That way, my bare legs wouldn't show like Tessa's did. Overseer commented when I came close. "What? You ain't showin no legs today. I don't think I seen them legs since that day I had to catch you like a wild boar. Maybe I'm gonna have to steal a glance when you ain't lookin."

Tessa paraded between me and Overseer with her skirt held high, her bulging knees, grey with ash. "Here some legs for ya." She giggled, and I wasn't sure if she was mocking me or saving me, but I was grateful.

October 1861

I WAS IN THE SUNDAY PROCESSION NOW, as opposed to watching it through trees on the veranda. With the others, I crossed the quarter yard and walked past the red and orange leaves that lay on the green lawn of the big house. The Sunday meeting was held in the old servant house that had been restored for Bartlette's slaves to attend Missionary's word. Though the shack wasn't far, just up the slight hill, it was enough to make me feel as if I went away from the plantation.

Old Raymond said, "Massa finally said yes to the Missionary from the North, not because he think this man is gonna make us want freedom, but because this man gonna preach some words that's gonna make us appreciate what we have as a blessin from God, and we'll never want to leave it." He giggled through his nose, in slight high pitched tones.

Tessa, and a few of the young slave men sat around the fire at night doubting, and telling fabricated stories about relatives on other plantations who had been turned into zombies by the voodoo words of sweating, white Missionaries, but I knew like many of the older slaves, that this was an opportunity to dress finer, to maybe even try my hand at singing. That was something I looked forward to as I remembered longing to understand the singing I heard every Sunday in the quarters at LeFlore.

I put on the handed down dress from the Bartlette girls. "Fine dress, fine," Old Raymond said smiling as I crossed the quarter yard, a half foot taller than when I'd come to Bartlette's, and a young lady now. I held my head up as I ascended the two stairs and filed into the small space with the others. Inside the meeting house I felt like Lilly LeFlore again.

I was awakened the next morning, by the smell of my own blood. My dress clung to the covers and my thighs held the thick odor of raw meat. The omen of life and death filled the morning darkness, damp air, stillness outside the door. I could hear Sybil's voice, *Trouble's comin little miss, and God ain't gonna spare you no more than he spare them who ain't done nothin but serve you.* I sat up and could hear my own rapid breath in opposition to Anna's long drawn out snores. Deep breaths brought the smell of smoked hickory through the damp air, brought the memory of Overseer's words, "Is you bleedin yet?" His hands between my unguarded legs. My belly cramped, and I realized it was early enough, and I could clean myself, make rags of the old worn sheet that covered the bottom part of my straw bed.

My hands shook, and my shoulders ached in stress as I tiptoed from the pump to the outhouse. I washed my night dress, washed between my legs over and over before wadding the rags, tying extra around my waist, all the while, not certain in the darkness if I'd left the color red to be revealed by the morning sun.

That morning, I worked the smokehouse, two layers of skirt, the handed down petticoat for wearing on Sundays. I was grateful for the cold morning, the extra clothes bringing me no more attention than Tessa, who wore two pair of torn wool stockings. She tried to make conversation with Overseer, who said he couldn't stand the tone of her voice. "Weather just changed like that. Did you read about any thang like it in the Almanac Overseer?"

"Hush gal!" He said, leaning against the tree, half asleep with drunkenness, his rifle across his lap. I worked in harmony with the smoke, walking inside the billow of grey. Walking kept the pain in my belly quiet. When ever possible, I remained invisible to Overseer, and when he slept, I quieted my mind with whispered conversation: a competition between Tessa's bolstered omniscience and my bolstered affluence. Each of us fantasizing that we were soon to rejoin our true fate.

She bragged about not having to stay if she didn't want to. "I know all kinds of folks around these parts—free Negroes, folks on other plantations, drivers even. If I got a good mind to get sick of this place, I could just move on, go marry some free Negro with some land, and be done with this place."

I told her what I could remember of my father's promise to leave me the fortune for my future. "He'll leave everything I need, in a place of bleeding rocks and tragedy, or..." I stammered. I could barely remember my father's words. "He'll leave it in a place of still water and trees like knees. "

His words blended with my mother's story of her father's last words to her. I froze there in the telling, trying to separate the memories.

Tessa interrupted. "Well, which is it; blood, or trees like knees? Cain't be a good story and it be both. Anyway, that sound like a bunch of voodoo, and I ain't studyin no voodoo." But she went on asking me, "What's gonna be in this fortune anyway, gold coins?"

I thought about it for a while. "Probably coins, fine china, and pelts and things like that."

"Pelts? What's that be?"

"Animal fur, the valuable kind," I said, squirming slightly to adjust the tattered rags saturated with blood beneath my skirt. Tessa blew the smoke away from her direction.

"Well, I think you need to come up with a better story tomorrow."

I did not sleep that night, but quietly cranked the pump to wash the rags. I made a small rack with two thick branches and several long twigs for drying them, a trick that I hoped would keep me safe from breeding. My mind chased itself around in circles, all that fantasizing with Tessa bringing down the pain of being brought to Bartlette's, punishment for a crime my father didn't commit.

The next morning, Old Raymond passed me in the yard on my way to the smokehouse. "Stay strong, Lilly," he said and we both turned to follow each others eyes: mine bloodshot with tears, his bright with some mysterious happiness.

I used the smoke from the smokehouse to hide the redness in my eyes. I kept them open, and passed the unpatched hole where smoke escaped. The pain in my gut was so sharp, that I could only endure it in silence. Tessa didn't let me stay quiet. She whispered, "What story you got for me today?"

"I don't," I answered her without looking up.

"You got to tell me something to while away the sound of Overseer snoring, then scratching at his pants and fiddling with that rifle every time he hear something."

A big knot in my throat made it hard to swallow away the pain that welled up in my gut and made my legs quiver with fatigue. The cramping in my womb signified that time was rolling on and soon I'd be more Lilly slave, than Lilly, Grey Fox's little girl. The tears came, but I kept my lips together to hold my sound. Tessa, leaned into the cloud of smoke with big questioning eyes, and I confided in her the true reason why I had been captured.

"Bartlette was very angry with my father for selling him a sick slave, but I think he just wanted to drive my father off his land. My grandfather will make them pay for this someday, for making me accountable for some old slave woman's death." The tears were bitter in the corner of my mouth.

Tessa turned away from me in disgust, "I don't think my ears is fit to hear anymore about why you don't think you belong here." She raised her voice out of a whisper, making a sad face to mock me, "Who is gonna suffer for Miss Lilly's anguish? Who is gonna save Miss Lilly from the slavery?" She chuckled, picked up her skirt, and went back to the grunge of our work.

The billows of smoke from the opening in the smokehouse followed Tessa, and in their wake a boy's eyes appeared first, white in the sockets of his dark skin. My heart doubled in beats, and blood gushed into the bulge of rags between my legs. I looked at Overseer, waiting for him to grab his gun, and shoot the boy, but his beard and mustache moved apart as he mouthed the word "Mornin." I looked away in confusion.

The Negro boy said to Overseer, "Pine chips? Won't that smoke strange?" He talked like a white man's child, he talked like me.

Overseer said, "Never you mind, little Satan. Ask too many questions, and you'll be over in here slavin too." The boy giggled, and hung on to the tree limb, his fine cowhide vest hung free at his side. I watched on suspicious, studying him, but trying not to pause too long. Then he caught sight of me as if he was seeing someone he had lost and was glad to find.

"She is quite the prize," he said, talking to Overseer but grinning at me. Both of them chuckled. Then Overseer stopped abruptly to put an end to any assumed camaraderie with the boy, who stepped a little closer. "What's your name, gal?" His shirt was clean beneath his vest, like the missionary man's shirt on Sunday morning, and I could smell the talc on his skin, the way that my father smelled, fresh when he came to the dinner table.

He was tall as a man, though he was just a boy, and I wanted to fall into him, and fly away on the levity in his voice, on the fresh smell of his skin, on his freedom.

No one moved, the two slave women, me, Overseer or Tessa, who broke the silence. "Willie, she don't talk much and she a mean heathen too." Tessa giggled, showing her pink gums.

Overseer said, "Shut up, gal, before I burn yo tongue out and you don't talk no more, God willing." Tessa looked away and made a face.

Overseer responded like a raccoon awakened in the daylight. "Get on out'a here Willie Killem. Ain't nothin here for you, so don't be lookin." Smoke rose on the wind, and when it cleared, Willie Killem was gone.

"Shovel that on in there Lilly," Overseer said, settling back into his slumber, but I was entranced by the clean voice of freedom, *Willie Killem*. I left the safety of the smoke and stepped closer to the twigs behind the smokehouse, no longer aware of Overseer and his rifle. The color red was cool as it trailed down my ankle, where there was no camouflage of red leaves fallen from the trees—red, made its way through my layers of protection. My heart pumped fast enough to pound in my ears as I looked into the untouchable wonderland of trees and leaves to where the young man had disappeared. I stared until I heard the sound of shovel and pine chips again and turned to see Overseer's eyes trailing down the white petticoat, to the space where my skirt did not conceal the truth. The blood seeming to whisper, "Here she is."

In the grey of that morning, the layer of clouds did not move, but lay flat on the sky above us. There was no variation in the women's eyes when Overseer lunged and grabbed me by the neck with one hand.

Tessa, yelled, "Oh Lord!" and ran to get Old Raymond.

Overseer gripped neck bones, trachea, my cool stands of hair, warm skin that covered my jugular. The only sounds were the ones inside my body, while I scratched and beat on his hairy arm, the vibration traveling up to my ears. I could not breathe, or straighten my legs to stand while he dragged me like hunted game behind the smoke house.

His teeth were clinched in anger. "Keeping damn secrets from me? Huh? Are you?"

His one hand held me up on my tiptoes, the other hand held the rifle, cradled in the length of his arm. I felt as though my skull cap opened up and let the coolness of the morning in. I could not think well enough to tell myself not to look at him, to grab the rifle. I struggled to breathe and could not move my stare from the blue of his eyes, like the same blue of the dress I wore the day I was captured.

I heard small grunting sounds, that did not sound like my voice, come from inside my throat, as hands that did not feel attached to me slapped and scratched at his sleeved arm. He pulled down my petticoat. The bloody rags fell away, releasing the rancid smell of life and death into the air. My legs were numb when he threw me on the damp leaves. I heard the sound of Overseer's belt buckle, then the sound of Old Raymond's limp gait, furious on a sinking bed of fallen leaves.

From beneath the veil of my breath going still, and the sound of my arms flailing to grab Overseer's hairy arms, I saw Old Raymond grab the shovel from one of the slave women, who held it poised, but could not strike. I saw Old Raymond's face all around me, his eyes, fiery with the anger I imagined in the eyes of Missionary's God.

I smelled the dampness of the earth, not orange but dark brown with decomposed hickory where his old heart beat furious inside his big drum chest. My eyes cut away to the split-log mortar walls of the smokehouse, and I did not hear what Tessa later said sounded like a stick against an empty cow bell. The shovel came down with all of Old Raymond's strength, and struck Overseer Yates, across the back.

Overseer got off me to bend backwards and grab his shoulder blades. In the same move, he fell on one knee, pivoted around and with the surprising precision of a dying man firing at circling buzzards, he fired one shot with the already cocked rifle, and Old Raymond crumpled, and fell like a great oak.

HE WAS BURIED THAT AFTERNOON, or at least that's what the slaves were told. Janie from the kitchen said, Master Bartlette did not want the few slaves he had, getting mournful, then angry, then wanting to rise up against him. The slave men left the fields and came to the back door pleading, "Massa please let us bury him." They were told by the voice that rarely addressed slaves, "No, now get on back to the fields, and don't ever come up here again unless you are called."

I sat in the cabin, the only light was from the small window. I stared at the orange, yellow and red leaves, until my emotions burrowed so deep in my center, that my eyes could not see the color of the leaves, the cardinal, the color that had brought death to Old Raymond. I bit my nails until the colorless liquid dripped from the chewed places. I replayed the events over and over, blaming myself for being weak like Old Raymond had said, for bringing bad on everybody else with my ways. *It was a bad thing,* I decided, *for any slave to come near me.*

Slave men from the Gamble plantation came in on a wagon, their quiet bodies bouncing over rocks, shovels in their hands. They loaded the thick body onto the back of the wagon, the blood having drained, and the organs gone rigid. They strained the way the men did the day the Bartlett girls got the new piano. From the window, I watched them drag his body over the dirt. I imagined the loose wood splintering, where they strained to push him onto the wagon. The reflection of my own eyes in the glass was empty, but I screamed inside myself as the wagon and the slave men rode away, my protector's head of soft wool, limp and bobbing outside the wagon.

Overseer could not come down to the quarters with the cracked shoulder blades, but stayed in the darkness of his cabin, wincing at night as he held his body upright to tap Bartlette's dwindling supply of brandy, dwindling in this time because supplies were cut off as roads were closed by Union troops. The pending doom of defeat closed in on any plantation that was not self sustained.

John Bartlette took to his journals more, and with low supervision, the slave girl Martha who had been taught to read on her plantation in

Georgia, but had been taught to use it as a secret weapon, read the entries, and reported to the quarters so the slaves would know the news straight from Bartlette's head, know his fears, his weakness, and plan an escape.

The night after Old Raymond's murder, Bartlette sent word, via Janie that Old Anna wouldn't be needed in the house anymore. Young Martha would take her place. Anna was told that she would go back to the shucking of corn, spinning of wool, churning of butter, and that it could all be done from the barn, not the cabin, because that's where defiant old slaves who pampered unruly Indian children would sleep. When she packed her things, she didn't seem angry with me like so many of the others, who said *I* killed Old Raymond, but she didn't have any parting words as she kept her face stern and hurried down to the barn with her things wrapped in a sheet.

Tessa was moved into the cabin with me, for the two of us to live up to our purchase. The thick odor of Old Raymond's stew pot wafted over to the circle, stirred, by various hands, and I sat inside the circle, my nose burning while I refused to cry at their angry stares. I stayed at the fire, numb, pretending Old Raymond would come and fill my bowl, like Sybil did when I was a child.

"You alright?" Tessa asked, looking more bewildered than concerned. I whispered in one tone without looking toward the others. "I'm scared Tessa. Overseer sitting in his cabin practicing his rifle shooting by shooting out toward the quarters. You not scared about getting stuck with me? Everybody thinks I'm cursed. You not scared about who it is supposed to be laying with us? You not scared?" I did not show expression, but my temples throbbed beneath the rag tied on my head.

Tessa sat with her fists on both hips. "I don't reckon I ever heard you talk that fast Lilly. Them folks just actin like they mad, but every one of them would have felt good to end their journey like Old Raymond, by doin somethin about that old buzzard who's sittin in his cabin with a back infection.

"Only thing you need to be worried about is that he gonna be meaner than ever on you now."

The blood gushed again, along with my escaping tears.

Tessa turned to me and frowned in discontent over my crying. "Folks probably mad 'cause you always feelin sorry for your self. Like you some white gal, but you ain't. You ain't strong worth nothin. Old Raymond dead for trying to save your Lilly white ass. Least you could do is quit actin all the time like you ain't got no back bone." Tessa walked away, thudding her bare feet on the cool October earth, having found her way of blaming me too.

Someone started out the tune, in low gutteral sounds, and the other slaves joined in song for Old Raymond, the way the slaves at LeFlore sang for Josephine.

When I'm tired
and weary
He's comin to take me home
When I'm tired
and weary
Comin to take me home
Oh Lord, oh Lord
Comin to take me home
Hallelujia
Hallelujia
Amen

The song repeated over and over until the bodies around the fire, were still, but their spirits stirred in the air like the lightening before a storm. I was moved, outside of self-consciousness, and stood up with those who sang, and for the first time let my voice come soft into the air, "Oh Lord, forgive me." The other voices dropped away, leaving the paper thin airiness of my cry on the night air, alone, above the sound of autumn's last crickets. Alone, the voice of the one who brought death to Old Raymond, the very fate that he warned me of: bringing bad down of everybody in my midst.

When the tears subsided, I did not run, but went quietly to me and Tessa's cabin and shut the door. All night I repeated something Old Raymond had told me, "Know yo self, chile, and don't act weak against other people's thoughts of you." I slept in a knot of legs and arms.

Late in the night, cold hands eased beneath the blanket, bringing with them the smell of liniment and whisky. The two soft, warm pillows of my new breasts froze in the closed fists that squeezed till pain shot out to my arms and legs. I lay still inside the nightmare, images of odd contraptions of torture compressing my limbs, my tongue, my nipples.

And then, my own voice coming in short breathy screeches inside the cabin. In the darkness I felt my fists colliding with thick, hairy arms. I heard my voice in the space of the open darkness, call out, "Tessa, Tessa," but there was no answer, then the flicker of yellow light, and a lantern floated out the cabin door, a brown hand above the dome.

"Tessa," I called after her.

I felt something warm and limp, like a hairless rat on my thigh, then felt it caught in the tangle of sheets. I slipped into a dream, and saw the bull standing in the field, and he caught sight of me, his penis hanging from his body, his stare rabid and evil. I saw the shovel handle gripped by Old Raymond's hand come across Overseer's back, and I struck him there. In the stale air of our cabin, I screamed out, "Anna, Raymond," and Overseer's hand muted my scream, the way Old Raymond quieted me that first day, just before he gave me a meal and assured me with his eyes that he would take care of me, the same promise broken by my father who did not return. I did not cry out into Overseer's filthy hand, but sucked air in through my nose to accommodate the long sobs.

I did not fight now, and Overseer pushed himself inside of me. A grunt escaped with the heat of whisky on unbrushed teeth, and his knuckles hammered against my face, my neck, my back as I tried to curl into myself and disappear. Then there was the floating, unconsciousness, my body on the creek of cold water, the boulders beneath me bowed in sorrow for my childhood self passing, for the paranoia that would lodge itself in my bones and weight me down to the bottom where muddy sediment would swallow me. Before he was done, the icy waters of the creek entered my body between my legs and made me one with all that was dead.

I woke to the stillness of breath. The cabin door swung open, a flash of light from Tessa's lantern. She stood quiet and unscathed, just beyond the threshold, and I saw Overseer's silhouette: his body bent, with hands crippled by the cracked shoulder blades, his stench creating a luminescence of yellow around his body as he exited.

The lantern entered. "Jesus Christ Lilly, why didn't you just let him have his way and be done with it." Tessa sat down on her bed, held the light out over my long body. I contracted into a centipede's coil, and Tessa blew out the light, and she fell into an exhausted sleep.

In the window, the sky shifted to a dawn light. I opened my eyes and felt like that's all I was, just bone and eyes lying there in the cabin. My stomach turned at the odor of Overseer's liniment, the puss in the wound on his back, and the semen that had spilled out lazily from his penis. I looked over at Old Anna's bed, and sitting on the edge there like a crow, staring was Tessa. Her face was dark, like the deep purple of pokeberries. Her pink lips were speckled with the dark color of her face. There was nothing readable in her stare, no hint of sympathy, no sense of ridicule, just a still face that felt familiar and cold to me. The rag tied on her head concealed the bulk of braids.

"What are you looking at?"

I was surprised at the sound of my own voice, like sugar boiled down to liquor it was coarse and angry.

"Well, least I know gettin beat that hard don't keep you from still bein a mean ole heathen." Tessa got up to prepare for the fields. "Smoke house or shukin corn, which one you fit for today Lilly?"

I sat up shaking my head. "Tessa, I can't go out to work this morning. I need to hide," I explained, looking for things to take with me, "Maybe to the barn where Anna can help me know where to go. Maybe somewhere around here that makes a good hiding place from Overseer until I can run away from here." I thought about the wolf hiding under the barn at LeFlore to birth her pups, and the place on the side of my head throbbed with the thought of Overseer inside of me, of birthing some evil baby that bore his stench.

I ran out the door, grabbing the bucket on the way to the pump. The dawn light glowed on my torn night dress, revealed the fresh ripe red of the bruise on the side of my face, my neck, my outer thighs. I fetched the water, and splashed back to the cabin looking up to the house, down near the fire pit, to the fields.

Tessa stood in the doorway, and held her hands out for the bucket, and she helped me bathe, stern like Old Anna, Tessa rubbed hard against my tears. "Lilly, what Overseer done to you ain't nothin more than what he done to all the women, includin me last spring. He gonna been forgot about it by next week. He just works himself up on you for weeks, then tears into the cabin like a bandit, and then forgets about you, and finds another one to go after. Folks say he been run off the Gamble place twice, and Massa and Gamble argue a heap about that old drunk try'n to get at them gals over there."

It was quiet for a while, Tessa wrung the rag and wiped the sore place between my leg. The moment was familiar and comforting, like Emma or Earleen bathing me before bedtime, but the pain was like knives cutting into me, and I stomped one foot to make Tessa stop, to keep from beating her, to keep the fit of anger inside my body.

"Don't go turnin on me Miss Lilly. I'm just try'n to help. Don't nobody else around here give two shakes about you no how after Raymond dead. Yep, nobody care, except Massa, who gonna think you worth a lot more for having babies in these troubled times. Don't go try'n to run. That'll bring a mighty price on yo head. Yes, ma'am, Injun niggers bound to be strong field hands. Overseer say ya'll babies worth a plenty." She laughed, wiping her nose on her head rag before putting it on.

I sat down. Nausea swam in the center of my being. "Tessa, shut up. Overseer didn't tell you anything. You walk around here like you know everything about everything, like you know all that goes on around the plantation and off the plantation. If you're so smart, how come you ran out of here last night?"

She laughed again, loud enough to wake the other slaves. She put her hands on her hips. "Hell, you such a proud, well-to-do Injun, how come you ain't free?"

"Nigger. Bitch!" Before the words lit on the air, they came across my tongue like a jagged blade cutting me away from childhood, permanently, cutting me away from the possibility of being friend to any of the women on the plantation, who saw me as privileged, and a danger to all of them.

"Well, Lilly, you a woman now, got big nasty words like Overseer, but look like you the bitch now. I guess you best finish cleaning yo own self up before the light comes in good and all the men be beggin to be your bull. Here." She tossed me a head rag. "It's gonna be a long hot day in November, maybe today you can pay attention to your work rather than lookin off in the distance for that old Willie Killem. That fool Raymond thought he was powerful enough to have Willie steal you away before Overseer could test your waters." She headed out the door, her words still cackling in the yard where the light floated between the slats of our walls. "You sho is ignorant about so many commonsense things, Miss Lilly LeFlore."

I could not leave the cabin that morning. Each time I tried, my breaths came in such succession, that my lungs threatened to collapse. Old Anna came out of the barn, slowly in the warmth of the day, and approached where I stood with the cabin door propped open. She smelled like the cow manure and hay. "Come on," was all she said, and took me by the hand to the barn where the older women shucked the piles of harvested corn. The black woman, whose skin was like charcoal, looked down from where she sat on three bails of hay, "Soon you'll be good for somethin, 'cause half the time you don't even move fast enough to keep yo self warm."

"Go to hell old woman," I yelled out, though I kept my head hanging, hair over my bruised face, I felt powerful in my new anger, my teeth clinched behind red lips. I pulled the husk away and tossed it sideways onto the pile, and no one said anything back, and that day, being ostracized from the others didn't feel so bad, because it was my decision.

The barn for shucking, the fall garden for Bartlette's kitchen, but never the smokehouse, never the far end of the fields. It was too far from the cabin. I managed to slip back inside the cabin two or three times a day, just for the comfort of the walls. I moved the chair against the door, my heart beating in my hands. I waited until my breathing steadied, and I'd slip back out, undetected. My paranoia set in like the infected wound on Overseer's back, which never seemed to completely heal.

One day I worked the fall garden with Tessa, and something white moved out near the trees. My heart leapt into my throat. I dropped the scalding wash water, when I saw the pattern of his face camouflaged in the shadows and leaves. Willie Killem. The same sensation to run to him before it was too late tingled in my legs, but the longing turned to anger as I remembered Old Raymond with blood pouring from his gut in that same place where I first saw Willie, out near the smoke house. *If Old Raymond told him to come for me, why didn't he before now?*

"Hey Gal, slip out with me tonight," he whispered in the distance, and I responded by stabbing the soil with the hoe. Tessa reared back, cupped her hands over her eyes, but all she saw was the white tail of a deer bobbing off into the woods. "Was somebody out there?" she questioned, but I did not look up from my work.

That night, Tessa stuck her head out past the candlelight. "You ain't liking him, is you? I know you don't think you runnin off with the likes of Willie Killem." I lay on my bed pretending I didn't hear a word Tessa said. "Good, 'cause free blacks and Injuns don't need to mix."

"Free," left her mouth and hovered around the warmth of the lantern flame, ringing out in the darkness.

September 15, 1863

COOL AIR moved in on an early fall day that had promised searing temperatures. That day, we picked baskets of greens, and dug up carrots for Tessa to take up to the house. With Overseer laid up sick in his cabin again, Tessa took long breaks to sit down in the dirt and chewed on the sweet tough skin she stole from the smokehouse. Tessa was never caught, always with something special just for herself to gnaw on. She looked out toward the woods for a glimpse of Willie the way she had for two years, and worked hard to get me to confess to having a plan.

"You know, everybody but you is gettin themselves a plan about runnin on away from here. Janie say a crowd of newly freed Negroes and Yankee soldiers gathered at the courthouse at Vicksburg. The Union occupation is a victory to all Negroes. She say they done raised Stars and Stripes over the town's center right in the heart of Mississippi." She laughed the way the adults did between their words about good news. "Janie say if we lucky, the Union troops is coming out here to Oktibbeha Country next. What you think of that Injun girl?" I didn't answer her, but snatched a whole turnip plant from the ground. "Girl what's the matter with you? Them greens ain't gonna grow back without no root or nothin in the ground. I know you actin all high and mighty, and mean to everybody, 'cause you got some kind of sure fire plan." I continued to pretend like I couldn't hear her.

"Well if you thinkin 'bout that old Willie, you best know what I heard. The only reason why Willie's father be a free man and he be a free boy is 'cause his father got a dirty job doing lookout on the back fields of Massa's land and Massa's brother's land." She stuck her neck out and whispered. I raised up and took off my head rag, twisted my hair again, and put the dirty rag back on my head. I kept cutting through the thick mustard green stems with my thumbnail, the only nail I hadn't chewed down to a nub. I filled the basket, and glared at Tessa, imagining digging the nail into her round arm.

Tessa smacked her lips at my show of anger. "Willie's father be the friendly face that tricks slaves into comin with him when they run off. They think they done left and ain't goin back no matter what. Then Satan returns them to their massa, who sells them right away." Tessa leaned over to make her face level where I bent over. "You too scared to leave the quarter yard though, ain't you Lilly? It's like there's a big rope tied around your ankle or somethin. Nah, I don't think nobody gots to worry about you runnin, but just so you know.

"Ain't none of us that's living here now ever seen Willie's father. I try to imagine what he looks like by seeing Willie's face turning old, and his head getting big with gray hair, but I don't conjure up nothing in my head. We call Willie's father Satan 'cause you cain't see him, but the last thing you want is to see him, 'cause by the time you see him you know you dead and in hell."

I shifted restlessly on the dirt, trying to get warm, and her thick body odor wafted up into the cool air.

"When somebody starts to talk about running away, Old Anna changes their mind by saying," Tessa lowered her voice, "'Do you wanna see Satan or do you want to wait for yo freedom?' Folks say if ever you get a notion to run away from here, don't look for no tall strong man that looks like the nigger devil. But there's a woman folks who run-aways do look for, a woman with hair red like a fox, little and quick, who lives among the alligators and snakes. Anybody brave enough to go to where she lives has got a refuge from they massa. Whatever you do, don't go tryin to run off with Willie."

She talked so fast and with more and more ridiculous detail, finally I couldn't stand the pressure I was exerting on my teeth where I held my tongue still in my mouth. "Shut up Tessa! Shut up! Shut up!" A loud whistle startled me just before the itching in my chest sent my angry shout into angry screams. It was like Old Raymond's whistle, but it came from where Old Driver rode on Overseer's old horse, temporary foreman he called himself, but he was the only Negro Bartlette trusted in these times of potential uprising. The cold air moved in between us, and when he passed, I ran to the safety of the cabin where I ranted out loud for everything that Tessa said, and for all the pain that I felt with no sympathetic ear to listen. "Get back to work Tessa, and get up from that ground now," I heard Driver say, and I heard Tessa yell out, "Get back to driving a wagon you old goat."

There was no more order. I dried my eyes with the head rag, and comforted myself with knowing that the chaos meant there was no plan to make more Bartlette slaves, but also nobody watching to make sure slave men didn't just come and take what they wanted. If I could stay clear of the men, and stay clear of Overseer who was sick in his cabin with one ailment or another, then I would be all right.

For the rest of the day, my mind obsessed on a plan, so I wouldn't be left behind if there came a time to escape, but my thoughts settled over and over on images from Tessa's story; half-human creatures, giant men and tiny red haired Negro women, gods of the free spaces around the plantation.

I fell asleep that night, and against my wishes, dreamed myself the wife of a free black man. I stood on the front porch of my house, rain coming down but a roof to keep me dry. I looked out on the crops, at the good work my slaves had done. Like my mother, I was intrigued for hours until fanning the flies was too much work. My husband, Willie Kellem, in his crisp, clean white shirts, his teeth and eyes bright, his words clear like he had never been beaten.

The next week, Massa Bartlette's twin nephews came home from the war to warn the men that Grierson's raiders were moving in.

Janie, who was always cooking and canning in the kitchen of Massa's house heard the men talking in the parlor. What she heard, she told the boys who rode back and forth to the house, bringing food from the fields.

Sometimes an entire page of John Bartlette's journal would be memorized, and made its way from the house slave girl, Martha, who was taking Old Anna's place, the girl who shuffled along, acting dumb in order to keep things clean and keep Massa warm at night, but she could read words as well as I could. They sat around at the evening meal wishing for winter; melancholy skies, cold, chilled breezes, working the weaving and spinning and the smokehouse. They listened to one another recite Bartlette's journal, as if they were there while he wrote things down.

The tall stout man named Tom who wanted to preach like Missionary recited best: *"My wife stay with her brother. She stays away. It's better for the war. Better for me. I don't know her anyway. I haven't been a husband to her. I can't think that way. Even in the dark I can see her eyes and then I cannot bring myself to pleasure. Her eyes look hungry and make me feel empty and ashamed, and lost, and my body yields."*

They all got a good laugh. *"And my body yields?"* one of the men said, laughing hard and slapping his knee at white people's way of talking. Then, Janie, stood tall and thin, the cook gracing us with her presence on a Saturday night. She lowered her voice like a white man and recited:

"I can't be around those girls and their noise, colds, needs, wanting to be hugged. It's best that they are gone, for things are dangerous now, and slowly growing scarce. I told the men to sell both bulls and six of the milking cows. The cotton is still plentiful though, and the hogs will make a good yield of pork."

Most of us never really got more than a glimpse of Bartlette; hat and black suit in the winter, white suit in the summer, hopping in the buggy, or going on down the road in the back of the carriage.

Old Anna recited: *"My nephews, my nephews. May God watch over them as they fight in the battle."*

Tessa stood up, with something to say, looked over at me and recited an entry.

"I'm going to get what Grey Fox owes me. Indian heathen think he's on par with the rest of us. Think I'm going to settle for being hoodwinked? It's time somebody showed him that his father was the only thing of his fate that kept him in good standing, but with him dead, and nothing bequeathed to the cause, it's time I was the one who stood up to the potential enemy. Not another day will I sit, disgusted by his greasy skin and hair, sip brandy from glasses where heathens and niggers have placed their lips. I want, in exchange for his poor trade, his child. I will not 'yield' to this.

They all broke into laughter and clapping, except Janie, whose voice came gently. "Everybody, I think we done heard enough. Let's put out the fire."

I sat on the rock outside the fire circle, only my eyes moved. Tessa had finally done the job, broken through my anger, and found the place to produce hurt again. The others were twisted in laughter. I did not want to give them the satisfaction of my tears. *Besides,* I defended, *It was not true; my father and I had both been the victim of Bartlette's treachery.*

I glared at Tessa across the fire, and she glared back. The laughing died down, and without so much as another word about it, they started another story. I listened on, heat in my face greater than the fire's warmth. *Never,* I thought *will I confide in Tessa again, no amount of loneliness or boredom will take me to a place of aligning myself with a heartless thief.*

I returned to the safety of the cabin, where I sat on the edge of my bed, plotting my revenge on Tessa. Outside, a young man perked up and talked about those high and mighty twin nephews of Massa Bartlette, how they left the battlefield, because in plentiful times their father provided good for the Confederacy, and they felt like they had the privilege to travel on home to bring word to their father and his brother of the coming Yanks. Old Anna stood up in revelation.

"Listen now, that got a miscalculation in it. I worked beside Massa for a long time, and I know them twins stops and gets drunk, and get waylaid at brothels and cockfights every time they break free from battle, and so when they gets to the plantation, Massa gonna be relyin on a truth that be several days old."

Everyone understood the implication of her words, and they all got up from the fire when the carriages came down the road; men coming from all around that night to get the report on how many days they had to prepare their plantations before the Union troops were coming. I sat inside the cabin, and heard the chatter go silent, nothing but wagon wheels and the crackling of logs turning to coal. "Get ready!" I heard a voice whisper at the door, and I ran to the window to see everybody else who shuffled in the dark, gathering close under the night sky to get their plans set. I heard Tessa and some of the others say they were going to be ready to run in any direction except north, where Satan would be watching.

In a waking dream, I saw my long-haired father, his faithful dark suit dusty and limp around his body; his face relaxed while the world around him collapsed, bricks flying away, smoke, clouds of dust, voices, and my father's hair free on the mist of rubble dust, clouds, his hair on the wind, his body lean and forward in his escape; and I could hear the tenor of his voice sing. I had never heard him sing, but in the vision he wailed a song of few words. *Stay, stay, stay, I am coming to take you home.* A song sweet and painful, deep sweet like the scent of magnolia, deep pain like the high-pitched, sharp pain of frostbite, so pure in the way it creeps into the fingers and up the arm, that surrender is the only thought. In the vision, I heard his song, and felt warm.

Stay, stay, stay, I am coming to take you home. And I floated there just above my straw bed, held up by my soul's belief in his words.

From the window I looked to see the fire die out while folks talked in little groups. Nobody looked to see if Overseer was coming, nobody motioned for me. They were all lost in the ritual of leaving. In the distance visitors' buggies sat in the glow of lanterns full ablaze outside Massa's house, white men busy with their plans while in the quarters voices whispered, "Everybody get yo things."

The sound of a rifle echoed, and screams came in intervals, the sound of horses thundering, up near the house where the landowners sat in ambush. The smell of gunpowder filled the air and burned the back of my throat, and I remembered again the vision of the horses' hooves on the morning I was captured, my mother lying cold, staring soulless, like the carcass of a deer.

I remembered that in the last days at LeFlore my mother was on edge. Anything distracted her, the wind blowing through high bushy pines. "Winter's coming," she'd say. "Death to many things."

The leaves danced in what I thought was the wrong direction. She raised her head from her tea. "Rains coming." She'd be telling me a story. "Dogs came running from the woods with death on the sweat of their fur...," and right in the suspense, she'd look up at me. "Did you ride far again today? Were you at the creek with your horse?"

"No, Mother."

"Then do not go. Betrayal is on the wind. Betrayal is on the wind," she said again the night before my capture, and that night, I rolled over in my bed separating myself from her madness.

The moon was just a sliver. The sounds were too many to focus on just one, and the walls of the cabin vibrated from the chaos.

Off in the distance I heard hounds baying, heard gunshots. A bugle blew a message to the men of the Union troop. Old Anna's voice was among them all. "Now is the time. It be time now to be free. Run now, run." I peeped out the window to see Tessa running with her eyes wide open, her dress hem in one hand. I flung the door open, and we embraced. I let myself fall into Tessa's soft pillowy body. In that moment we were both little girls, frightened by what would befall us. Another bout of rifle fire, and Tessa fell to her knees in prayer.

"Get up Tessa, get up. We have to run." I pleaded, knowing I would never be able to leave unless I had searched every fleeing face to make sure my father's was not among them.

Pain gripped in my chest, and in the deep way back of my belly as I watched Tessa, the ornery person I knew, reduced. *Everyone's leaving. What should I do? What should I do?* Things outside the window moved too fast for me to make out any one object, black night, orange hot fire light, the soft glow of lanterns, and dust, so much dust. "Death to many things," I heard my mother's spirit whisper, and I strained to listen above the sounds for some guidance from my father.

My arms shook as I gathered my few belongings, including the two pig skin shakers Old Raymond had made for me. I bundled everything in the sheet, and sat down on the bed, perspiration soaking my body, as I recalled my last night at LeFlore, and the suspicious layers of Sybil's clothes that hid the stolen items.

Other slaves vanished in flight beyond the firelight. Some of Massa's friends came past the cabins yelling, "We need the strong ones out here to fight. Come on, ya'll." But people were running every which way, ignoring the command. A woman screamed, someone was crying. I felt the sweat roll down my face as the cabin became an island in the chaos. Tessa lay down on the floor, spread out with her face looking up, saying some of the prayers Missionary had taught us.

"Tessa," an unknown Negro man called, "Tessa," and she sprang up and ran out the door, her thick hair still in braids for the night, her skirt worn at the bottom, her bare feet fleeing into the flashes of light and sounds, and she was gone without another word to me.

I sat alone in the cabin, and hugged my bundle, held it tight to my chest, which rose and fell in tremors. "Run, run," I heard, but held myself there against the shaking to be free. Behind my closed eyes I could see broken images of my mother running across the open field. I heard... "Lilly." Somebody called outside the door of the cabin.

There were so many sounds, too many sounds, and I could not make out the voice saying my name. The door of the cabin flew open, and it was the boy with black skin and a white shirt, now a man, Willie, son of Satan. He grabbed me. The smell of his body, soap and talc, and the musk of his underarms engulfed me, as I struggled to get free. The chaos sent my mind into a jumble of hateful images: the fantasy of my fists beating on Overseer's back, pounding his bones like pestle pounding corn to meal. I wrestled with Willie, whose dark persona turned into Overseer. In the darkness, I searched for something sharp, but my feet left the ground, as Willie flung me over his shoulder, an act that seemed impossible for his small stature.

"Come on, Lilly, we gots to run, come on." My eyes were not able to separate images. I yelled out, "Willie no!"

Sweat trailed down the side of Willie's head, where he fell to the earth under my weight. Out of breath, his voice cracking in fear, he explained, "We got to run, gal. Ain't nothin but Union men comin to do some mighty thievin and damage. You go back in there and you sure to get raped and killed."

I stayed there on my knees, in a suspended state: my mind told me to run with Willie, but my heart pounded, the sounds of horses, whinnying, guns firing, the darkness refusing to give me enough light to even fully make out the boy, who looked so different two years later. What could I trust? At the sound of a shot fired so near, Willie covered his ears and dropped to the ground. My body went rigid, and atrophied along with my thoughts, which shut off at the sight of Willie's fine shoes, kicking up small clumps of mud into the deceptive night light in his escape.

Part Three

September 21, 1863

I WALKED AND RAN ALL NIGHT, avoiding the direction of gun fire and the direction of coyote howls. The overcast morning brought unfamiliar trees, brush, and rough grass. I was the only creature in their midst after the night's destruction. I picked up my bundle and with the instincts of a wolf fallen from the pack, I walked toward what I hoped would be home. I saw other folks, some black, some white men in Confederate uniforms looking withered from their journey. I shied away, but none of the soldiers paid me any attention. A slave man with an old cotton basket atop his head ran over the flat dry space of land that stretched out before me, and I held tight to my belongings, the few tattered skirts, with the head rags, my other top, and one of Old Raymond's rattles, the other, I tucked into my pocket so I would still have it if the bundle was stolen. It rattled against my thigh, and the sound of it kept my mind still, able to focus without spinning into panic.

Clouds cleared, crickets and hard-shelled bugs hummed and rattled loud in the heat of late afternoon, and my nerves stirred again like disturbed fire ants. I could not continue to walk across the expanse of land where the sun spied me, a rabbit in an open field, birds of prey cawing overhead. There was too much space around me; the trees seemed too far away.

Some man's voice rang out behind me, "What plantation you from?" and I did not turn around, but took off running. I ran out beyond rows of corn, and did not navigate direction as I journeyed over landscapes of rocks, brush, past trees.

It was the sound of a church bell ringing that let me know I had traveled far from Bartlette's. The folks on foot grew from sparse to dense and I figured I must be nearing the ravaged county station. The road looked slightly familiar as one I'd traveled with my father. The smell of smoke was strong in the air, and dry in my throat.

"The county station!" some woman called out, like it was celebration time. "I'm headed to the county station to get my freedom papers, then off to see my sister in Vicksburg."

The Negro man walking with her said, "Woman, you cain't travel between counties yet, don't jump da gun."

Where had all the slaves come from? I wondered, *Where had the patrollers gone?*

The people on the road grew more dense, and I could not bare the constriction of the air. Someone nudged me on the way passed, and the touch caused me to turn inward, I hurried away from the town where I might be saved, but did not feel safe.

Other slaves were also displaced but intent in their travels. *Who was I going to? What was my plan?* In my panic to get away from the people, I imagined what they saw, young Indian woman, with hair dangling, and eyes attempting to steady themselves in the vaguely familiar surroundings.

I tried to follow the sun; *East of the creek? West of the other fields.* I was careful not to look in their eyes, but glanced at their bodies, the hands that held dress hems. I hoped to recognize a familiar gait like Janie's or Tessa's. Loneliness sunk in my middle along with the hunger and exhaustion, as the sun threatened to set. I mustered the courage to ask a passer by. "Which way to the LeFlore plantation?"

"Gal, ain't nobody studyin about gettin to a plantation. You best get you self off the road if you ain't with a group, and you a mulatto girl too." The two Negro women shook their heads and hurried on their way.

I searched for a good place to leave the road; not into a field of high weeds, snakes might lurk there, not into a ravine of cattails and high thorned brush, dead soldiers might lie there, not where hungry soldiers walked lost and starved for a woman's flesh.

The healed welts from the day Overseer whipped me itched beneath the cotton dress, as I focused my sight, stepped over a wooden fence and headed toward what looked like an abandoned home.

I crossed the dry crunchy lawn. My feet throbbed inside the too-small-shoes, the prospect of rest bringing with it an ache in my whole body. I called out gently, from the other side of the broken picket fence, but no one answered. Clouds moved into the sky and comforted me from the sun. A damp warm breeze circled from the front of the house and brought with it the smell of rotting animal, a stench so high in its rancid pitch, but my lungs had already filled with the odor that invaded my whole body. I stepped away, back to the road, and as I ran past the front fence, the sound of flies humming was deafening. The shiny chestnut hides of four horses, dead in the yard, the men who rode them, lying prostrate to the silver sky, with necks ballooned like swollen pig bladders. I ran, the sky and road above and below me, as I tripped wildly in flight.

Before dusk, I stopped running in a ravaged tobacco field. The dry weeds lay down and made a comfortable bed for my throbbing feet.

I noticed, growing way off, on the side of a run-down barn, a fruit tree, and as water shot into my parched mouth, I realized I was hungry, and imagined myself having the strength to walk to get some of the fruit, and like walking inside sleep, I did.

I sat under the tree, bumblebees hovering around the juice of a fall peach, half rotted as it ran out of the corners of my grateful mouth. The peaches, my skin, the evening sky all one color, my hair and the tree bark the only dark contrast. The peaches were coolest in the center, near the hard pit, and I almost broke my teeth to bite in deep.

Full and tired, I relaxed with the liquor scent of fermented peaches beneath me. I watched the sun set slow, and a fear of darkness came on, as I imagined the ghosts of the dead soldiers waking, and accosting my sleepy body. I told myself, *Don't cry, be brave,* like my father had said, and I rested beneath a fruit tree, heavy with peaches and laden with bumblebees and flies. I ate my fill, then surrendering loneliness and fear for a heavy sleep that held dreams of a distant morning.

In the dream, I was young Lilly LeFlore again, my body, new and clean beneath the nightdress, dawn in the sky at LeFlore. I sat awake in the rocking chair all night. I waited for my mother to return from a journey that sent her off into the night in her hooded cloak, waited for my father to return from some day long journey to right what ever wrong brought men to the house to question him, and each of them did not return until just before dawn. First I remembered my mother tiptoeing on the squeaky wooden floor, then a few moments later my father. The two of them snored in unison while I let my worries about where each of them had been, build into a fear of being left by my parents. I fantasized that they, like Alice in the stories from London, would someday disappear into another world, the way that they eventually did.

I woke, exhausted and worn, with the question of my father's life, of Jacques LeFlore's life. Soon, I was fully awakened by the sharp light that lifted the mist, and brought stomach cramps from sun heated peaches and the occasional, accidentally eaten fly. I heard Old Raymond's voice, *Get on to your chores. Eat what you got in front of you.* For a moment I relinquished fear for a feeling of pride, for feeding myself, for surviving.

The air was already swollen with the heat of the coming day. I swallowed back the foam that rose in my throat, while the memory of the men's engorged bodies, slunk into memories of Old Raymond's stiff corpse enduring the bumps in the road like shot deer. I held onto my stomach, which convulsed, and the peaches foamed from my heaving belly until the convulsions were dry like the trail of salty tears on my sunburned face.

I told myself, *Don't think, don't think,* in an attempt to keep the fruit in my stomach. I tied my bundle and slung it over my shoulder, and walked on.

I headed out in the direction that in my memories, I had seen my horse, Spirit running. Mist lifted fast in the haze of the sun. I got happy at the prospect of food and shelter when I thought I saw someplace that looked like the quarters at LeFlore, but I couldn't tell from the edge of the woods. I walked on across the wagon road, looked both ways at what seemed strange and familiar; cabins, but there weren't any people, or crops, just a few burned shacks and a sheet of blackness over the burned fields.

I bit the skin on my calloused fingers, trying to remember the day I had run away from my father, with two slave children, through the cornfield and to the quarters. *What had the quarters looked like?* I remembered that feeling of familiarity, and like that day, I froze at the sight of the scene before me, wondering why it felt known to me.

Off in the distance, bending and picking alone, like a ghost, was an older woman. She came away from pulling up the weeds, pushed the wheelbarrow to the edge of the field, and headed out in my direction. Her hand cupped her forehead for clearer sight.

"Mornin." She looked at me long her face like worn leather.

"Mornin ma'am," I said, holding tight to my sack, wondering if I knew her, where she stood, a shadow with the sun behind her head. She looked like one of the slaves at LeFlore, but her face was more pruned with worry. "Ma'am, what plantation is this?"

"You on the Bartlette place, gal. Ain't no plantation no more. Folks gonna be getin shares here now." She looked on again, staring, and she put the wheelbarrow down.

"Lilly, is that you?"

It was Janie, the cook who had called to have me beaten for eating the bread that she herself had baked but wasn't allowed to eat. I stepped back, and let out a sigh as deep as the groan of a toad. The disappointment and embarrassment rolled over me, like the breeze that snuck up from behind, bringing the familiar smells of a few nights before, the gun powder, the smell of blood on dry earth. How could this place, and Janie look so different from the freedom side of the road?

Janie reached out for me, to embrace someone familiar, but I curled in on myself. "Lord, girl, the last days done you good. Yeah, you kind of burned up by the sun, but I swear you look taller and healthy too. You a little smellin bad too, but a little lye soap, and you'll be alright.

"I heard you ran off with that Willie." Janie stood away from me like she was examining a loaf of bread that didn't quite brown right. She tried to see around the hair that hung as I looked down not letting my worn shoes out of my sight. Janie smirked, "I guess you thought you really had gotten somewhere, but you back where you started. You'll get over the shock in a minute. I know you; soon as you get your footing, you'll be mean as a pole cat."

My eyes made a quick scan of the land for any sign of Overseer. I stopped on the house, which a few days ago was not visible with all of the overgrown brush, but after the raiders came through, the place sat, raw and vulnerable in the sun. *Someone has taken the world and turned it upside down with me in it,* I thought, ignoring the over enthusiastic tone in Janie's voice, the woman who always thought I was too high and mighty, and now wanted me as familiar. My breath came quick and unsteady, when my eyes landed on the larger cabin, Overseer's place, where someone had put a rocking chair out front, and a couple of sun flowers in a water filled slop jar.

The land was quiet, and cracked with drought. The charred piles of wood from burned cabins drew heat with their black coals. The crickets didn't sing loud, their population burned out. The remaining cotton crop was small and sat still in that moment, no breeze to bend the stalks. I remained quiet, expecting to see Overseer appear in that doorway.

I tasted the sickness from the peaches, and my stomach turned; the same taste of Overseer's poisoned mouth, his tongue prying open my teeth, the same way he strengthened his penis by forcing the tunnel to my womb to open.

"Janie," I said, not looking at her. "I have to move on."

"Well," Janie said in a less deliberate voice. "These are hard times. Yeah." She hummed bent backward for a while to relieve her back.

I asked, "Is Overseer around here?"

"Don't fret about it, Lilly. Massa had some men come yesterday and buried him way off in the woods behind the house. The infection was so bad. Turns out he was dead sometime before the Union soldiers even brought their crazy brand of liberation through here. Yeah, but Tom and I cleaned the place down real good all day yesterday, and if you ever did see it before, you wouldn't know it. It's a good home for us.

"You know, Tom and I is the only ones that stayed? Made a deal with Massa to sharecrop thirty acres, rebuilding the crops, which we'll bring in till we make enough money for our own place. Tom, didn't go in for buying any of the equipment on credit. He say he'll preach and pay for stuff so the land can make a profit. He say what we cain't afford, we cain't have, but don't buy nothin on credit. He said, 'We'll abide by this contract we done swore on for a year, turn a profit, and we free to buy a piece of this, or buy our own land. But, we cain't owe nothin but the rent. Don't buy no soap, no tools, no seed, less we can pay for it.'

"That's what Tom say gonna make us different. That's the best deal. Humph, Folks acted like they had it all figured out, but didn't none of'em know the Union was gonna secure the county. Everybody still around here somewhere, 'cause we all still slaves, except for right here in this here piece of Mississippi."

Janie talked to explain new situations to herself that I couldn't understand. She walked in a larger circle around me, picking up broken glass and talking to bring me back from panic, and I exhaled deeper with each breath, until the light didn't seem awkward, the sounds didn't seem piercing, and I could hold my head up. She talked on, "Most of ya'll been runnin around in circles, the past few days, talkin 'bout findin this kinfolk and that one. I heard John and Joseph who used to talk all the time about how they wasn't gonna get old and die like Raymond, they done wondered over the county line that night and is workin on a plantation again. They probly don't mind, neither. You ain't the only one scared Lilly, you ain't the only one who cain't find they people and some kinda home."

The word home did not comfort me. I had grown to resent the way *home* and *mama* made an insatiable hunger twist tight in my belly.

Old Janie asked me to stay and work the share that she and her husband, Tom, were clearing and cleaning. Tom decided to follow the ways of Missionary and set out to become the preacher man for blacks around the county. Janie said, "It ain't easy for me either, it's work I ain't done since I was your age, but look, gal." Janie used the hand that didn't smell of cow manure to wipe the sweat from her brow. "You needs a place to be, and you a mighty strong lookin gal these days. So you works the share with me, and you gets fed."

My twelve-year-old mind ran itself around in circles of an imagined life with Willie, of an imagined life with my father in Oklahoma, but I looked out at the trees and fields that seemed impossible to navigate, and the words freedom, and rape pulled and tugged in the same place of my hunger, until I reluctantly agreed, "Thank you Janie, I guess I'll stay a while."

Turning burned out cotton fields into something that could flourish again was like trying to turn chicken feathers into dove feathers. When Janie and I took breaks from the hot sun for drinking water and to stretch our backs, Janie gave me advice for the time that I would surely feel stronger, and leave Bartlette's land. "If you want somethin, Lilly, do what Preacher say, don't ever buy it on time. If you ain't got cash you best leave it be, 'cause for most of the Negroes this share croppin business ain't provin to be no different than slavery was. Most of them women's could'a been workin for some missus in her kitchen, and makin a little money. But, Tom he has his work, and I'm glad, 'cause that's gonna mean somethin different for us. You ain't nothin but a girl. Don't be like the rest of'em; let shackles you cain't even see keep a hold on you."

She wiped her sweat, and in realizing that she was directing me to leave her, she bent back over to the work, and contradiction to her own words, "But try'na go anywhere anyway is a bit foolish. We only free as long as the Union man standin there enforcin it, but it ain't the truth, if you don't know how to go, and where to go, you gonna end up beaten again."

I took her words in, like I took in the sparse food, the small place where I slept on the other side of a wall made from curtains and scrap lumber, like I drank the water from the creek, that after the raid was muddy and disturbed, but each day ran clearer. "Yes, Ma'am."

For weeks, the two of us worked side by side picking the cotton that hadn't burned, in the same old rhythm, pick, pick, pick, stuff, step, and removing the burned debris of the destroyed fields, for both of us there seemed to be some momentary peace and solitude in it; no feeling that a foreman or overseer was about to sneak up out of the humid air.

One day Janie said, "I ain't had no intentions of havin no more children, 'cause all they do is get sold off to work someplace else, after I does the nursing them and lovin on em." She grimaced a smile in the heat, her teeth yellow against her black face. We paused, and she reached across and took my hands in hers, turned the pink side of them up to see where the softness of my girlhood days; tea parties with the Bartlette girls; had turned to cuts and calluses. "Us in our torn straw hats, look at us, chile." She laughed and looked up to the sky, squinting in the sun, then looked long and tired at the cotton that stretched out before us. I shied away, remembering the turn in my mother, the way she talked as though things were over, as if she had only a few days to give her ten-year-old daughter the language, and history of a whole people. I pulled my hands away.

Janie kept talking to the cotton field, "We's late gettin it all picked 'cause of the heat, but next spring, we plant enough to get Massa, I mean Bartlette, to knock down the balance to buy a little plot. All the rest, we sell for profit." Her voice was sometimes lost in the movements while we both sweated, hunched over in the sun. *Next spring?* My mind settled there. Without effort I had taken the first step in leaving. I couldn't imagine being anywhere else, but couldn't imagine being at Bartlette's next spring.

I moved through the cotton each day, the sun passing over me effortlessly as I gained some strength and found myself musing on the possibility of leaving. My voice became clearer, and I looked Janie in the eyes when we talked.

Janie stood and fanned with her hat, looking out on what the two of us had left to pick. "These white clouds of cotton sure look tempting to the touch, but it sits crouched in these hard sharp spikes ready to poke and prick. My hands is just sick from it all. I wasn't intendin on none of this kind of work after I got myself to the kitchen. Have mercy. It didn't even look like that much cotton to pick. Lord, wait till we set out to pick what we plant next year." She dabbed the sweat and tears, and commenced the rhythm; pick, pick, pick, stuff, step.

Janie told me to call her Maw Janie, and a quick feeling of resentment came over me like the clouds that threatened rain. She said for me to listen to Preacher, because he made a way on Sunday to sacrifice the extra rows that could be picked so he could bring the word to the people. I had seen the church. It was at the old warehouse that used to store firewood for the stove in that fancy restaurant in town before the place burned down. Now there was just the old shed, small and set way back like a tooth, crooked and pushed back in a row of good teeth. The people walked all the way from their own sharecropping work, every day, and gave him a coin here and there from their own debt. They came to the county station, horses, tired from not enough feed. Preacher would spring out from the crooked roofed building, his white shirt yellowed under the arms, suspenders pulled too tight making his trousers ride up too high over his belly. Black, like the color purple in black berries, his neck, folds of skin that I feared trapped small dead insects in sweat and dirt. But Maw Janie said listen to him, said it was the way to salvation.

My defiant questions came when we'd ventured to the county station. I breathed unsteady all the way, and my accomplishment in arriving there made me feel strong for questioning her. *Maw Janie, when we go to the county station with the few coins Preacher gives you, it doesn't amount to anything but a new blade for the plow, and flour. Why should I stay at Bartlettes when I can read, when I can marry a free man, and be Lilly LeFlore again?* My questions were more for myself, but I directed them at her.

On our third trip to the county station, I walked with confidence. The fear had faded away with the practice of being near people. The feeling returned of wanting something to be just mine. I stuck my calloused hand in the sugar barrel and licked my fingers slow, one at a time, and nobody stopped me, because Janie was the diversion. When Janie stood too close to the flour barrel, with her big satchel, laying half open after our long trip, the white man stood with his aproned belly pressed against the cash register. He looked angry for even having to sell her anything, said she was an uppity Nigger for thinking she didn't need to get it on Bartlette's account. He talked to Janie like she was a child. "Gal, get away from there. If you need flour take it from the bags that already been dished up. I don't won't your nigger hands over in that barrel."

But, I stuck my hand in for more sugar, and watched Janie move like she was trying to keep an angry bear from getting riled. She kept her eyes cast down to the floor, "Yes sir."

In town, Janie and I were separated as suspect and invisible. When we got to the porch, Janie stormed over to the side of the street where the likes of us could walk. With no need to talk about it, we both knew that with some cleaning up, I could pass as privileged. But, that day, I was a tall yellow girl, with straight dark hair, oily from no time to wash it. When I caught up to Janie, she grabbed me by the nape of the neck, "You a nigger just like me girl, and acting like you better is gonna get me in bad standing with the whites who I gotta rely on for everything. This ain't no different than you risking other folks gettin beat by Overseer 'cause you actin like you own the right to hot bread."

"I didn't do anything Janie."

"That's just it. You didn't do anything, but steal something for it help yoself while I was being reprimanded."

I knew that the thing I was about to say was not said out of ignorance, but anger. "Should I have stolen some sugar for both of us?"

Janie stopped, and stared at me, both of us the same height. The disappointment in her yellow eyes so deep, the pain of her whole life on me, and tears welled up in my eyes, as my emotions became disoriented by both sorrow and resentment for Janie, who looked at me the way Sybil did on the morning she turned on me and told me I was no better than her.

As the two of us passed the courthouse square, the white people went slow in their walk: clean clothes, time to chat with one another, ignoring the glances that I shot in their direction envious of the leisure and camaraderie of the upper class. Their feet trod on green lawn, in white shoes, not the same kind of worries about when they were going be able to buy some of the good things in the barrels and jars, ham cured in the back; while out at the road, dust was raised by blacks moving fast to return to their duties. Union men sat outside the courthouse, outside the tavern, and on the steps of the church, keeping this order in place, while maintaining the delicate, balance of new freedom.

On the way home I stepped quick to avoid the hot rocks of an unusually warm October. Flies buzzed slow at my saliva-and-sugar fingers. Janie's raggedy dress hem waved with her stride, torn from the cotton stalks; no thread for sewing it. I walked fast looking at the ground, not sparing an uneven step.

"We losin good time coming here for this little bundle of things. Time we done spent here not affordin nothin could have been time spent getting some more cotton bailed, or planting greens for the winter garden so at least we'd have somethin to eat or trade or somethin," Janie said.

I followed two steps behind not wanting to incense her further, but still angry for being scolded. I looked over at my shadow and saw, elongated in the burnt grass, a woman, my arms and the tattered dress hem flowing with my movement. I interrupted Janie's complaining, and spoke, with pouting in my voice. "Maw Janie, I think maybe I'll be leaving Massa Bartlette's land and goin on to live somewhere else."

I heard my own voice, the way it had changed over the months and thudded on the humid air like Janie's, slack in the way it slid over my tongue, vowel sounds dropped deep into the back of my throat. "At least if I go on somewhere else there might be finer things," Somewhere else meant Willie's where I felt I could have a home of my own. Where I could escape the contradiction of belonging to Janie, and not wanting to be seen with her.

"Ain't nowhere to go, Lilly. We gots a mess of work and hard labor every day. Massa Bartlette'll send out a search party if we don't do what we say. Cain't just go runnin off with a share of the crops owed to Massa. He and Tom struck a deal in order for us to have somewhere to live. We got a whole season of cotton to plant and tend after the winter thaw. I done measured things out for next year accordin to havin yo help."

I skipped right over what Janie said and spoke my mind.

"I'm not eatin any more hot water bread for dinner. I want some ham or somethin like those big loaves of bread you used to make for Massa."

Maw Janie put her hands on her bony hips and leaned back on the diagonal, to recognize me.

To rebuttal her look, I continued, "I was eating better out of Old Raymond's stew pot, and looks like I can still get whipped if I don't get my behind to the fields every mornin, only difference is I don't even have a plate of chitlins to show for it." I was hungry, and tired, and was in the first day of my bleeding. Sweat rolled over the old scars on my back, rubbing against the abrasiveness of me and Janie's morning, and frustration came into my voice. "I'm fit for better than this."

Janie didn't show me any sympathy, but fixed her mouth into a frown, "You best watch yo mouth, gal. Same as always, you got a heap of tears with yo head hanging down half the time cain't even look up to see where you go'n, but don't let somebody get on yo bad side, then you all spoiled little slave master's gal, with a temper that cain't be relieved." She took a few steps, wiped her face with the rag from her neck, then her mouth. She turned back, gesturing with the rag. "You done had freedom befo, but I just got it myself. Look here at me, I am goin up the road with you like we both experiencin somethin new. But no, I guess you always felt like you can go where every you please." She straightened up and walked tall the way she used to in Bartlette's kitchen.

Her words set me back into the truth, that I wasn't Lilly LeFlore, that I was Lilly with no belonging, and did not want to be cut loose from the only nurturing that kept me whole. We did not talk for the rest of the walk home. I caught up and walked beside Janie, who remained cold and separate.

By the time we arrived at the half picked cotton, Janie's face had relaxed. "Look Lilly, you ain't doin nothin so wrong. You just at the age where you stuck right in the middle, actin' like a girl half the time, and wantin' to be a woman the other half. I guess it just don't help that I look at you and see the difference between you and me; one cain't help but be a nigga, and one can just up and choose to be free."

"Just forget it Maw Janie. I'm sorry," I said above her words, hoping to dismiss the short notions that I could be free; Maw Janie not understanding what I was slowly beginning to accept, that Negro or Indian, any rights me or my parents had been afforded, were only as long as we did not in any way cross a white man, or deny that our prominence was a product of his charity, privileges revoked at his will.

January 1864

T HE WAR WAS QUIET in the wintertime, too cold for soldiers to hold the grip of a gun or sleep in a tent. Icy rain kept them held up somewhere, but not in Mississippi. The Union soldiers controlled most of the state now. Every evening, we had to listen to Preacher Tom talk at us about the war, like he was preaching a penny out of a Negro pocket.

"Mississippi used to be the gopher hollow for the rebels, but the Union smoked them out of this ole hole, and keep watch to make sure they don't take hold again. Yes." He wiped the crumbs and spit from his mouth and stuffed the handkerchief back in his pocket.

Maw Janie and I listened by the light of the fire, knitting hats to sell to the fat old mercantile man who cheated us every time. He subtracted and added to make sure we never got more than the time before, even if every hat had been sold off the shelf. Maw Janie didn't know the difference, and wouldn't allow me to say anything about it.

Tom cautioned Janie and me, "Be careful going to town, when ya'll pick up yarn for the knitting, even when you pick up laundry to do. Without the army, those white boys who ain't run off to fight somewhere else gots to prove they ain't cowards, and that type ain't nothin but trouble. Lilly don't nobody know I can read the bible, but the Negroes, ain't nobody got to know that you can do figures but us. It'll come in handy someday, but don't be lookin at the mercantile man like you know he done somethin wrong. That ain't gonna bring nothin but trouble."

The winter was hard for Maw Janie, keeping warm by the fire for laundry water, hanging the clothes in the bitter cold, that cramped her knuckles, but we made due, until time to plant again.

Spring 1864

SOMEWHERE IN THE PLANTING, hauling of water, setting rabbit traps, and being exhausted, being the mule for the plow, I turned thirteen.

And Janie's new sadness made me want to run, reminded me of the discomfort and panic I felt when my mother cried for no apparent reason. Janie spoke in confident terms, but as the two of us tilled the soil, our hats shading and hiding our faces, I noticed the occasional tear drops that fell into the broken earth. "It's a blessin that my Thomas preaches the word," Janie said, with a slight chuckle.

But I did not see Thomas the way Janie did. In my eyes, Thomas used preaching as an easy way out of the work, left the women to keep up the cotton field, and the other half the time he came looking for something to eat from the little bit of food Maw Janie and I could scrape together. In my mind, he was too much like the foreman or Overseer, and the two of us the slaves. At night he counted up what we had and doled out a penny or two for what we needed, then shook his head at me and Janie's slow progress all the while scratching the stubble on his round black cheeks; a shave offered by one of his women followers. He picked his teeth, stew meat from some pot other than ours which simmered nothing but soon-to-rot root vegetables. "Janie, Lilly, y'all gonna have to find a way to speed all this up, else I'll be dead and in my grave when we finally get enough to get off this old place." And Janie smiled and cried, just thinking about his sacrifices.

One afternoon of planting, I interrupted Janie's praise for Thomas, "Who are you tryin to convince, Maw Janie?"

She folded back the brim of her hat, "Don't speak about what you don't know, chile," and familiar words came up from her quiet hurt place. "You being angry ain't gonna make it that you can see or hear which way to go, so you may as well just be still till you know somethin better, till you can get some kinda plan. In the meantime you best be grateful that Preacher and I workin as hard as we are to pay for some land. Workin in his way, but that ain't for no young folks to judge."

Summer 1864

BLACK STALKS AROUND WHITE COTTON. Summertime came with it's dizzying heat. The cotton grew, because twice as much was planted that spring, and the two of us picked and picked in the same rotation of how we planted: weeding the new stalks of the last stuff planted, and picking the first planted. With no end in sight, the heat pushed down on us and made the days quiet in the field aside from bug noises, the occasional cry of a hawk, and the occasional hot breeze through distant trees. My stomach often cramped for water, but stopping for water meant a longer time before getting the cotton picked, less of the profit going to the illusion of purchased land.

The whole season passed before I spoke to Janie about leaving again. "Maw Janie, what you think about me going on to be with Willie?"

We were so close to getting all the cotton bailed before fall rains, so close that I felt that it would be a good time to brave the spaces out-side the old Bartlette place and just go. Janie spoke, but kept picking. She held her stare solid on the cotton, her lip stiffened the way she did when she didn't want to show what she might be feeling.

"Well," Janie started out, playing the only card she had remaining in hopes of keeping me with her, "What if your father or some other kin is still alive. They are certain to come look for you in the place where you was traded off."

I stood up and smiled. A year with Janie had taught me that this kind of manipulation was more a show of love, than any attempt to hurt me by bringing up the past. "Well, yes, ma'am, I did think about that, but like you said, everybody looking for they kin and ain't nobody find-ing them. Life done moved on. I'm a grown woman. I don't know what ever happened to my father, but he sure isn't comin for me here, and I don't think I can stand another day of pickin cotton."

Maw Janie stood up, took her hat all the way off, and wiped her forehead where the rag didn't stop the sweat. Her open hand was bright pink against her sun-blackened skin. "You know, chile? It hurts my feelings the way you act like what Preacher and me give you ain't enough."

I stood there blowing air out, my leg shaking from the aggravation of trying to tell her how I felt without insulting her. Rows of cotton between us, my two long braids hung from under the rag on my head, my arms and legs tanned light brown in the scorching sun, I was both handsome and beautiful, and looked every bit of the woman I claimed to be.

"Maw Janie, I just want something of mine. You and Preacher have something to work for. If my father had come, I'd have had something in going on to Oklahoma, but I don't. I need something, somebody that's just mine."

Janie saw the way my cotton sack hung off my shoulder as if it didn't truly belong there, the same way the drag of my language didn't fit over my proper words. This time Maw Janie lit in with a true concern. "What you gonna do when he starts actin like you his slave?"

"I'm not going to be treated that way."

"Gal, outside the comfort of everyday good treatment, you just turns back into a scared little rabbit. It ain't so easy to shake being beaten and raped, when you got somebody mean hanging over you. Dont' you know you just gonna be shying away from every little thing always waiting for him to get mad and hit you again. What you gonna do to stop it? Ain't like you got somewhere to go. You'll be his property then."

I paused, and blurted out the only thing that came to mind. "No I don't have anywhere else to go, but I'm taller than him," and the two of us giggled: me half laughing, half whining, a new sound that made me laugh harder and harder in embarrassment. Maw Janie, laughing deep and hoarse. It was a good sound to hear in the fields at Bartlette's.

"I reckon you got a point, Lilly, but a man of small stature can have some mean and bullying ways for provin himself. Size don't determine humility. Look at my Tom. He a big heavy set man, but humble as the day is long."

I huffed and mumbled, "Humble and fat," and turned to the cotton, not wanting to show my ill feelings about Preacher hardly ever working the crops.

"What you huffin for?"

"Nothing," I said back, done with it.

After a while I quit picking again, unable to stop thinking about Preacher Tom and his absence from the dirty work. "What I do know Maw Janie, is that some folks like Preacher have what they haven't worked for, while we have to make our own way and hope for the best that he is gonna own this land, or that land or some land, if we keeps starving while the crops get tended. We can't even buy a pouch of tobacco or a bit of coffee to relax with at night, just sit around with our fingers sore mending our old torn skirts with thread we unraveled from some other old rag."

Janie stopped picking. "Look down at yo belly, Lilly. Don't look like you starvin to me.

"Tell me you ain't lucky you livin in a liberated county. Maybe you go on up to Tennessee where you can be caught in the crossfire, stripped of your purity again and beat to death. You don't know nothing, chile. You been spared, I tell you. Who you think gonna let you keep up your highfalutin, white-actin ways, when the truth is, you been slave long enough that you about look like the rest of us, and sure 'nuf talk like the rest of us?"

I didn't answer, but held my anger so tight that I drew blood from my own lip. *Willie Kellem, Lillie Kellem. Maybe being Willie's wife wouldn't have been so awful, my only kin having died or forgotten about me.* I decided while picking that day, that if I was strong enough for this haulin and bailing and picking, that I was strong enough to steady my fears and try my luck at finding Willie.

Janie kept up with her work, almost snatching the whole stalk each time she picked. "I know whatcha thinkin, and who you thinkin about, but havin a whole buncha thangs ain't gonna make you free. Specially if you got em with folks who do dishonest work."

That night the two of us barely spoke, and Tom sopped up his vegetable and bean stew with his biscuits, never asking me or Janie what we did that day, what we worried about, talked about, he just shot off his mouth about news of the war from the county station, punctuating every sentence with, "Yes," and a pass of the handkerchief over his pink well fed lips.

"They bring dead bodies home on that new road every day. Look like it was run through here for no reason but to roll them out alive, and bring em back dead. Yes. I sho don't like no white crackas, but I prayed for em anyway. Don't want they souls hangin round here hauntin thangs up. Praise be, the Union done finally killed the most. Yes." He reared back in his chair, finally making eye contact with us. "Hmm, ya'll sho is quiet, Anyway, they done took the Shenandoah Valley now. The rebels ain't got no supplies, ain't got no mo soldiers to send, cain't cross the Mississippi River. Ain't nothin to do now but wait. Yes." He burped. "Thank you, Lord" and got up to wash outside, his belly so full he could barely stand.

When he passed me from behind, he said, "Lilly why you restin yo head on your hand like that?"

Maw Janie volunteered, "She gettin her behind up on her shoulders again, like she got somewhere to go."

"Gal, don't let the word freedom fool you. It ain't right out there. White folks still praying for a miracle, and they'll take it all out on somebody like you. Ya'll was the ones that made them mad long before the Negroes did."

October 1864

I DIDN'T KNOW AT THE BEGINNING of the day that it was going to end the way it did. Maw Janie and me got out to the cotton as soon as the sky gave us enough light to see the white, before the early October heat came looking for a little piece of exposed skin to burn it back. About the time that the calluses got soft, which was shortly after noon, Preacher came waving through the field. I stood there watching him approach. Bugs and seeds rose up in the wake of debris behind his large body.

He came closer and closer, just waving something in his hand. He showed Maw Janie first, and she squinted in the sun, her eyes burned with sweat. She held it away and pretended like she could read, "That be a good thing to preach," she said. But I figured it was something more important than Tom's sermon, so I snatched it away and read it. I looked at my Maw Janie, sweating and wondering if I understood what I had just read. The deed to some ten acres of land in Oktibbeha County, Mississippi, with Tom's initials in the place where it said "Buyer." I studied Tom for a reaction. He grinned, and I remembered him as Thomas the driver, then Thomas the part time Overseer, gaining weight as he climbed in status. Now, he would have his own land.

Sweat poured from the crown of his nappy black hair, and from the pinched corner of his eyes. He was still catching his breath, and began exhaling short laughs.

"Janie," he said, "we own ten acres. The contract is up after this here crop, and we'll have more than enough to give Bartlette his, and move on to our new land. Bartlette can get some of them niggers standing in line, wanting to be a tenant to work this now, ain't got to work it no more."

"Ten acres where?" Janie, squinted at him in the sun.

"Right here in Oktibbeha County, woman. Gonna take us a bit to get there though. I was good to buy on the fertile side of the creek."

A feeling that I didn't ever remember, warmth inside my chest like a cauldron threatening to boil over, and I reached to embrace Janie, but she turned around and went back to the cotton.

Preacher stood there grinning and panting hard, his preaching hat in his hand, his old white preaching shirt wet under the arms and around his thick neck. Horseflies collided in his tight dark naps of hair. The buttons pulled away from the round of his fat belly, full from all the food women folk cooked for him. He had nickeled and dimed his flock and taken care to get himself and Maw Janie out of that situation; a feat that was both despicable and admirable. I felt a new respect for him that had been reserved only for my father.

Tom, finally hooped and hollered and threw his hat up to the sky, and I let the abundance of warmth pour out in hard laughter. Thomas put his arm out and the two of us do-si-doed and raised the dust up to the sun. "Stop all that foolishness," is all that Maw Janie said.

The sun shone different for the rest of the afternoon and evening as the three of us made good on bailing the last sacks of cotton. I breathed deeper in my thoughts about moving on, about things seeming better. The coolness of autumn moved in on us.

"Woo," Janie smiled quietly, "the air is changing." She shook her head while we finished up the work, then after a while she picked that cotton fast and sprightly like she was a young woman again. She smiled so big that it seemed her face might tear. All her teeth showed, the good ones and rotten ones alike. "Well, some things I guess finally do just change. You wait and wait thinkin ain't nothin happenin, but it's happenin all the while by and by and then...things is changed. And you know? Much as I'm proud of Tom, I know when it's time for a change to come, it don't matter who do the honors; good deeds or bad deeds, change come like a storm that don't worry 'bout whether you was standing on the inside or outside of the house when it blow down, 'cause it's time for the house to blow down."

She talked herself into freedom, but the closer we got to finishing, the more her face turned solemn again. "Soon be over," she said. "Been wantin to tell you somethin Lilly." Her brow furrowed, and her bottom lip poked out, to hold her face proud, "I ain't had no right to keep you here, 'cept selfishness. I knowed after while when you look like you wasn't the same kind of weak girl that you was, that you was wanting to get on yo way."

"It's all right, Maw Janie. I didn't have any place else to go."

"Well." She looked out the cabin window at the dusk; the sky streaked a harvest orange. "Well, I was tryin to see 'bout you, 'cause you and that other gal was the best I could do to be close to Josephine."

"Who?" I remembered hearing about this Josephine before, but couldn't place the familiarity of the name. Maw Janie waved her hand with her back to me, reminding me of Sybil looking out the kitchen window on the morning before my capture, and I remembered: Josephine, the slave woman, Jo, who the slaves at LeFlore gave ceremony even though she was no longer on our plantation. Josephine, Tessa's mother, Tessa's dead mother.

"Why," I asked Maw Janie, "are you talking to me about Josephine?"

With the sunset behind her head she was a silhouette with the whites of her eyes the only part of her visible. "Hush. We'll talk about it in the morning. I will tell you, though, if you decide on goin yo separate way, don't go to that Satan and his son, that ain't nothin but trouble, you hear me? Find the redhead woman of the swamp, and maybe she know somethin about which way yo father went. I think that's a good thing to do." She turned back to the window.

I frowned on one side of my face not wanting her to see my reaction about talk of the red headed woman.

Janie kept rambling. "'Course I ain't never seen that woman of the swamp myself, but I know she lives in the swampland, and I know it must be somethin to see a woman that look like a fox and a Negro woman at the same time."

"It's getting late, Maw Janie. We better eat supper. It doesn't matter any more anyway, I'm thirteen years old. I don't have much need for trying to find my father any more." I shrugged my shoulders, brushing away the possibility of feeling. "I don't know what happened, and it doesn't matter any more. I don't need to know."

Janie dried her already dry hands on her skirt. "Trust me child, you don't never get too old for wanting to have a Mama or Papa or somebody to call your kin. Well, here come Tom from the rest of settling up with Bartlette. Let's eat."

Janie lit the lanterns, and we had a dinner of chitlins with apple cider vinegar and corn bread, and Tom asked, "Janie, how come you don't look glad?"

She said, looking down at her dry feet, "The fields may not be simple to work Tom, but much as all my life I wanted to steel myself away to somethin better, I believed, sho 'nuf..." She paused and laughed a bit. "I done got too old and comfortable livin right where I been livin all my life, on Massa Bartlette's land. I'm just gonna get lonely and half crazy with not another soul around on ten acres."

He ate voraciously, "Umm, You'll be alright. Yes." He wiped his mouth, as if something had been decreed.

I ate the rest of my food, nervous inside for Maw Janie, for myself, wondering if I was going to get so old and used to not having my way that I would fear anything good. All the more reason, I thought, to force myself to walk off of this land. I sat, chewing and convincing myself that death would be the worst fate that I would encounter tomorrow, and if I could make death a better fate then staying with the two of them, then I would be alright.

I got up from my place, picked up the plates, and took them all to the pump. I stood there beside Janie in the dark drying the dishes. "You ain't got to do that, Lilly. You best be gettin yourself ready for goin on your way. We don't wanna see the sun rise all the way up tomorrow and you still be here, and I guess you already know, don't take no cut-throughs, stick to the Union roads."

"I already have my bundle set, Maw Janie, and Tom done already instructed me on how to get me back to Willie's. He even told me folks' houses along the way in case I get tired." I used my open hand to move my hair out of my face.

"Hmm, and you need to quit talkin like me, 'cause that ain't gonna get you nowhere out there. Go on back to talkin like you did when you was little."

I stood there trying to hear some other, more proper voice in my head, but nothing came. "Hmm," Janie sighed again, and I stepped close to her, a surrogate embrace for the women who had seen me back to strength. Janie took the last plate away from me and dried it herself. "Lilly," she said, looking off the way Old Anna used to, "I think you might be good to go on and see that fox woman before you carry yo self on to Willie's. Ain't gonna hurt nothin to just go see if she might know somethin, least it'll put yo mind to rest."

"I'll think about it, Maw Janie. Mostly I'm just ready to get on."

"No, why don't you promise me. That's all I'm askin. You got to pass near that way, so just go."

I couldn't figure why it mattered to her, some expectation that I could remedy her longing for lost parents. I barely talked above a whisper, "Okay, I'll go by there, but I see an alligator, and I'm on my way out. Besides, what if Willie 'bout to marry somebody or move?"

"You should think about all that before makin yourself one plan with no back up plan."

"Seems like I'm damned if I do, and damned if I don't."

Janie kept her lips pressed tight. "Let's leave it on a good note Lilly." My hair hung around my face where I bent over to stack the clean, dry pots and dishes, and my mind slipped to the space just before dreaming: the sound of Tessa's voice, *Her name was Josephine. I got to remember that so I'll find her in heaven.* I jerked out of a nod.

"Go on ta bed." Maw Janie squeezed my shoulder and touched me on the back. "Good night."

I looked over at Janie and etched her facial lines into my memory. "I'll think about the swamp, Maw Janie. I'll think about it." I wanted to hug her, but I rubbed my eyes and went to my bed.

I slept restlessly on the other side of the makeshift wall, and listened long into the night to Maw Janie's restless sleep, the same way I once listened and worried for my mother. Through the night Janie chuckled in her sleep, then cried a bit, and called out, "Lilly, yo mother will be waiting, just walk around in heaven callin her name," and I listened painfully while Tom shushed her until I was pulled into colorless dreams.

At the start of the new day, I stretched myself long on my hay bed, inhaled the smell of a free dawn, and felt my cheeks rise into a smile. The welts from where I was once whipped, itched, but I knew in that moment, that they would one day be flat and smooth and faded away with no memory of the Bartlette place. I figured if Willie would still have me, then I was going to him, someplace where things came easy, meat, sugar, coffee. If he would not have me, I'd come back here and be with Maw Janie.

I inhaled the dampness of morning, and smiled again realizing I didn't have to get myself set for the fields, just had to get my bundle and say good bye. I crept across the floor, sticky under my feet. I lingered in a moment to myself, and looked over the fields, knowing that work wasn't mine to do any more, and the rest of my living awaited.

The blanket of early morning humidity hid the black cotton stalks, and I watched quiet and satisfied as the mist lifted slow, moving around those cussed stalks like long fingers coming my way. I caught a chill in my spine, and I steadied myself in the doorway and fixed my mouth to call Maw Janie, but a black crow came strutting and walked right over my bare feet, then flew off graceful. The sun entered in the place where it pierced the sky, and I heard Tom yell out, "Janie Mae? Janie?"

In her sleep, Janie had gone, peaceful, drifting off in the disconnected images of some dream. Her soul tunneled down through the old boards of the cabin and out into the cotton field where she was happy to stay, "too old to be traveling."

I stood numb in that doorway with my back to Janie's resting body. The sun smiled slow and deceitful on my face, and I couldn't move, wondering if somehow my decision to leave had motivated Janie's decision to do the same.

I listened to Tom cry, saying Janie's name over and over in his prayer voice, the voice that had come through the curtain in a whisper each night, "Lord, bless me with prosperity," while I massaged the blisters on my fingers.

I stood just outside the curtains watching the fat on Tom's back quiver as he struggled to kneel at her bedside. His huge discolored underpants hung low on his sweaty, misshaped hips. His lips contorted like twisted slugs, and his voice shrieked out like the rooster at dawn, "Lord, bring her back. Lord, forgive my ways," and then he choked up a continuous laughing, grieving surge of tears, his eyes pinched shut. I wanted to disappear from the moment, not bear witness, not show any sympathy for fear that it would bind me to him, not show any mourning for fear that it would take away my courage to be a woman outside of Bartlette's. I imagined working the fields alone, cooking for Tom, and being too afraid to leave the plantation. With a shortness of breath and the sweaty palms returning, I grabbed my bundle and fled.

All Hallows Eve 1864

WHEN I REACHED THE OPEN FIELDS beyond the woods, I took a deep breath to try and steady myself, to keep my mind connected to my body. I looked to the woods and wanted to run into the orange, yellow, and brown fall colors where I would be camouflaged, but I remembered Tom's words, *Stick to the road.*

I would try to find out if the redheaded woman knew anything, and then, quickly, I would get on to Willie's. The sun was hot on my face, not my neck, the way it was every day in the fields, and I shut my mind from the experience, reminding myself, *She's happy,* knowing that Maw Janie would have been as tortured off that land as I was on it.

I walked till late afternoon and came upon the place at the edge of the woods, where new, dark grass flourished in the shade of the trees. I remembered Tessa saying, in her know-everything voice, on one of our nights so long ago, "That is the sign for the swamp."

Little violet flowers cushioned my feet as I followed the green through the woods, then lush ground cover and fern, the smell of rich mud. My knees and elbows stiffened in the new dampness, and my field shoes sloshed in the first piece of damp earth.

I took off my shoes to feel the coolness of mud squishing between my naked toes. I clinched my body in an embrace of excitement at being alone, away from the possibility of being seen, and I was proud of myself for staying quiet inside my mind, inside my panic. It was enchanting like the secret lands in fairy tales. Toads grunted like old men, and I stopped to listen to things around me. My breath found a new, comfortable rhythm, and I reminded myself that I was to find the woman, ask about my father, and get on my way.

It was peaceful in this place. Beneath a canopy of tree moss, I lingered on the possibility of my father, gone on to Oklahoma still alive, and I remembered my mother's story; her father's directions for her to run to the swamp.

I stepped on, deeper into the color green, less enchanted now, but contemplating my mother's life, my life, had she been able to get here before the men had murdered everyone. I wondered if it would have mattered, but shook the thoughts from my head, not wanting the trap of emotions to take me from my journey. The trees reached tall to the sky, and their trunks grew thicker until above the muddy ground their bodies fanned out like skirts, some of them like knobby knees. I heard in my memory Tessa's chatter one winter morning at the laundry pot. *The swamp is a place where niggers get eaten alive sometimes, nothin left but bone,* and above the sound of her voice I heard an animal moan, saw a great gray bird fly off from the edge of the mud, saw a small furry animal struggling to get out of the mud, then sitting still, then struggling and sitting still, nothing but its head exposed. I reached out to free it and stepped into a dark green slime.

My feet maneuvered in the thickness for something stable beneath the mud, but there was nothing, and I stepped forward for more solid ground beneath me; the small animal, its eyes still and quiet above the water, its fur brown and slick, sank and disappeared beneath the surface.

MUD! Niggers drown in sink mud every time. Tessa's high-pitched voice across the small space of our cabin as I drifted off to sleep those nights, dreaming of the cotton fields turning to mud, and me disappearing beneath the orange earth.

Standing still in the green-black thickness, my weight began to sink, up to my ankles. *Think, Lilly,* I looked around for a branch to pull. I lifted my leg hard against the sucking, and the other foot sank further. I took a deep breath and stepped quickly toward the dry island just next to me, and tried to fall over on it so that I could pull myself out by the sticks and gnarly brush there, but each movement sank me deeper until I was waist deep, my clean skirt ballooned around me. I caught my breath and looked around at this peaceful place the way the brown rodent was, a victim of the same fix. The ridges of something near the surface looked like a thing I could grip, but there was a blink, film over an eye. An alligator stared lazily at my whole self sinking.

Dammit. My ballooned skirt sunken now, my legs numb. Mud collapsed the hard nipples beneath my clean blouse. My eyes relaxed and let in more light. I wanted to scream, but knew the likelihood of attracting some white man. I thought about what it would have been like at Willie's, and imagined the children I'd never have; sweet and round, their hands and hair with sweat like the two little Negro children I played with at LeFlore one day. I breathed deep against the pressure on my chest. *This was not my end,* I thought, and let out a short laugh thick with tears, the mud put pressure on my ribs. And, I screamed out, "Help!" then I was silent, listening before yelling again, realizing that the sound of my own voice yelling may be the last thing I would hear. I struggled to lift my arms out and pull against the mud, but my arms were already numb. I tilted my head back for air and took deep painful breaths to muster another scream, but the pain in my chest silenced me to a wheeze.

Father, I cried, barely able to exhale or inhale. Tears rolled into my mouth, and I thought, *Be at peace,* but I was angry, so angry at leaving like this.

Tense breathing fell off and my breath came steady and short, my heart beat slow. The colors of the swamp faded away from green to black against my fight to breathe. My thoughts loosened and I saw my mother's face soft and comforting, *Hush,* and I was drifting, floating out of the swamp, my father next to me like two quiet canoes, small flowers over each eye on beds of reeds that we built with our own hands. Mosquitoes hummed in one sweet voice, making a calming song for my journey home.

The hand that was wrapped around the mud and slime of my hand was warm in the slow dripping rain, then two hands were around my midriff. The pulling was slow. The hands unclasped from mine for a while. Deep breaths. Recovering. "You ain't no little girl. Gots to do this one piece at a time."

She pulled me up away from the place where my shoes remained, but my curled toes mingled with roots that tunneled deep toward solid earth. When it was done, the small woman with fox red hair and chestnut skin lay next to me, both of us limp on an island of mossy earth.

The air was too thick and too warm for us to catch our breath. My dress was covered in green-black water and mud.

"I don't suppose you got nothin to pay me for savin you from being swallowed alive," she said in a voice raspy and high pitched. She shook the rattle that had been in my skirt pocket. "I'll be keepin this for my pay. Conjure don't come cheap."

Her voice helped bring me back. She rolled to her knees. Her hair was like the red ball of sun setting over the cotton field in early fall, and I was unsteadied by her confidence. "Get up," she commanded, and I obeyed and got up like a child being scolded to rise up with the dawn. She was the most freakish thing I'd seen since my own reflection in the rain barrel.

For a promise of warm bread, I trudged through the swamp behind her. The taste of Maw Janie's feast of chitlins and corn bread was still on the back of my tongue, my mind still dwelled there as if I'd go home to help Janie make the biscuits at the end of this day.

Mosquitoes hummed around the fleshy part of my ear, and I was careful to place my feet only where the small woman placed hers. I spoke in broken sentences, trying to figure how to find a place to start with the questions, but she spoke first.

"I know slavery is comin to be over. I knowed that longer than you knowed your own name."

My name. I listened to the low hum of the frogs, and stopped in my journey to listen for the sounds of my name. *What was it? What was my name?* The stuffy air told me nothing.

"Breathe," the woman said cautioning. "You cain't think if you ain't breathin. You know, you had stopped takin breath for a couple seconds. That ain't good for the mind."

She talked through our journey. "Don't let this kinda air catch you standin still. It'll wrap you up and send you on to yo next life. That's what yo problem was just now. You ought to know better than to stand still and stop breathin. Worms and beetles be just a'calling you, child. Hmph. You better breathe and let some air get in your brain." The woman motioned to coax me on.

Sometimes the dark water was knee high, sometimes just mushy earth. "You gots to resist the mud when it be pulling you like that, by standing still and lifting each limb slow like you crawlin, and the mud will make steps beneath yo feet. Takes time, though." She turned around, looking up into my brown eyes, hers different colors, dark brown and hazel.

"I wasn't scramblin." I explained, but she laughed, and kept talking like she had recited these words many times. "Yo journey gonna be too short, too soon, if you don't stop fightin without thinkin things out."

"I wasn't fightin." I defended myself the way I did with Maw Janie, not wanting to be seen as weak. But I felt heavy and the mud was caked on the bottom of my good shirt, my good skirt, dripping in big clumps, making me look dumb for being caught in such a fix.

She rambled on, "I thought yo people knew all kinds of things about how to work with the land, avoid mud-fish holes. What was you, offering yourself up to alligators?"

I grimaced knowing that arguing with old women had always been useless.

"No, ma'am," I said quick and terse, thinking I'd get the bread, ask the question about my father, not expecting that she would know much, and see if I could find Willie's house. I prepared what I'd say to him as we walked on. "I'll be yo wife, but I ain't interested in bein no bed warmer, ain't interested in bein you and Satan's slave." I'd let Willie know that right away.

The redheaded woman and I were in the middle of a field of stagnant water and tall, petrified trees. "I'm freezing, I can't cross any more water," I said.

"Unless you some kinda hante, you can cross it like everybody else."

It was getting late, and the sky reflected on the water like a sheet of glass, making it impossible to see what I was stepping into. The air was chilled with the weakening light of day. This part of the swamp was like the place Missionary said a sinner would be stuck after death. "Not heaven, not hell, just repenting all day and night wantin to be saved."

"Ma'am," I said, "I gots to get outta this place soon as I get a piece of somethin to eat, and I appreciate you gonna give me somethin. Which away do I go afterwards?"

"Which way? You ain't even to the bread yet and you askin about the next direction. Just hold on to yo self, and maybe I got some questions of my own." She shook the rattle, and whistled along to herself. Her high boots were strung up to her knees, her damp stained pants looked like they had once been white. "Whistlin and rattlin keeps that ole black bear away from the water while I'm here."

I laughed in a hiss, the way I'd taught myself to do, to keep from being afraid.

Bears, mud holes; I wanted out of the place, bread or not, so I spoke my peace. "I'm lookin for my father, Grey Fox, half Mississippi Choctaw, half French, son of Jacques LeFlore, master of LeFlore plantation."

She turned to me slow, her one hazel eye being the last to stop there, her colors the only red in the dark hues of humid air around us. She paused there, her eyes journeying into mine before she turned to resume the walk across the water field.

The mating sound of a gator moaned like the slave men farting around the fire after mealtime, and I picked up my feet to catch up. A fear of being left alone itched in little red bumps on my chest.

"Ma'am," I shouted out to keep her in sight, "you seen any Choctaw people, anybody but me?" And she kept walking on.

In the middle of the swamp the land was higher and across wood planks we walked to her cabin, where a snakeskin hung coiled on a nail. The two of us sat quiet around the small table made of a tree trunk, the stools made of smaller stumps. The smell of mildew saturated the dank place.

"I reckon you 'bouts the only Indian still roaming around these parts."

I chewed the stale bread, barely able to swallow past the hard painful knot in my throat, and I looked away. *The only Indian?*

It had been a buried truth, calm pain to reckon with some other day, but hearing someone else confess it brought the knowing to the surface. I remembered the sound of Tessa's feet thudding on the dirt of the cabin floor as she chased the call of her name into the night, Maw Janie's tunneling warm beneath the slave quarters having found her freedom before me. Loneliness overtook my exhaustion and I felt like the small ten-year-old girl of LeFlore, watching from the window as I saw my father for the last time.

Heat swelled in my nose, but I ate the bread with my head tilted back to keep the tears and snot from spilling. I sipped water from the tin cup to wash the bread down, and the taste of the bread in my mouth reminded me. *Home,* I whispered inside myself. I wanted to go home, to see again the dancing room, the great fireplace, my mother sitting there with her dress ballooned around her, my bed turned down and waiting for me. I looked at my long fingers around the cup handle and wished they were brown, so the memories of Lilly LeFlore would fade away, and my life here would make sense.

She sat across from me at the table made from a tree trunk "Gettin dark," was the only thing she said as she stared at my sinking face. I looked away to avoid her. Few things were visible in the candlelight, an old guitar leaning against the wall behind the ladder to her platform bed, jars of pickled things on a shelf; the smell of the place like old meat decaying. The little flame of light from the wood stove, where the plate atop was tilted off to one side, lit the far wall.

I spoke, quiet and soft in the departing light, restating my question more clearly, so that I'd get a clear answer. "Have you seen anybody, for years back, anybody who looks like me, who is Indian?"

"I reckon you can ask that question without feelin so sorry for yo self, cain't you?" She lit a corncob pipe, reminding me that it was dark, and I was at her mercy.

She went on not answering me. "Being Indian don't make yo journey more ill-fated than nobody else's."

I wiped the stream of frustrated tears from my cheeks, and quickly asked the question again.

"You seen a big Indian man; tall, with narrow shoulders?" I was raising my voice, and getting angry that she was forcing me to remember the details of my mother and father, making me long for their smell of starch, sun and talc. She walked away with the candle toward the bottom of the ladder for her bed, and I continued on yelling with tears in my throat. "Hair long and flowing dark like the river at night? You some kind of conjure, can't you answer me with what you've seen?"

She halted in climbing up to her bed, she held the candle out to take a look at me, but I could tell from her squinting that I had breathed air on an unstitched wound. She took a deep breath and looked off into the darkness of her cabin, her eyes red now. "I sleeps up here 'cause the rats cain't climb up there. You can sleep where you are for the night. You welcome to sleep on the table, then I'll see you off to your whereabouts in the mornin."

I spoke up again, ignoring her sudden grief. "No thank you."

She chuckled, putting the shame back on me, and when she leaned into the light of her candle, her fuzzy red hair tempted the flickering flame. She inhaled and a tear escaped and doused the light.

Before sunrise she was shaking my arm. The candle rocked nervously on the stump table. I raised my head at the sound of a distant rooster crowing. "The table would'a suited yo tired body. Don't you think?" she said, pulling my arm in the grip of her strong, squat hands.

"I was fine right where I am." I turned to go back to sleep.

"Sun comin up soon," she said, "and I'm seeing you on yo way before such a time as a new day comes for me." She pulled again anxious, like pulling me out of the mud, but realizing I was a worthless find, she was throwing me back to the river before the sun could rise and mock her misfortune.

What had I said that made her cry? I searched my mind, but in my exhaustion I couldn't recall the words from my mouth, just the frustration. What had Maw Janie been thinking to send me to this woman, time wasted from getting on with my life? Everybody else had found a way of some kind after the county had been liberated, and here I was, marrying-age, and messing around asking questions about things that long since passed.

The air outside her cabin was thick but fresh, and I realized how rank her cabin smelled by comparison to the air outside. Had she ever bathed, used lye soap to kill the things that surely crawled in her matted hair?

The mud on my dress was dry now, and I was silent as we headed for an exit to the swamp, a maze I could never retrace, humid smells of life emerging and decaying in the waters around us. Lazy alligators on the dry land slithered into the water as we passed. In the distance was the sound of the railways being hammered down by the black men who had not obeyed the new laws, and we stood silent listening to the clanking.

The red woman spoke, glad to be rid of me, but obliged to give me her bidding, "Well, you watch yo self, and don't spend no time tempting death to come by yo way. Just get what you can get in this world like everybody else. The war soon to be over, won't bring no misfortune to folks who know how to bide their time and mind their business." She pointed in the direction where the sun shone brighter; "That away will take you in the direction of the cold end of the river, the way where I believe you wanna go." She looked up at me in the thick air, the cold first day of November morning about to get warm, the sun baking our heads.

"Do me a favor," she said, breaking our locked stare. "Don't come back by here, unless you and me the last things breathin on the earth." I stared her down, stunned by her insult, knowing from my days with Tessa that questions about kin and memory could bring down hurt that was best warded off with meanness. I looked away to the clearing she had pointed out, wondering about her name. I turned and watched her disappear around the curve of a few thick trees.

When I turned back to the clearing, Willie and the man who must have been Satan stood shoulder-to-shoulder watching me.

November 1864

O N   T H E   F I R S T   M O R N I N G   I was grateful for dawn in my new home. Willie slept gentle like a boy, his lashes long and quiet. The warmth of another body was a comfort I had never known. I almost kissed him: the way his face was surrounded by the dark tight naps of hair cupped by the feather mattress. I had already heard Satan's hard shoes on the other side of the wall. Out to the barn, I milked the cow slow so I could take in the peace, listen to the hooves of Satan's horse cloddding, restless for the ride at dawn. Willie's horse scooted hay with its hooves and snorting at the prospect of being hitched to a wagon instead of saddled and ridden. I came to the kitchen to do what I hadn't had the chance to ever do, cook.

I put the pitcher down still warm from the cow's body, and felt my chest broaden at the sight of all that was mine. Everything was in a tin in the cupboard or on the shelves of the kitchen. All around the walls, there were things in canisters: cornmeal, flour, sugar, salt, grits, oats. I opened every canister and bag, and took a deep satisfying breath for not having to be hungry anymore. Maw Janie must have had many good bites of Massa's food back when she cooked. I commenced to making my first loaf of bread.

Willie came into the kitchen dressed for wherever he went each day. Satan came, tall behind Willie, took one look at my mess, shook his head, giggled, and turned to leave the house, patting Willie on the shoulder in sympathy. "Hope you can break her in, boy."

My pride hardened. Willie stood in shock. "Damn, Lilly. What the hell are you doing?"

"Don't be ungrateful," I defended myself. "I made you some bread."

He looked at me suspicious and sat down in the chair carefully clearing the flour from the spot where I placed his plate. The wood stove cracked and I jumped at the sound of damp wood. "What you so jumpy for? These little black things ain't pokeberries, are they?"

I folded my arms and stared on, letting him wonder.

I said back at him, "Here, eat," and I poured plenty of hot molasses and butter on his bread. Willie was looking at me with one eye while he chewed, then both eyes got big and round and he spit the food out. "You ought to be ashamed. You cain't even cook."

He stormed out, placing his hat on his pea head. "You best learn or go back to roaming around the swamp." I went over to taste a slice of the abandoned bread; salt and sugar had been in similar containers. The humiliation rose in my chest and burned steady and hot there.

I sat on the porch half the morning, working Willie's insult over and over in my head, each time conjuring up a better response for the next time he saw fit to embarrass me. I had told Maw Janie that I wasn't going to be no slave to Willie, and I meant it.

Before cooking the noon meal, I tasted everything in the tins to see what was what.

That night, I scrubbed extra well, and put on the clean night dress, clothes Willie had already bought for me. The night dress that reminded me of my own mother's sleeping gowns. I used the lemon scented toilet water, and lay quiet in our bed telling myself not to think of Overseer, but to think of the lovers in aunt Doves novels that lay open on the lace table cloth for ten-year-old eyes to see. Lantern light and the big bed, the house silent, I couldn't keep my mind from reeling, on what it would be like. I put my hands between my legs to see if the space there would even open up after bein clinched so long to mend Overseer's crime. I thought to go to the kitchen and put lard there, to make his manhood less abrasive against my insides, but I heard his wagon pull up. When the door shut, I gasped inward, and held my breath like that, my back to the door as he entered the room. "Evenin," was all he said before he blew out the lantern, then the rustling sound of clothes being removed over dry skin, his cold hands and penis on my thighs. He pried me open, and with the motion of a butter churn, he moved on top of me, until he held himself still, held me tight his voice grunting as he strained, and then he collapsed, rolled over, and was snoring. I went in the darkness to the wash basin, cleaned myself up, and stayed awake, pondering the disturbing emptiness I felt, not afraid, panicked or defiled, just empty.

December 1864

O NE QUIET EVENING the sun set in beautiful streaks of violet and peach. I stoked the fire and watched through the panes of glass as the sky changed, wanting for something to do and then remembered that I had wanted to measure myself by the flat piece of wood that was nailed to one of the kitchen beams. Figures were marked on it all the way from one at the bottom to seven, at the top. "W" was marked several times from the three mark, steady on up, and I traced the carving with my dry finger, wondering if Willie's mother lived here one day and made the marks, or if Satan made them. I closed my eyes and saw a thin black girl no older than me refusing to take orders; the "W's" didn't go higher than the line right between the five and the six, and that "W" looked like the way Willie wrote his name on the sheets of papers before they were stuffed back in his satchel, figures like those Preacher scratched with the pencil stick to keep track of what we owed.

Outside I heard the clank of Willie's wagon in the cold air. The wheels came over rocks and I measured myself quick; my hair, not yet being washed, made an oily mark right below the six.

Way bigger than Willie, I thought, smirking in his absence. At the sound of him climbing the three stairs, I scuffled in my stocking feet to the kitchen to turn his meal over in the skillet.

"Lilly!" he yelled, forcing his voice to go deep, not letting the words slip gently off his tongue the way they did in his sleep.

He sat at the table like Preacher, talking without asking me a thing about my day. "You make sure you stay around here. Don't go to the county station or anywhere." It seemed he hadn't noticed that in the five weeks that I'd been with him, I hadn't set foot off the property.

He moved the perfected bread around his plate to collect the gravy. "Sherman has taken Savannah. That's a good thing for our side, but there's plenty of white men at the county station who's talking about killing the Union soldiers who sit watching over them. Plenty of those white men talking about turning Oktibbeha County back over to the rebels, lynchin all the Negroes."

I listened, but didn't want to think about war. This place seemed untouched by it, the way LeFlore seemed for so long. I didn't want to leave, didn't want to go out to the county station and have the white people ruin my peace. Here, I was the lady of the house.

Each day Willie left by morning and came back for a spell in the afternoon, then left again till late at night. Satan came and went like a ghost, never saying much of anything. "What folks do you do work for Willie?" I asked nervously.

"I ain't a common nigger Lilly. Be satisfied that what I do keeps a roof over your head."

I thought about Maw Janie, never questioning Tom, and I felt foolish for wanting the peaceful days over any information about Willie's whereabouts.

Winter locked me into the rhythm of running to the shed for wood, a pile for the porch, a pile for the kitchen stove. Keeping the fires is how I spent my days—laundry fire, cooking fire, house-warming fire. I sat in the big room at night by lantern light and fireplace light, remembering the bright chandeliers at LeFlore, how I never thought about the work it took for Sybil, Earleen, and Emma to keep all the large and small fires of the house lit. I went to bed each night afraid of every sound; raccoons, deer, until either Willie or Satan came into the house.

April 20, 1865

W ILLIE KEPT A CALENDAR, that he picked up at the post office, with pretty drawings like the *Farmer's Almanac*, a book Willie and Satan kept, but did not use. It was my birthday. I debated about whether or not to tell Willie that I was fourteen years old. Willie was eighteen, and he thought I was too. I liked having that secret.

Willie left for his regular morning, and before I could get the water hot for the laundry or get the chickens fed, his wagon came back up the road. A few other Negroes who had built houses near by also came looking misplaced from their day. He came into the house and went to the bedroom and sat on the edge of the bed. I went in and stood in the doorway just staring at him. He looked like someone had died. "What's the matter, Willie?"

He sat, strange, his elbows on his knees, looking at the floor, "Father been back here this mornin?"

"No," I said with a question in my throat.

The words rolled off his tongue without preparation. "Lincoln's dead. Shot by a crazy white man."

Willie's hat dangled between his knees, where his hands trembled to hold it there. He placed it on his head, and without looking at me, he walked past me. "Stay around here," he said, a coating of yellow pollen on the shoulders of his suit, visible from where I stood slightly above him. He hurried back out into the morning and left me speechless and shaken by the news.

The first assassination, they said, but I remembered my mother's stories of her mother, father, a whole clan of people killed for their land, and I still remembered the smell of the creek that morning of my assassination as Lilly LeFlore. I remembered the smell of tar rope and blood, and my mother dead by the water's edge.

That evening I put on my good top in celebration of myself, and sorrow for the dead president. The stains from that day in the swamp were yellow and barely visible. I wore my good skirt, and Willie came in with a package for me. He threw it on the table, and took his skinny self to his chair.

"Where's the meal? Oh, happy birthday."

He looked over at me, and I expected him to smile, but I didn't know what he was feeling, his face was perfectly blank; a black purple slate, his eyes without a curve of the eyebrow, without a widening or squinting.

"How did you know?" I asked, not giving him an expression either.

Satan came into the front door, rounded the corner, the heels of fine, heavy soled boots, his hair speckled with gray these days, his body less kept. He hunched a bit, but was still taller than me. He pulled up a chair and began eating the stew I ladled for myself, and talked while he gulped. "He knew, I knew." He laughed. "Hell, you drew little flowers on the calendar next to the date. Either you was born on this day, or you planning on taking flowers to Lincoln's grave." His laugh was baritone and deep up to the rafters. Willie didn't laugh, but stared a strained look at his father. Satan reached over, slapped him on the back, and turned his bowl up.

Outside, voices clamored with wagon wheels on the road. Darkness had already taken the sky. Satan cracked his back and went to the front, grabbing his revolver from his boot jacket. Candles from across the road, lanterns, all bounced both jubilant and frantic.

The three of us stood on the porch trying to understand the commotion. *A lynching party coming to burn us out?* I thought, but the voices were Negro.

Somebody whooped, as loud as they could, and yelled up to us. "The Confederates done surrendered. Wooooo!" they hollered. "Freedom!" I heard some man yell.

The little crowd of people was just singing and clapping, calling out names of people outside the county they were going to hurry up and go find. Somebody yelled, "I'm gonna lay down in a shady Northern grove."

Somebody else yelled, "I ain't workin the share no mo. Catch me if you can. I'm gonna go see my baby."

The three of us stood like carved figures; Satan tall and separate, with the revolver in his hand, Willie slight with artificial confidence, separate in his arrogance. I was lost in the trance of the voices, nothing different from the voices in the quarters the night Tessa took off without looking back. My bitter face was the only face visible on the porch.

"Seem like a good birthday present. Guess Lincoln was the sacrifice. There's always a sacrifice, before somethin good comes," Satan said quiet.

I licked the tear in the corner of my mouth. Freedom didn't ever seem to work for me the way it did the people around me; it didn't satisfy a hunger but gouged the pit of my belly out more and more hollow.

The next morning I opened the package, and I threw the thing in a corner. I couldn't look at it all day. Then, before Willie came home, I picked it up with one hand, looking the other way, and hung it on a hook inside the cedar chifforobe, pulling Willie's suits in front of the cloak, and shutting the door. It was just like the one my father once bought my mother from New Orleans, just like the one Missus Bartlette had said was quite tacky and resembled a conjure woman's getup. It hung there for years to come, ignored by me while I worked inside each day motivated by belonging.

Summer 1868

THE INSIDE OF THE HOUSE and the yard became my world. Unlike the world around me, it did not change. So I fed the chickens, tended the cooking and laundry, fed our one cow, swept the porch, and mended the hole in the basket weave of Satan's porch rocker over and over.

Three years had passed, with uneventful birthdays, removing the curse of tragedy that always seemed to strike on the day of my birth. I was careful not to curse the day, and made flowers around April 20th, with my eyes, not the quill pen.

Satan turned from a surly giant to a pitiful old man who limped a little, bathed himself less often, and complained about everything, angry that he couldn't get around the way he used to. The thought of needing anybody wrecked his every day, and I couldn't feel sympathy for him. He claimed in his deep voice, "Ain't feelin too right," only moments after yelling at me for not cutting his bread the right way.

The piss bowl by his bed was sometimes pink with blood, and I ignored his complaining, knowing that if it had been me, he would leave me to rot before lifting a finger to help. Willie paced in worry every time Satan grimaced in pain, and walked around acting like it was my fault, just finding things to be cross with me about.

I kept to feeding the chickens, keeping the fires, and cooking. I got as good as Maw Janie; biscuits, stew, and bread good enough to steal. We had fine meat that Willie bought at the county station, because Willie said he didn't eat nigger food like chitlins, pig feet, and tripe.

Good food or not, Satan got slow and looked like he was sitting back looking off into the distance more. The more Satan got sick, the more Willie acted like Satan, checking behind himself always to make sure the horse was saddled right, or that the horse was bedded down right. He was sure to always follow up with me about milking the cows, feeding the chickens, fetching eggs, sweeping, making sure the rocking chair was free of spider webs so Satan had a proper place to sit if he so chose. I wished they would both go back to disappearing every day and leave me alone. The house didn't feel the same with them in it telling me to do things I'd done for years without supervision.

"What you, some kinda field nigger that you didn't learn how to tuck a sheet?"

Then one day the thing Willie was dreading came to pass. The worms and beetles that the woman with red hair told me to be deaf to, called old Satan's hard body down.

The sun parched the ground, cracking under the weight of Satan's stiff body, and Willie pressed his head to Satan's chest and asked for God's help. I hadn't ever heard Willie ask the Lord for anything. I hadn't ever heard him ask me for anything. I put my head to Satan's massive black chest, still rising and falling. He talked out of his head, lingering somewhere between his childhood, and his days as a young man. "I'm gonna go out to Jacks place and see if there's any work for me to do." He chuckled in a way that was kin to a cry of defeat, and looked over at Willie, the passing clouds in his eyes taking his soul away, "Willie, take her to the flowers."

"Papa?" Willie, whispered, "Come on Lilly; Lord help him," Willie cried. His small head lay on his father like a boy's, and I watched on, struck by the tenderness of Willie touching. He looked up to scold me. "Ain't you got some kind of heathen medicine?"

I looked away and saw not with my eyes, but the way my mother saw; sap running slow from tall trees, trees bending over for water; and it didn't feel right to deprive them of the sacrifice of such a massive carcass like Satan flowing back into the pores of the earth, roots, branches, leaves needing the food.

"There's always a sacrifice, before somethin good comes." I said, without compassion in my voice, without allowing myself to be astonished that I had a vision, with my eyes wide and awake.

I had seen summer only seventeen times, but I had grown numb to the grief of death.

The sun beat down on the three of us in the yard. I looked down and saw Willie's life through the slow passage of Satan. I closed my eyes and saw Willie, weaker than the day he stood in the shadow of Satan waiting for me at the edge of the swamp. I looked into his sunken eyes and tried to imagine his mother.

I saw the round belly of a Negro woman against a background of other brown hands in candlelight, a male child at her open blouse, her breast sweating into his purple lips. I saw Satan riding with the bundle strapped to his body, the horse approaching, its eyes covered for forgetting. I saw into a warm night beneath the blue light of the moon, the boy on a bed of feathers, the woman's bare feet over sharp rocks and tree roots, the two of them embracing, and then a dirt road, her hands and feet bound, flung over Satan's saddle like a sack of grain to be sold at the trading post.

"You useless heifer," Willie said rising off his knees, his father lifeless on the ground, Willie's good pants stained with red earth. "You ain't good for a damned thing," He mumbled, clearing the tears from his dark stern face, and nudged past me.

I was indifferent to Willie's pleading, cold to somebody who didn't want anything but maid's work from me. I was no more to Willie than Old Anna and Maw Janie were to Massa Bartlette. Both of them died away slow, their power stolen by men who wanted their meals cooked and bread sliced by hands that were good for no other purpose than to feed them and keep them satisfied at night.

I looked off across the road into the distant field, ignoring Willie's grief.

In the days that followed, Willie started commanding me like Satan. "Lilly!" he shouted.

I responded, trying not to show that I was growing weary of his harshness. "A man of small stature can have some mean and bullying ways for provin himself," Maw Janie had warned me.

"Don't call my name like I'm your slave," I reminded Willie in a tone that wore down over the months.

"You can do what I say or be put out for the wolves, gal."

I huffed in response, but each time I did not show him that I could leave, he grew more confident in his insults, and I grew more certain that there was no other life for me.

Winter 1869

ALL THOSE TIMES Willie turned over on me in bed, I never got pregnant. He didn't even stay around the house long enough anymore for us to have an argument let alone make a baby. He rose up before light in the morning and ate the breakfast I prepared for him, then put his white shirt on, his nice pants, and a suit jacket meticulously buttoned and straightened with smooth hands, and was gone off to who knows where.

Sometimes he returned for lunch, but I prepared it whether he came for it or not. Watchful for Willie inside the brown log walls of our home, I amused myself with how light entered through the glass window at the front, disappeared, then reappeared in the bedroom window, then set red in the trees out back beyond the freezing water at the pump. I spread out the task of doing the laundry, a little every other day, so there would be something to do.

Sometimes I rocked quiet on the porch. Folding the sheets, I took the time to smell the winter sun in each one, and remembered Maw Janie, wishing I could apologize to her for being so ungrateful, accepting the invitation to be her child, all the while complaining about what I didn't have and what Preacher didn't provide.

With the loneliness of watching the sun in its arc, day after day with nobody to talk to, I came to wish for a child of my own so hard, that my body ached with the desire for Willie to have his way with me. A child was what could make me happy. All the fear I once had of being taken by force by Overseer faded off, I was eighteen years old and Willie treated me more like a sister that he didn't quite like than his wife. I thought long each day on the feeling of his manhood-inside me. I imagined having a baby to bring the sound of life into the house.

One afternoon I stood there on my porch, as my mother used to stand on the veranda, rain falling but not on my head, and I thought maybe I wasn't going to find what I was needing here with Willie, my life being wasted in boredom, still not really having home. I listened to the distant train and thought about Oklahoma, about how family could be found only with family, how over and over I was trying to get something from Negro people that I could get only from my own.

I thought to leave, to put on the shoes Willie brought for me and head up to the county station, maybe to a job like the other folks who went to work each day. I wondered how much things changed there since Maw Janie and I went to use the credits. Must have changed a mighty lot with people going that way for work after harvest. In the distance more and more houses could be seen, in each direction, a few acres between each, just enough for good planting. I craned my neck off the porch watching until folks turned the bend in the road and disappeared.

I packed a small handbag one night and stuffed it under the bed. I figured I'd spend a few days getting my nerve up to be in the company of that many people again, then I would try my luck walking there, maybe go up and read all the postings about Oklahoma, get a sense of the place before going, but on that night, Willie turned over on me, and this time made me a mother.

Spring 1870

BEING PREGNANT didn't make me any less lonely. Each day I watched the ritual of the man across the way; off to the grain warehouse at the county station like the other black men in wintertime. Then came spring, and he plowed, seeded, weeded, sometimes with the rain pouring down on him. Watching him was the event I looked forward to each day. I wondered who he worked so hard for; a wife, a landlord? I ran to the stew pot in the kitchen, stirred it up, and fled back to the porch to see how far he'd gotten in his farming.

Sweet wisteria hung from the vine on the porch rails, and my belly grew round as I watched the man's cycles. He tended his field in a big circle of sunrise and sunset; hands rose above an unyielding field, mule and plow, seed dropped gentle by his faraway hands. I looked at my own forefinger and thumb and imagined rolling the seeds out of his warm palm. I placed my hand on my growing belly and went inside until the next day.

September 1870

ONE DAY, a cold autumn rain came down, hard like the cold rain of day of my beating from Overseer; a river poured down on the house, causing me to breathe out of rhythm. Someone ran up the road yelling, "Come a tide!" The sky was almost like dusk even though it was afternoon. The rain kicked up the smell of my musty pregnant body, and the talc of dry dirt. Thunder shook the walls, then lightning hit the oak tree out front in an explosion like gunfire. My ears rang high pitched, my whole body hummed. Then another horrible sound; the tree creaked and split in two, and it hit the ground, sending the shudder up through the posts of the house, up through my bare feet. Tiny yellow leaves rained down on me, and my first birthing pain came hard.

The baby's body was warm like bread fresh from the oven, hands still in fists where lifelines charted a path like mine, a map hidden in her clutch. Eyes still innocent, not submitting yet to all this noise; crickets, and the barn door swinging loose and banging again and again.

When her eyes opened, they were perfect round pebbles, night skies without stars, her soul sunken deep in that place. I shook, cold for a moment inside the quiet prayers that whispered in my mind, and I lay back in the lamplight on the wooden floor, not wanting to soil the bed with my birthing blood. I fed her there, her brown body tiny against my pale breasts. I knew what to do, but felt awkward with the chord in my lap going dry and the wet sack wrapped in the sheets where I had birthed her.

What would I name her? A bird lit on the window, the black space of the night turned to dawn where the lamp still glowed in my room. The bird called, "Su-die." A mate answered, "Su-die," and I let it be that simple. I closed my eyes vowing in a whispered wish to protect her until she was old enough to walk alone.

Once I had my Suddie, I couldn't understand how I had endured the isolation of each day without her, small and needing of my constant care. Feeding, awake, sleeping, my pattern was set now to hers. Colors died out in the cool fall air; winter was long, with nothing to make the difference between one day and the next; then bug noises in the spring, high corn in the summer. The baby grew like seed planted in early spring. She made cheerful cooing noises in the dark old house, like the ones my mother said once filled the halls of LeFlore. This child was my family.

Summer 1871

T HE MORE I paid attention to Suddie, I didn't so much pay attention to Willie commanding in Satan's voice. I didn't so much care about where he went each day to do his work, or why it was such a secret. I remembered how my mother clung to my father, not wanting him to go each morning, and now, I didn't understand why. Willie disappeared each day before we could have a cross word, and I liked it better this way.

The summer was sweeter with a baby to tend: suckling babe, sweet face, brown like Tessa. I sat with Baby Suddie on the porch every morning and night, and Willie complained when he came in for some food. "Damn it, Lilly, there's other things to be done here too. Baby's big enough, and don't need all that tendin' still." Dishes often sat next to the pump covered in ants before I'd lay her down and wash them. For months I crawled in and out of bed without ever fixing the covers or washing the sheets.

Willie complained about everything whether I did it or not, but he wasn't ever around anyway, so I ignored all his noise. When he did have me lying right next to him at night, he pushed me to scoot over. "What is that smell? You still smell like blood nine months after birth. What is that smell?"

"Willie, you gonna wake the baby," I'd say, and the next day I'd sniff around the folds of my body trying to see what it was he smelled.

Then I remembered the smell of Sybil each month, her arms reaching up into the glare of the sun to take down the dresses and blankets, wet with the smell of deep well water, the hair beneath her arms holding the odor of her sweat, the curtain of her dress moving just above me, the dark hidden odor of her blood, calming.

I sat sometimes rocking my baby on the front porch way past the damp chilled sunset of fall. I watched the man stroll up in the evenings now with a woman in a long dress, a bustle added to the butt that she was already toting. I watched them in the distance every evening from my sheltered porch.

Months passed; the baby pushed my hands away as she tried to stand. Suddie looked at me with wide accusing eyes, questioning new pains of teething. When she screamed it wasn't for milk, or for sleep, her gums were hard; long high-pitched piercing sounds, her eyes pinched shut.

It was the end of our peace. I ran around asking her what she wanted even though I knew she couldn't answer. "Suddie, what's the matter? Huh?" I paced and patted her back and tried to remind myself that she didn't know better. I sat down and cupped her head in my hand, offered my rough finger to her gums, but it looked like she was mad at me.

All the sweetness drained out of those moments of holding her, humming little songs, looking at how perfect her little lips were, her hands and toes still clenched and wrinkled. How did other women find patience for the constant helpless screaming? The screaming—why did it send alarm up my spine, why did it make me fear being severed from life itself?

I sat there with night coming on, unable to think of anything else to soothe her. The sky turned orange like the dirt and the maple leaves, the dank wood of the house like the color of my baby, and me more like the color of the sunset. The isolation rushed back after months of being drunk with the sweetness of her; brown baked-bread cheeks. I thought to sing some old song and rock away the pain of new teeth, say sweet things no matter how much screaming, the way Old Anna used to do for Massa's girls, but I stayed there in the heat with her until she exhausted herself, and I pulled the blanket tighter around her body, resisting the urge to suffocate her in my disappointed arms, my whole body aching in a fight against panic.

The sky faded to the dull blue gray of a Union soldier's uniform, and when she slept I was numb, with my ears still ringing.

With Baby Suddie always screaming now for one thing or another, I developed a stern tone, much like my bitter ways before my first menses. At the end of each day I comforted myself with knowing I was taking care of her the best way that I could, never striking her, though the image of Overseer's elbow catching just above my nose, striking over and over, satisfied me until the screaming subsided.

I tended to the daily chores again, with Suddie swung on my hip screaming, or sometimes she was distracted by the chickens running in the yard, but the only way I could keep my mind away from beating thoughts was to do what I needed to do, whether she was screaming or not, an effort that required my face to stay stern. Now Willie had a mirror image of his own joyless face, and he looked assured when he saw the dishes done, beds made, and breakfast, lunch, and dinner there on the table again whether he ate it or not.

Evenings, I stayed in off the porch with the baby, trying to stay with myself as Lilly Kellem, not as the child whose initial wounds I could barely remember, the child with her mouth open waiting for her father to reappear on the edge of the nest, young rodents in his talons.

Night after night memories came less often as I dug my dry yellow hands into my life, not much different from Old Anna's and Maw Janie's: shitty baby, Willie's white shirts needing cold rinse water hauled from the creek, not the pump. Seemed like there was never time any-more for musing about another life, for fixing and playing with my hair while I sat in boredom watching the trees blossom. I didn't have time to care about how I looked, and there wasn't anybody to appreciate it anyway.

Summer 1872

BABY SUDDIE'S FEET fit into store-bought shoes that trailed along behind my bare feet in the heat of our summer journeys down to the creek for washing water for Willie's shirts. Sun baked us; tall color-of-sun woman and little brown girl. Sometimes I looked at her and thought, she is cute, like Willie, softened and innocent, but then the harmony of June bugs and horseflies with their shimmery blue-and-green bodies reminded me of how much trouble it was to get her to mind me on the way to the creek for water.

I was quiet and careful not to show her any sweetness, less she'd be wanting it always, the way I had wanted molasses candy with nothing but sharecropping credit to exchange, but wanted it anyway because Maw Janie had given it once.

Sybil had said children needed more teaching than spoiling, and Suddie was hard enough to be with without new stuff for her to be testy about. She could talk good for a baby not yet two, and was smart about things, but not from my teaching, from hearing Willie talk. She said anything that came to mind. "Mud fish, mud fish, makin bubbles, mud fish, mud fish on the double." The more she conjured up songs, the more quiet I stayed, even if it was funny. I didn't want her thinking I thought Willie's old silly songs were funny when she should have been learning about how to plant, or help with the wash. There was a time when teaching a little girl songs and how to read would have meant something, but that time was long since over. I told Willie she needed to learn how to take care of herself, not learn a bunch of things that would make her want for what she couldn't have, but she already knew some of her figures, "One potato, two potato, three potato, four."

Suddie's sounds filled up the silence like Tessa, always making sounds with her mouth. I stayed more quiet and got on about the chores, serious. "Hush, Baby Suddie," I said, frowning, the sun pruning my skin. Baby Suddie looked like the slave babies, wool hair, with songs like the Negros, my Baby Suddie more like them than me.

I tilted my wooden bucket down in the water and from Suddie's small body came a whole string of words.

"Poppy said it can't be still water, gotta be still running when it's fetched like a scared nigger looking for freedom." Sometimes her words scared me, grown-up words from a little bitty body, and she'd just look at me with ancient eyes after saying something like that.

I saw myself bending there with my dress hem getting wet, and I wondered why I was putting up with such foolishness on such a hot day. Willie wasn't coming home anyway. How was he going to know where the water was fetched from? "Hush, gal, that's grown folks' talk," I said, confused over whether or not my two-year-old baby had called me a nigger.

Summer 1873

THE OLDER SUDDIE GOT, the more her legs found their way to running away from me. Her eyes came out of wanting, and came into her own way of knowing, understanding what she saw between me and Willie; me obedient to him for the promise of meat on the table, a porch with a roof over my head. Already Suddie knew survival well, because she picked the ways of Willie over the ways of her mother. She spoke to me in commands.

"I want something to eat, Mommy."

She paused, reluctant to call me that, but whenever she tried to call me Lilly, it came out as Willie, and damned if she didn't get more upset at making her own error. Next thing that would come was she'd say, "No," and go to swat at me.

New words came that I didn't teach her, words she heard Willie say to me. "Shut up," she said and turned away from my lazy discipline: a scolding look, and then back to my chores.

Half the time I didn't know what to do, and the more time that went by with me confused, just like her father, the more power she took to say whatever she wanted. I was always having to remind myself that she was a baby, like I once was, and I tried to remember being two, but nothing came until the memory of riding on a carved wooden horse, my father proud, and smiling.

One day I napped with Suddie, grateful for a break from the heat, and I dreamed of myself as a little girl. I was leading the two slave children through the cornfield, little Netta and Little W, on a day already filled with too many stresses for the adults. We wanted to scare the old nigger woman by throwing things from the high stalks to the perch where she sat keeping watch over the corn, and now I understood, she was keeping watch for my father or Uncle Golden.

When Suddie woke from her nap, the heat was as bad as it had ever been, but the air was light, not thick. I went down by the creek with Suddie, and stuck my aching head into the numbing cold, my hair on the water like weeds. I imagined the water taking me downstream to the place where I played in the creek as a girl. Suddie held her head down too, and the water lifted her hair, puffy like foam from floodwater. She had hair like Tessa had and when she wasn't looking at me, I was looking at her and wondering how I had birthed a baby that didn't look like me, how I had birthed a baby at all.

When we rose up, our eyes met, through sheets of dripping water, and she looked at me like I was somebody who had tricked her into feeling something for me. The smooth perfection of her skin wet and precious, but her stare mean.

I walked back slow telling myself I needed to quit acting like a girl, and find my strength as a mother. Through the thorned brush and young dry saplings I stepped, with Suddie behind me, and she got to singing some song Willie or somebody at the county station taught her:

The Freedmen and Mr. Revels
Got together with the Devils,
Took the white man by the hand,
Gagged him down in Dixie Land.

I switched hands with the heavy bucket and reached for Suddie's little brown hand without looking at her. I said, sounding like Old Raymond, "Don't sing stuff like that out loud, you'll get us both killed."

The Negro man Hiram Revels had just finished a term representing Mississippi in the white government, and other black folks were trying to get elected to be next. Willie said all of it was causing white men to be meaner than ever in town, said the Klu Klux Klan was a secret group of raiders who exterminated men who stepped out of line. Said they were like white people's Santa Claus, sent by God to watch you all the time, then when he put that suit on, you were getting what was coming to you, depending on how you been behaving.

I didn't want any of the news of all the wrongdoing, not even from a two-year-old town cryer. I had seen horrors of war, been beneath the whip, the weight of a white man's body, seen a dozen of them dead by their own brother's hands. Keeping the thought of even pending conflict out of my head, out of my home was necessary to my having any strength to deal with Suddie and Willie.

I kept walking with my one free hand out behind me, thinking Suddie was coming along, but when I turned around she stood way back, her face frowned in the sun, not happy as she had been on the way to the water.

"No," she said, "I want to sing my song."

"You didn't nap long enough. You tired, now hush and come on."

But she just stood there on the path with her lip poked out, a little bitty brown girl acting like a grown woman, acting like she didn't know what it meant to obey because of fear of being whipped.

The few trees rustled in a little bit of a breeze. We stood there in the broken shade of green leaves, the orange dirt all dusty on my ankles, dusty on her black shoes. I searched for something wise or loving to say, and remembered my father's speech of misunderstood words the day before Overseer took me, the day before my mother died running with me, the day before I began to know better than to be defiant for defiance's sake.

Suddie and I stared each other down in heat only the flies could survive.

"Come on, Suddie." The way Tessa told me to come on to the fields, I motioned for her, but she stomped, making clouds of orange dirt, and I went cold in the heat. I rubbed my arms to keep my hands occupied, to held myself still though something clawed to make it's way out of my chest. The glare of the sun turned a blinding, head-ache white. Suddie poked her lips out letting me know once and for all that I could not make her do what she did not want to do.

Her nappy hair glistened in the sun, and I struggled to remember that she wasn't trying to frustrate me like Willie, she was just a baby, and I saw the image; two faces standing over me, one hooded, sad eyes, another with large eyes that rained tears down on me, the heat inside the darkness so intense, my thirst so overwhelming, that my chest ached with the same clawing, something trying to make its way out of my body, and into the crying woman's arms.

I was startled out of the anxiety of that vision, by the piercing screech of Suddie's voice, "No," and I could not hold on.

"I cain't take the heat no more. If you ain't comin, then stay the hell here." My head ached from the hurt of being shunned by my own baby, of being shunned, left abandoned by my own parents. She was still standing there even though I was halfway up the path. I doubled back fast, seeing myself approach from her eyes, a child whose mother could not see her for seeing all the people who reminded her that she couldn't go home.

"Come on here."

I felt my hand come down, and I tried to stop, but I was swinging and smacked her across the backside. The sweat beneath her little dress made the sting on her back loud and accusing in the stiff heat. Cicadas stopped shrilling. I heard my own voice, "Do what I say."

What was I doing? Suddie was crying louder now into the heat. The trees bent over me in a stare. I commenced walking away from her and the woods, my guilty hands shaking like Old Raymond's the day he smacked me to make me be still in Overseer's presence. I ran to the clearing beside the house, singing a song from Maw Janie's work in order steady my breath, and be still the chaos in my aching head. I paused in my journey toward the porch to sing some words out loud above her scream and the trees' accusations.

Gonna shout trouble over,
  When I get home.
Gonna shout trouble over,
  When I get home.
No mo prayin no mo dyin
  When I get home.
No mo prayin an no mo dying
  When I get home.
Meet my father
  When I get home.
Meet my father
  When I get home.

I cried, and begged as I ascended the stairs, "Suddie, stop screamin!"

Her screams like an alarm inside of me, like the men hammering on the railway, the vibration traveling across miles and miles of memory, to say that someone is leaving, someone is leaving. Her cries, took me somewhere so deep inside of grief that no air, light or sound existed there. I got myself to the porch and curled up in the rocking chair, where I felt safe.

As dusk approached, I took one of Willie's pipes from the table on the porch and lit it. I rocked and took long draws of sweet calming tobacco into my mouth, then exhaled slow to still my mind. I didn't know what I looked like sitting there, but I felt as old as prayer itself, ancient and haggard at twenty-two. My butt bones, cut into the chair, my hair hung in my face, making blinders for the world outside the porch and the pipe.

The pipe fared better in calming me than biting the dry skin off of my fingers, which were now stinging from my own sweat. I listened to her, still crying out in the trees. I heard myself, *What are you doing?* but I didn't have an answer. In long exhales of smoke, I blew the pain out from my core.

Suddie's crying came up from the trees disturbing all the life; the people in distant houses across quiet fields must have been wondering for sure. The man across the way was probably wondering, past the ears of corn that made the wall again between my life and his. I took another long puff on Willie's pipe and let the cool burning in my throat calm me enough to go fetch her.

I kept my hands quiet where I held her thigh around my hip. Her body convulsed against mine in stressful sobs, but I looked stern toward the house like Old Anna, not letting the child come into my heart.

The next day when Willie came home at midday, Suddie smiled, pushing back her difficult self, and presented him with the sweetness of a two-year-old girl. I stood there like a goose fallen loose from the flock. I wiped my hands on the lap of my old cotton dress wondering what I didn't know how to do that Willie, never being around, knew how to do well. *How did he make Suddie his family?* I looked around for something to occupy me, deciding I would stay away from both of them, as they managed to make kin with each other and a fool out of me.

I went over to the butcher block and commenced to cutting the stew meat Willie brought home for the night's meal.

"I would like to have that for stew tonight," he said.

I watched the two of them out the corner of my eye, him tickling her and reaching in his satchel for the big lollipop. My eyes watered in disbelief of his gifts, of his smile, of Suddie acting like the child I wanted.

I spoke up, stiff against their laughter. "I cain't make it for stew. It's too hot out for that. I'll cook it over the laundry fire and make it like barbecue."

Willie got up and put Suddie in the warmth of his chair, next to the cold iron of the wood stove.

"Light this damn thing and make me a pot of stew, Lilly. I don't ask for much. I work hard and want what I want. Don't question me."

"You work hard where, for who?"

"I work hard for you, and if I ever have to tell you to stay out my business again, you ain't gonna have to worry about where and for who no more."

He didn't raise his voice. His lips were close enough to my ear that I could smell the talc on his chest, the mint leaves on his breath. "Now, listen here, ain't no wife of mine gonna be cookin outside like some common slave set out to the quarters at night. "I want this as stew tonight," he said again, standing at my side, so close to my face, his perfect smooth brown skin, his scent of lye and lavender.

Suddie napped in the chair now, and I wanted him to touch me, to stay. He slapped his hand on the butcher block triumphantly. "Gotta be gettin on." He pushed past me to head out the door, and I let go of my tense, anticipating breath, disappointed in myself for wanting him in the same moment that he threatened to hit me.

I spent the rest of the afternoon over the fire of a wood stove in August. I shook my head at the thought of me insisting that Sybil make biscuits on mid-July mornings. The sweat stung where it dripped in my eyes, and the weight of my wet hair made my neck ache. The house heat up so terrible, it sent me and Suddie out to move every single black seed pod so we could lie under the magnolia.

Stay, I heard Old Raymond say as I looked off down the road waiting for some black angel to come take me away.

The next morning Willie sat at the breakfast table after having come home in the middle of the night. The humidity of the coming day already heavy as dawn broke.

"The cow's got to have some hay, put it out before dark. Don't let yourself forget."

I asked him, "Does that mean you ain't comin back till after dark?" He didn't bother to answer me, just sat there and didn't look at me when

I let my backside brush against his shoulder on my way to stack his dish. He stopped on his way out the door, smacked his lips, a piece of cornmeal from the breakfast stuck in his teeth, and I imagined he was the man from across the road, waking up from a hard sleep and smiling at me like I was the best thing he laid eyes on. He would say something like, "That was better grub than I reckon I'm gonna get in heaven." Then he would reach across the table and take my face in his, his lips full with desire and love for me, and he'd kiss me long.

I hadn't been kissed by Willie or anybody else, ever. Willie had rolled over on me in my sleep and thrust until it was over, but never a kiss. I looked at him, his hands around the glass where he took a departing sip, his lips full and supple, and I wanted his touch; even being pushed away or grabbed by the thick of my arm would have been welcomed. My skin crawled, bare in the heat, nothing but thin cotton covering my body.

He wiped his hands on the napkin that he insisted be dried in the sun and folded, and he tossed the crumpled heap on the table the way Satan used to. On his way out the door he cleared his throat. "You should put on some clothes, Lilly." Then he was gone.

Willie still called himself that, free, as if we all weren't free now. I didn't ask how come other Negro folks looked shabby and run-down, like they couldn't get anything to show for their time working the land, while Willie Kellem's land was overgrown with blackberry vines, fallen branches, and weeds, while he rode a real good horse and buggy, had nice clothes. Didn't none of it make sense. Whenever I said Suddie needed shoes or that something in the house was broken, things got thrown on the eating table still wrapped in brown paper and string, with no trace of the bloody fingers that had to pick the cotton, sheer the wool, or skin the beast.

"You like the bed I got for Suddie?" He asked this for every new possession.

"Yes, Willie, it sure is nice."

"Yeah, it's nice wood, heavy, high priced," he said, poking out his chest like a rooster.

I didn't ask anything about what didn't make sense, because

I remembered what Maw Janie said. "Don't always be askin questions, just be grateful for what you have."

I remembered the crazed look in my mother's eyes when she tried to see where my father had gone each night. And I vowed to never become obsessed.

So, without asking anything, I turned the crib up on end and put good sheets on Suddie's new bed in Satan's old room, making room for Willie to roll over on me again, his eyes blank without notice of me.

July 1874

WHEN I WAS BIG with the next child I tripped over myself every time I took too many steps too fast. My awkward body, long legs and arms, huge belly threw me off balance, badly enough sometimes that I was practically running to keep from falling, and Suddie ran around in front of me laughing, thinking I was finally being playful.

One day the sun beat down, drying and cracking the earth after many days without rain. Trying to catch Suddie before she pumped all the good water out the well, I fell on my way to her. My elbows crashed on the hard orange dirt like I was falling on bricks, sending a shock through my whole body, and my water came out in big gushes.

I walked to the bedroom with Suddie in tow, and it felt like the baby inside me forced her head like a cornmeal stone grinding on the bowl of my womanhood. I resisted the instinctive push.

I took the sheets from the feather bed, placed them on the floor, propped myself upright, and pushed. Suddie lay on the bed above me, asking a whirlwind of questions that faded below my pain. My body rose and fell in waves of gripping stabs, and I didn't feel when the baby was coming, but I pushed with the last pain that rolled through my body like the earth quaking slow from one mountain to the next, until there, sticky with life, was my new daughter. I chuckled at the sight of her, laid her on the deflated sack of my belly, and rested before nursing her.

She was dark like Willie, but her hair was slick and long to her narrow bruised shoulders; like my mother's story of Aunt Dove, the new baby that had been brought out into the light after several days with the women singing and healing. Her father marveled at the dark-haired child. "Chito; a warrior, protector he will be," he said, clapping. My mother's aunt hushed him, "Binili," waving for him to sit down and be quiet. "She is strong, she is a girl." And her father smiled. "Yes, Alla Chitoh."

My mother was lost in the story, lost in her insanity, and she whispered, *"Chi hohchifo nanta?"* What is your name, child? And she did not care that I rolled over and went to sleep, knowing she was lost again, knowing she was not talking to me.

I looked down at my new baby, and I vowed that I would never take refuge inside my own mind and leave my daughters defenseless.

My body opened up to let the afterbirth flow, tears, blood, pain in my every breath. I felt the strangling grip of memory. I wanted for my mother's song, her hands. I remembered a voice deeper than my mother's, sultry and dark like the grieving voices that sang for Old Raymond. Someone singing over me, her arms full of me. I hushed my thoughts, and let myself hold my new baby. Her lips struggled to receive food, but there was nothing while her cord still fed on my life.

She opened her eyes, and they were familiar eyes, eyes that I longed for from someplace far beneath layers of leaves on some distant forest floor. I heard the word "Ishki" inside my head, and without understanding the current of my grief, I cried in deep sadness as the rain fell in sheets, as Suddie dozed on an off, on the feather bed above me.

Suddie's head came and rested there on my shoulder. "Three is a strong bond," I remember my mother saying one night when she was afraid my father would not come home from the meetings.

After a while, I felt strong enough to clean up. My one hand swirled the towel around in the basin of water, to reveal her brown skin, like the faces around the fire at Bartlette's. I wondered if she would grow to look like them, shoulders and hips nudging in the shuffle of a dance around the fire, all the grown-ups the same color brown, their bodies all the same, the scent of boiled pork, and beans satisfying after a long day of harvesting. I shook loose the familiar image and wiped my baby's skin, so dark brown beneath my blood. I swirled the rag in the clear water, then pink water, then red water, and I took the three of us to the kitchen; the baby in the crook of my arm, Suddie's hand in mine, and I lit the lanterns, heated the meat knife, and cut the baby loose from me.

In the morning I woke up hearing the same voice of the songs, a gentle, familiar voice whisper, "Sleep by day, little one, sleep. It's time for me to go to the fields." I woke up thinking I would give anything to go back to the innocence of my childhood mornings at LeFlore, to go back and never get lost. Then I heard Virginia coo for her first feeding, and knew this was home.

That day I rocked in the shade of the porch, and Suddie chased the chickens, chased flies, chased ants into the cracks of the earth. I was so tired, I couldn't do anything but sit there on the porch, feed the baby, and watch the other one play.

I watched the people go about their business, planting, walking to the county station, to church. It seemed like every time I looked off the porch in any direction, there was a new house dispersed among the trees. Willie said if the new jobs for the railroad, and Northern textile keep moving South, there won't be any space between us, and town. The thought of it made me feel the trapped feeling of Overseer's body on top of mine. I shook my mind loose from almost sleep, and watched the movement of the people to keep me awake. I couldn't figure what made other folks have so much energy, and seem so happy. Willie came up the road in the wagon and parted the folks walking to church. He held his head up and forward. His hat made him look taller as folks clinched their teeth to keep from using the Lord's name in vain while the horse hooves and wagon wheels raised a huge cloud of dust that settled on their good clothes. He had missed the whole thing. Another child appeared like the meat he brought home, packaged up and tied without him ever having to see or smell the mess.

He lifted the clean bundle of child from my arms and grinned and giggled like a boy getting a new toy. "Look at her, Lilly. Look just like me. My girls. I think ya'll both look like schoolteachers to me, maybe nurses. I can see this one is as smart as Suddie. What did you name her?"

"Mm hm." I folded my arms across my leaking breasts and left the three of them outside.

The next day, I watched the man toiling in the heat. He seemed happy to work so hard. "Hee-aw" to the mule, and she dragged the load of fallen branches, dead stalks, and weeds out of the fields, in the same backbreaking fashion that Maw Janie and I cleared the fields after the Union raid.

Over the years the man had been the seasons for me. He commanded and the mule pulled. At harvest time, his woman emerged and tended to the picking and hauling of the summer crop. Now there was a little one almost Suddie's age. Every now and then the boy ran in and around and between the woman's legs, disappearing in the rows of vegetables.

They were something to watch, so happy, and I reckon I was like Massa's daughters peering from behind the curtains, except I held a straw broom in one hand, baby at my open blouse with the other. I wondered if this was what my mother felt like, not much to worry about, but not much to make life worth something.

Vanishing just out of my sight, Suddie ran to find mischief. She would have been the one to have her feet branded back on Massa's plantation, to teach her that feet were for stepping in the cotton-picking rhythm, not running.

Later in the morning I peered off the porch as long as I could, till the heat couldn't be tolerated. I thought to myself, *I'd rather be sweatin in the field alongside the man, my baby running round my feet, my other baby tied to my body, than to be in this big house with everything I wanted, unhappy with no man around who would treat me like he wanted me.* I saw his head bobbing, and I knew the man was singing. I closed my eyes and listened real close to the faint memory of Maw Janie singing in the field, her song absorbed by the cotton, his song coming to me through the rustle of corn grass.

My ol missus promis me,
When she die she set me free.
Lived so long her haid got ball,
Give up the notion of dyin atall.

Come along, little chillun, come along,
Wile the moon is shinin bright
Git on board, down the river float,
We gonna raise a ruckus tonight.

My ol missus say to me,
John, Ize gonna set you free.
But when dat haid got slick an ball,
Couldn't killed her wid a big green maul.

My ol missus nevah die,
Wid her nose all hooked and skin all dry.
But when ol miss she somehow gone,
She lef po John a-hillin up de corn.

Ol mosser likewise promise me,
When he die he set me free.
But ol mosser go an mak his will,
For to leave me plowin ol Beck still.

Way down yonder in Chittlin Switch,
Bullfrog jump fum ditch to ditch.
Bullfrog jump fum de bottom of de well,
Swore, my Lawd, he jumped fum Hell.

His laughter was absorbed by the humid air. When I opened my eyes he looked like a nigger bending and stepping, so I closed my eyes again and just listened to his voice. Didn't have any idea what his song meant, but he sounded like a swarm of locusts coming cross the distance of quiet hot air. Every time Virginia went to cry a little, I sang, "Hush, hush," put my teat back in her mouth. Every time Suddie asked for something, "I need some bread," I ran to the darkness of the kitchen, snatched it up for her, and bent my ears back in the direction of the man.

One day he halted his work and looked up to wipe the sweat, and I thought he saw me way in the distance, heat wavering in his vision. He looked with his hand up near his forehead like he noticed for the first time that a woman was watching. Embarrassment almost made me holler, "How do, sir?" but I scurried out of the rocking chair, about tripped over the edge of my skirt. I scooped up Suddie in the free arm and made my way inside, locking the heat outside. I tried to stop the thumping in my chest before I got the baby all upset. I didn't know what was wrong with me, I had never felt overcome like that.

Later I felt foolish for acting that way, but I sat up late that night feeling flush. A rush of energy went through me every time I thought about him looking at me. I put my free hand on the tense place of my womanhood. I thought about him until I barely had enough strength to reach over and turn down the lantern.

For the rest of summer gathering and fall planting, I stood bold on the porch, making sure to put my hair in a bun, to wear the clean skirt and blouse, but I couldn't tell if he was looking my way, the way he wiped his brow, then drank water from the flask. I milked the cow before the light was clear enough to make out any figure, and I watched for him then, like I watched for him all day.

Fall 1874

THE CRISP SMELL OF FALL, leaves settled at the bottom of distant water. The remains of crops dried up and surrendered to the coming winter. The chatter of birds arrived from faraway places, giving thanks for their rest. Life stirred in my chest as I watched the man brace against the warning of frost, to bed down his fields till spring. I knew that soon he'd be walking to the county station for work, and that would bring me closer in his view.

A hat covered his big hair and I could barely see his gentle face. Gloves covered his hands, a wool shirt and an old suit coat covered his chest on his way to the town work. His woman strolled beside him all bundled up, but I didn't pay her any mind. In the evenings, he strode home in the procession of other folks with a lantern. His light broke away from the bobbing lights like a firefly, across his fields, then he disappeared to the place. Surely his home was warm each night with the woman who had come home much earlier, her child, a fire, words and glances. I imagined myself in her chair, smiling at my strong husband, the glow of a crackling fire on us, our son resting across the room in the tiny house.

The air was filled with the smell of hickory and pork. Folks smoked up the meat for winter, and I closed my eyes and saw myself quiet, holding the hickory chips in my skirt and listening to Tessa carry on about getting married to a handsome man of wealth like Massa Bartlette, some man with money like Willie.

That night Willie brought our smoked meat home from town wrapped in brown paper with string, and when the fire burned out in the middle of the night, he turned over on me. Seemed like every night now, way late after he came in, he turned over on me. Right when I was getting a mind to drift off in my sleep, I'd be thinking sweet thoughts about the man across the way, and he'd turn over on me, like he somehow got it in his head that my hair up in a bun, and my blouses washed white was all for him.

I got an itching on the back of my neck, each time, hoping that he wouldn't get himself to the point of flowing into me, hoping I wouldn't get pregnant again.

I kept my eyes closed and drifted away to a dream where I was a baby, and some slave woman danced over me. The round part of her hips led her movements, her hands soft on the air. I listened and her words rained down on me. "Lilly, I'm gonna look for you in heaven." Then her face rose up from mine, and her pink lips came down and almost swallowed me. It was dark, and I could feel the damp warmth of her breath and smell the sun in her kinky braided hair.

I stayed still there waiting for the sound of her voice again, but another voice came heavy. "Lilly!" I opened my eyes and couldn't feel my body beneath Willie's.

Seemed like the sun rose late that morning. When I woke, a light frost coated the picture window. The fire was long since out. Willie had fled the house without so much as nudging me for his breakfast, and my head was heavy there on my pillow. When I put my hand on the frosty glass of the picture window, the heat made water in my palm. Virginia shied away from my sweaty touch, and I sat her close on the rug, where I intended to keep her in my sight while I stoked the fire. Suddie sat there wrapped in my shawl, Willie's long underwear, the baby's blankets, and a pair of my bloomers, which sat lopsided to keep her head warm.

When my shaking started I tried to hold my hands steady while I stacked kindling in a scattered fashion, tried to resist the slanting of the floor and the fireplace. I put the driest logs on top, and fanned. My girls were grateful for the warmth as the flames grew, but the throbbing in my skull set to boil. I thought, *Must be a cold coming on. I'll light the fire, then rest,* but my body fell limp to the floor. I felt myself floating, a peacefulness like being a girl bathing in the tin tub in the warm sun that came through my window in a shaft of light holding me safe, comforted by the sight of Earleen and Emma's dancing dress hems waltzing around me to fetch a towel, my toy boat.

My spirit rose above my own head, above the rug, the girls, the table and chairs high into the rafters of the dark wooden house. I saw the three of us there where the glow of the firelight kept us locked in a trance; the sweet smell of the wood reminded me of someplace distant and damp that felt like home, and through the ceiling my spirit rose up through the wood grain of the rafters and to the cool white clouds and sky blue. I saw little particles of light, and heard that voice again. *Lilly, I'm gonna see you in heaven.*

I heard Suddie call, "Mommy; Mommy," like the caw of a crow, like my own voice so long ago in Overseer's wagon, the jolt of the rough road hushing me. My new wings beat slow and hesitant at her sound, and the sound of the woman's voice, so sweet and intoxicating.

Doubting too long, wings caught in the cobweb clouds of the ceiling and sent me plummeting down into my yellow whip welted body, into the hot blood of my fever.

There is strong, like the mule pulling the plow with the force of muscle and bone, and there is strong, like the shock of a solid hand, cool, on a feverish forehead. His spirit moved through his hand and stirred my soul.

"Lilly," a voice called. The face was not far now, was not shielded by the dust of parched earth turned up in early summer, not shielded by the hat bending against a brisk wind. His face was gentle and right with me by the light of a candle.

All the blankets, all the clothing of my house, his coat, were all piled on me. His hand was wide and whole where it rested on my forehead, a comfort like the weight of a good blanket on a cold night.

"I'm sorry to be up in yo house, Mrs. Willie Kellem. I just knowed somethin was wrong from the sound of that spirited gal of yours. I could hear her screaming for you all the way to the road. I had to leave my journey goin to workin, and get up in here. I is sorry though if my bein here is any embarrassment. Sometimes folks cain't hear after sufferin such a bad fever with this awful influenza. Can you hear me?"

He stammered on his words, but his voice was sturdy, deep, and honest. "I sho hopes you can talk, ma'am. Is you hearin me?"

I didn't know what to say.

"I'm fine." I said, "I must've caught a chill or somethin." The sound of my voice talking to somebody who was not Willie or the girls was strange.

"My name is Emmanuel Jenkins. You was on fire with fever, but I sees you better now." Out of the corner of my eye I could see the window, dark, only the reflections of the room. On the night table sat the chamber pot that I used to teach Suddie to use the outhouse full of pump water and a rag. I looked away and smiled a bit, too uncomfortable to say anything, and I felt the muscles in my face quiver from where they hadn't smiled for so long. The candle glowed in the room to bring light to the winter darkness and I felt like the warm sun was shining on my smiling face right then.

"I best be goin," he said, ashamed, grabbing his hat, and I struggled for some words that wouldn't make him embarrassed, but would keep him with me a while longer. I sat up on my elbows and spoke out to him.

"I ain't tryin to laugh at you in no way, but that there basin is for teachin my child how to go to the outhouse." He turned around and took a long look at the bowl on the table. His dark puff of hair stood high in the rafters, and I giggled again, in embarrassment of his beautiful broad face, sweet brown and smooth. He covered his mouth with his hat, and the two of us laughed; him like the sound of a horse neighing, me like the squawk of a guinea fowl. It was the best sound I ever heard in that house, my giggles and his laugh in harmony like the men and women heading up the road singing together on their way to church.

"Hush now, yo babys is sleepin in the other room, and you fine enough now to be left to you own keeper."

He calmed his chuckling, gently lifted his coat off me, and we looked into each others eyes until I felt naked and looked away. Emmanuel Jenkins cleared his throat and looked around at the room. "It's getting late in the evening now, a whole day gone from my work."

"Where your woman?" I asked, looking at the wall.

"Oh," he said, stammering a bit, "she goes to tend a woman of the church every now and then. You know, takes her turn among the other womenfolk. She takes the boy with her."

He folded the rim of his hat, nervousness in his hands. He looked over his broad shoulder at the door, and before I could thank him, he was gone from Willie Kellem's house.

I remembered that song Old Raymond sang for Missionary Man.

Yes, I am glad,
Lord, I been born again.
Yes, I am happy,
Bless the Lord.
I been born again.

February 1875

I DID THE CHORES, and rested between each one. Weaned Virginia with the cow's milk so she wouldn't get the illness. One of the women from further down the road, closer to town had died of it, and I was grateful for my body's ability to regain its strength.

I walked every day to the chicken house, milked the cows, fed my children. Ever since that night, I couldn't think about anything but Man-Across-the-Way. I took the privilege of calling him Man in all my imagined conversations, and those conversations helped me to be more happy when I dealt with Virginia and with Suddie. Sometimes. I even smiled at Suddie's silly old songs, and at Virginia pulling up and falling trying too early to learn to stand up. Suddie softened to me, but every time I buttoned her and Virginia up to go into town with Willie, I caught myself putting his wishes before mine, "Mind your poppy," and I kept buttoning without looking into eyes that questioned my strength the way I questioned Old Raymond's and Maw Janie's.

February and March, winter set in deeper than in December. Sun came less often, but I got up spirited every morning, saw Willie off; waited for a glimpse of Man at the window, and as he passed by way of the road he was all bundled up. He had such big fuzzy hair now to keep his head warm, and every bit of him seemed precious to me, precious, like hidden treasures visited for a while and then tucked away from other hands. When he wasn't with the woman, he waved a quick one for me, and I imagined him smiling at me. The girls and I danced around the room; Suddie doing a shuffle dance, and the baby on my hip. They didn't know what was all the fuss, but Virginia screamed and giggled, and Suddie unfolded her strong brown body and danced hard like a little girl ought to. The fire crackled in the background for our music, and we danced and laughed; I was the only one knowing what brought that kind of joy.

"Mrs. Lilly Kellem?" Man said, and I stood there in shock. The cold air whipped at his back. The fire crackled with the sounds of my cold children whining behind me. "Maw-mee, shut the door," Suddie demanded.

"Ma'am, you be well these days?" he said, and I was quick to quit looking dumbfounded.

"Course I am. It be a few weeks now. What I be made out of if I'm still sick after all this time, Man?" All the imagined conversations helped the words come smooth. We grinned a bit, and my whole body relaxed in warmth.

"I like that, Man."

He shuffled his feet a little in the bit of snow that dusted the porch. He looked at me and smiled. I smiled back until it seemed silly to keep straining my face that way.

"Maw-mee." The girls were caught in the cold draft of air sweeping over the floor of the big room. Suddie sat too close to the fire, and Virginia crawled to get closer too.

Finally, Man saw fit to back away, waved a bit, and bowed. He almost fell backward off the porch like a silly little boy. He turned and jumped down, his shoes smacked in a cold landing. He threw his sack over his shoulder and got on down the road. And sure enough, I thought I was going to sprout wings right out of the welted flesh on my back. Every happy song from the plantation fireside rung in my head.

Almost every day following that day, Man found some kind of way around his woman's coming and going, and Willie's coming and going, to stop by to give a hello and a smile. It was all I could do every day to pay any attention to Suddie begging for things, "I want some bread, Mommy," and Virginia cooing and still reaching for my breast after being weaned for months. All I could think was, *Is Man stopping by?* I looked to see where he might be watching from, the bare gray trees, the tiny windows of his house, across the fields awaking to spring. Every sound was his footsteps on the porch, and any day he did come, I was like the sun after a long dreary winter.

One spring morning, Willie looked at me, looked at me direct to figure on me, and my new nature. He stared across a fork full of eggs, paused with the fork just beneath his nose. His eyes were like that day when I saw him appear out from the woods behind the smokehouse, innocent, but spoiled in having his way. I wasn't hypnotized and longing for his touch anymore. I just stared back. Time had taken everything but his eyes; they still were clear, and white inside the dark sockets. "Hey, gal," I heard him say inside my head, but I brushed my hair away from the old whipping scars on my neck.

"Cut it," is all he said to me, and I stopped my staring, looked away to the back door, and to him again.

"Cut what?" I said back, hiding my new confidence behind the old shame.

"Your hair," he said, eating the fork full of eggs. He seemed satisfied to have found something to say that would have me responding right away.

"Cut your hair, Lilly. It's just ugly like that. You'll be happier if you look more like the women around here." He wiped his mouth with the napkin he said needed to be washed, dried in the sun, and folded.

"I wouldn't know, Willie. Guess I best get to town and see what them women's hair do look like."

There was a time when bickering with Willie left me feeling like I still had hold of something that was mine. I felt my confidence rise like the fur on a bear's neck, my voice deeper and clear.

He tossed his napkin on the table like he always did to let me know that my show of power didn't lessen his idea of my place in things. He sauntered out of the kitchen, looked at the rafters and beams like

Satan used to do, checked to see that everything was still in the same place. I wanted to say to him that I got another man that is going to know how to treat me, that somebody likes my hair, but I heard a voice from way back say, *Be still Lilly, and latch hold of something.* I thought, *Let Willie think I'm down under him, let him think it, 'cause in the meantime I'm gonna be fixin myself to go off with Man.*

I looked out the window at the girls playing in the dirt. Suddie chased the chickens in her good shoes. I looked out past the field that Man and his wife tended well, and already the cornstalks were knee high, soon to block the view of their house in the distance. I looked up the road as far as I could toward town, and down the other way, toward the river, and felt my heart tighten in my chest as I imagined going out past the yard, but relaxed in thinking Man and I would leave together, and two or three days would pass before Willie would turn over in bed and wouldn't find me there.

The cleaver that I used for chopping sat on the block beside the stew meat that was already going rank. My head began to ache like the day Suddie screamed in the woods. I laid my head down on the chopping board and brought the cleaver down across the length of my long dark hair, which had never been cut, and it fell heavy to the floor in sacrifice. I got up, numb, thinking, *Man gonna like it just the same.* I called the girls in for their lunch and a nap knowing that Man might be coming by soon.

Suddie came past me all sweaty and smelling like spring. "Mommy, you look like a heathen," she said, reminding me that I was Choctaw and she was Negro. Her leather shoes and white socks ran past me to get to the kitchen, where I had prepared buttered bread. Virginia came slow, struggling to get up each step, and without looking at me she toddled to catch up with her sister; nine months old and walking away from me like her sister. The two of them were brown like walnuts. They ate their bread and butter, looking at each other with eyes squinted, and then giggling.

Days, weeks, months passed without Man standing up in the fields to look my way. I spent days thinking about why he didn't come for me, and nights dreaming about him. When the leaves turned and everything got harvested he started up the road every morning with his woman, both of them more and more bundled up as the days got cold. My hair longer, but still uneven, I stood there in the door every day wondering what I was needed for, my hair like an uneven skirt, a few inches at one end, and the length to my shoulder on the other side.

April 20, 1876

I T WAS MY twenty-fifth birthday, the rain came across the land like sheets blowing on the clothesline. "Tide's comin up the river. Come a tide!" folks shouted on the road on the way to higher ground. Willie came running out of the down pour of water, unhitched the horse in the barn and ran to the shelter of the porch, looking like an ant, his suit all shiny and black-wet around his skinny body.

"Is we leavin Willie?" I said, holding Virginia in my shawl, and with Suddie dressed for travel, excited for the adventure.

"No," is all he said.

The next day the floodwaters made the road disappear. Willie got up, looked out the door with me, and said, "Well, light up the stove, we stuck here. I suppose we have to eat."

I put breakfast on the table for Willie and let the girls sleep. I shuffled across the floor to pour the thick melted sugar and butter for his pancakes. I dragged myself joyless around the kitchen with the grief of wanting Man. I didn't look at Willie, but allowed myself to be with my thoughts.

Why do I stay? New baby isn't the excuse anymore. I tried to come up with reasons the way I did when things were quiet around the house, just Virginia and me, Suddie gone to the freedman's school on Willie's insistence. I would make lists of reasons to stay while I waited for Willie to bring Virginia back each day. But, all my lists ended in knowing that I was Willie's property by law, and all I was allowed to own was the notion that what was his was mine. I rocked by the quiet fireplace those days, not going out of the house or out of the yard. *Man not coming around anymore, Why don't I leave?*

The sound of a silver ring pinged against the black iron of the stove and it lay there on the ashy stone. Willie chewed his food like a cow, not looking at me when he said, "Happy Birthday. There it is; now quit pouting and actin like you ain't been properly married."

I realized then, staring at Willie, the light coming slow in the window on the side of his head, that I stayed because being a woman was kin to being a slave; free only if a man says, just like being a slave and free only if a white person says. My life was just a cycle of waiting: waiting for my father to say run, waiting for Willie to say run, now waiting for Man to say lets run.

My thoughts tangled in and around one other. "My birthday was yesterday," I said stiffly as I wiped the table, angry at both Man and Willie for making me wait the way my mother waited.

By the time Virginia woke, and I sat by the stove feeding her, my thoughts had calmed and returned to the whirlpool of questions. The ring lay there on the ashy stone beneath the hard black iron stove, and Willie didn't say anything until an unexpected tear spilled out of my eye. The empty place in my chest where nothing existed opened up defenseless, and Virginia struggled to get out of my lap. I put my hand over my mouth, surprised at the whimpers that escaped, and Willie said without looking up at me, "It's nice, isn't it? Well, put it on," and I picked up the silver band that said, *Lilly Kellem* on the inside, and slid it over my crocked middle finger.

That afternoon, the tide came. We watched from the open door, and Virginia ran from the safety of the house to fetch her precious glass marbles which were taken into the current in one sweeping motion of a strong wave. Suddie ran down the steps to try and grab Virginia's flailing arm, but her feet faltered and they were both swept into the muddy water to the sound of my scream. Willie and I both ran to rescue them. We slid down the front steps on the shifting muddy slant of the yard, and into each other, grabbing clothes and skin before disappearing into the gush of brown water.

The current was swift, and each time the water submerged me; my eyes still wide open; my arms and legs flung loose and separate in the under current that guided me around the threatening wood planks of someone's barn. *My babies will die. Why wasn't I paying attention? Thinking of Man.* I bobbed to the surface with enough time to release air and grab another deep breath before being pulled again into the agitated water, the sounds so muffled, then the roar of water raging above the faint sound of Virginia's screams. She was still alive.

I struggled to keep myself breathing in the current, and wondered how Suddie and Virginia would ever know to do the same. The cage of my ribs burned and each breath threatened to rip me open there in cold foam. *If the girls die, I don't want to live.* I offered my truth to the white sky above me.

The moss-covered coolness of angled rocks beneath my clinging feet guided me along toward saving Virginia, and then shifted me toward near misses of my skull against the walls of some well-built shed.

My hands caressed and then grabbed the raised roots of a tree, and I was above the water gasping for air, afraid that the water would take me from where I squirmed to stay on the flat piece of barn door that had wedged itself precariously between two great oaks. They had surely been planted by the old white people who must have owned the house in the distance, white pillars as big around as the oaks, an old proud couple who were certain to see their great-grandchildren climb among the limbs.

Using the bottom of my feet to suction me to the wet slick door, I stood up, but did not see the girls or Willie, just crests of brown that confused the lines of where the road once was, the fields, the yards of the big houses, and rooftops of the sharecropping cabins. I leaned into the growing rage of the creek and became one among the goat turds, stray work boot, and fancy women's underpants, and there on a tall gray rock was Willie, shirtless. Virginia flailed, full of life, in one of his arms. He reached into the turbulent water where Suddie held tight to the rusted fencing that had once kept our chickens in the coop. In my rising and sinking vision, I saw her first struggling to hold on to his arms. His arms never looked strong beneath the white shirt, but now I saw the lean muscle of a resilient body straining to keep Virginia and Suddie from slipping away. I watched on growing heavier as my skin wrinkled in the chilled water. Willie summoned up the will and strength and pulled to keep his children to him as I drifted past them in the swollen creek, unseen.

The water sucked me down, and when I rose above the foam, I saw the three of them downstream. They ran tight, like a pack of dogs dripping and filthy. They ran through a line of woods, graceful in dodging the jagged trees. Willie's eyes guided their flight and charted my journey. I almost felt love for him, felt the energy to fight for my life, felt the circle, the cool ring, on my finger, and thought that if I did not drown, I would not think again of leaving.

The waters slowed and subsided where the roads of Oktibbeha county station made unnatural gullies. Sacks of dirt were piled around the high decks of the weathered wood of buildings. Exhausted whites and Negroes, dead animals, tree limbs washed up there, and so did I.

Suddie and Virginia waded through the shallow, slow water to where my weak body quivered like a new calf. I stood and fell back, weak, into the raw waters. Willie and Suddie each pulled me up by one arm.

"She's all right Poppy," Suddie yelled obedient, Willie's scout giving details of her mission, "She's all right," and Willie slid down with Virginia on his hip, his eyes wide as he came to where I struggled, in the place where he thought he might lose me.

When he saw me walking on my own, he stepped back on the Negro side of the planked sidewalk, buttoning the dripping shirt that somehow followed him downstream, he looked around and composed himself.

Even with the roads filled with silt, I could see that the county station had not changed, except for the deck and overhang built for a train whose tracks were concealed by the boardwalk and row of establishments.

Willie sat Virginia down in front of me, and rubbed his muddy shirtsleeves in embarrassment. He looked to where the girls and I still wobbled, and then nodded grimly at the white folks who waded along, fetching themselves and their belongings to the white people's side of the road. "She's all right." He gestured to some old white man in fine clothes who paid him no mind. We walked home by way of high ground through the woods. Willie talked to the girls but acted like he didn't know me. I twirled the ring to keep it from setting in the caked mud on my fingers, and wished I'd thought sooner to lose it in the floodwaters.

In the days that passed, Willie wouldn't accept help recovering like the other folks did. Each group took turns at one another's places. Folks who worked shares all banned together to right things after the tragedy of lost crops and dead cattle.

"Willie, don't you think we ought to talk to some folks about sharing the load?" I suggested gentle, though I was resentful about hauling dirty water out and clean water in for wiping things while Willie just paced, worried, and fussed over how long it would be before things were dry enough to get the wagon out and get on up the road.

"Naw, Lilly," he said, moving around the girls and pushing past me to get to the window again. "And don't ask me again. I got enough on my mind."

"Willie, I got Suddie till the schoolhouse gets cleaned up, but that ain't good enough help to get the house clean. It'll take months. It's going to be summer before we get this cleaned up by ourselves. The least you could do is stay around and help with our house." He asked me to be quiet, and I turned away, mold making the whipped wounds on my back itch. I ignored my irritation and fussed on about having to do the work myself.

Old Raymond had stood at the stew pot one night, keeping me near him when I told him that the healing wounds itched like fire ants. He said, "Fire is present in all things; the light of the moon, the veins inside ripe fruit, the dry stacks of wood not yet split, the hatchet waiting for the time to lay metal to wood." It was present in the flat, smooth flesh of Willie's open hand. He gestured with his right hand open and shaking at the side of his own head. I could see that he wanted to strike me, hammer his smooth hand against my sun-toughed cheek. I knew that he longed in that moment to see my lopsided hair fly in the direction of the collision. My eyes returned an angry stare at the short-statured man Maw Janie had warned me of. We both stood on the wood floors turned dirt floors in Willie Kellem's house. He turned around still shaking his hand in response to me.

"Maw mee?" Virginia whispered, and reminded Willie and me that the girls watched on with rags in their hands and tied on their heads. Virginia stared up at Willie frightened that the ceiling and walls of her home would melt into the same mush of the floor. She broke down into the same screams that carried her downstream, but Suddie turned away to the scrubbing of the table legs. I stood quiet in the storm of tension.

"Damn it, Lilly. I said don't rile me now. I have my own worries. Least you can do is quit acting like a kept nigger and clean the goddamn house."

The horse bore the whip for his anger. He yelled with each lash, "Hee yaw," and she strained baring teeth to haul Willie and the wagon through the muck of our yard and up the muddy path to wherever he found exile.

Summer 1876

THE SMELL OF HONEYSUCKLE was strong with the intensity of the summer heat. The wisteria petals floated purple through the warm air, the vine wrapped around the porch, like the desire that crept up my legs, up my spine, unsatisfied passion for Man. I watched again each day to see him framed by the vibrant yellow and orange of tiger lilies.

The height of the corn blocked my sight and I took to pretending I could see Man, weeding, and toting water to keep the corn alive. My hair pushed out long from the roots on the energy of my longing. The music in my heart was wild and erratic like a high-strung banjo, and the more I waited, all knotted up the more the imagined conversations with Man grew resentful. *You too busy to find time to come callin on me again?*

The girls ran and played with the butterflies, and I thought how much I wanted to feel that way again, not worrying about anything, just playing, free, and I slipped from resentment to grief. *Did man still care about me? Was he still there across the way?* Laundry piled itself up for weeks at the back door while I questioned and aged.

One day I just kept thinking about what the redheaded woman had said; "Don't be caught standin still like that;" and I got angry with Man and with myself. Then I heard Tessa's voice, "You know, everybody but you is gettin themselves a plan about runnin on away from here." *Do somethin Lilly, do somethin,* I thought as I put water in the cauldron and stirred the clothes, then scrubbed them, a labor for my heavy grieving arms and legs. When the chore was done Suddie and Virginia slept in the shade of the magnolia tree, lazy taking for granted that other kids were working the share all spring and summer till harvest, and they just played, napped, and waited for school to start up.

I watched past the edge of the yard for something moving besides the treetops and high grass in the slight breeze of late summer. Nobody was going up the road, nobody coming down. I sat there on the ground, my cotton dress getting even dirtier than it already was. I tried to calm my own thoughts. I picked at my dry feet and thought I saw the top of his straw hat past the corn. I smoothed the cool ring on my finger. *Who did Man think he was, comin for to see me when he felt like it and me not having no say on when I see him?*

Willie's underwear peeped from behind the house in the exhausted air, clapping out answers in the breeze that went past the clothesline and slunk around the corner of the house to where I sat.

I chewed back the skin on my sun-browned fingers, chewed it back to the yellow skin of winter. I sat there listening to the sound of bugs, then the sound of something that felt like death sneaking up on me. It was a fear of dying like this; napping under the magnolia, as the tree stretched out wide, like big hips to accommodate new children. I stared at the wall of Emmanuel's corn, cussing it for keeping me out. My tanned legs quivered in a shock of nerves, my butt bones pressed into the earth with restless rocking, and in the moment of pondering, I was on my feet.

I stood up and looked around at the yard: the hum of bugs, green trees, burned brown bushes, clay earth smelling rich out back where the wash water was dumped, the barn worn and gray. The cow out behind the house grazed and left warm piles for me to step in. The outhouse door was cracked open, waiting for somebody to tend to shoveling clean earth in over the stench where flies hummed. Across the road, the corn wall reached its stalks rustling slightly.

Curiosity pulled at my collarbone. I needed to know if Man was still there, if he was thinking about me the way I was thinking about him. I crossed the yard, I crossed the road. I looked back at the two little heaps of life resting. I looked down at my feet, bare and dry, pale against the orange earth. The heat of summer baked my neck, the cry of cicadas rose in warning. I asked myself, *What am I doing?* and I entered the corn slow and stealthy.

I came up on his house and looked through the window. My heart throbbed in my neck, as I heard man's voice, almost a whisper inside the house, the sound of bugs drowning him out. "You ain't gettin fresh on me is you?" I heard him say playfully. I thought to run, *What am I doing?* But realized he might see me. I heard giggles in between the sounds he made. My head was almost pressed to the screen, staring off into the distance, lost in the reality of the life I imagined them having. My hair blew in the hot breeze and somebody approached fast from the side of the house.

"Ma'am!" Man yelled out. "You sick again?"

I stood there trying not to squint in the sun for it might make me look old and tired. I brushed my hair out of my face and didn't look to where his pants were still undone.

"Ma'am?" he said again like he couldn't remember my name.

"No, Man, I ain't sick," I whispered. I was fighting back the pain in my head, the bright sun blinding me and making me nauseous. I was lost hearing his voice, hearing him act like I was a stranger, and I was not thinking much about what I was going to say if his woman came out, maybe, "Good afternoon, I'm the neighbor come to call."

I heard her strange voice, "Who that, Man?" All this time, she didn't seem real to me, no face, no voice, but a woman somewhere beyond the dirty screen waited for her man to come back and be with her before going back to the fields. His woman's voice called again, "Man?" and the bumps rose on my skin, instinctual in defense. She called him by the same name I used for him. I looked at Man trying to figure how I was going to explain myself as I heard feet shuffling across the wood floor behind the screen. He and I stared wide-eyed, but he fixed it. "Ain't nothin, Tessa, go on back to the dishes."

I stood there buck-eyed. Tessa, her voice clearer, but still high-pitched. I recognized it now. "Man?" I saw her shadow on the back wall, like her shadow in our cabin in lantern light. She stood, and worked fast to button her top. It was the same two thick braids, the same thick body, that from my distant porch had no form. I stared back at Man. My lunch bubbled into my throat where I swallowed it back. He sported a slight smile, proud of himself for keeping her at bay, having no idea who she was to me. I gathered up my dress and took off in the heat of that Saturday afternoon. My long legs ran and stumbled through mature rows of food. "Lilly," Man whispered after me.

I rested my head in the dirt next to where the girls still slept, and I let myself cry real quiet. I was a fool. Tessa was his wife, and Man had never been my man.

That night I felt my body turning inside out while the girls slept in their room. My head swelled in the heat of a restless night, and even when I thought my mind was done with the matter, a cool tear trailed down my cheek.

In the morning I sat on the porch after Willie had departed at dawn. I tried to collect myself before the girls woke. I wondered, had Tessa known about me and Man? Had she seen me across the way and mocked me for being the wife of Willie Kellem? "Heathens and free niggers don't need to mix." Had she talked to my children in town?

I sobbed into my hands. Laundry from the day before still clapped out back on the dry morning breeze, and I dried my eyes and went to take it down so things would appear normal for the girls, and they did, all day, as I went about my chores without any more expression than a squint in the sun.

Willie did not come in that night as I lay there with the drought moon shining in on me. Just after the girls were breathing deep in the difficult sleep of the thick heat is when I heard him cross the fields. I was drifting in and out of dream while I listened to feet over dry grass. I dreamed about my father running around Bartlette's plantation looking for me, and through my window like a horse jumping the stable gate came Man.

Half asleep, I stood up in the darkness and I tried to collect myself there, to remember my anger with him; acting like he wanted me when he was with Tessa. A wild herd of thoughts stampeded through my mind, until he put his arms around me and I melted into his touch. He hushed me like he was hushing a restless mare. Every part of my body rose and fell with the movement of his hands. He kissed me hard, and I could not stop the rush of sweat and tears that came over me.

The night sky spilled into the room, smelling like water. Coolness came into me and our bodies were one, shuddering and releasing. Summer rain came down to the dry Mississippi earth and my body shimmered like moonlit drops of water. I had never felt this way: gaping open with unquenchable thirst.

My body relaxed beneath his thick, solid strength. The smell of his sweat was sweet on my cool, bare skin. I heard the songs of freedom from around the Saturday fires. The softness of his full lips on mine reminded me of peaches, when I was a little girl, small feet in leather boots dangling from tree limbs, giggles, sweetness running out the corners of my full mouth, until the search party, Nathan, Sybil, Earleen, Emma, and my mother turned up the little girl of LeFlore.

Lying next to him, I felt close to newborn, and as close to death as gnats and butterflies. I was everything I'd ever be. I was a Lilly, nigger woman, who couldn't remember her name under Man's spell. I was young woman hollering in her chest, hungry for her home. I was long-time-ago woman in my mother's stories, power rising and falling, like the river in flood time.

My breath steadied, and concrete thoughts came again: Tessa's Man, the strength of the plow on top of me in Willie Kellem's bed. I thought I must be crazy, but crazy felt like having won something, like having snuck into the smokehouse for salt pork and ham, and lying awake eating without sharing.

As I drifted on the smell of the rain, my exhaustion carried my body sweetly, floating just above sleep, and then into dream. I could see Tessa and me tending the fields together, her singing slave songs and looking up every now and then to say, "What you lookin at? I cain't keep my mind on my work for minding what you lookin for." And I stared at her quiet, not telling her my secret plan. There were flies around my sweat, and I did not flinch so as not to reveal that her children were behind my back. Then I could see the sun beaming down on us brutal, and scorching. I could see the whip that Willie kept hung in the barn, hear the sound of it cutting through the air, see Overseer's hand strained around it, the color red everywhere. I startled awake.

Man and I both heard Willie's horse sigh in weariness, the metal of her harness being undone, and in one move Man had his shirt on, his pants on, and was out the window, headed across the road, where the sound of the heavy rain hushed his flight.

I held on to myself tight, fearing Willie would catch the scent of the head that rested in his place. I turned his pillow over, and steadied my breath into the long exhales of sleep. He climbed onto the feathered mattress, clearing his throat of the damp air, and was snoring before his head lay down.

The next morning, fall opened up like seeds bursting from poppy flowers. I sat on the porch watching Tessa bring down the stalks, Man with his back to her. I wondered if she could see me in the distance. I wondered if she remembered me.

I missed her, but I wanted Man. My spine straightened up in the chair, and I hoped she couldn't see me watching, and she walked on like she didn't even see the girls running in the yard, my rocking kept time with her rhythms.

I wrapped my shawl in a hug of satisfaction, and watched Suddie and Virginia in the cloudy light after such needed rain. A gentle rainbow arched in the distance, and the new colors of red and yellow and maple laughed against the gray sky and made light where there was none.

I took the girls down to the creek that afternoon and we enjoyed hours of cool, early autumn water rushing over our feet. We stayed until the blood in our veins was one with the water. For the second time in my life, I laughed with my girls, my joy contagious.

Man came at least once a week with Tessa gone to tend the dying elder of the church, and every morning I let the bacon burn on the stove. It smoked up the house so bad that I had to let the damp fall air and the bitter winter air flow into the house, waking Willie to a suspicious dawn.

He came into the kitchen after a night stiff in the body because I did not tend the fire after Man left the night before.

"I can smell that burnt meat on my shirt, you know? I cain't wear somethin that looks right but smells wrong."

He snapped his suspenders in place. "You gettin feebleminded, woman."

I kept my back to him and cut the bread, smiling. My hair had grown back, the missing strands, the sacrifice of unloved, unwanted mornings. Maw Janie was wrong. I had what I wanted, in a new way that my mother couldn't have fathomed.

Winter 1876

WILLIE HAD BOUGHT both girls good sweaters that year. He said now both of his girls were going to the freedman's school.

"But Will, she ain't but three yet, Virginia needs to be with me."

He didn't look at me, but kept unwrapping the big package of clothes for her.

"She's tall like you Lilly, almost tall as her sister, and has good talking skills. Don't nobody need to know she ain't five.

"I can't let nothing ignorant come of my girls like it has you."

I turned away from all of them, and went to the back to peel apples for a pie, but after a while I let that alone, because I was scared the knife would get a mind of its own, and cut Willie across the throat.

Willie talked over the bundle of clothes and told the girls they would be wearing the finest clothes to show that white Northern teacher that his girls could speak fine, dress fine, and do fine.

One Saturday morning the air was nice enough for play outside. The dead leaves itched on the back of my throat while the girls ran and kicked the leaf mold into the cool dry air. They played in their good school sweaters, and I let them wear them too, because Willie wasn't there to tell anybody what to be wearing. I wanted Man to get a glimpse of how fine they looked if he came past to give me the signal to let me know if he was coming by that night.

Virginia etched in the dirt with a stick, and called me off the porch to see her drawing, and I wasn't annoyed with the familiarity of her voice, but happy in seeing her little white teeth like corn kernels, something to stop me from making myself crazy with thinking about Man. Her black face looked up at me on the porch, and if it weren't for her dark skin, I would wonder if I wasn't seeing my child self reflected in a pool of water. I stood over her and watched her draw lines in the dirt. "Look, Maw." Long fingers plowing trenches through the orange dirt, her dark brown fingers, innocent, and deliberate. Then I heard the sound of my father's voice, *Do not leave LeFlore. Wait for me,* then the sound of horses muted. My girls hummed while they played, but the sound of horse hooves thundered around me. I was engulfed by white darkness, the curtain beneath the cupboard where I hid that morning, my eyes seeing the men coming for me, my mother standing in the dining room, her eyeballs white, madness in her song. I looked around, frantic in my search to find Sybil, there in the yard, where my girls stood, strangers, staring with wide eyes; *slave children,* I thought, not recognizing Suddie and Virginia, *slave children.* I screamed at them, "Where is my mother? Where is my father?"

The girls froze watching me. I could not stand them watching me. Then I heard the guns, the sky was dark now. *Where is my father?*

I heard the voice calling Tessa. I stared at Virginia for understanding of what was happening. Suddie frowned in disgust. The straw from my slave bed itched in the healed wounds from my beating. *Where am I?* I couldn't stand the way the girls stared at me. Tessa's voice, *You a breeder now, worth more. Here come Overseer.* I hurried across the yard trying not to scream, and grabbed the hands of the two girl children who I did not know, but knew they needed protecting, because Overseer was coming.

Overseer held the tar rope over us. *He can't take them away.* The memories pushed at my back like the force of tornado winds. The sound of the whip. Some woman's voice yelling, *Run, child.* I heard my mother scream. I had never heard my mother scream, then my own voice screaming through time, *Where am I?*

I knew what would come next. *This time*, I thought, *I'll hide.*

As the day passed over and evening fell, I stayed huddled with my girls beneath Willie's bed. There was the sound of buzzing flies trapped and dying after a false spring day. My nervous hands swatted. It was the buzzing that brought me back, slow and certain, to the house of a free man. His name was Willie Kellem. The tall yellow woman, I couldn't remember my name. The wide eyes of the two brown faces beneath the bed were frightening but familiar. I saw my reflection on their eyeballs. The woman with the hair always braided back, always in the cotton dress of a faded nameless color, always with the two ornery brown girls at her bare feet, we were breathing heavy together, then slow as I remembered who we were.

Through the evening, my thoughts wavered between sane and insanity. I hurried around the place doing chores in the lantern-lit dark, trying to stay busy to keep the thoughts off me, like my mother, going mad. Suddie chased behind me. "Who was coming, Mommy? Is somebody coming to do harm? Is it Klansmen? Schoolteacher said we got to mind ourselves and not be uppidy niggers, 'cause of Klansmen."

I scrubbed harder, not taking in her words.

"What about Poppy?" she asked, nervous, as I had never heard her voice before. "What about Poppy?"

I rocked there on the frozen dark porch where hell had consumed me earlier that day. The girls slept in their solid oak beds safe from their mother. I took long drags on Willie's pipe, and exhaled myself to a space of calm. That night in my dreams, I saw Virginia's fingers again, then my father's fingers, long lines and shallow small waves beneath them. The hands turned into Emmanuel's hands, then the hands of the little red fox woman, her one hazel eye stared at me for understanding, then the lines again like trees ascending to the heavens. They turned into Virginia's thin brown legs standing in stagnant water. I woke sweating, and looked around the dim light of the bedroom to see if Willie was beneath the crisp white sheets with me. But my eyes adjusted, and I was free to let go of my breath, and try to steady myself before he was home. I cried there, hoping Man would come. I cried until the weight of my head forced me to lie down again.

"Mommy," Suddie called from the next room.

"Yes," I answered stern.

"You all right?"

"Yes," I answered again, ashamed of myself, and remembering the nights I lay awake listening to my mother toss on the sun-dried sheets, screaming sometimes, calling out in Choctaw that word that I didn't understand, the last word she spoke to me. "Ishki, Ishki."

My heart had opened for Emmanuel, and out came a flock of memories, like trapped doves set free. That night Emmanuel didn't come. Willie came toward morning. I heard him come in, but I was deep in my dream, where I stood in a doorway watching a tall brown woman with a white rag tied tightly on her head in candlelight. She was facing a ghost in a black-hooded cloak, a cloak like the one Willie bought for me, the one that hung in the cedar chifforobe haunting me. In the corner a horse stood over a trough guarding what I did not see, but I knew a child slept there.

I was in the floodwater again, swimming backward, away from Virginia and Suddie. I opened my mouth to scream, and Willie pushed himself into me, his face invisible in the dark. When his movement stopped, his stale sweat dripped onto my cheek and I was awake to see his eyes opened and white.

I lay quietly beneath the sheets, aching inside my body, way deep where the meat of my bones held the fate of that unnamed child in my dream. I drifted away to Missionary screaming, *Sinner, nigger, heathen bitch, adulteress, adulteress.* He pointed at me, and the image shifted to feet yellow, and feet brown, Emmanuel's feet over hard flat earth, hands beating on tree trunks with the sound of our feet leaving.

The next morning, I stayed in bed.

"What, you sick?" Willie asked, not turning around to look at me.

"Yes," I answered without taking the covers from over my head.

"I'll get the girls off to school. You best get some baking soda, and get better, 'cause the cow won't do all day without being milked. And, we for sure can't have you being sick like you were with the influenza."

For months I lay with Emmanuel, never telling him about the dreams and the sleeplessness, the way I walked on eggshells to keep my mind from slipping off to places I didn't recognize. I held on to him like he was the only thing, floating in rushing floodwaters, dreaming with my head on his chest; hushed by his whisper of promises. "Gal, you and me gonna be together one day." And that satisfied me when we laid together. He called me, "Lilly, Lilly," the way a voice called Tessa away from the slave quarters on the night of our freedom.

Seasons passed, our children grew, and our sin settled into the rhythm of satisfying lies.

April 20, 1878

THE NIGHT OF MY twenty-seventh birthday, Emmanuel and I lay butt to butt, Tessa gone off to tend to some always ailing elder of the church, and Willie never home early in the night. The sound of acorns fell to the barn top, mocking the sound of wagon wheels over earth, which kept us alert.

"Lilly," Man whispered below Suddie's earshot. "Tell me, who is Grey Fox? You've been calling out for him in your dreams, sometimes scary the way you sound. Who the hell is he?" He shifted uncomfortably on the feathered mattress.

"The dreams are about my mother's story of her father's last words, and the the dreams turn and are about my father, about the swamp, his hand drawing lines in the dirt for trees, and a pool of still water, telling me that all that is mine will be there. Then he is always fleeing on a horse with the sound of the hooves so loud that I feel like my head is gonna explode, as he gets further and further from me. I just feel like I'm gonna die." I turned over and held on to myself, wanting to keep these two things separate: the dreams and Man.

He shifted again, his broad back rising in uncomfortable breaths beneath the sheets, "Even if your father hid somethin there in the swamp for you, it could be at the bottom of thick, dark green water now."

I sat up, "I didn't necessarily say he left me anything in the swamp. I just remember bits and pieces of stories. There are things in the dream about my mother, about some baby that I don't know..." Man cut me off with a stern voice. He asked what might have been in it, as if he hadn't heard me say that there wasn't necessarily something left for me. He held me gentle until I spoke to him about my made-up treasures, the same way I confessed to Tessa to soothe her curious mind. "I guess, animal fur, maybe some gold pieces, or silver and things he would have wanted to keep safe. I don't even care about that stuff, but sometimes I figure maybe I'll go back to the swamp and will end my nightmares, maybe I'll go there and find out what happened to him.

I've been there before, but I was just a girl then. I think about going back."

Man said, "If you askin me to go up in there where frogs, snakes, alligators, and voodoo chases Christian folks to the grave, you got another thing comin." I held my breath, hoping to take us back into silence, but he continued, "Look, Lilly, niggers is always puttin themselves in the way of a challenge to claim back some losses of slavery, but the best thing be to get what you can, honest, and move forward, not to be bettin on a bad plan, or taking money for doing dirty deeds. My father was free because he was allowed to work outside the plantation on weekends, and that man 'bout killed himself so I could be free, free to marry, free to have a son that ain't had to be no slave. I ain't about to start steppin in the wrong places, disrespecting who came before. If you think you better than the rest of us, and you got some treasure stored up someplace, don't think you gonna take me to hell with you."

He had never spoken a harsh word to me, but there was so much poison and judgment in the way he spoke now. I felt myself shrinking away from him. The feathers of the plush bed multiplied in the space between us.

I lay flat, my hair undone, surrounding my face like waterweed. Age crept up my spine like vines reaching up to pull down solid brick walls, and I whispered into the silence of the night, "I ain't no nigger."

He sat up and looked at me like he was needing to recognize who I was. He swung his heavy legs to the floor, and gave me a slight nod in the darkness. "Good night, Mrs. Willie Kellem." And with his leaving that night, our stolen moments went into the quiet ways of men and women. Not having much to say, he came those nights, mumbled on and off about the difficulty of being a man with land in a place of angry whites, did what he needed, and left.

In one breath of me speaking my mind, Man had turned cold to me, like the Negro people around the fire not wanting me to speak of my hurt or to sing for Old Raymond. There I was again. I wasn't a slave, but had scars all over my body to prove I wasn't free.

In the morning, I looked out the window at things staying cold, keeping spring at bay even though it was April. I saw the girls out the door and up the road to the schoolhouse, and I stood at the glass watching Man and Tessa going on down the road cloaked and huddled together, going to their jobs in town. She didn't even look my way to the window where I was peering out, so proud with him on her arm, strolling past. *Did she not recognize me?* Man had his coat up around his ears, hair in a big fluff of black wool. He cut his eyes in my direction, then went back to having his shoulders hunched up against the cold walk to town, and the pain twisted in my gut. Everybody was changing except me, Man about to leave me behind because of the fact that he and I were different, and that wasn't my fault. Tessa had changed: going to the county station to work, raising a child, but going away on weekends to do what she wanted to do. I was still looking out a window, waiting for something to happen. If I was Negro, or a woman, or white, I would have been able to enjoy the changes around me, or rebel against them, but I was Indian, and there wasn't no bunch of folks to band with and make a cause. Man and I separated like clay and sand.

I had made all manner of excuses about not going to town, figuring that the folks trudging to town didn't look any happier than me, thinking there wasn't anything special about it when I used to be there; a bunch of places just for blacks, a bunch of places just for white folks, and nothing about Indians. My daughters went there and got fancy shoes, and lollipops, and things that didn't seem right for kids to be worrying themselves away from home over.

Another Sunday came, and I saw Emmanuel and Tessa walking past for church, their boy getting bigger, all of them matching in who they were, and that made sense. Then I imagined me on Willie's arm with the girls skipping behind, and it didn't match. It didn't make no sense. I was the thing that didn't fit in it all. Emmanuel had his woman, a child, land, a life all the Negroes wanted, all in harmony, and I watched it from the front porch.

Spring finally warmed the soil and made things ready for planting. One night Tessa was away again and Man came to lie with me in me and Willie's bed, middle of the night, the fire burned out early, and I was thinking about the girls getting cold in their room, and waking up, and I was thinking on lots of things, and through the front door he came like he was the man of the house.

When he was done, I blurted it out. "What you doin with me? You said you had yo eye on me, that we was gonna be somethin if I kept things lookin right with Willie. We been together for years, and Don't look like you got no plans for me, none. Cain't even come with me to find out about my father?" I sat up and stared him in the eyes in the darkness, my nerves so frayed that I could see my hair shake with my heartbeat. I let myself be bare-chested away from the sheets and blankets. I sat there in the pause, goose bumps rising on my body, my nipples standing up, reminding me that my body was still young. I had never felt the muscles in my arms from wringing the clothes, from lifting wood, and storing the hay, but I felt them then, stress tightening my body. My heart beat faster, and my teeth clinched in a nervous grip. And I waited.

"You be...," he said, and then paused. "I gots to have somethin that ain't about obligation to make good, to do better, to make the wife proud and give my son a good future with land to plow. I got to have somethin of mine," he said, like it was his last breath, then he turned over and pulled the covers up over himself, leaving me cold. Shortly he turned over on me again, no kiss, just turned over on me like he was Willie. I pushed him away, and he cussed me. "Damn woman."

He got up to leave, and I sat there, shaking in the cold air of the house, pondering how his words went around in a circle, but didn't include anything about me; didn't name my name, didn't say anything about love, or beautiful, didn't even let on that there was anything other than the fact that I was a woman that made our being together important. The house seemed so big; the girls' tiny snores rose and fell in the distant cold. Man, huge and strong, shuffled quietly and familiar across the floor in his leaving. He looked out the door for Willie coming in the night the way he always did, the two of us old in this routine. "Good-bye. Don't forget to reload the fire," he whispered.

I said back, "Good-bye, and don't come back by here no more." He paused and turned to me, his sillhouette, like his spirit, massive in its weight and height. He blew a breath of air like the horse, and left.

Many times the moon went full without him challenging my wish.

Summer 1879

I TOOK TO STAYING INSIDE AGAIN UNLESS IT was early morning, or late after dark, or unless I was behind the house. That way I couldn't see the corn, wouldn't anticipate it being harvested, wouldn't smell the stalks burning sweet in the coming autumn. Now, the green stalks sprouted yellow hair from all the hauling water. Suddie, acting grown now, reported like her father, "That nigger cross the way sure hauls a lot of water for that corn. The drought don't stop him none."

Every time I got lost in my regrets of wanting Man to touch my body like that first night, I forced my thoughts to the list of chores. I washed the clothes watching the blood of my knuckles flow red into the water. And I refused to think at all about Tessa, least I be consumed in shame. I let myself stiffen to life again like a carcass hardening, my shadow in the summer sun, long and weary, my hair always swinging, unkempt over my eyes.

There wasn't enough rain that summer. I spared what I pumped, because Willie said there wasn't much left to pump. But even with sparing the well water, one day the water came up with earth in it. The girls' lips had little dry cracks. Virginia asked for cow's milk, "I want some muck Mommy?" But the cow wasn't giving milk on account of not having any water. I needed then to go by the heat of the day to the cold creek in hopes of water still running.

I thought to leave the girls in the cool shadows of the house, and go alone to the creek, but then I thought about the possibility of seeing Man, or Tessa out across the road. I'd just as soon she never found out it was me who lived across the way, never get the chance to mock me.

The girls would keep me to the task of fetching the water, keep the thoughts of Man or Tessa at bay. I told the girls, "Put on your sturdy shoes, and sunbonnets. We got water to fetch." I made them both carry a bucket. I took a pole with the other four milking buckets hanging on it, and we set out, east of Man and Tessa's house.

The buckets shook in my nervousness below the watchful eye of the trees and sun, which might look down at who I'd become and shun me. I counted up the years, twenty-eight, and this is who I was, and how my life was going to be.

Leaving the house was like starting over. I hadn't been to the creek since Suddie was six. Now she was about nine and looked at me from under that bonnet like I didn't know what the hell I was doing, looked at me sideways the way Willie often did, making me doubt my own instincts.

Virginia struggled to keep up, being six years old, her legs still too short, feet still too small for long journeys, and she was obedient from being Suddie's little sister. Virginia's hair fell heavy and silky from under the bonnet, and she looked at Suddie like she wished she'd slow down. We traipsed off like that, ornery, hot, and thirsty.

River otters didn't ever come that far down, but they went sleek, sometimes walking, sometimes swimming down the middle of the creek, and we stood there sweating, happy for the cool running water after our journey. I took deep breaths and reminded myself not to be nervous, watching the clearest water rush over rocks in the middle of the creek. With my hand on the gritty back of my neck I figured on the situation just the way my Maw Janie would have. I thought long and decided to leave the girls in the shade, not sure of my decision, but certain from Suddie's squinted stare that I needed to do something to get to the middle of the creek where the water ran clear. I tied my dress in a knot, put all the buckets onto my pole, and set out across the creek, clanking and balancing to the place where water ran deep in the otters' path. I did what I had to, like Maw Janie or Old Raymond.

I balanced on aching knees while I held the pole on my shoulders and looked for another dry rock to step on. The slow creek moved below me. My mind darted back to the safety of the house, its dark walls and creaking wood floors, the smell of the fireplace saturating everything. I swallowed dryness and fixed my mind on fetching the water, focused on the girls' parched lips, on the cow sitting thirsty in the shade of the barn. In my concentrating so heavy, I had not stepped mindfully, and it was too late. The head rose stiff and took a striking position. The bare skin on my ankles was wet with the sweat of the creek.

The explosion was so loud, ricocheting off rocks and water.

Virginia screamed muted above the echo, and my eyes darted counting them, Suddie, Virginia, and Man. He stood next to them holding the rifle at his side, his bare chest rising and falling in relief. His suspenders held the work pants to his wide naked chest. The snake was dead at my feet, and I heard the redheaded woman's voice from long ago, *Don't let life catch you standing still.* The water carried the snake's body away and my long legs were safe, sticking out from under my knotted dress, the buckets still in balance on the pole.

I stared at Man, and my girls far from my reach, and could remember all the moments that brought me there. The girl that was Lilly who had wished herself dead, hair floating on the water at dusk. I stood on that rock gritting my teeth, agitated with myself for being so happy to see Man's face.

"Lilly," he yelled to me, not caring that the girls stared at him, then at me, wondering what would happen next. I stood there on the rock balancing, and I worked on filling my four buckets of water until he was gone.

I lay numb and nauseous next to Willie, thinking about the years I pretended to be meek and knuckling under so he wouldn't suspect I was seeing somebody. *And what difference did it make now?* I thought. I was just a fool for having ever thought I was going to get something from sneaking around with Emmanuel behind Tessa and Willie's back, like Tessa taking pleasure in the risk of stealing right out of the overseer's pocket, a fool for thinking that little bit of power was going to make her feel better.

I lay there in bed next to Willie and let myself claim the truth. Man had called out Tessa's name many times when we were together those first nights, and I had been numb to it. "Tessa." He pushed himself into me until he came to pulling himself out and releasing himself into the washbasin. He called her name in the voice that summoned her on the night of freedom from Bartlette's plantation, called her up from the frantic prayers on the dirt floor where she left me alone, not even a word of good-bye after all that shared misery.

The next day, I stood on the porch not knowing for myself how to ward off the fear of leaving and being left, and called out brave and foolish, to the proud couple headed to their Sunday meeting, "Tessa!"

I called the way he did that night, knowing that my connection with Tessa would take the "havin somethin of his own" out of his hands. "Tessa, it's me, Lilly." Man stood like a deer, his eyes wide and humbled by what he could not understand.

Tessa squinted hard at the woman with the yellow girl's voice, standing in shadow of the porch. "Lilly? Lilly, is that you?"

I couldn't tell from her flat tone if she was lying to me and had known all along, or if she was holding back, because she was stunned to see the past staring at her, fifteen years later, two kids later, standing on the porch of Willie Kellem's house. I frowned at her flat tone, but lured her away from the road, into the yard by holding my arms out. She tilted her head to one side.

"Lord you done married Willie?"

And she walked up to the steps, her hair braided neatly under her summer hat. She let me put my arms around her, while I was sure she was peering over my shoulder into the house, then she pulled away.

"I gots to get on to my meetin, but Lilly, I sure am glad to know its you livin here." The glow of our old lantern gone, her eyes were flat as the gray sky. She stepped closer again and peeked around the side of my head to see into the house.

She chattered just like in the days when we were young. "I makes it a point not to even look this way. I always say a prayer so I don't get the sins of this house hoppin off on me. But you livin here? Things must done lost they vex, 'cause ain't a whole lot of people or spirits alike more ornery than you. Don't see how you can live in the house of Satan's ghost." She peeped around again, craning her neck around to behold the dark silence of the house.

Guilt climbed over the welts on my back. I looked down at her shoes and up her body. She was the same, but more round. Her thick hair was bound up on her head, the first gray hairs sprouted, and I could smell her stale-water sweat beneath the Sunday dress. I wanted her arms around me, because seeing her was like seeing kin. I hadn't realized that I needed her, needed somebody who knew me from way back, some reflection of who I was, but if she ever found out what I had done with Man, there would be no hopes of kinship.

A parched wind rushed around our bodies. She reached her hesitant hand up and touched my cheek where an unwelcomed tear flowed.

"Mrs. Lilly Kellem?" she said, smiling in a way that left me not knowing if she pitied or mocked me.

I wrapped my arms tight around my body. "You gots to get on to your meeting, don't you?"

"Yeah, it's a long hot journey," she said, stepping away, the round whites of her eyes still on me as she walked off.

Man stood at the road dabbing his sweat and looking distraught by our interaction, and I did a slight wave and turned to keep him from seeing my tears. Tessa marched back to him, chattering loud. "Her and I go way back to the same shack on Massa Bartlette's place. Lord, I cain't believe it been Lilly livin there all this time. Lord, ain't that somethin?" From the window I watched her go up the road. Her hands gestured telling Man all kinds of things about my beating at the hitching post, my wanting to die, things I didn't want Man knowing anything about.

Tessa was so at peace with her life, the same way she seemed at ease on Massa Bartlette's place, but not much had changed in me; still dreaming about what I was going to do, but not having a plan of my own.

I watched as Man and Tessa turned the bend in the road, exchanging my secrets, and I decided to let the whole thing alone, just let it alone, because thinking about spending time with Tessa was already bringing on a wealth of old grief; Tessa's mouth telling everything, not letting one thought be solitary or sacred, and Man walking along like the innocent farmer. I hated them both.

Fall 1879

S OMETIMES THINGS JUST stay how they are because nothing significant happens to change them. Nobody gets up and does anything in particular. I remember my question to Old Raymond, "How come we don't just run, knowing Massa's men can only catch so many of us, knowing a fox hunter can catch one, but not a whole den of foxes unless they just stand there shocked in the trail of the first fox, waiting for the hound to backtrack on a second scent?"

That "questioning Lilly" and "attitude Lilly" was hibernating, deep in her slumber, while I walked through my days obsessed with Man; wanting him, hating him and wondering what he and Tessa were saying about me. Virginia and Suddie were always off to school, and I sat on the porch rocking, my feet crossed at the ankles. I chewed back all the calloused skin on my raw lye-soap fingers.

The winter came on cold and hard before it snapped into spring. Folks got a heap of glory out of it turning to the year 1880; Suddie all the time bragging to me about how the black folks kept the celebration to themselves because the white people try to act like blacks in town celebrating meant somebody needed to be lynched. I told her not to tell me anything about celebrating, or lynching, that I didn't want to hear anything about it. She said they had been building a cotton mill, that people had come to Oktibbeha County to live and build the houses all the way from Alabama, and I felt old and ignorant. I had read books in my childhood from London, had gotten gifts my father brought back from New Orleans, had picked out fine things in catalogues from New York, but I didn't know any Alabama. I didn't know anything that had been written down since the things I read as a ten-year-old Southern lady.

I lay in the nights hearing my girls snoring in the other room, Willie out there in the big world beyond the land doing who knows what, Emmanuel over across the way staying safe, and I was inside the square of my house, sharp angles around my caged thoughts.

I tried to find reasons to be on the porch all the time, sweeping powdery snow or pollen, or blossoms or whatnot, so Man would come past the road and see me in the distance. Then I could catch his eye and let him know that if he wanted to come by here again, it would be all right with me. We wouldn't have to talk about anything he didn't want to talk about. Maybe Tessa would stop thinking about hantes and look this way, come and have coffee with me; melt away the loneliness with the girls both gone to school every day. I felt pathetic, wanting both of them, either of them, just somebody to make the drowsiness of my lonely days disappear.

One Sunday when he was all matched up with Tessa and the boy, he didn't look my way at all, but Tessa waved and veered in her footsteps to come speak, and Man snatched her gloved hand, and they headed up the road, her looking back and waving.

In the morning Tessa came past in the same old travelling shoes, fixed up for going to work at her missus's house. I watched her from the door biting my nails, and wondered to myself yet again, *How come she always was like that... free in whatever she was doing like there wasn't no misery in wearing worn-out shoes, no misery in goin all day to be slave again for some white people, nothing but a little bit of money and some leftovers from their table to show for the hard work?*

I knew the answer to my questions. She was a thief. She had the man I wanted. She had an understanding of how to get and have within the suffering. I followed her with my eyes the way I used to follow Emmanuel. I followed her trying to understand her by her walk, reading her steps. *How did she find peace?*

The girls had left for school. Man and Tessa and their young man had gone up the road, the fog of their breath on the spring morning air as they talked, and walked fast to stay warm. Through the gray air of that day, past the unturned cornfield stood their house. It was small and worn, and my obsession with cracking the code to my loneliness drew me to it.

I went to the cedar chifforobe in the bedroom, swallowed back the lump in my throat as I opened the doors. The earthy smell of the cedar wood made my head light. I couldn't even look at it; Willie's pants, Willies's white shirts, Willie's jackets, and the hooded cloak. My breath caught in my throat, and I reached for it, ready to undo whatever spell kept me prisoner while everyone else walked free.

I put on the black hooded cloak and headed across the field looking for the right places to step.

Hard stalks, dead pieces of coarse things. My exposed legs above the boots were the only part of me that felt visible. I felt shielded from anyone who might see me, though I walked under the flat white clouds of a stormy spring sky. My cloak caught twice in my journey as I put one foot in front of the other. My eyes cut away to the road, where I thought someone might be watching. Our house was brown, and shrinking in the distance behind me. The posts held up the roof of the porch where a shadow made the front door invisible, the barn almost invisible among the dusty gray and light green of thin trees with soft new green buds.

I knocked at their door, though I had seen them all leave, the boy running ahead of Suddie and Virginia, the strap that bound his books dangling as he hurried, glad to be headed to the schoolhouse rather than the fields.

Tessa had painted the door white, like the white of Massa's house. The door creaked on its hinges. "Hello," I said peeping in. The smell was sweet and warm, the smell of life even in their absence. There was the thick odor of chitlins in the air, the sweetness of the stove's wood, smoked into the walls. Herbs hung drying from their garden, smelling like earth after a good rain. Their walls brown worn wood that a child's fingers surely found splinters in, much like the walls of my home. The ceiling was low just above my head, and I felt hugged where I stood, no drafts of air from raftered ceilings, silence in the house, but no loneliness.

The boy's clothes hung over three chairs near the cook-stove. Tessa was a mother, taking care for the needs of somebody else, and I was bewildered remembering her so crass and selfish. I imagined her voice too harsh in talking to a child. "You ain't gettin out of the work. Get out to them fields now."

The fireplace in the room was still slightly warm. I touched the metal handle that reached out where a pot must have hung the night before, and it squeaked, unoiled.

I sat down in the rocking chair. A basket of yarns died yellow from onion skin, purple from pokeberries, a knitted hat for the boy. The thought of Tessa's restless hands knitting seemed silly. I smirked, thinking, *Who is she tryin to fool here?* I crossed the small room to the other rocking chair, where Man's wool shirt hung still damp. I sat down and wrapped the arms of the shirt around me, breathed deep, and felt pain curl me away from the small space. Man, he should have been mine not Tessa's.

I comforted myself by making a cup of tea using the last warmth from in the stove; rosemary, mint, licorice root. I sat in her rocker, lay on the straw mattress against the wall where she and Man had made love and brought their son into being; his smaller bed in the nook behind the curtain of sheets.

I napped there, Tessa's dreams crawling like mites off the pillow and into my ears. I dreamed of a woman, the contour of her brown breast just above me, a slave woman, her arms strong, where she laid me down in a little space, the glow of candlelight on her cheeks, and strange words. *Good morning, now go to sleep, and don't be cryin. You hush, be still and wait.* Wait, wait, wait, the message came in one voice, then many confusing voices until the sound was so chaotic I couldn't breathe.

I woke up to the harsh and soothing sound of crows and doves cawing and cooing in the gray afternoon. It was getting late. I walked in my foggy state around the little house, put each thing back where it had been before, rinsed the cup at the pump, tracking a bit of water and mud into the house on my boots, half hoping that they'd find my dried tracks there and wonder who had come into their perfect world. I inhaled a last breath of mint herbs, chitlins, and the oil of familiar hair and skin, and I turned to the window, where neat piles of seeds laid out to dry planting when the spring rains were over. I rubbed them between my thumb and fingers; pure, smooth from the womb of Man and Tessa's garden. I put one bean in my mouth, tumbled the dirt and dust around and chewed it, raw and bitter, then picked another bean, like picking up the few precious pebbles that wouldn't be missed from the creek. I stole a few from each small heap and tucked them into my skirt pocket.

I turned to leave, and heard two quick steps on the porch before the door swung open.

"Man?"

He stood, not startled, but out of breath. "On my way to town I saw you cross the field." His face was more soft than I remembered, moistened by the dampness of that morning. His hands were stern on the door latch. "I done worked as fast as I could to get back here early to make sure you ain't been in here. What you doin here, Lilly?" His voice cracked and he looked out the window near the bed where he and Tessa slept. He bit his bottom lip in some effort to hold himself back from something, looked away from me and pointed me to the door.

I held still and reached for his hand, letting myself stay in pretending that I was Tessa, letting myself lose my mind, and it felt good, because as things were, I didn't much reason to do right. I stared into his eyes without wavering and asked him to call me by her name. Man lifted my hand from his and kissed it, refusing still to look at me, and he lifted me onto their bed and took me like the very first night he came through the window.

Willie's sleep was different those days, more restless. He made the room warm with his slow aging body. He came home early in the night, and spent most of the sleeping time going back and forth to the picture window in the big room, then to the kitchen for a spell, then back to bed, and I worried a bit that he suspected something between me and Emmanuel. I cain't say we were as careful as we used to be, I cain't say I had any reason to hope for anything with him, didn't care what would happen the way Willie or Tessa, or even Man, might, because I didn't have anything, and nothing take away Man was even more nothing.

One night I slept restless and went to the window, where I heard a voice, and realized Willie was on the porch in the rocking chair, smoking and speaking. I wasn't sure if to himself or me.

"That's one foolish nigger across the way, think he can just go on about being a Negro with no concessions to the white folks, no deals made, no bowing and scraping, just being Negro, like that's good enough." The tobacco in his pipe glowed red in the dark when he paused. "They gonna come for that prime piece of land sure enough. Um hum. What he got over there is a whole lot more attractive than what I got over here. And all his struttin and pride gonna be the draw to it."

What? I wondered what was he talking about, mumbling like Satan, looking off into the yard. I stared on, quiet at the window, seeing how the hard work of keeping secrets aged both of us beyond our years.

In the morning, I got the girls up for school and I went to the window the same way Willie did the night before, wondering who he was looking at or looking for.

"Mommy," Suddie said, reprimanding me like Willie. "Why you standin there like that?" I didn't answer her, and she snatched Virginia by the hand, as if she was saving her from the likes of me. They headed on off to school in the boots, the spring skirts, and the bonnet hats that Willie bought, but spring was about as chilly that year as winter had been. I yelled after Suddie to come back for her coat, and she ignored me.

I stood there watching the girls as they trailed up the road. I thought on the month, the days I had been counting since I should have been bleeding. Time had passed on quiet with me not needing more from Man than the occasional touch. I fiddled with the stolen seeds from Tessa's windowsill quiet in my skirt pocket. I counted the seeds, and the weeks, tried to remember if the moon had been full again since my last menses. Too much time had passed.

I stood there feeling the blood inside my body troubling up in the pit of my womb. My rags stayed in the bureau drawer, sheets not needing washing from monthly bloodstains. I looked out the window wondering, *What I'm gonna do if the bleeding just don't come?*

Tessa hurried up the road to keep from being late to her missus, and Man came behind her. In my shawl and nightdress I ran to the damp boards of the porch. I waved for him. *What we gonna do?* I was planning on asking him, but he turned onto the road never looking my way.

I brought my hand down seeing the other men and women, with coats and bonnets up around their ears, brown skin and the accusing whites of their eyes. I felt the first stirring of the life like a tadpole, blind and innocent for the coming of things.

April 19, 1880

IN MY SLEEP early before light, I thought, *Tomorrow is my birthday,* and pain seized in my chest at the curse of my birthday. It was not a good thing. My birthday remembered was always my birthday regretted.

The next morning the hair on the back of my neck stood up from the roots when Willie climbed out of the bed with the dawn coming. The covers rose up and down, leaving the warmth of his restless body. The sky was just before the rooster crowed, and an unfamiliar dawn eased me out of slumber.

The blaze rose up before the rising sun. The blades of grass outside my window wilted in a heat that raped the sky of its cool colors. The flames leaped in the spot where Man and Tessa's house once stood.

Their half-tended fields glowed in the distance. I looked on confused about this waking nightmare, a scream caught in my throat. "Man. Tessa." I gasped inward reminding myself to breathe. The scent of honeysuckle blossoms mixed with the thick air, tasting rancid on my tongue. The burning cross glowed. Ironies of Missionary's words ran hysterical through the blaze in my mind: the fires of hell, the fish and loaves of bread, a dead man rising free from the confines of his grave. The rocking chair creaked against its own dying wood. Willie sat right outside the window, bundled in his good coat. "I told you this day would come." And I heard Tessa scream, heard her son scream out. I could not breathe, waiting to hear Man's voice too, but his cry did not come.

Willie struck a match for his pipe, and it illuminated his face like the blaze illuminated the other objects that we witnessed. Willie got up, left the rocking chair, and slowly took steps toward the road, where a few others stood, watching.

I thought, *Run*. Run into the flames and save Man from the white men dressed like ghosts. My Suddie had warned me once about the Klansmen who might rip my skin from my body if I looked the wrong way, and here they'd come, where I stood, where I lived, they came and ripped Man away like fruit snatched at harvest. My body trembled where I stood in the middle of the bedroom floor, in that house that had become my solitary prison. The life inside me swam, panicked in the heated waters of my womb. Things spun: brown floors, walls, the patterns of the crocheted blanket on our bed, and I fell to the bed swallowing back the vomit that rose bitter in my throat.

Willie's words were stiff and emotionless when he scooted under the covers, negotiating around where I lay on top, curled tight in a knot of nightgown and long dark hair. "They done hung that fool across the way, and the woman and the boy went on with some folks up the road. Everybody gone on back home now. It's over." Like Old Raymond. *Go on back to the quarters now, it's over.*

I fumbled the dried seeds in the rough palm of my hand over and around my ringed finger, and the seeds moved slow in the puddle of warm tears.

The sins of that day lifted in the veil of smoke and mist to reveal Man, swinging from the end of a scuppernong vine at the edge of his own land. My face was fixed with new aging. The tears flowed in regret of not having run to Man in the procession of workers headed to town to tell him that I was pregnant, for not having run into the inferno of white men. Maybe we could have run away from Tessa, and the responsibility of tilling the land, away from Willie and this house.

My thirtieth birthday: gray hairs sprouted at the nape of my neck and the peak of my hairline. My skin sagged away from my face like my mother's.

Man had said, "Niggers is always puttin themselves in the way of a challenge to claim back some losses of slavery," and his words whistled through the hollow of my bones.

Late morning, the people carried his body on shoulders past the house on his journey on to another world. The sun of a reluctant spring shined down onto the light green new crops, and trees snowed petals. The people in dusty black clothes moaned a song, like a swarm of bees rising and falling in their hum. Tessa wept on the shoulder of some older woman, her hair in a braided bun, her boy almost her height, stout in body like her.

I stood in the doorway resenting the sun for shining down on me, revealing me in my stupor of guilt and grief. Virginia and Suddie watched the procession from the porch, captivated by the omen of voices grieving, curious but not mournful, the same way I had watched the slaves of LeFlore mourn for the dead woman, Josephine. They had all mourned her, even the people on Bartlette's place, even Tessa, the child she had birthed, and left behind. They had mourned her.

My cotton dress hung lifeless around my body and I let my hair hang with new gray streaks where the girls could not see that tears streamed over my high cheekbones.

"Courage," I remembered my Old Raymond saying, "is something you build inside yourself, and like a snake storing up poison, you strike when the time is right." But always I waited, until life struck out at me, until Old Raymond was dead, until my own mother lay at the edge of the creek bed.

The girls turned around confused at my noise. Suddie glanced my way, but continued to watch from the porch. Virginia asked, "Mommy, is somebody comin to get you again?" They had obeyed the sugar cube and molasses pact of silence so well that Man was a stranger to them. "Go on and play down near the creek," I had said, pulling the dusty sugar jar from the top shelf. They were so grateful that they never questioned, but reached their dirty hands in over and over until I pulled the jar away.

The sight of figures in black, moving slow against new green, did not rile them. Ex-slaves with the lynched-one cut down from the tree did not strike a chord of fear in them. They were Willie Kellem's daughters.

Willie stepped right over me on his way to wherever he went every morning. He pretended not to notice the slight bulge of my gut. He pretended not to notice my crying on hands and knees now with my hair curtained around my anguished face. Even the birds flying overhead could see fit to recognize that death was passing that way, swooping low and graceful, they sang their calls in long notes. But Willie Kellem went out of the darkness of his house into the sun, across the yard to the barn to hitch the wagon: the only black man in the county not affected by the prophecy of vines and ropes in trees.

Nausea came every morning, and I stood over the fried eggs swallowing over and over so Willie wouldn't suspect anything more because I hadn't figured what I was going to do; both hearts beating inside me, troubling my insides with responsibility for my own life, and the baby's, not yet affected by the miseries.

I was glad the girls went to school every day, because I couldn't imagine enduring their noise without taking my agitation to their backsides.

Willie watched me like Overseer watched me at the smokehouse. I needed to keep the walls from falling down before I could figure out what I was going to do. I had wet the monthly rags and laid them in a wad near the back door, a decoy for any curiosity over a missed menses. I wondered if he smelled the evidence of new life above the odor of his eggs scrambled up yellow, a smear of blood in them signifying that life had almost come.

"Suddie, are you gettin yourself ready for the schoolhouse?" I yelled out. The skin on my forehead itched, as I wondered if I had accidentally said "ready for the smokehouse."

My clothes felt tight like ropes binding me. I couldn't help but to yell. I needed to flee the sickening smell of food. I took my cold bare feet over the dusty boards of the floor, out the front door, across the cool muddy yard, and to the side of the barn, where I vomited until nothing came, then made my way to the chicken coop to scatter the feed and disguise my footprints.

I watched my Suddie and Virginia run hand in hand. They hurried up the road to the schoolhouse. I called out, "Good-bye," but Suddie kept running. *Who was I to her?* She wasn't defiant with Willie, but disregarded my wishes, just frowned, annoyed when I spoke, embarrassed of my looks and my way of talking. I wondered if she knew. *Was she close enough to womanhood to see the bags under my eyes. Could she tell by remembering the days of Virginia growing in me?*

Behind me I heard Willie hitching the wagon. He rode past where I stood in the yard. Wagon wheels over dirt, the sound of an unnecessary whip to the horse's hide startled me, and he was off to his day without a good-bye. I took a deep breath, glad they were all away from me, glad that I could endure the tension I felt welling up in me without their scrutiny. I watched him ride slow past the girls, waving to them with his gloved hand. I watched the girls turn the bend in the road, and my eyes swept across the field where the little house once stood, nothing but the stone chimney remaining. In that house, I had rocked in Man's chair, been taken into the righteous places of spirits with him inside me. Next to the chimney I thought I saw movement, and realized someone stood there.

She came across the field like a ghost, still in the black dress that she wore weeks ago when they carted Man up the road, her head not wrapped in the damp air, her shawl; one end almost dragging the ground.

"Tessa," I said, greeting her, then letting my eyes wander back to the road, where I waved, pretending to still see the girls. She stared at me, without her face grinning the way it always was, without meanness or spite. Just stared.

She stuck her finger in her ear to guard against the wind that came curiously around from the back of the house, and she spoke.

"You'd think winter would let go, and let spring be here. Things ain't supposed to feel this damp in May. Usually by now we would be plowing and planting. The kids'll be out of school soon. Make good for field work."

I took my hair in both hands and started braiding to calm the aggravation. I couldn't talk to anybody, be near anybody, least of all Tessa. I felt like I could take my nails to my own skin and claw the flesh away if I wasn't let be. I felt anger well up at the sound of Tessa's voice.

"Ain't you chilled Lilly? You ain't wearing nothin but a dress, no shawl, ain't even got on shoes."

"I'm actually quite warm." I leaned my head in her direction as I finished the braid. I didn't want to ask the question, but felt foolish standing there not inviting her in. I was sure her superstitions about the ghost of Satan would cause her to turn down the invite. But I had to invite her in, else she might wonder why not, might think I had something to hide, might see "widow" in my eyes.

"Tessa, if you want to come in, just say so."

"It's a long walk back to the church. That's where me and Davis been staying."

Davis, I had never asked Emmanuel what the boy's name was.

"Things are a mess, but come on in," I said in a discouraging tone, and she stepped toward the house.

The smell of the eggs was still lingering, and I sat nearest the fireplace so that the smoked wood overwhelmed the smell of the eggs. Tessa brought another straight-backed chair close to where I sat, and looked around at the ceiling the walls.

She looked down at my shaking foot, my whole body quaking from my fidgety movement. Her ebony skin beamed with a smile. "Look at us. We ain't sat around a fire since we sat around the smokehouse hopin to stay warm." She giggled, that old sound, like milk caught, slimy in her throat.

Then she got serious again. "I ain't sure what I'm gonna do next, Lilly. I ain't planned on nothin except being with Man."

I sat in the chair across from her, feeling exhausted from my own grief and agitation. I worked hard to keep my eyes on her. I scratched my temple and looked down. "Well Tessa, sometimes people don't have a plan. Sometimes life just catches you on the end of a hook, and you have to figure out how to get off before you're caught."

She ignored my bitter sarcasm.

"Is Willie treatin you good? You sho look tired, and I ain't never thought of you walkin around with no shoes on." I rubbed one eye, knowing I could not do this. The fantasy of friendship with her died with Man, and I could not have her sit in my house and find reason to insult me the way she always had. I could not tolerate the fact that I did not feel sorry for her being without Man. In that moment,

I was the widow, and she was a chigger boring beneath already irritated skin.

"Tessa, I'm sorry for your loss, but I need you to go."

She didn't get up from her chair, but leaned forward, evening the lengths of her shawl. "Lilly, I came here 'cause you's my sister. I ain't got nobody else, and you's my sister, and we need to be with that."

I stayed sitting in the chair, and folded my arms against the cold as the fire died down to embers. "Tessa, we done come a whole lot of years from Bartlette's place, and I... I don't think you understand that I don't feel that way about you. You just about the only person I know who I can say I truly don't like." My tongue was forked like the streak of gray in my hair.

I stared her down, convinced that she was trying to lure me into one of her old tricks of pretending to like me, make me weak, then tell me she knew about me and Man, tell me about the two of them laughing at me in their warm house at night. So I got to her before she could get to me.

"I'm not your sister. I hated having to spend those nights listening to your mouth."

Tessa's eyes got big and she moved her head back on her neck. "Naw, Lilly, you my sistah." Her face was heavy and darker with the fire dying, nothing but the gray light from the window to reveal her.

"With Man gone, I sit in that church crying all night, for everything, not just for him, and I remembered my mama, remembered coming to the plantation, I remembered." She laughed. "It's foolish that I didn't remember everything she told me about you before now, that I was so hurt it took another wound just as deep to make me remember. Foolish that didn't nobody back at Bartlette's place knock me beside the head and say to quit treatin you that way 'cause you my sister."

I sat there with my arms in my lap now. My mouth was slightly open and taken aback by her insanity, taken aback that my insults couldn't penetrate her foolishness. I relaxed in surrender knowing that I was trapped listening to her until she shut up and left.

I quieted my voice, put my hand on my shaking knee, and tried one last attempt to get her to go. "I ain't feelin too good these days, Tessa, and I wish I could help you in your grief, but;" I looked away and shook my head, because a tear had gotten loose and trailed down my face, my long neck, and dripped onto my veiled chest; "Tessa, I got my own problems." *Why was I crying, like my mother in those last days, angry and shouting in one moment, unannounced tears the next?*

She sat down on the floor, her dress ballooned around her the way my mother's once did. "Lilly, I know you angry at me for the way I used to be, and I ain't trying to be mean. My mother's name was Josephine. Her and I came to Bartlette's, but we used to live at LeFlore. I remember that woman Sybil, how she used to come bring the good fruit from ya'll rich Indian folks' stash. She used to shine the apples up for me 'cause I loved the way they looked in the firelight.

"After Motha and I went to Bartlette's, she started saying she wasn't gonna live to see her other children again, but said she had named me and another one, and would meet us both in heaven. She told me not to ever forget her name, and told me not to ever forget the sister named Lilly, Lilly LeFlore, first flower of summer. Said she had made that baby with her old Master Grey Fox."

Tessa stopped and scooted over to the fire to pick up the poker and stir the embers, not like she had just desecrated my father's name and poured acid on my mother's life, but like she had just finished some delightful fairy tale. I saw her face in the slight glow of the embers the same way I saw her face the night she held the lantern out to leave me to be raped by Overseer, and without thinking about what I was doing, I let my barefoot fly up from the floor, and kick her in the face.

She dropped the poker and stood up so fast it took her time to steady herself.

"What the hell you do that for?"

I must have looked crazy, my hair hanging in my face, my eyes red from crying angry tears for who or what I did not know. I couldn't control my hands. If I touched her, I would kill her. In my outburst, my words came down like wild horses frozen into the side of a mountain, until heat gave way to a stampede.

"Tessa, you mean heifer, who, ain't never cared about anybody but yo self. You cain't stand that I got Willie and yo husband dead." I backed her out of the door. She dropped the poker on the floor and the sweet smell of seared wood filled the room, making me want to vomit. I shook my head. "You can be so evil you would take my stories and twist them up into yo bad fate, just to make somebody else feel bad like you, just 'cause you don't know yo mother or father. I would tell you an evil thing or two that would make you wonder about the life you thought you had with Man, but I ain't that kind of woman. This time, you can run out the door, and leave me, and I don't care. Time for you to be a sista to me was when I needed you on freedom day."

She stood on the porch now, with me in the doorway. She twisted her face and looked down at my hand. I did not remember picking up the poker, but I held it on the hot end.

"You my sistah," she said, with no tears, but snot running down over her full lips, "and I already know you was spendin time with Man, just like I know the old white man whose burnin everybody out of their homes to claim some Mississippi land, but see, I bein who I am, I couldn't do nothin about either truth, so I just live my life for what is good."

She turned around, and her church shoes resounded in my aching head.

I ran out behind her. "If you knew then why didn't you say somethin?"

She turned around at the road, her jaw sliding away to a frown. "I did, but I didn't say it to you. I said it to the one who made a promise to never forsake me."

The pale sun shone weak in the sky, and I opened my hand to drop the poker. The white hot pain shot up my arm and into my chest. I went to the chair, the fire dying to cold. I tried not to think, but I couldn't stop the jumble of faces and voices of all the people who were once in my life, and how I didn't trust any of them, not Willie, not Tessa, not my children, not even the ghost of Man. Unwelcome tears flowed all day.

The girls came in from the schoolhouse, bringing their noise, and questions about supper. Suddie glanced at me and turned in disgust to bring wood for the fireplace.

The next morning seemed long and drawn out, with the girls taking forever to get ready for school, and Willie in his new fashion of staying long in the morning to eat his breakfast, to watch me, to wonder at me.

The waves of nausea moved up my spine and settled in my gut. *Leave, leave,* I chanted in my head to the three of them. I just wanted to be in the house alone so I could go to the feather bed and sleep, numb and momentarily dead, escape the frustration and rage, kill the madness that grew in me; my hatred for my own children, even for the dead man who said he'd take me away, and then hung from the vine with deceptive bulging eyes.

I breathed deep, thinking on what kind of thing I should do or say to try and look normal until the three of them were gone from the house.

"Well, got chores to do," I hollered out in the direction of the kitchen, realizing that I had never done the laundry from the day before. The cauldron out back sat with cold water now, the decoy menstrual rags at the back door in a cold sculpted clump. I grabbed my hooded cloak and headed out the front door with laundry for the cauldron at the back door.

I lit the fire, and wrapped the paddle in an old cloth to protect my branded hand, and poked in the hot pot of water, stirring Virginia's pissy sheets and the girls' underpants. I watched the girls turn the bend in the road. The steam rose up in the cold, as I stood tall and hooded contemplating the coming days. *Would Tessa come back to tell Willie about me and Man? Would she come with a gun and shoot me?* I peered out past where the girls had disappeared at the bend in the road to see if she was coming, looked around the front of the house to see if she stood at the chimney contemplating my death. *Would she kill me slow, find even more things to say to make me feel like the slave she wanted me to be?* My mind was unravelling with the thoughts. *Maybe I'll go to Willie and tell him we having another baby and let that be the truth. Did Tessa know I was pregnant?*

I was startled from my thoughts by Willie standing there at the back door. He was all ready to go in his fine coat, and he held the little clump of damp monthly rags in his grip and came toward the pot. *He and Tessa are after me,* I thought, then quieted my mind and brought my eyes back to a smaller stare.

His hat still did not make him my height, but he looked in my eyes, and I concentrated against the instincts of pregnancy; I concentrated not to lift the scalding paddle in defense of myself and the baby.

He said in a tone deeper than he usually spoke, "Do you need to clean these rags too?" And he dumped the already clean rags into the water, and off he strode to the barn. I had hoped he was hitching up the horse, but he came out with his whip in hand, standing there in his suit and hat like Overseer, except he was clean, except he was Negro. "Hmph," he shook his head, an accumulation of anger in his eyes, and he proclaimed. "Old Raymond told me, 'Don't beat her. Don't you ever beat her.' I should have whipped you a long time ago."

I couldn't even see him now, in the steam, just his hand where he held the whip in a circle, loop of my fear, his dry hand uncertain, his eyes losing their conviction as I continued to glare back at him. Both sides of my body had been burned by the sun, my back whipped, my front whipped.

The tight-wrapped tail of leather hung from his hand and snaked along the ground ready to fly and sting. *Why had he ever come for me at Massa Bartlette's?* The image of the two of us running through the shadow of trees, the smell of gunpowder poisoning the air.

Overseer's brown teeth grinned down at me at the splintered hitching post, Old Raymond's feet in the shoes with soles curled up going to tell it in the quarters for to see the girl whipped, stripped down with her hands bound, flat ceiling without clouds.

I could see Willie now. He was fixed in the gray morning, his eyes like two worlds suspended in the vague heavens. With one eye I saw his arm lifted. His teeth bit firm his bottom lip the way Overseer gathered strength, and I saw the whip, slow, coming down on me and the baby.

My tall body cloaked next to the cauldron, steam rising, I raised the wooden paddle in the stillness of a silver May sky, and Willie's head collided with the flat end of the stick.

The knees of his clean pants landed in the mud where the horse clodded. His face went gentle. His one hand opened to brace his fall. His other hand held the bleeding side of his head, and his body struck the earth like a thick tree surrendering to its own weight in falling.

I stood there, on the wicked side of my mother's death, of my father abandoning of me; stood there having struck the blow. The laundry still swam in the hot cauldron, the girls' sheets, my old menstrual rags sending up the signal of our scent rising in steam over Willie's fallen body, and I ran. Like having heard the ancient women in my mother's stories for the first time, my instincts responded. *Run, child, run.*

The cloak resounded with my invisible steps, heavy thuds from my long body's stride. Over the yard, the road, around Emmanuel and Tessa's fallen charred walls, and away in a streak of black.

From a tall poplar tree two crows descended and took flight in kinship with my journey, wings over the fields. They cawed like mothers telling their child to flee, the two of them cut the air as they flew across the white sky to protect me from the men who would surely come for me. They flew toward the dome of the swamp and I ran to catch their long slender bodies against the lynching light of the sky.

Among the green, the gray moss, and black shadows, they faded momentarily, and reappeared among the high limbs of cypress trees, and the fog of my own heated breath, their sleek shifting images again, and then they were gone, spirits, not choosing to fly over still black water.

My heart made tight fists in my chest. I splashed and tripped desperately until I could not breathe. I stopped and inhaled deep like the redheaded woman told me never to do. The frogs hummed in the places where shackles rusted, red, orange, dissolving in the water and on the back of my nauseous throat.

I remembered my father sitting with me the day before my capture.

"Lilly." He said my name slow, confiding in his only child. "You are my only child. I have not done right by you. I have visited the same motherless sins on you that I have lived. I will do what is right, I will." I had not remembered these words before. I stared at him confused, the walls of my bedroom at dawn, storybooks, porcelain dolls, vases with fresh honeysuckle behind his head.

I waded to an island and stood in the late afternoon cold, watching the slender white egret fish, it's black bill and legs in stark contrast to it's ghostly body. The sleeves of my cloak covered my murdering hands.

I will die, I thought to myself, cold clouds of breath before me. *I will breathe no more, see no more, hurt no more. I will die. They will come for me, and I will die.*

Alligators waited lazily at the edge of the still water for my surrender. I rocked steady to the sound of my own moaning, my hands on my slightly round belly where the baby waited to be spared life as my child. The children I already had were at the schoolhouse learning. This was not the end I ever pictured. I never imagined Man dead, Tessa across the way, me doing something as awful as killing Willie, and running away. The cold wet cloak made me heavy where I stood. I didn't want to think, I just wanted to sleep, to lie down and never wake. I rested back on my heels and lifted my face to the place where the clouds moved quickly above the ancient trees. "Please take me," I whispered to whatever God would listen. "Please take me."

Then came the sound of calloused fingers over metal. With my eyes closed I felt the sun come warm to the vulnerable inside of my hand, my face, the light red beneath my eyelids. The sound of the music rose in the trees that canopied above my black cloak and got louder still, the guitar sweet and triumphant over my trance. I stood up and walked out into the still water. My bare feet slid over objects, roots catching around my toes like fingers, the roundness of stone, of skull. I hoped this death would come swiftly, gentle.

I woke from a sleep, so far away; and she was sitting there in an old rocking chair made from thick swamp vines. Sage burned in the humid cool air and tree moss hung down above me. She sent smoke up from her corncob pipe, while she plucked the rusty strings of her guitar.

"I'm sending up some smoke," she whispered, her voice more raspy than I remembered. "Got to let the vultures know that you and your yoke not available for their supper."

I saw her brown legs thick in my sight. Her stockingless feet rested in a pair of old leather shoes too big for her, but tied tight. Short pants in the cool air, cut off at the knees, and an oversized suit jacket with holes worn through to the long underwear buttoned high. The redheaded woman blew the smoke again. "I'm guessing you think I'm the only person still livin, 'cause here you is again."

I lay there on her deck, like a bird washed up on the riverbank waiting for her feathers to dry. She picked at the old guitar, and commenced sliding her hand up and down, making the sweet sounds again. I listened to the music, and the sound of hungry plants devouring flies and beetles in the distance.

I looked at the sky, the sun about to fall to evening. Suddie had probably found him. Virginia, "Mmm," I moaned in disgust and wanted to turn it all back. I moaned and curled into myself, my black cloak filthy on the moss green boards of her unsheltered porch. I was still alive, I had not wanted to see evening, to think of the girls mourning for Willie and for their lost mother. I moved the moss off my body and looked down the length of breasts and hips and legs that I had not paid attention to since I was here before, a girl, arrogant in what I wanted.

"Hush," she said. "Just hush. It don't matter now. What you done did ain't as awful as you makin it out to be, and things have changed for good, Lilly Kellem.

"Cain't tell you the number of mornings I was glad to be alone, so agitated I'd a killed somebody who had somethin to say to me."

I rolled over, troubled by what my girls would see: *Suddie, Virginia.* I remembered seeing my own mother's eyes staring, and the sound of the frogs in this swamp was suddenly deafening.

"Hush," she shouted to the creatures, to me, annoyed with mourning. "Hush; dammit." And I was quiet and numb like the gray moss in a small mound next to my head.

She plucked on the rusty strings, and began to speak, like Tessa speaking all manner of things I didn't need to hear when I was healing from the whipping.

"The man I loved was a powerful man once too, but the darkness of the world outside the swamp turned his skin from copper to green, metal gone bad like the shoe buckles." She paused in playing the guitar, rocked forward to catch my eyes, but kept patting her oversized worn shoe. She veered from the things she was saying like she wasn't sure she wanted to keep talking about it. "I was always finding white men's buckles, their shoes sunken in mud after they agreed with themselves not to keep trying to find their way out of the swamp.

"The swamp was their challenge. White men always have to be challenging themselves. So, they couldn't help but to follow their prey in, but they rarely found their way out. The pointy stumps signified to many that they had come as far as they were able, 'cause around them stumps you cain't spot the difference in what's a gator, and what's a stump. They knew then, it was time to declare their restless property useless. Hounds couldn't follow the scent through muddy water, through water full of small eggs of all kinds of livin things hatching. After a while I guess they stopped worrying with comin in here lookin for their property, just kept an eye on the edge.

"Chains and shackles are among the other metals in the swamp. They are heavier than buckles, made to fasten tighter, made to weigh a nigger down, but shackles always float to the surface. If they still holdin hands or feet, though, they go down in burial."

She pulled down on the ragged pants to warm her legs in the evening air. She lit her pipe again and filled her lungs with the smoke, looking off into sunset.

"Folks thinks 'cause I can help 'em a piece here and there, 'cause I can hear and sometimes see things other folks cain't, that I don't have things that scare me, that I don't need things like everybody else."

I curled around to listen to her, talking like she was continuing some old conversation.

"Hell, I need to survive like every other nigger, gotta figure how I'm gonna eat every day and who gonna pay me some mine like everybody else. You understand me?" And she looked over to me, her hair and the sky the same color now, but I didn't respond, just let my eyes make patterns of the color of the sky, the color of her hair, the moss, her worn clothes.

"Well, the man I loved," she went on as if I'd agreed with her. So I spoke up.

"I don't know for sure what I'm gonna do. Miss...What is yo name?" I sat on my knees and removed the hood, slicked the cool dampness from my face, over my hair. I held the small round space of my belly and cried again.

She paced her response, and leaned in, put the guitar down, and rested her chin on her fist. "Well, you sho can be evil, cain't ya? Just walk around like you scared of yo own shadow. Then out come the evil. Don't you wonder where yo wildness been hiding all this time?" She frowned when I didn't answer, and she shook her head.

"They calls me Verdeen, and you know, everybody got their own way slavery time affected them. Folks want me listenin, but ain't got no room for my stories or my questions."

She repeated herself, but I was still unresponsive, floating as if I'd awakened from a bad dream and was still realizing the atrocity of it.

We sat for a long time, not saying anything. Dusk came over the swamp like something divine from Missionary's old sermons. I bit back the skin from around my fingernails, my back getting cold against the changing breeze. I squinted off into the dark.

She turned to me and said, "Hush," annoyed with the sound of me inhaling and sighing. I tried to speak back to her, but again she said, "Hush." Then, before I could even get words to my lips, she said hush again, and I let the frustration come out in sobs.

"Hush. Come inside for goodness sake. Cryin ain't gonna do no good now. Don't mean nothin now. Hell, it been over, and you askin in yo head what you gonna do, when it ain't about none of that."

I was overwhelmed with frustration. She wouldn't let me speak, and now I couldn't remember what I had to say.

"Oh, just breathe," She waved her hand in the dark. "I ain't try'na aggravate you. I'm try'na telling you somethin because you all caught up and angry about your man being dead. That was his life, to live, and to leave when he got ready. You ain't loved him because you loved him. Hell, you been here twice, and ain't never mentioned loving nobody. You wanted him because he reminded you of somebody who said they was gonna save you, take you away from your own misery. The man who really was supposed to do that for you was your father.

"When you was young and cocky you said to me, 'You some kind of conjure, can't you answer me with what you've seen?' and I knew

I couldn't answer you with nothin that was gonna satisfy you, 'cause you spent all that time as a slave. Your predicament no better or worse than nobody elses, and you didn't even know yo self well enough than to be askin somebody you didn't even know for answers to your own questions."

Darkness reached over us as mysterious as her rant.

"You talkin in riddles," I said with my hair hanging on either side of my face like blinders.

We moved around each other quietly, lighting candles on the table in her cabin. The sweet smell of decayed bone and wet soil from the swamp was eternally trapped in those walls. She lit the wood stove; its lids each tilted off giving light, and for a moment I caught a whiff of feeling at home.

She came to me with a pair of beeswax candles, and I reached out to take them, and saw; the vision again. A tall brown woman with a white rag tied tightly over her head. Candlelight. She was facing a ghost in a black hooded cloak, a cloak like the one Willie bought for me, the one that once hung in the cedar chifforobe haunting me, the one that comforted me now like a quilt. My mother's face in profile when the hood was lifted. In the corner a horse stood over a trough guarding, where I did not see, but knew a child slept, and I knew that child was me. This time, the horse turned into my father, his face younger, his words clear, "I will see to it that Josephine stays with you, my child." And then his face, in the white light of a room, my mother's face next to his. "What will you name her?"

I managed to get my hand away from one of Verdeen's hands, but her grip held like talons. Her eyes were turned back in her head, and a prayer unraveled backward from her lips, and I was gone again; Josephine clung to the table's edge before giving over to the dizziness. Together Verdeen and I saw Josephine fall from her chair to the worn boards of my old slave cabin. Tessa's round face made a shadow over Josephine's strained expression. Tears fell, and in them I saw babies coming like seeds from Josephine's chest bursting into the stale air, their faces blending into the work of the fields, into the eyes of the Negro women, eyes like the colors of the swamp, eyes like mine.

There was a short silence like the sound of muffled darkness in the deep middle of the river. Verdeen's hands let go of the candles, and I collapsed on the table, my black and gray hair making a drape to protect my unsteady mind.

I lifted my head from Verdeen's table, the sounds of morning rising in the swamp. My streak of gray made a fuzzy veil where I watched her descend the ladder. "Miss Verdeen," I spoke up, my voice raspy, my head in a vice of pain, the smell of my breath rancid, "did you bring me beeswax candles last night?" I rubbed my eyes again, looking around and not seeing anything like the candles. "I was dreaming, the same dream again," I said aloud, and I was embarrassed sitting on the little stool. "When did I fall asleep?"

She did not answer me, but started talking as she came the rest of the way down the ladder. "I'm leaving this place soon. It's time for me to go. It don't matter where. I've been carrying the past around like a sack of cured bones. It's time to leave it where it lay, and move on."

I held my weak head up. "Are you leaving now?" My mind returned to my need to be guided out of the swamp, on to whatever it was I would do, run or surrender my life.

"Well soon as I get you a piece of this corn bread so you don't fall out…I'll think on it, but that ain't for you to worry about."

I saw the way she turned her body to go to fetch the bread. She was afraid to leave this place. Her shoulders were rounded like the wear of the walls around her. Afraid as I had been afraid to leave Bartlette's, then Willie's.

I ate the bread and thought about thanking her, but I kept chewing.

I said in one exhausted tone, "I don't really think I should stay here. Folks gonna be lookin for the only Indian woman around here."

"For right now you in about the best hiding place."

She started to continue but I interrupted her. "I really just wanna get on my way. I'm thinkin I'll go to the county station, have a good meal like I never have had my whole grown-up life, and then turn myself in."

She blew air out of her body in a sneeze of laughter.

"You done found a little freedom, boosted up by your rage, and you makin it out to be like you black and done lynched a white man."

Verdeen's voice quieted, and she bit her lip looking off to the dusty jars of pickled food that had been given to her as payment for her time, her help, her sight.

I watched her, assuming she was signifying the need to be paid, "I can leave you my cloak. I won't be needing it anymore."

She paused still, looking off at her belongings, then up to her bed high on the posts. "That'll be good. That's a fine coat, everybody cain't afford a coat like that. Miss Raven had a coat like that." My head moved slowly away, but I kept my eyes on her.

"What did you say?"

She looked at me sideways and fiddled with a knot in her red fluff of hair. "Nothin," she said.

And I questioned first my own sanity, and then hers. "Please don't say anything else." I held my forehead where the pounding was great, but she was not looking at me anymore.

"Didn't that corn bread do you any good?"

"Please do not say anything else."

She kept talking while I pleaded with her to stop. I held down the need to vomit. I sat there rubbing my weary eyes, unable to stop thinking about my mother begging my father not to go that morning, about the girls finding their father dead, wondering now if Willie had already been put in the ground, if his spirit would come for me.

"Hantes cain't cross water!" Verdeen shouted, minding my thoughts. Both elbows on her knees, she puffed her pipe in satisfaction of having hopped into my mind again at the expense of my already drained spirit. She spoke in riddles, putting on the cloak, which seemed to shrink her with its length.

"It's a gift, to be told other people's stories, even if it ain't all about you, even if it is. But it's a gift to be told."

I spoke with the awful taste in my mouth. "I gots to go, Miss Verdeen. They'll be lookin for me, and I cain't entertain in no more disconnected stories."

"Ain't nobody gonna be lookin for you. Only folks care anything about the son of Satan just as soon see him dead for his land," she said, glancing down at my belly, and I caught her arm.

"Listen to me."

I was struck by another pang of agitation and rage.

"Oh, what you gonna do, hit me beside the head too?"

The child twisted in my restless belly and Verdeen shifted her eyes to where she could hear it screaming for its life.

I steadied my tone, and pleaded with her, "If you can see...tell me what to do. I have another life to protect, but if I go back there I'll be hung." I sat back on the wood of the stump, thinking out loud now. "Maybe the girls gonna be better off once some black woman is raisin them."

Verdeen started in with the same abrupt tone I used with her. "I don't see for you or nobody else no more. I's done set myself free of all that. See for yo self if you need to see." And she laughed, amused at herself.

She looked down at the quiet pipe in her rough hands. "I sees for me. But I tell you what," she said just above a whisper. "You get out of this mess you in, then make sure you come back by here to see me." For the first time I noticed her teeth. They were stained brown, some of them broken. She was older than the cypress trees. "I has some riches I'd like to pass on to ya. I'm gonna be movin on and there's things that might benefit a woman who got trouble seein for herself. Would give'm to ya now, but I don't think you fit enough woman for 'em."

"Miss Verdeen, it'll be riches enough if you can lead me out of here."

The sun caught in her always-suspicious hazel eye and she looked out long into the swamp morning.

"The air is clear... Trouble," she said, and then said, "Gets yourself together 'cause I ain't got a need for trouble, and I don't want to have to be part of it. Come on." She grabbed me up from my rest.

She shut the door behind us and hung the old snakeskin there. Her life hadn't seemed to amount to much since I'd last seen her, and as I had feared the day I saw Old Anna sold away, nor had mine.

She hurried down the plank in my cloak that was too long for her. I was ashamed for us both; me pregnant with another man's child, no shoes on my feet, my husband's death on my hands, running, finally running.

We passed by the places of the swamp that were familiar from the first time I had been there. I spoke out into the cool spring morning. "My whole life done passed me by..."

"Yo life? You ain't even old enough to done started no life."

"I got thirty years, and nothin to show."

I towered above her in the journey, keeping my eyes on her red hair above the cloak as she dragged the hem through shallow cold water.

"Oh Lord here we go again." She mocked me, " 'I ain't got nothin. My life is so bad.'

"You got some gray hairs, don't ya?" She laughed at herself for a while before continuing. "You ain't even dreamed yet. Ain't dreamed nothin but stuff about what done already happened, and ain't even growed up enough to know the difference between foolish make-believy dreams and visions.

"Ain't dreamed yet about what you want to see happen or what folks might be bringin down to happen. Hell, I'm old as dirt, and I'm just about to start livin. Ain't gonna be everybody's eyes and ears no more. Folks come all bleary-eyed"; she slumped her body over and sloshed like a tired old man; "then I show them the truth they came for, and they straighten up, act healed, and deny everything I tell 'em, then they shuns me, and go on off happy in they lazy lives. I ain't got time for none of ya'll no more. I'm about to do some powerful livin."

She turned around, looking past me, and I turned to look too, but there was nothing but moss hanging, and a blue heron watching us with one eye.

Was the sheriff the trouble that was coming? Was it a mob of men, coming to hang a defiant wife?

She led me through the muddy places. My heart beat into my ears, keeping me from freezing when we waded through the water. Her short body sunk to her thighs, but she moved fast. With the water only up to my knees, I could barely keep up for the cold trying to seize in my bones.

Verdeen motioned for me, her red hair against the green of the swamp, and in the new sunlight, she was painful to look at; red hair, one hazel eye, light brown face, freckled cheeks, painful like looking at the truth with no skin over it.

In the black cloak she moved like an otter through the water, then abruptly she stopped.

"Well, I'll fix myself to say only what I feel like I know, and I ain't gonna try and attach more to it, or attach yo fate to it, 'cause that kind of pretendin just bring about messes. I do know that you spend an awful bunch of time askin questions and feeling sorry for yo self, and don't spend a whole lot of time even knowin who you feelin sorry for. Hell, girl, you don't know yo self.

"Here. I got's to get on now." She handed me a wad of bills. My hands and nose were cold now. I wondered where someone like her got that kind of money. She looked toward her cabin again. "This all that's left, and it's better you have some of what everybody else done had on your head. Go on now, go."

And I turned with the urgency of her words and ran, hearing the slosh of water behind me in the swamp.

May 15, 1881

M
Y LAST DAY would be spent with fine clothes, food in my belly. I ran with the wad of bills in my hand toward the county station. The sun was clean in the way it shined in a cloudless sky, clean like spring on the early mornings of my childhood.

Lilly. My mother's voice calling from the bottom of the stairs, gently, her voice among the chatter of new birds excited about starting new lives. I ran and watched the clouds clear to blue above me. I slipped into a gentle skip just like a child. My mind was free, and I did not care about anything, didn't care if people saw me, how many people, what they thought. The images of my execution dissolved behind me as I ran across the clearing, tall Choctaw woman, long dark hair, off-white cotton, bare feet in my raw departure.

New, fine clothes. I told myself I'd get dressed up like one of them mulatto women who strode by the house last Easter; put my hair up under a fine hat, and get a meal at the place the Negro folks went to eat, calm my nervous mind, and walk among the proudest ones. Have them all look at me wondering if this be the same adulteress that killed her husband. It had turned out to be a promising sunny spring day, clear and good for me.

At the county station the air smelled like wildflowers. The store that I had once stood in with Maw Janie counting up our credit for flour and a plow blade was now a fine Negro general merchandise place. I was greeted with a nod but little regard, until I showed the dollar bills.

They had stacks of hats and fine dresses, and a big oval mirror, clear and sharp, with gold leaves on the rim. The first time in my adult life I ever saw my whole body in the mirror, my face dirty and dry, my hair frayed from the long braids. A little Negro girl sat in the corner on a stool playing a banjo with three strings. I thought for a moment of Virginia, but closed my eyes and only saw the little girl. The music was happy. The woman of the store was proud to take me behind the curtain and help me try on the finest dress. She got for me all manner of under-garments that I hadn't seen since watching Emma and Earleen pull the laces tight while my mother held her breath. I ignored the life in my belly and let the woman squeeze it into a small space.

I had lost my fear of being out there. The money brought me peace, and knowing that my fate was soon to be decided by men who would bring punishment for what I'd done, relieved the pain I once felt; always out of place, always wondering what I should do, when, how I should do it. All of the men in my life dead, all of the women dead. There was freedom in being orphaned.

I decided on the sky blue dress. It reminded me of my mother, and wearing it, I felt complete. I had done something, and the things that would come next would at least lead me somewhere, to a jail cell, a workhouse, to my death, but somewhere.

The woman came with the bowl and water and welcomed me to wash my face, gave me toilet water to spray around my body for a sweet scent of roses, and she washed my feet with gentle hands.

I went back to the mirror and saw a fancy woman there in her light-blue, high-neck, lacy-on-the-edges, and big skirt like Missus Bartlette's.

My lips were strange and beautiful with the color red contrasting the light blue, like wild roses against a clear sky. I thought I'd see my mother's lips, but I did not see her at all. I could see my father's narrow French and Choctaw features. I searched but I could not see Raven LeFlore.

I stood there trying to reconcile the familiar shape of my eyes, like Tessa's when she came that Sunday morning and greeted me for the first time in fifteen years, my lips like the lips in my dream; the woman hovering over me with the strange command, *Sleep now, the sun is rising.*

The storekeeper placed the hat atop the bun of hair. With the hat I was ready for the parade of my last day. I was ready, like the hog made beautiful for the smokehouse. But in the mirror, I noticed the tiny bumps on my cheeks, the one curly hair growing on my chin, and behind me the streets that awaited my entry.

Past the panes of the window, in the streets, a man walked among the hurried crowd, walked somehow separate in my sight from the other bodies moving in the river of workers. Horses and wagons passed, then the man again, like a precious thing caught in the current, a bandage on the side of his head. He walked swiftly like Willie heading to the barn for the whip. The flesh beneath the high lace neck of my dress rose in heated bumps.

A ghost, I thought, and I turned away from the mirror. There was no ghost, it was Willie, walking urgent. He walked by the store, and I ran to the porch to confirm the reflection. The peculiar heels of my new shoes threatened to throw me to the hollow boards.

The sounds of the streets; metal on wood, wagon wheels rolling over deep spots in the road, worn by the old flood. Drivers yelled, "Hee yaw," to their horses, laughter echoed, someone yelled for the ice truck from a window, the smell of meat rose from barbecues behind buildings. All the Negro people hurried along on my side of the road, and the white people took up all the rest of the space. A white man yelled out, "Ma'am," and I waited in my long blue dress, my face in shadow under my fine hat. I waited for my beating. He came past the Negro people like stepping through troubled water, his face evil, but he stopped gentle on me, tipping his hat. He took me by the arm and led me to the other side of the road where the white women walked along in dresses as fine as mine.

"May I escort you someplace?"

"No thank you," I answered, trying not to let my teeth chatter, and he hopped on to his wagon and tipped his hat again.

Willie was striding fast with the other Negroes, and I followed him from my side of the road. I had never watched him when he didn't see me watching him. He was hard to distinguish from the others in the crowd. Many of the women were in clean black dresses and white shawls like Tessa's clothes for working at her missus'. The men and women walked in the same direction and wore white shirts, dark suit coats, and so did Willie, but his back was straight, his manner righteous.

The sounds of the street faded behind us, past one big house, then another; bushes high and even-cut, like Willie's hair. I had to drop farther behind, pull my hat down, and make myself look to be one of the women heading slowly for a visit, slowly, without a care in the world, for tea, or out for a stroll.

Far ahead of me, Willie opened a black iron gate to one of the houses and it squeaked on its hinges. He looked in my direction but did not look at my face, where he would have seen the woman who tried to kill him.

Was this the sheriff's house? Was this the place where Willie came each day and night in secret, like his father, telling Klans men when and where to strike, for the salvation of his own free hide and the exchange of fine things? Would he send them to rape and hang me? I walked slowly past the iron gate, my movement gentle and calm; myself a ghost, already dead from this life. No one stopped to ask me questions. Willie walked up the path that cut through the lawn, almost to the front steps, and then he headed around the back, a stone wall and shrubs obscuring him.

This house was all painted white, three white rocking chairs on the porch, and the glass in the windows looked like when the frost covered the windows in Willie's house while a pot of stew boiled on the stove. Fancy flowers were carved into the frost, permanent, the way Suddie drew in the steam of the picture window, and I longed to go inside and be home, the way I had always understood home.

[I was on the porch now, a quiet spirit remembering my mother standing on the porch of our house, and I knew that Verdeen had been wrong. I knew the difference between dreams and visions. I had seen things I wanted, seen that I stood in a dress like Missus Bartlette's on a sunny day, a white porch shielding me from the sun, a fine hat atop my head. I stood there listening to the sound of the nearby creek, rushing in the spring breeze.]

The knocker was cold. My gloved hand; intricate patterns of lace covering the flesh of a cotton picker. I lifted the knocker and rapped three times on the door.

Willie answered, and stood there in his perfectly clean white shirt, his white-gloved hand around the brass doorknob of this place. He did not lift his head but looked at my shoes like Old Raymond in Overseer's presence, and I saw the gray hairs there curled in tight among the dark ones. "Good morning ma'am, LeFlore residence." And he looked up to see me.

We stared like two cold fish, depressed at the sight of each other. The odor of mildew; white people's money going stale beneath where they sat on it with their pride keeping it warm; the air of stale lives came past Willie to the porch.

I thought about the slave girl at Massa Bartlette's, standing on the wall pretending to have no desire for living beyond servitude, invisible while Massa talked about his idea of her people's fate, her standing there with a silver tea set. I remembered Sybil's last night, her skirt pockets each weighted with one piece of tradable silverware. Willie with the good furniture on the back of the wagon, good furniture that he'd been given in fulfillment of some promise. It stood proud in our house, the pockets of Willie's good pants sagging with lies.

The lies had weighed more than iron, and held me down in the saltwater end of the swamp. Willie's lies and mine, circles, spinning my waterlogged face to the sun, the moon, the sun. We had collected sticks, stones, crumbs to have something to hold on to. Old Raymond had spoken one sweltering night, ["Joy...freedom, faith, spirit, the foot on the ground, the gracefulness in the bend of the back picking cotton, dancing, flying, is all the same; Truth. When you can move according to the truth, you are free, free, free. Always your feet will fall in accordance, and love will be as sure as meat on the table."

I had come to Willie looking for fresh meat, a roof beneath the sometimes harsh sky, and he had given me his poisonous gifts, never offering the source, and me never asking.

In the distance somewhere his own mother decayed slow into the earth. *Who were we, grown old with all these sins repeating?* Verdeen was right, I did not know myself, but stood on that porch in a familiar costume, much like the one my mother wore. She was Choctaw, she was the child in her stories. Surely fine fabrics, tight corsets were not her truth.

"Lilly," Willie gasped, awakening me from my seeing of all our lives and deaths.

"Willie," I called back to him, struggling with the limit of words to express my regrets.

A white man's voice called out proper-like, "Willie, has someone come calling for morning tea?" His eyes widened and filled with water; the bandage comforted the left side of his head. The man's voice: "Is that a nigger girl's voice I hear?"

"No sir."

The man's voice was rancid like the smell of the green-wood cross burning high above a blaze of Man and Tessa's crops. And Willie shut the door, leaving me staring at the engraving on the brass knocker. "Jacques LeFlore."

My mouth went dry from the quickened rhythm of my breathing. My eyes moved involuntarily in their sockets. I opened my thoughts to try to understand, but my thoughts shut down, shut me out like Willie slamming the door. I could hear the old man's voice muffled. "I told you never to let her come here, ever. How many other promises have you broken, look at her, people are going to think she's of some kin to me." The curtains parted, and a face like my father's, but on an old white man small and worn, my father's lips, and his eyes evil on me.

One lace glove cupped over my mouth to try and conceal the cry that came up from the mortar bowl of my pelvis, silent. I picked up the hoops of dress and ran, not taking the street, but cutting through the large plots of land that cultivated well-kept lawns.

When I got to the quiet roads, I had to stop and rest, my breath short with the nausea reviving in my gut. Verdeen was right, I didn't know myself, I didn't know Willie. *He lied to me!* I thought about Willie with the horse and buggy, sometimes coming home for food, probably before going back to my grandfather's, paid more than any other servant to keep me well, but keep me away from him. *He had lied to me!* "Hey gal," on that first day, sent then to steal the granddaughter away from the man who took his son's child. My fate caught up in their piracy. I wiped the sweat from my forehead. My dress was too heavy in my flight. The smell of the toilet water made me sick, the same odor on the shawl that used to be Massa's daughter's curtains.

I couldn't bear wearing the dress, Jacque LeFlore's money connected to everything outside and inside of me. The dirt beneath my feet, the blood in my veins fed by every piece of meat ever brought home by Willie, fed and housed like a family dog. The sky blue adornment constricted the illness growing in my stomach. I stood beside the open cotton field and stripped down to the fine corset and long underpants, like my mother on our last morning. I left the dress, the hat, the boots by the side of the road. I ran again, letting my hair flow on the wind where I cut through thin woods, not knowing where I'd end up.

I looked up to the shadow of trees and saw myself from high atop a vulture's perch, half naked, half dead with the secret baby inside me. My throat burned from inhaling the pollinated air, and a feeling of helplessness washed over me, as I whined the word "help."

I had returned to the swamp, hoping to find my way to Verdeen's cabin. She had said she was leaving this place, had said I was good company. I could not do the things that I needed to do, and so I hoped I could run with her.

Without the sound of her guitar guiding me, I walked across the land bridges and islands. I staggered onto the deck. Darkness crept up behind me. The air of my gasping lungs burned inside my body, reminding me that I was still living.

I stood there, my undergarments showing light blue in the last faint light, and I waited, expecting to hear her guitar signifying for me to come in, but the snakeskin was gone and there were no sounds, no young frogs peeping, no birds. I stood there, my breath coming and going while I waited for something. I imagined her appearing in the door. I stood ready to go with her, away from this place.

I opened the door, forced its swollen wood. The smell was like the meat wrapped in brown paper when Willie didn't bring it home soon enough for the icebox. I went to the table where I remembered the lantern to be, and lit it with the match on the rough side of the table. I looked around the room, waiting for my eyes to adjust in the darkness. The jarred food was gone from the shelves, where a rat scampered across. The herbs that hung at the back window compromising the already dim light were gone. Verdeen had left. I exhaled. The hope of leaving Oktibbeha County drained out of my body, the reality settled in my exhaustion. *I should have known she would leave without me.* How had I convinced myself that she cared?

I looked around the lifeless, empty cabin, and on the floor I spotted a leather satchel, bulky and worn. My black cloak, my mother's black cloak lay lifeless on the stump chair beside it. I blew air from my nose like a tired mare.

I picked up the leather satchel, and I recognized it. My hands shook. I rocked on the uneven stump. I rocked there silent and insistent in my struggle to breathe. This was my father's saddlebag.

I undid the buckle and rummaged hungrily through the sack, but there was nothing but a letter in shaky script on yellowing paper.

September 1863

Dear Father,

The prison was burned down by abolitionist raiders. I have escaped into the swamp. Why have you not answered my letters?

My heart is lonesome without your words, and I write you this letter because my mind is lonesome without ever having confessed a truth that only two people share, one of them now dead.

I must tell you this father, not to injure your position with all of your current and potential allies, but because I wish to save my child.

You are my only living kin besides her, and if I fail in finding her, you must.

Please forgive me, Father, but they have taken the land, our home, and they have taken Lilly away from me, because the codes that you have helped to write and you and I have both lived by have been violated. I wish that I were not ashamed of this truth, but I am. I loved my wife, Raven, and I loved Josephine, the slave breeder you purchased before your leaving. When she came to LeFlore, she was young and lost without her family, and so was I. As Raven once reminded me of mother, Josephine did as well, strong in spirit, but lost. Over the years I followed my duty to breed her among the strong field hands, but I always made sure that she had the best to eat, a cabin of her own. I have both protected her and committed the greatest sins against her.

My daughter, your grandchild, Lilly, was Josephine's and my child. On April 20, 1851, she was born. A slave, but Raven saved her from that fate.

Do not put this letter aside, Father.

I have learned many things in my imprisonment, in the loss of our home; money and privilege did not spare me the truth. I saw my mother mistreated by you, I saw my mother die at the hands of patrollers. I have always lived with the guilt of not having saved her, and I have tried never to lose the women I love, but I have lost them all.

I have learned that privilege did not spare me my fate.

Please help me in saving Lilly. Tonight, the moon is a sliver of hope in the night sky. Union troops are in the distance, coming to raid the nearby plantations, and thereby weaken the Confederates by annihilating their supply of food. Tonight I will attempt to steal her from the Bartlette plantation. If we do not arrive in the Territory within a week, you must come and look for her.

Please do what is right for her, for my mother's spirit, for your wife's spirit and to save Lilly from an ill fate as a slave.

*You have not answered my other letters, Father, and I pray you
heed my plea, I pray you are alive.*

Your Devoted Son,
Hatta Tchula LeFlore

The cap of my skull went hot, and a scream spewed from deep in
the center of my body, a scream like the sounds so loud ears cannot
perceive. I wailed like a tree shrieking in pain when the metal blade
cuts through veins for timber, the sound of tiny rocks crying way into
the night after dynamite rips and contorts the mountain, the sound of
a slave girl breathing inside dreams of her promised rape; I screamed.

Hush, hush, I could hear Verdeen say, annoyed and nurturing above
me. *Hush. It already been done now.* And I quieted.

Quiet, I said to my mind the way Maw Janie said it when I cried
a little piece in the morning because my legs still ached from the
picking cotton all the day before. *Quiet now. You got to be strong, 'cause
we got to make do.* I summoned all the comfort of women who had
mothered me.

Sound and color came back slow, and I adjusted the wick and read
the letter again and again.

I took a deep breath, all the smells of the cabin going into my veins.
I realized that somewhere inside of me, I always knew that my mother
was Raven, but that she did not birth me. I always knew from the way
her hand hesitated before touching me, hesitated like the touch had to
be a thought before it was an impulse, but she was the mother I knew,
and I loved her.

I sat there with the dreams of the woman with the rag tied around her
head, the softness of the brown nurturing moon of her breast over me,
the dream becoming my waking memory. Tessa's mother, my mother,
slave woman, Josephine, Josephine, Josephine. Sybil's voice, *Why don't
you ask your uncle, and your father if they got any niggers in they family.*

My eyes darted around, for something to keep me still. *Latch hold
of something, Lilly, and stay, stay.*

The frogs and snakes, the trees, everything of the swamp hummed deep, and I joined them in a moan, a primal sound coming up from where my veins were hot beneath my scalp. I felt alone; alone like the day of my birth, forever severed from my first kin, every day taking me further away from her, alone. I moaned from the abandoned place inside me where grief and birth and death are the same. No kin, alone.

In the cold darkness of my grief my soul rose out of the top of my skull and into the air, sensing the odor of white men's whisky rising into the rafters, and I saw. I saw the hooded men, my girls running. My girls.

The letter itched in my hands like fire ants, my feet itched with the pinpricks of bad poison, like a snakebite taking hold. The papers floated down like autumn leaves to Verdeen's floor.

The girls, the girls. My whole body went cold in a chill. I could see the girls, quiet in the house, their hands folded in the laps of new skirts; Virginia's face soft and accepting, Suddie's face stern and untrusting. They had been left alone in Willie Kellem's house, his deal gone bad with Jacques LeFlore. My girls where no longer protected in a county where lynching was common except on the land on which they flourished, untouched.

I could see the white men descending upon my children. White bags tied over their own heads, holes for their eyes, no drums for the ceremony of their evil, but fire.

In my vision, the girls ran from window to window of the house looking for a way out without flame, and Suddie went to the back door, remembering the place where I always dumped the wash water too close to the house.

I was no longer in Verdeen's cabin, I crossed the maze of land bridges and islands in the swamp. My feet drummed on the hard earth. Leaves, sticks, and rocks beat my approach to signal the girls to run from the men who came for Willie's land, the same men who hanged Emmanuel, the men who had chased me down so long ago, overseers turned white farmers, who would chase my daughters into the woods, hurrying, drunk, their smell like wet hound dogs, whisky and sweat, chasing the scent of the starch I had put in the girl's school dresses.

I listened and saw with my eyes glassed over beneath the before-dawn shadows of the woods.

I saw the flames again, the house burning; the girls' old cradle standing on end, dusty in the corner of the bedroom. I saw the place I stood barefoot when the fever brought my body down in front of the fireplace on that cold day, the table where the thick wood was smooth and dark from all of our hands, the blanket crocheted on my bed, the place where Man and I had lain together.

They were running toward flame. Suddie grabbed Virginia's hand and ran. I tried to calm the thoughts so I could see them clearly and know where to run, but I ran following muddied boots that stumbled drunk in my path. I could hear the men clear now. Flashes of green and brown whizzed past me, and out of the woods I emerged drenched with sweat in the dawn, the white corset and underpants like armor.

My legs were thick right down to my ankles with the new life changing my shape. My face was solid like my father's. I was the vision of the vulture sitting on a high branch, seeing and knowing; the rope that had once swung there on a night when dark faces escaped LeFlore. I foresaw the girls raped and discarded, loss twisted around their wrists and ankles like grape vines.

My feet carried me over land trodden by all my escaping ancestors, the golden ones of the sun, the dark ones of the night. The light of dawn revealed me in the clearing. A fire burned there in my chest, and showed a glow in the windows of the log house. I was at Willie Kellem's house, where the grass beneath my feet was deceitfully damp.

The sweet calls of mating birds, frog's voices not yet gone deep in the season warned me, and I crept barefoot toward where a small flame grew in the windows; the house still standing, fire and rape on the wind, my vision cast ahead.

Quietly up the steps of my own home I crept with my whole foot touching the boards, and I opened that door that I had hid behind for so many years.

Willie sat on the floor, a small lantern next to him, both hands full of kindling, where the flames grew to push away the chill of a spring morning. The lantern flame illuminated the white bandage, illuminated the whites of his eyes, innocent like the day he begged me to do something, anything, inside my powers to save Satan from the certainty of death.

"Lilly?" He startled, and stood uncomfortable like a child.

Virginia came first from the room where she huddled beneath my sheets in the feather bed.

"Maw maw," she cried, and hugged my legs. Scent of Josephine, spring air on her sun bleached blouse, the same sweetness of my sheets in the house of LeFlore. The comfort of Virginia's touch loosened the noose that I had imagined around my neck the morning before, and I let go a cry for having been left, for having been lost, for having been hostage.

Willie watched on quietly, the same way I watched his hands touch his dying father, riveted by the possibility of his caress. Behind me, mature heels on the porch. Suddie opened the door. Only eleven years old, she stood there like a woman, her arms full of stacked wood, her starched skirt filthy with wood chips from the barn. She stood, with her wool hair in two thick braids, her eyes quiet and harsh on the scene.

The cool air of morning moved around her body, and brought the scent of her blood, soon bringing her to womanhood. I heard a whisper on the wind, *Run.*

From across the road, *Run,* across the field. I saw the white hoods, specks of white circling, the fire of their torches on the horizon. *Again?* I questioned from the eternal place in the pit of my belly where the new life stirred. *Again,* like my ten-year-old self, shocked at the sight of death coming for me and my mother.

But I was tall flesh and bone now, with thick firm weighted metal in my feet; feathers sprouting from the whip wounds on my back.

Willie laid down the kindling and grabbed his satchel, filling it with the small precious things; a belt buckle thick and well made that belonged to his father, coins emptied from a box on our bedroom dresser. I ran to the butcher block, and with one of the three most precious things swimming in my gut, I grabbed the cleaver and placed it in Willie's satchel along with the bundle of things from slavery time, one of Old Raymond's rattles, the old skirt; an assortment of odd things hastily thrown together. Suddie stood silent in the middle of the big room lost in the images of evil coming for her. Virginia ran close around me and Willie.

Willie and I glanced at each other in a moment that extended itself, where we recognized each other for the first time; both shaken down to the roughness of man and woman hued from dark clay, our truths beaten and contorted into hard crystalline stares. We stood there at the back door among the sounds and sights of the white men's voices hooping and hollering on approach of their sport, the call of a barred owl, the light of the moon giving over to the heavy shades of morning, the girls' eyes wide open and soft with fear.

Willie grabbed the small willing hand of Virginia, and I grabbed the coarse familiar hand of Suddie. The frogs resounded, the birds returned from the night's hunt, and fire roared like the last remains torched of the dead.

Disturbing the black glass surface of the swamp water, we splashed and tripped in flight. Willie and the girls followed the pattern of my movement through the dawn-lit swamp; sharp cleaver from the cutting block in my shaking grip. Behind us, the smell of our whole lives being reduced to ashes.

When we reached the swamp, the light of morning lit, yellow, on the tree tops behind us, and the sun hummed loud and thunderous in the sky, hummed a deep guttural song about land, wars, reservations, plantations, hummed for the tree limbs that never intended to bare the weight of murder, hummed to summon all the blades of grass, the rivers and streams, the rattling bones in the river bed, summon them to guide Ishki, Inki and Allas home.

About the Author

ZELDA LOCKHART is author of the novel *Fifth Born*, which was a 2002 Barnes & Noble Discovery selection and won a finalist award for debut fiction from the Zora Neale Hurston/Richard Wright Legacy Foundation. Ms. Lockhart holds a Bachlor's in English from Norfolk State University, a Masters in English from Old Dominion University, and a certificate in writing, directing and editing film from the New York Film Academy. Her other works of fiction, poetry and essays can be found in anthologies, journals and magazines. Lockhart is also the author of *The Evolution*, a serial novella, currently appearing in the archives of USAToday.com's Open Book series. She is currently working on her third novel, and facilitating a variety of workshops that empower adults and children to self-define through writing. Ms. Lockhart welcomes inquiries about her workshops and writing at www.zeldalockhart.com. She lives in North Carolina with her two children.